The Thunder
The Star of Delhi

TWO CLASSIC ADVENTURES OF

by Walter B. Gibson
writing as Maxwell Grant

plus **"THE WITCH DRUMS OF SALEM"**
a classic from the Golden Age of Radio

and new historical essays
by Will Murray and Anthony Tollin

SANCTUM BOOKS

This Sanctum Books edition is an unabridged republication of the text and illustrations of two stories from *The Shadow Magazine,* as originally published by Street & Smith Publications, Inc., N.Y.: *The Thunder King* from the June 15, 1941 issue and *The Star of Dehli* from the July 1, 1941 issue, plus "The Witch Drums of Salem" broadcast (as "The Witch Drums) the week of September 11, 1938 on *The Shadow* radio series. These stories are works of their time. Consequently, the text is reprinted intact in its original historical form, including occasional out-of-date ethnic and cultural stereotyping. Typographical errors have been tacitly corrected in this edition.

International Standard Book Number:
978-1-60877-100-4

First printing: December 2012

Series editor: Anthony Tollin
anthonytollin@shadowsanctum.com

Consulting editor: Will Murray

Copy editor: Joseph Wrzos

Cover and photo restoration: Michael Piper

The editors gratefully appreciate the contributions of Margot Avery, Bernard A. Drew, Karl Schadow and William Nadel in the preparation of this volume.

Published by Sanctum Books
P.O. Box 761474, San Antonio, TX 78245-1474

Visit The Shadow at www.shadowsanctum.com.

Volume 68

CONTENTS

Two Complete Novels
From The Shadow's Private Annals
As told to
Maxwell Grant

Thrilling Tales and Features

Cover art by Graves Gladney
Back cover art by George Rozen and Graves Gladney
Interior illustrations by Paul Orban and Edd Cartier

THE THUNDER KING

Meeting lightning bolt with a blast from a .45, The Shadow stages a terrific battle with Thor, master of thunder!

CHAPTER I
OUT OF THE BLACK

THE café lounge of the Hotel Metrolite was a quiet, comfortable place to wait for someone, but Margo Lane had been waiting too long. She was waiting for Lamont Cranston, and he was ten minutes overdue, which meant that he had probably forgotten the appointment; usually, he was very punctual.

An added annoyance was the man at a near table, who kept ogling looks in Margo's direction. Perhaps he admired brunettes of Margo's type, but his appearance didn't impress Margo favorably. Though sleek and well dressed, the fellow had rat-like eyes that darted from his sharp, sallow face.

He'd given his name to a waiter, loud enough for Margo to overhear. He'd asked if there had been any calls for Harvey Quade, and the waiter had gone to find out. Just now, the waiter was returning to tell Quade that there were no messages.

Rather than appear interested, Margo let her eyes drift toward the door, hoping that Lamont would appear.

Her eyes riveted.

Coming through the door was a man she recognized by his stooped shoulders and the long face above them. The blinks of the man's colorless eyes clinched his identity. He was Louis Wilbert, private investigator working for Universal Industries, a concern with which Lamont Cranston was associated.

Margo had seen Wilbert talking to Cranston outside the Cobalt Club, a few days ago. At the time, she had been waiting in Cranston's limousine; hence Wilbert hadn't seen her. Later, Lamont had told her who Wilbert was, and had been rather noncommittal in his opinions regarding the investigator.

Margo had gathered that Wilbert might be capable, but that his methods were somewhat doubtful. Her opinion was strengthened as she watched Wilbert cross the café lounge.

Wilbert came directly to Quade's table. There, the long-faced investigator shook hands with the ratlike man. They ordered drinks from the waiter, and began a buzzing conversation. Margo was quite confident that their talk must concern Universal Industries.

Feigning indifference, Margo stopped the waiter as he passed her table and ordered a Mirage cocktail; then, with no change of demeanor, she strained to listen to the neighboring conversation.

Margo understood the setup of Universal Industries. It was a huge, new corporation organized by a financier named Oswald Kelber, and Universal Industries had taken on tremendous contracts to build and equip new factory units that would turn out materials for national defense.

Universal Industries would lose those contracts if deliveries were not made within a specified time; hence Kelber, fearing unforeseen delays, had hired Wilbert to check conditions at the various plants connected with Universal Industries.

One man would probably be very glad if Universal Industries should fail to deliver. That man's name was Jerome Thorden, and he headed a large business group known as Thorden Enterprises. Thorden had been after the very same contracts but Kelber had underbid him. Should Kelber be forced to drop the contracts, Thorden would take them over.

Wilbert and Quade had finished their drinks and were ready for another round, when Margo's Mirage cocktail arrived. The Mirage was a pinkish concoction that looked like a very powerful cocktail, but it actually contained nothing stronger than grape juice. Margo could drink Mirages all evening without losing any of her wits, and at present, her choice of such a drink was bringing dividends.

Seeing Quade glance at Margo's table, Wilbert did the same. Both mistook the Mirage for a rum concoction, and they decided that the brunette wasn't in a listening mood. Unconsciously, they let their voices rise a trifle. Margo overheard them.

"I've finished most of the work that Kelber wants," said Wilbert. "So far, it's been mostly a routine job."

"Has he paid you off yet?" inquired Quade.

"Not yet," returned Wilbert. "He's still expecting a final bill. Which makes me think"—Wilbert was stroking his long chin—"that if I showed him the correspondence you mention, it would be worth plenty—to both of us."

"It ought to be," grunted Quade. "It would give you proof of everything you suspect."

Wilbert nodded; then Margo heard him say:

"There's just one question, Quade: how much Kelber will pay. You see, I'm working for him—"

"But this comes outside your regular job," interposed Quade. Then, with a sharp laugh, he added: "Away outside!"

"Kelber may not see it that way."

"Let him make an offer," suggested Quade. "If it isn't enough, take it up with Thorden. I'll bet that he'd pay double."

Wilbert gave Quade an indignant stare, and queried:

"You'd want me to double-cross the man I'm working for?"

The question brought a guffaw from Quade, who seemed to consider honesty on Wilbert's part as worthy of a jest. The guffaw was overloud and caused Wilbert to glance in Margo's direction.

Fortunately, a waiter was passing the brunette's table, and she promptly pointed to her empty glass and ordered: "Another."

Nevertheless, Wilbert and Quade lowered their voices as they resumed their conversation.

Margo caught snatches of their talk as she sipped the next Mirage. They seemed to agree that they would have to acquire the correspondence that they had previously mentioned, before negotiating with either Kelber or Thorden. Margo heard Wilbert ask:

"How long would it take us to get out there, Quade?"

"About three hours," Quade replied. "We take Highway 95, over in New Jersey, and follow it as far as—"

He paused abruptly, flashed a ratty look toward Margo. Then, even though the girl didn't appear to be noticing, Quade buried the rest of his statement in a mumble that Wilbert could hear, but Margo could not. Wilbert nodded as he listened. He beckoned to the waiter and paid the check. The two went out.

Promptly, Margo hurried to a telephone. She called the Cobalt Club, to see if Cranston was there; but he wasn't. So, she tried his home in New Jersey, and gave a pleased ejaculation when she heard Cranston's quiet, even tone across the wire.

"Sorry, Margo," said Cranston. "I was going to call you, to say I'd be late. Some business acquaintances stopped by, and I didn't notice the time until they left. We were talking about Universal Industries—"

"And so am I!" put in Margo. "Lamont, I've just seen Wilbert. He was making some sort of a deal with a man named Quade. Listen, while I give the details—"

Cranston listened, but seemed only mildly interested. When Margo emphasized the final point—that Wilbert and Quade were starting on a mysterious mission along Highway 95—Cranston interposed with a tired drawl.

"I suppose you think that I should try to follow them," he said, "or have someone trail them for me. Very ridiculous, Margo. It would be nothing but a wild-goose chase!"

"Then I'm a wild goose!" snapped Margo. "I have my car here, and I still can overtake that pair. You'll hear from me later, Lamont!"

SLAMMING the telephone receiver, Margo flaunted from the hotel, took her coupé from the parking space that an obliging doorman had found for her, and started toward the Lincoln Tunnel. She was still boiling when she drove into the tube, but as she neared the New Jersey exit, she cooled.

Odd, thought Margo, that her appointment with Cranston should have enabled her to witness the meeting between Wilbert and Quade.

Perhaps Lamont had known that Wilbert was to meet someone at the Metrolite and had deliberately arranged for Margo to be there, in case he should be detained elsewhere. If so, it was natural that he should have pretended indifference later, for when Lamont Cranston played any part, he carried it to the full. For example, the matter of The Shadow.

Everyone knew of The Shadow, that strange, mysterious fighter in black who battled crime to its doom. But few suspected that The Shadow, in private life, posed as Lamont Cranston, wealthy New York clubman.

Margo was one of the few who did suspect it, but even she could not always be sure. The Shadow certainly had ways of appearing in places when Lamont Cranston didn't seem to be anywhere around!

Probably The Shadow wanted Margo to take up this trail, and therefore, when speaking as Cranston, he was true to form when he discouraged her. But the point was that Margo *hadn't* been discouraged. She was actually on the trail, *despite* Cranston. Things could work that way, where The Shadow was concerned.

Thus convinced, Margo glued herself to the task of picking up the trail, and was successful as she neared the beginning of Highway 95. She saw a car turn off ahead of her, just as a traffic light changed to green, and the glow from a service station gave her a view of the men in the other coupé.

Harvey Quade was at the wheel, and his companion was Louis Wilbert.

The night was moonless, and stars afforded very little light as Margo followed the other car along the devious turns of Highway 95. She was careful to keep well behind, so that if Wilbert or Quade noticed her headlights in their rear-view mirror, they would simply think that another car had chanced to take the same road.

Route 95 was an old one, and for once, short hills and sharp bends were Margo's idea of perfect driving conditions. Time and again, she was able to close in on the car ahead and spot it taking a slope, or a curve.

This was rugged country, and the highway followed the deep ravine of a creek. At times, it dipped and crossed the stream over bridges; more often, it skirted the fringes of the gorge, where heavy guardrails protected motorists from skidding into the threatening depths. At intervals, Margo noted great buttresses of ghostly gray that loomed to a higher level.

They marked the new superhighway that was soon to replace Route 95. Having driven the old road before, Margo knew that soon it would swing beneath the arch of a great concrete span that stretched across the deep ravine.

There would be a climb first, a steep side road to the left, a short level stretch, and then a gradual gradual left-ward curve that would take the old road under the new bridge.

A good place to gain on the car ahead. Margo recognized the upgrade as she neared it and gave her car a spurt. She was doing forty as she passed the side road, and she held that speed along the level.

At the curve, she let her foot go to the brake pedal, though she expected that the motor itself would sufficiently reduce her speed. Still, it was best to play safe, for the ravine was on her right and Margo didn't care to test the strength of the guard rail.

She caught the gleam of a taillight as she took the bend. There was only one car that it could be—the one containing Wilbert and Quade.

Just ahead of the other car, looming like a cavernous maw, was the archway of the great new span. The other car was curving into it, as though some monster were receiving it in a side-mouthed gulp. The thought gave Margo a momentary shudder. It was curious how she could imagine things.

But nothing, in all of Margo's wildest fancy, could have matched what did occur.

IT came before Quade's car even reached the harmless gullet of the bridge. Margo had heard of bolts from the blue; this was a bolt from the black. It struck downward from the blocked-off glow of the stars above the huge concrete bridge.

It was a flash of forked lightning, jagged, brilliant in its gleam, terrific in its stroke. A blinding flash, accompanied by a smash of thunder that seemed to burst Margo's ears and jar her from the wheel.

Her own car lurched over toward the guard rail, as her foot instinctively drove down on the brake pedal. But the jounce that she took was as nothing compared to what happened to the car ahead

Like a shaft of doom hurled by some ancient thunder god, the bolt struck the car containing Wilbert and Quade, made it twist and writhe like a living creature in agony.

Wrenched out of shape as the lightning lashed it, the car actually somersaulted toward the guard rail. It didn't have to bounce across the barrier, for the rail itself was cloven by the bolt, and with it went a chunk of roadway ripped up by lightning's power.

Margo had a momentary glimpse of the doomed car plunging into the ravine; then blackness was back again, in all its intensity.

Then, as a final touch to those loud, but short-lived peals, Margo heard a dull, metallic crash drift upward from the depths of the ravine.

It marked the final halt of the doomed car beside the rock-strewn creek, a hundred feet below. A token of double death that had come to Louis Wilbert and Harvey Quade, whose scheme for mutual profit had perished with them!

CHAPTER II
MEN OF THE NIGHT

MARGO'S car was perched against the guard rail, some thirty feet short of the spot where the barrier had broken to let Wilbert and Quade take their plunge from the old highway.

Probably the drop hadn't been needed to seal their doom, for Margo's recollection of the lightning stroke was vivid enough to include a picture of a car so twisted that death could have come instantly to the occupants.

There was something else that Margo remembered, though it came back to her gradually. The concrete bridge had been plainly shown in the glare that had turned blackness into something more brilliant than daylight. She recalled tall towers, skeleton structures, on the bridge itself, and a truck parked beside them. She wondered if the truck had occupants, too; if so, how they had fared.

Her own plight didn't bother her, chiefly because it did not seem serious. She was safe—alive; that much was certain. She couldn't wonder what to do next because she felt too dazed. Besides, her eyes still saw jagged flashes—after-images of the lightning—and she was wondering, vaguely, why no thunderclaps accompanied the brilliance.

Her eyes tightly shut, Margo pressed them with her hands, and gradually the forked light faded. Then, oddly, she thought she heard the thunder rumbling from somewhere up above her. It didn't come with a loud burst, nor did it echo as it had before, and very suddenly, Margo realized that it wasn't thunder at all.

The noise was the motor of the truck that she had seen on the bridge. It was pulling away from the span above.

Margo reached for the door of the coupé. She couldn't find it at first, because she was lying on it. At last, she recognized the tilt at which the car had stopped. Pulling herself up against the wheel, she groped for the door handle.

The door gave of its own accord and Margo rolled out into the arms of two men, who had opened the door from the outside.

She couldn't see their faces, even though there was a slight trace of starlight, for her eyes were just recovering from the ordeal of the lightning. But Margo, taking these arrivals for friends, thought she must tell them what had happened.

"One car went off the road," she gasped. "It had two men in it! The lightning struck it! There was a truck ... up on the bridge—"

One man was hauling Margo to her feet. The other pushed something cold against her neck. The pressure, plus the man's growl, told Margo that the object was a gun.

"All right, wise dame," the man said. "You're coming with us, and no squawks!"

Margo made no squawk. She was too dazed even to stay on her feet. The road wasn't tilted the way her car was, and she lost her sense of balance. Before gripping hands could halt her, she slumped back into the car. Her head rolled away from the gun and angled across the wheel. The first man was trying to haul her out through the door again, when the fellow with the gun gruffed:

"Hold it! Here comes a car the other way."

The tone was half gloating, and Margo saw why,

when she half opened her eyes. Headlights were swinging from beneath the arch of the concrete bridge, and only by a sudden maneuver did the arriving car escape disaster.

The lightning had carved the narrow highway almost to its center, and the left wheels of the car just missed the fissure, as the driver swung the right ones against the embankment.

Chunks dropped from the center of the road as the car pushed past. It veered slightly, and its headlights fully illuminated Margo's coupé and the men beside it. With a glance, the girl observed the pair.

They looked rough, but fairly respectable; more like a pair of truckers than the thugs that Margo knew they must be.

Half hidden by his companion, the man with the gun was sliding the weapon away, but Margo saw that both were keeping their hands in their coat pockets.

As the other car arrived, a clatter told that the door had opened on the driver's side. The two thugs couldn't see the man who was getting out, because he was in back of the lights. Thinking that Margo had gone back into her daze, the pair stepped forward, rather affably. Margo heard one speaking to the man that he couldn't see.

"You'd better hop along the road," he said, "and warn people about the cave-in, so they won't come through. The girl's all right"—he was gesturing back in Margo's direction—"and we'll look after her."

Desperately, Margo raised her head.

"No, no!" she called. "I'm not all right! Look out; those men have guns!"

THE thugs were turning when they heard Margo's outcry, and she thought they were going to pounce back to her car, to silence her; hence, she sped the rest of the warning. But the mere mention of guns produced a reverse effect.

Wheeling, the thugs yanked their weapons and sprang for the driver of the rescue car, hoping to suppress him.

They were going into blackness beyond the lights; at least, so they thought. Instead, that blackness surged out to meet them. It came in the shape of a cloaked fighter, who already carried a drawn automatic; a figure whose challenging laugh was an added token of identity.

The Shadow!

How he had come here from the wrong direction, was as much a mystery to Margo as to the would-be captors who had hoped to suppress her. However, sight of crime's archfoe blotted trifling matters from their minds. Their guns already drawn, they tried to use them.

It was a foolish effort, considering that The Shadow already held them covered, and his speed with a gun trigger would easily have enabled him to jab two shots before either thug could supply one.

But The Shadow wasn't wasting bullets at this moment, nor did he care to deliver death where other measures would suffice. He made a slash at one crook's gun, while his other hand sped for the second man's wrist and plucked it upward.

The first gun flew to the roadway; the second spouted a harmless shot in the air. With a twist, The Shadow not only wrenched the gun from the hand that had fired it; his leverage on the man's arm somersaulted the thug a dozen feet from Margo's car.

The first man, scrambling to regain his lost revolver, was halted by The Shadow's laugh; while the other, on hands and knees, looked more dazed than Margo had when she rolled from the coupé.

It would have been an easy victory for The Shadow, but for the seemingly useless shot that one of the foemen had fired. That shot proved a signal.

Before The Shadow could huddle the two prisoners together, guns began to blast from down the road. Bullets whizzed past Margo's coupé; wide shots, but close enough to prove that marksmen would soon find the range, with The Shadow as their target, if he remained where he was.

Oddly, The Shadow did remain. He seemed bewildered, as he wheeled toward Margo's car. The thugs close by grabbed up their guns and sprang for their black-clad foe, thinking that it was now their turn for victory.

Ending his bewildered pretense, The Shadow twisted hard upon them, giving a mocking laugh that told how ably he had tricked them. It was too late, then, for the pair to change their misguided tactics.

The Shadow was upon them. Slashing with his automatic, gripping with his free hand, he was knocking other guns aside, and at the same time hauling his foemen into a grapple that they could not escape. The Shadow wasn't slugging them into submission, as he could easily have done; he was letting them continue a groggy struggle, so that they served as human shields against the distant gunfire.

Always, the two buffeted thugs were between The Shadow and the marksmen somewhere down the road; hence the spasmodic shots continued to be wide. Sharpshooters were yelling for their pals to wrest away, to allow clear aim at The Shadow; but the two thugs couldn't.

One person, alone, failed to realize The Shadow's strategy. That person was Margo Lane, at present back behind the wheel of her tilted coupé. From Margo's restricted viewpoint, The Shadow's grapple with two foemen looked legitimate enough. Indeed, the way he reeled to turn his antagonists toward the gunfire, made it seem that they were gaining the upper hand.

They were swinging their guns, those thugs, and Margo didn't realize that The Shadow was letting them. Each time he parried a wild stroke, Margo thought that luck was partly responsible. The grapplers were at the very door of the car, and Margo valiantly tried to equalize the struggle by grabbing at the first man she could reach.

At that moment, The Shadow was voicing a sharp command, apparently meant for someone in his own car. Too late to countermand the order, he hurled one thug aside and lunged for the other, who was turning to beat off Margo's clutch.

The lights of The Shadow's roadster were suddenly extinguished, a result of his command, bringing a blanket of absolute blackness upon the scene.

THINGS happened quickly, and blindly. The Shadow hooked the second thug as the fellow's swinging gun was descending toward Margo's

Blackness surged out to meet the thugs. It came in the shape of a figure whose challenging laugh was an added token of identity. The Shadow!

head. The action would have fully diverted the stroke, if Margo, thanks to her tenacious grip, hadn't come along.

As it was, she took a glancing blow that gave her the sensation of bursts of light amid the darkness, a miniature reminder of the lightning flash that she had seen earlier.

Margo's grip was gone. She rolled back into the car, while the slugging thug, caught by the full fury of The Shadow's fling, took off for the other side of the road in a spinning plunge that landed him headlong.

Hurled like chaff, The Shadow's two antagonists were gone, while Margo's moan, coming from within the coupé, revealed that she was not too badly hurt. With darkness laying its deep shroud over all, The Shadow had attained the setting that he needed.

Again, The Shadow's laugh; this time a taunt that carried its sardonic mirth to distant men who had halted their useless gunfire. The challenge that only The Shadow could utter, a tone that carried prophecy along with its note of triumph.

A relentless laugh, promising victory in the greater fray that was to come. Victory, not for those marksmen who no longer had a target, but for the avenger who opposed them, The Shadow!

CHAPTER III
THE WRONG ROAD

THE SHADOW'S gun was talking from deep darkness, its stabs directed toward the enemies who had tried to clip him from long range. Uncannily, he had gauged their position from their earlier fire and was placing shots too close for their comfort. They began an immediate retreat, supplying a wild return fire as they went.

The thing that baffled that crew completely was the way The Shadow's fire shifted. The spurts of his gun came from varied angles, in a style that they could not fathom.

At one moment, he seemed to be shooting from the rail that bordered the ravine; at the next, from somewhere on the other side of the road. The range of his fire also fluctuated, making it impossible to guess where he had gone.

It didn't occur to those retiring gunners that they were dealing with two opponents, instead of one. Having lost sight of The Shadow during his struggle beside Margo's coupé, they supposed that he had gotten back to his own car and turned off the lights himself.

Actually, the lights were blotted out by Harry Vincent, one of The Shadow's secret agents, who had accompanied his chief on this expedition. Harry had simply awaited The Shadow's order.

Once given, the order was also Harry's cue to join the fray. He was out of the car, pumping shots along with The Shadow's. Perfectly teamed, The Shadow and his agent were alternating their fire, each picking up where the other left off. Such sporadic gunnery bewildered the opposition, making them think that The Shadow might be anywhere—or everywhere.

Indeed, The Shadow intended to further that impression. Drawing a fresh automatic, he delivered two quick shots—a signal for Harry to continue the fire alone. Crossing to the inside of the road, The Shadow was ready to move in rapidly upon his foemen, to reveal himself among them while they still believed him to be elsewhere.

He had calculated their number to be no more than four, and a surprise attack from their midst would be sufficient to scatter a group of that small size.

But before The Shadow could make his advance through darkness, his opponents received a warning. It came from the two thugs who had taken those sprawls in the road.

Finding their feet and their guns, they were too chary to attempt new combat with The Shadow. Instead, they crept to the inside of the road and began climbing up among rocks and slender trees, to reach the higher level.

Loosened stones began to tumble down, while saplings crackled as the fugitives gripped them. Realizing that they were giving themselves away, they went the limit.

"Look out for The Shadow!" yelled one. "He's moving in on you!"

"He's got other guys with him!" howled the other. "A bunch of them—"

The rest was drowned by the burst of guns. Turning, The Shadow was shooting in the direction of the voices, largely for Harry's benefit. The Shadow's own position was unknown; that of his agent could be spotted. The thing was to spur the flight of the two fugitives before they could get in deadly work. The Shadow succeeded—and more.

Not only did his bullets ricochet among the rocks; those slugs nicked the fleeing men, for the wild shots that they sent back were interspersed with howls. After that, they fired no more; the only sounds from their direction were stumbling clambers toward the top of the steep slope.

They wouldn't have taken that precipitous route unless it offered safety, and The Shadow promptly linked their flight with the calls that they had given.

Down the road, four other men were in rapid retreat past the shelter of the bend. Unquestionably they had a car awaiting them; hence, there was only one way to overtake them, along with the crippled fugitives who had scaled the height.

Springing toward his roadster, The Shadow met Harry on the way. He sliced a flashlight's gleam toward Margo's tilted coupé, revealing the half-stunned girl behind the wheel. He gave quick orders to his agent, then leaped to the wheel of his own roadster. Big lights glimmered; The Shadow shot the car into gear and was away with a roar.

By then, Harry was at the coupé, pushing Margo to the high side of the car. Backing the coupé, Harry worked it to the middle of the road, then started forward. Since The Shadow's car was gone, the way was clear.

Bearing to the left, Harry avoided the cleft in the road and continued beneath the great arch of the concrete bridge, carrying Margo off to safety.

MEANWHILE, The Shadow, speeding in the opposite direction, caught the shine of lights off to his right and above. Crooks had reached their car and were starting it up the steep side road that Margo had noted when she passed it earlier.

Veering hard to the left, The Shadow skimmed the guard rail, applying the brakes after yanking the wheel hard to the right. The sudden jolt actually put the big roadster into a skid that enabled him to make the hairpin turn. Then, accelerator shoved to the floorboard, he was spurting up the steep slope of the narrow side road, on the trail of the car that carried the fugitive mob.

Crooks couldn't have supposed that The Shadow would make the U-turn in one sweep; otherwise, they wouldn't have slackened their flight to take on the two men who had clambered up from the rocky slope.

Those two were hardly on the running board, before The Shadow's lights loomed into sight from the rear, fully disclosing the fugitive car as a rakish sedan, the very sort that mobbies would prefer.

The man at the wheel of the sedan did not wait for others to open the doors and take the wounded thugs on board. He gave his car all the speed he could, took it over a sharp rise, and made a sudden turn to the right.

Perhaps he hoped that the swerve would deceive The Shadow, but it didn't. The pursuing roadster was too close to lose the trail.

Therewith, The Shadow made a valuable discovery. In cutting off to the right, the sedan was picking a road not yet opened for public travel. It was leading The Shadow across the great span that formed a link in the new superhighway that crossed above Route 95.

Where one car was going, another could have preceded it. And that fact told its own story. The Shadow knew, without Margo's testimony, that the disaster that overwhelmed Wilbert and Quade must have come from the bridge top.

There was no sign of the truck that Margo had observed coincident with the lightning flash, for it had gone; but The Shadow recognized the existence of such a vehicle and knew that the fleeing sedan was nothing but a cover-up car, that had come along Route 95 to make sure that murder was properly delivered.

The roadbed of the great bridge was a level of rough concrete that had not yet been surfaced; hence it could not show telltale tire marks. But by forcing the sedan along that route, The Shadow was driving it on the trail of the truck. The farther such a trail continued, the better; so, to spur it, The Shadow leaned from beside his wheel and fired after the sedan.

Beyond the big bridge, the other car swerved. Apparently, its driver wanted to cut away on another dirt road, but was afraid to take the risk while harried by The Shadow's shots. He kept straight ahead, hoping to outspeed the roadster; but The Shadow kept the distance constant.

Gunners were firing back, without avail, for The Shadow had already gauged the limit of their accuracy and was keeping just beyond it.

The superhighway was tricky, sometimes broad and finished, at other stretches no more than a single lane. At the end of a mile, the sedan went smacking through a barrier, knocking it to splinters and keeping right ahead.

Flimsiness of the blocking fence made The Shadow assume that murderers, in fleeing earlier, had paused to replace the barrier. He could still force the sedan to keep to the right track.

The sedan took a sharp jerk to the left, so suddenly that one of the wounded thugs was flung from the running board on the right. The sedan was gone, down a ramp that led from the superhighways, and in its place The Shadow's headlights showed the rolling figure of the fellow who had been thrown off.

Braking his car, The Shadow heard a wild scream as the sliding man reached the road edge; then the human figure was gone, and the shriek was a trailing cry of hopeless horror.

Coming to a stop at the very brink, The Shadow saw a great gulf below. This was another ravine, not yet bridged. The unhappy thug had gone into its depths.

The road barrier was explained. Its purpose had been to keep cars from this stretch of unbridged highway. It followed, therefore, that the murder truck could not have continued this far along the route. It must have turned off earlier, before the barricade, and the sedan, in keeping straight through, had diverted The Shadow from the trail he really wanted.

There was only one course: to go after the

sedan and overtake it, forcing its crew to tell whatever they knew.

REVERSING the roadster, The Shadow guided it down the ramp, hitting a terrific speed along a slope of white concrete that might end nowhere. As the slope leveled, he saw dirt at the end; beyond, the lights of the sedan, which was darting toward a narrow bridge.

The Shadow struck the dirt with a jolt that bounced his roadster like a test plane making too sudden a landing. He righted it skillfully, but one great bound landed a front wheel against a jutting rock that encroached upon the road.

The front tire burst, hurling the car half over. The lights produced a whirl of green and gray trees and rocks—toward which the car was lurching.

To another driver, they might have signified calamity; but The Shadow's reverse twist of the steering wheel averted disaster. The roadster seemed to balance on its good front tire as its cloaked driver pivoted it full about, halting it straight across the road, with its rear toward the craggy embankment that had threatened to receive the crippled car.

Even as the headlights made their rapid sweep, The Shadow observed the scene ahead. He saw the fleeing sedan swing past the buttress of the old bridge and dart across, taking itself beyond gun reach. It swerved as sharply as when it had left the superhighway, and with the same result, for The Shadow caught a kaleidoscopic glimpse of a flinging figure that could no longer cling to the sedan's running board.

The fugitive sedan had lightened itself of the second wounded thug. Like the first, he had gone from sight, but his tumble was a shorter one, for the bridge was a low one, not much above the level of the creek.

To The Shadow, that one man, discarded by his fellow fugitives, might be as valuable as all the rest. Dropping from the disabled roadster, The Shadow hurried to the bridge.

From beside the bridgehead, The Shadow flicked a flashlight's beam to the creek bed. He saw a crazily sprawled figure, half in the water, half reclining on sharp rocks that bordered the bank. One look was sufficient proof that the victim was past recovery. Only a closer view would tell if he still had life in him.

The Shadow obtained that view by a quick drop from the abutment. Reaching the sprawled form, he tilted the thug's head upward and saw a face that was streaked with blood from a gash above the temple. Eyes opened, as if impelled by the focused flashlight. Tilting the beam, The Shadow let the dying man see his own hawkish visage, just above.

A shudder seized the dying thug. It might have been a natural spasm, but it seemed inspired by the burn of The Shadow's eyes and the whispered tone that reached the fellow's fading hearing.

There was accusation in The Shadow's whisper, but it was not directed toward this recent enemy. Instead, The Shadow's wrath was meant for those who had abandoned their companion. His words promised vengeance, and the dying man responded.

"We were covering up," the thug gasped. "For ... for Bayruth. Oliver Bayruth ... the guy in the truck ... on the bridge—"

"Bayruth," The Shadow repeated. "The man who murdered Wilbert and Quade."

Dying eyes were glaring, as their owner tried to nod; then, half raised from The Shadow's propping arm, he gulped:

"But it wasn't Bayruth who wanted them croaked. He isn't the big guy. I'll tell you who the brain is—"

A choke halted those all-important words. For a moment, it seemed that the dying crook would say no more, until, with a convulsive effort, he added:

"His name ... is Thor—"

There was a *click* from a rattling throat. Lips failed, as they sought to form a further phrase. Instead of closing, those lips widened in a death grin, as a dead weight settled back against The Shadow's arm.

Strange, sibilant, was The Shadow's mirthless laugh, when he eased the dead form to the rocks and turned to pick his way back to his car. A low-toned laugh, that blended with the chatter of the creek that licked the dead figure on the bank and continued its tumultuous path beneath the old and silent bridge.

CHAPTER IV
CRIME RETRACED

THE next afternoon Margo Lane still had a headache, which didn't help her recollections of the night before. In fact, the more that Margo thought about the happenings on Highway 95, the hazier they became. By three o'clock, she had managed to forget them, when Lamont Cranston called her, inviting her to lunch.

Usually, Margo lunched earlier than three, but today the late hour pleased her, for the cafe where she met Cranston was quiet and deserted. Cranston did not question her regarding the preceding evening, nor did his impassive features betray any curiosity about her adventures.

Margo stood it as long as she could, then emphatically opened her handbag and brought out some penciled notes.

"In case you're interested, Lamont," she said, "I'll tell you just what happened. I wrote it down this morning, at ten o'clock, which was when I woke up. Wilbert and Quade were getting along all right, until the lightning struck them—"

"The lightning?" came Cranston's query. "There were no thunder showers last night."

"I *saw* the lightning," Margo insisted. "A great flash of it! Right out of the sky, down past the bridge."

"Odd that it didn't strike the bridge."

"The br idge was made of concrete," reminded Margo, "and that's probably why it didn't attract the lightning. Don't try to tell me that there wasn't any bridge, because I saw it, too, with a truck on top of it, between the towers."

Cranston gave a slight smile.

"I suppose that the truck was made of concrete, too."

Margo hadn't considered that detail. She began to puzzle why the lightning hadn't struck the truck on the bridge, instead of the car coming beneath. Then, noting that Cranston had not relaxed his smile, she ignored that little matter and stuck to her story.

"Wilbert and Quade went off the road," declared Margo. "I nearly ditched my own car, and I was still in it when two men came along. They were very tough, or would have been, if The Shadow hadn't shown up. He was fighting them, and I was trying to help, when something hit me on the head."

"And you saw a lot of light?"

"Yes. Lots of it."

"Which probably explains the lightning flash you mentioned," decided Cranston. "Maybe you dreamed the whole thing, Margo, because it doesn't fit with the newspaper account. Here—you can read it for yourself."

Margo spent the rest of the lunch hour reading the newspaper version. It stated that the car containing Wilbert and Quade had gone to its destruction because of a cave-in on Route 95. There was no mention of any lightning, nor of a mystery truck.

As for thugs, two dead ones had been found, but they were far removed from the scene of doom that Margo had witnessed. So far removed, that the police believed them to be victims of a mob feud that had carried from Manhattan out to the hinterlands of New Jersey.

"Maybe The Shadow does know something about it," remarked Cranston in a musing tone. "Someone called the house last night and said that you were in your car a few miles from where the accident occurred. I sent Stanley to take you back New York."

Stanley was Cranston's chauffeur. Vaguely,

MARGO LANE

Margo could remember being in her car, near a crossroad, when Stanley arrived with Cranston's limousine. She recalled the trip into Manhattan, now that Cranston mentioned it. Watching her changes of expression, The Shadow observed that she was still unable to piece events in between.

It didn't occur to Margo that Cranston had come from his New Jersey estate and sped along Route 95 in the opposite direction, hoping to pick up the trail of Wilbert and Quade before they turned off from the old highway. Even though she identified Cranston with The Shadow, the arrival of the cloaked fighter seemed, as usual, something bordering upon the marvelous.

Nor did she guess that Harry Vincent had been with The Shadow. The fact was that Harry had called Stanley before Margo came out of her daze, which accounted for her being found a few miles from the scene of tragedy.

"We know, at least, that Wilbert and Quade are dead," declared Cranston, finally. "Suppose you let me look into the rest of it, Margo. I'm going over to see Oswald Kelber and find out what he thinks about it. I'll call you later."

THERE was just one place to see Oswald Kelber during business hours: namely, at the offices of Universal Industries, which were located on the fortieth story of an uptown office building.

Very few visitors were admitted to Kelber's

private office, but Lamont Cranston was one of the privileged. Passing a battery of secretaries, he was finally ushered into Kelber's presence, to receive an enthusiastic welcome.

Bulky, fat-faced and bushy-browed, Kelber wasn't the sort to show much enthusiasm; but on this occasion, he did. His warm, high-pressure handshake proved that he regarded Cranston as a friend in need.

"You've come to talk about Wilbert!" exclaimed Kelber in a booming tone. "You don't have to tell me, Cranston. You're one man, at least, who understands how serious this tragedy may prove. I wish that others could, particularly those whose own interests are concerned."

The Shadow gave a typically Cranston nod.

"You mean your associates in Universal Industries?"

"Certain of my associates," specified Kelber. "Sit down, Cranston, and let me give you a picture of the situation. I want you to judge for yourself whether I am right."

Seated, The Shadow watched Kelber pace back and forth. After a few pauses by the window, where he studied the panorama of Manhattan, Kelber swung about in his brusque but ponderous style.

"I have certain contracts to deliver," boomed Kelber. "I must equip important plants, so that they can turn out defense armaments. The total of those contracts amounts to some fifty million dollars, and they hinge upon certain key industries.

"For example, we need fireproof materials that can only be supplied by the Asbestile Co. The new plants must be bombproof, and I am depending upon the Orvis Engineering Corp. to design them. The government demands that every unit be protected against poison gas, which can only be done by installing air conditioning equipment manufactured by Vortex Circulators.

"Asbestile—Orvis—Vortex"—Kelber was counting them on his fingers—"they are the three bottlenecks. If any one of the three should fail me, my contracts will be lost. That is why I had Wilbert inspect their plants and make sure that they were safe. Wilbert's report was favorable."

The Shadow gave a nod. It was obvious that the reports would be favorable. Companies that manufactured fireproof materials, cantilever girders, and metal air circulators were not the vulnerable sort. On the surface, Kelber's worries seemed unfounded, but evidently his thoughts went deeper.

"Wilbert's reports were favorable," repeated Kelber. "But Wilbert is dead!" He stopped by his desk, to pound it. "Dead, I say! Killed by some unexplainable accident, in company with a man named Quade. Do you understand, Cranston?"

"I understand," replied The Shadow, calmly. "I have read all about it in the newspapers."

"You know who Louis Wilbert was," declared Kelber. "But did you ever hear of Harvey Quade before?"

The Shadow shook his head. Kelber picked up a sheaf of Wilbert's reports and thumbed through them. Finding the page he wanted, he raised his eyes and studied his visitor from beneath bushy brows

"You haven't heard of Harvey Quade," Kelber stated. "Tell me: do you know of Oliver Bayruth?"

That name meant much to The Shadow. Only the night before, it had been coughed by a dying thug upon the rocky bank of a creek. Moreover, The Shadow had looked into the case of Oliver Bayruth and knew quite well who the man was. Nevertheless, in playing the part of Cranston, it was better not to recognize the name. Therefore, The Shadow gazed questioningly at Kelber.

"I'll tell you who Bayruth is," confided Kelber, leaning across his big desk. "He is an inventor, an electrical wizard, once in the employ of Jerome Thorden. I don't have to ask you who Thorden is"—Kelber's tone became bitter—"because everyone knows that he is the one man who would profit if Universal Industries lost fifty million dollars in government contracts."

The Shadow's eyes took on a steady gaze. They lacked their habitual burn, but they had a strength that suited Cranston when his keen mind was aroused. In even tone, The Shadow stated:

"You mean there was a link between the dead man, Quade, and the living inventor, Bayruth."

"Precisely," affirmed Kelber. "My investigator, Wilbert, reported it. He was using Quade to find out what he could about Bayruth. What happened? There is your answer!" Kelber flung a newspaper across the desk. "Both Wilbert and Quade were killed!"

IN his ponderous style, Kelber resumed his pacing. He paused by the window, to turn around. The features of his heavy face had tightened; his tone was hollow, with a deep tremolo, as he declared:

"Wilbert and Quade, dead by accident. It was no accident, Cranston! Believe me, when I declare

★ ★

and cops alike—The Shadow, through his agents, gains knowledge of crime in the making and sets his plans accordingly. Criminals quail at his name, as the Master Fighter takes to their trail.

Cliff Marsland and Hawkeye are The Shadow's underworld contact men. Known as crooks, they are in reality in The Shadow's pay. From Clyde Burke, star reporter of the "Classic," comes information obtained by valuable newspaper contacts. Moe Shrevnitz, taxi driver "par excellence," takes the Crime Fighter Extraordinary on his secret missions. Harry Vincent—he owes his life to The Shadow—is the right-hand man of the Master of Darkness. The contact man is Burbank; through him clear all messages between The Shadow and his agents. Behind his occupation of investment broker, Rutledge Mann tenders invaluable aid to The Shadow.

These, and others, are the trusted agents of The Shadow.

Unknown to all but two trusted Xinca Indian servants, The Shadow's true identity is that of Kent Allard, internationally famous aviator. As such, he sometimes appears in public; but more often he takes on the guise of Lamont Cranston, well-known world traveler and explorer. There is a real Cranston, a man of deep understanding, and it is with his permission that The Shadow adopts his identity at such times when Cranston is away.

Such is The Shadow; only The Shadow knows!!

that it was death by design. Oliver Bayruth, the man who puts crazed inventions into the realm of reality, is responsible for the double murder!"

The Shadow gave the statement long consideration. It was impossible for Kelber to trace the thoughts behind the impassive mask of Cranston, even though the glow of the late afternoon sun was shining through the window, directly on the visitor's face. But the very calmness of Cranston's features, the length of time before he spoke, were proofs that he was tracing the case to a further conclusion.

At last, The Shadow spoke.

"Bayruth could gain nothing through such murders," came Cranston's verdict. "But Thorden could—"

He paused, awaiting Kelber's reaction. When it came, its note of caution was accentuated by a query.

"Can I accuse Thorden?" Kelber asked. Then, with an impatient headshake: "I can't even go to see him, nor can any of my associates. But there is one man, Cranston, who might."

Kelber's eyes narrowed as he spoke, and a faint smile crossed Cranston's lips. Very calmly, The Shadow nodded. Eagerly, Kelber questioned:

"You will, Cranston?"

"This afternoon," replied The Shadow, rising. "I am quite sure that Jerome Thorden will receive me. Perhaps, Kelber"—The Shadow's tone was casual—"I may be able to bring back the rest of Wilbert's unfinished report."

The two parted with a handshake. Turning toward the door, The Shadow let his lips relax into a smile that Kelber did not see. The assignment was to The Shadow's liking. As Cranston, he was embarking upon new adventure which promised results far more startling than those of the night before!

CHAPTER V
IN THE RIVAL CAMP

IN every way except one, Jerome Thorden was the opposite of Oswald Kelber. Both were men of grandiose ideas, who thought in terms of business contracts that totaled many millions; but there, the similarity ended.

Kelber, big and brusque, heavy in appearance and manner, insisted upon skyscraper offices where he could pace about and bellow orders to subordinates. Contrarily, Thorden was a retiring man, smooth of guise and tone, though he could be crisp when occasion called. Furthermore, Thorden never went to his offices at all.

Thorden preferred the quiet of his old brownstone mansion. The house stood on a secluded street and had the appearance of a mausoleum, inside as well as out. In fact, the old saying: "All hope abandon, ye who enter here" was bound to occur to every visitor who entered the ominous brownstone portals.

Never had Thorden's mansion looked so forbidding as it did when Cranston approached it that afternoon. The Shadow had seen the place often before, but never at this particular hour. Daylight took some of the grimness from the mansion, and darkness softened the formidable aspect of the walls; but this happened to be an in-between time.

The sun had just descended beyond tall buildings to the west of Thorden's mansion, and the result was a preternatural dusk. Elsewhere in Manhattan, the sun was still shining, but not upon Thorden's residence. It was as if the occupant, himself, had personally designed the setting.

Sensitive to unusual impressions, The Shadow was quite sure that eyes were watching him as he approached. Eyes that could have been concealed within recessed windows, looking for anyone who entered by the gate.

Reaching the great front door, The Shadow could actually feel the bulk of the building above him, and when the door opened in response to his ring, he wasn't at all surprised to meet a cadaverous servant who looked like something that the house had hatched.

Such a welcome could not faze The Shadow. Preserving the imperturbable calm of Cranston, he gave his name and asked to see Mr. Thorden. After a few minutes wait in a big, gloomy hall, The Shadow was conducted up a grand staircase, into a front room that served as Thorden's office.

It was exactly the setting that suited Jerome Thorden. The man was seated in a corner, behind a desk of quartered oak that matched the other furniture and the paneled wainscoting of the high but gloomy room. The windows were adorned with curtains of a lacy variety, which produced the effect of an encircling cobweb, with Thorden as the spider in the center of the lair.

The Shadow noted that the curtains were transparent when anyone looked outward, which fitted his impression that Thorden, from the desk, could watch for any visitors who approached by the front walk.

Thorden was darkish and his black hair, parted at one side, gave him a Napoleonic appearance. His eyes, too, were black, sharp beads peering from his tawny visage, but they seemed curious, rather than challenging. He had met Cranston rather frequently, and did not seem surprised by the calm man's visit. Merely curious was Thorden, but not at all hurried in his effort to learn why Cranston had come to the mansion.

IN Cranston's style, The Shadow gave an ostensible reason for the visit. Cranston held a sizable interest in the Equator Importing Co., which brought in various products from Central and South America. He could supply anything from antimony to mahogany, and wanted to know if Thorden had any uses for special imports.

Thorden's eyes became very wise.

"Thorden Enterprises are marking time," he said in an oily tone. "We have no large contracts at present, though, being equipped to handle them, we expect some in the future. I would say, Cranston"—Thorden's voice became crisp—"that the man for you to see is Oswald Kelber, head of Universal Industries."

"I have seen Kelber," responded The Shadow, blandly, scarcely noting the gimlet probe of Thorden's eyes. "In fact, I have just come from Kelber's office. He has already ordered certain imports, but is not ready for more. Perhaps"—The Shadow gave a shrug—"he found my prices too high."

Thorden relaxed, chuckling dryly.

"Kelber *would* find prices high," declared Thorden. "He went overboard when he underbid me on those government products. Fifty million dollars seems a lot of money, but Kelber will be lucky if he realizes any profit, at all."

Cranston's expression showed surprise; only a flicker of it, but enough for Thorden's sharp eyes to detect the facial change.

"Let me tell you something about Universal Industries," said Thorden, indulgently. "It is made up of a dozen corporations, some of which Kelber controls. But the key corporations, the real profit-makers, are in other hands. Kelber brought them into line, but he does not own them. He had to sublet contracts to them—on their terms.

"For example, Kelber needs a fireproof material called Asbestile, and he will have to pay for it. Jarvis Fralingham, who owns the Asbestile Co., is smart enough to insist upon his proper profit. So is Martin Orvis, head of the Orvis Engineering Corp. There is another company, too—"

Thorden paused, as though he couldn't remember the name of the concern. At last, he recalled it.

"Ah, yes," he remarked. "Vortex Circulators, which belong to Roy Darrison. He wants too much for everything, Darrison does. I know, because I once tried to make a deal with him, but had to acquire other air-conditioning equipment instead.

"Yes, Kelber will regret that he took those contracts." Thorden smiled smugly. "In fact, he has probably regretted it already. Those key companies will eat up all his profits. Possibly he mentioned the companies to you, Cranston. If he did, I'll wager he was worried."

Kelber *had* mentioned the three companies, expressing worry at the time, but not on the score that Thorden brought up. Kelber hadn't discussed profits; he was simply concerned because Asbestile, Orvis, and Vortex were vulnerable factors in Universal Industries.

It was obvious that Thorden must also recognize that point, but the oily man was either ignoring it, or preferred to conceal his knowledge. More than ever, Thorden was playing the spider, and he seemed to regard Cranston as a fly.

Absently, The Shadow tried to recall the things that Kelber had said; then, musingly, he remarked:

"Yes, Kelber was worried. Perhaps that was why we didn't get down to business. Kelber was quite upset over the death of some chap who worked for him. I believe that Wilbert was the fellow's name."

Thorden's eyes glittered. His head came forward, his hand drew up to receive his chin. His tone became crisp.

"Kelber *should* have been upset," Thorden declared. "Wilbert happened to be his prize snooper! Did he tell you that, Cranston?"

"He said that Wilbert was an investigator—"

"Another name for snooper," interrupted Thorden. "Among other things, Wilbert was checking on *my* business. He wanted to find out how Thorden Enterprises worked, so that he could sell such information to Kelber and thereby help Universal Industries. But Wilbert found out—nothing!"

LEANING back, Thorden spread his hands as a token of emptiness. Then, regretfully, he added:

"I'm sorry about Wilbert's death. The poor chap was harmless. In fact, last night he was riding on some sort of a wild-goose chase, along with a man named Quade. I really believe"—Thorden inserted a dryish laugh—"that Quade was taking him to see Oliver Bayruth."

The name didn't seem to register with Cranston. Thorden explained that Bayruth was an electrical wizard whose ideas, originally sound, had gone completely haywire. Ruefully, Thorden admitted that he had invested some fifty thousand dollars in Bayruth's inventions before learning that they were impractical.

"When Bayruth began to talk about perpetual motion, it was just too much," declared Thorden. "I paid him off and let him go. I haven't seen hide or hair of him since. I've had a little correspondence with him, none of it important. I suppose that Bayruth has tucked himself away in some retreat, to work on his impossible ideas and squander what money he has left."

The mention of correspondence interested The Shadow, even though Thorden defined it as unimportant. Thorden had a way of making important things seem just the opposite, and vice versa. Correspondence happened to be the subject that Wilbert had discussed with Quade in Margo's hearing. Obviously, they had referred to letters which were in Bayruth's possession.

The Shadow would have liked, very much, to have a look into Bayruth's files, particularly to see what sort of letters Thorden had actually written to the inventor. To do that, it would first be necessary to locate Bayruth.

Thorden was one man who might know Bayruth's present whereabouts but he had smoothly disclaimed such knowledge. Nevertheless, The Shadow still believed that he might obtain a clue through Thorden.

Abruptly, The Shadow arose, dropping the calm pose that suited Cranston. Thorden was quick to mark the change, which was precisely what The Shadow wanted.

As they shook hands at the door, The Shadow felt the gleam of beady eyes upon him. When he went downstairs and out the front door, he did not look back, for it was not necessary.

The Shadow knew, without benefit of such a glance, that Thorden must be watching him, and he suspected that the sharp-eyed man by this time had a companion. In that surmise, The Shadow was entirely correct.

With Cranston's departure, a blunt-faced, rangy man had stepped into Thorden's office through a revolving panel in the wall of oak. The rangy man had accompanied Thorden to a window, and both were staring through the webby curtain.

"There goes Cranston," said Thorden dryly. "I'm glad you agree with me, Blandle, when I say that he was sent here by Kelber. I want you to follow Cranston and find out where he goes next."

Blandle nodded.

"Stay on his trail," advised Thorden. "If you have difficulty, summon others to help you. Cranston is a man who knows too much. I don't like people who know too much."

That remark could well have included Wilbert and Quade, who, only the night before, had demonstrated that they knew too much. Turning from the window, Thorden gestured Blandle toward the door. As soon as the rangy man had left, Thorden indulged in a dry, harsh laugh.

Like Kelber, Thorden was classing Lamont Cranston as a mere go-between in this duel between two rival business giants. It had not yet occurred to Jerome Thorden that Lamont Cranston could be crime's master foe, The Shadow!

CHAPTER VI
TRAILS REVERSED

OUTSIDE Thorden's mansion, The Shadow stepped into his waiting limousine. From the moment that the big car pulled away, The Shadow knew that he was being trailed. The laugh that he gave was low, significant, yet carefully repressed within the confines of the car. The Shadow did not want Stanley to hear.

This happened to be Cranston's limousine, and to Stanley, the chauffeur, Cranston was Cranston only. Stanley regarded his master as quite eccentric, for Cranston liked to go to unusual places on occasion, leaving the car and returning to it whenever he so chose. But so far Stanley had never identified Lamont Cranston as The Shadow.

Others had: Margo Lane and Harry Vincent, for instance. Nevertheless, in a way, Stanley was more right than they were. Though The Shadow *did* appear as Cranston, there was another *Cranston*, also. The real Cranston was a globe-trotting millionaire who was seldom in New York. During Cranston's long periods of absence in foreign climes, The Shadow found it convenient to double for him.

Thus, to all intents and purposes, The Shadow was Lamont Cranston, and he was in such guise when he strolled from Thorden's. Hence, the laugh that he gave was especially strange, since it was The Shadow's laugh coming from Cranston's lips. The reason for the laugh was the car that pulled away from near Thorden's curb just as the limousine turned the corner. That car started just a trifle too soon to escape discovery.

Reaching for the speaking tube, The Shadow spoke in Cranston's tone. He instructed Stanley to drive in an aimless roundabout fashion while traveling to the exclusive Cobalt Club, of which Cranston was a member. Accustomed to such orders, Stanley obeyed them without question.

Dusk had gathered during The Shadow's stay at Thorden's, a dusk much deeper than the imitation which had shrouded the old mansion at the time of The Shadow's arrival. Within the limousine, The Shadow set to work to eliminate the guise of Cranston. He did it very simply.

Drawing a secret shelf from beneath the rear seat of the limousine, The Shadow took out a black cloak and a slouch hat. From the moment that he slid into those garments, he was obliterated. Passing streetlamps showed only darkness within the limousine.

That darkness contained The Shadow!

Packing a brace of automatics in holsters beneath his coat, The Shadow next drew on a pair of black gloves. He slid the secret drawer beneath the seat, and pressed a button in the partition that separated him from Stanley.

A panel came open, in the back of the front seat. From it, The Shadow took a pair of earphones. He turned a dial and spoke in whispered tone. A voice answered:

"Burbank speaking."

The Shadow had established shortwave radio contact with Burbank, the secret agent who forwarded instructions along to others. The Shadow's whisper continued; it brought a parting response in Burbank's methodical tone:

"Instructions received."

From then on, The Shadow sat back and waited. He didn't want the car behind to lose the trail; but it did, for a while. Stanley had a way of turning corners just as traffic lights turned red, and The Shadow's trailer had to wait, rather than show his hand. However, Stanley was a careful driver and the big limousine was very easy to identify, so the other car soon found it again.

When the limousine swung into the lighted area near Times Square, The Shadow drew back to a corner of the rear seat. He didn't want traffic cops looking in through the windows and noting the mysterious passenger.

Watching for a space beside a traffic island, where the street was not so brilliant, The Shadow eased forward and used Cranston's tone through the speaking tube.

"Six blocks north on Broadway," he told Stanley. "Then right. After you pass Sixth Avenue, look for the little cigar shop on the right. If it is closed, don't stop. Just keep on to the club."

AS the limousine crossed Sixth Avenue, other cars followed it. A taxicab, waiting on the avenue, swung in behind the procession. The crosstown street was quite dark, and The Shadow leaned forward in the limousine, his hand upon the door.

Stanley was looking for the cigar shop, and he was going to find it closed. The Shadow happened to know that the cigar shop in question had closed out its business two weeks before.

Naturally, Stanley slackened speed and was moving very slowly when he saw the darkened front of the cigar shop. At the same moment, The Shadow opened the door on his right and made a quick slide to the curb.

He was twisting as he went, and he didn't lose a step, even though the limousine was in motion. His spin, moreover, enabled him to sweep the door shut just as Stanley stepped on the gas.

The limousine was away, gathering speed, while The Shadow, no more than a blur in black, was wheeling across the curb into the shelter of the storefront. Other cars went past as he dissolved into blackness. The Shadow's blend with the gloom was so quick, so natural, that no eyes could discern him.

After a few cars had gone by, the cab came along. Its driver did not see The Shadow; nevertheless, the cab stopped.

Three quick strides and The Shadow was in the cab. The slam that he gave the door was a cue for the cabby to start again. The cabby happened to be Moe Shrevnitz, one of The Shadow's secret agents. Moe, or Shrevvy, as his fellow hackies called him, was one of the slickest drivers in Manhattan.

Leaning close to the front seat, The Shadow indicated two cars ahead and inquired in a whisper:

"Which was on the trail?"

"I'd say both," responded Moe. "Maybe it sounds funny, only—"

It didn't sound funny to The Shadow. His whispered laugh told that Moe was right. During the trip, The Shadow had observed two sets of lights behind him. Considering the peculiar route that Stanley had taken, one trailer could have signaled another to come along and help him; but The Shadow wasn't interested in that point, for the present. He was watching to see what happened next.

The two cars ahead were clinging rather closely to the limousine, as though they didn't care if they were noticed. However, in New York traffic, cars normally keep close together. The Shadow was sure that the trailers would ease a trifle when they turned a corner where traffic lessened.

They did, much to The Shadow's satisfaction.

That corner marked the Cobalt Club. By turning it, Stanley brought up squarely in front of the place.

The Cobalt Club had a very efficient doorman, who recognized the cars of members the moment that they turned the corner, and pounced for their door handles as soon as they stopped. He was up to form when Cranston's limousine arrived.

The doorman made his pounce, yanked the door open, and stood puzzled when he saw no sign of Cranston. Then, deciding that the limousine had come to pick up its owner instead of leaving him, the doorman closed the door and turned away.

He was closing the door when the trailing cars curved the corner, with Moe's cab behind them. It looked exactly as if Cranston had exited from the limousine and hurried into the Cobalt Club.

The trailing cars kept on their way.

From then on, it was a different sort of chase. The first car sped its pace, and the second car dogged it. Moe kept to the rear, guiding by the second car. Both had trailed Cranston to his destination; now, Cranston, otherwise The Shadow, was following them.

But the cars were much farther spaced than before. Moreover, the trail was moving away from the better part of town, into a neighborhood that was quite unsavory.

Streets were dark and sullen, the buildings that lined them were squalid and dilapidated. A low roof between two houses marked the narrow entrance of a grimy garage. Nearing it, the first car turned suddenly into the opening. As soon as it had gone through, the garage door was slid shut behind it. The second car kept on and turned the corner beyond, but Moe's cab no longer followed.

At an order from The Shadow, the cabby pulled into a darkened place beside the opposite curb and extinguished his lights. Like a specter of the night, The Shadow stepped from the cab and glided across the street.

To Moe, staring from behind the wheel, The Shadow's departure resembled the elusive way in which a cloud of blackish smoke would vanish.

CLOSE by the door of the garage, The Shadow merged with its darkness. Someone had clamped the door from the inside, but The Shadow settled that matter very readily. The door gave slightly, enough to produce a crack. Through the crack, The Shadow inserted a thin wedge of metal and kicked the clamp from its place.

Inching the door wider, he squeezed through and slid the door shut behind him. Since no one was in sight, The Shadow left the door unclamped.

It was one of those typical garages that ran from street to street. This was the rear entrance, and the garage men had all gone to the front. The Shadow saw the car that had just entered; it was a coupé, and its driver had run it over a grease pit, probably to make it look like a car that had been in the garage for quite a while, undergoing repair.

The garage was very gloomy, and in the farther wall The Shadow saw a crack of light issuing from the edges of a door. It looked like an office; probably the place where the coupé's driver had gone.

Reaching the door, The Shadow pressed it inward. He saw a roughly dressed man standing beside a battered desk, using a telephone. The fellow was stocky, and his garb gave him a squat look. His face, which The Shadow observed in partial profile, was ugly and thuggish.

No introduction was need to tell The Shadow that this man belonged to the cover-up crew that had patrolled Highway 95 the previous evening.

There was no way of telling what number the thug was calling, for the fellow had already obtained it. But it was easy enough to learn who he was, for he was stating his name across the wire, in a rough tone that fitted his appearance.

"Hello, chief," he was saying ... "Yeah, this is Matt Mardan ... Sure! It was a cinch picking up Cranston's car. It went right back to the Cobalt Club—"

There was a pause, which ended when Matt gave a gruff laugh.

"I'll say Cranston got wise," announced Matt. "You shoulda seen the way that big bus of his kept ducking ... Yeah, like a dog shaking off water, only too slow to shake me. Maybe the chauffeur uses gas with too much lead in it!"

Matt was laughing at his own idea of a joke, when a query across the wire stopped him.

"Cranston ducked into the club," returned Matt. "Yeah, in a hurry ... The chauffeur? He stayed right where he was ... No, he couldn't have tailed me here to the garage ... The boys? They're right here, chief—a couple of right guys, to make up for those two lugs we had to drop last night ... Yeah, they're all set to join up—"

Ending the call rather abruptly, Matt started to turn about. The Shadow was easing back through the door, when the stocky man apparently remembered another call. Matt turned to the telephone again and began to dial a number. He had trouble, due to a newspaper that was sticking from his hip pocket and getting in the way of his elbow.

Annoyed by the newspaper, Matt tried to tug it from his pocket. It wouldn't come, so he dug deeper and gave a yank. The rolled-up newspaper came flying from his pocket and scaled toward a blotch of blackness that was fading from the floor, just within the office door.

But, though the newspaper had gone from Matt's hand, the thug's fist wasn't empty. Under cover of the newspaper, he had brought out something else.

The other article was a glittering revolver, that Matt Mardan aimed for the door with the same sweep in which he tossed the newspaper. A triumphant snarl coming from his lips, Matt added punch by tugging the gun trigger.

Bullets ripped the door as the murderous thug drove toward it. Shots meant for The Shadow, whose presence Matt Mardan had detected from the infringing blotch upon the floor!

CHAPTER VII
CROSSED BATTLE

REACHING the door, Matt Mardan yanked it open, expecting to see sprawled blackness on the stone floor of the garage. Such blackness, in a solid mass, would indicate the bullet-riddled figure of The Shadow.

The blackness *was* outside the door, but it was closer than Matt expected. Instead of being huddled, motionless, it proved very much alive. It came lunging up from below the step that formed the threshold of the office—a cloaked attacker who sprang with incredible speed.

Matt's shots had not been quick enough. His gesture with the newspaper was a giveaway. The Shadow's fade was timed ahead of Matt's gunfire, and right now The Shadow's lunge was quicker than anything that Matt could produce.

A hand shoved Matt's gun upward as the killer tried to aim. Yanking his wrist free, Matt gave a swing that went a full foot wide, bringing his elbow against The Shadow's shoulder.

The Shadow had a gun, too; a heavy automatic that he swung sidewise at Matt's head. The thug dodged backward, which would not have helped him, except for the chance swing of the door.

It had a spring that brought it shut, and the door took some of the force from The Shadow's stroke.

Matt received the rest of the blow in glancing fashion, and reeled away, barely managing to retain his gun.

Though Matt's shots had failed to clip The Shadow, they did bring results. Those cracks from the revolver brought the garage men on the run.

As Matt's telephone conversation had evidenced, the garage was a hideaway for thugs of his own ilk, and the four men who appeared from around the corner were drawing guns as they came. They saw The Shadow, but he did not give them time to aim.

With his drawn automatic, The Shadow opened rapid fire that scattered his foemen instantly. He wasn't seeking results with those first shots, for he had the man he wanted: Matt Mardan. Other rats could flee if they wanted, but if any took to cover and tried to return the fire, it would be a different story.

One man attempted it. He dodged behind a stack of tires, poking his gun back as he went, hoping to blaze shots at The Shadow.

It happened that The Shadow's hand was quicker and his show of marksmanship amazing. He jabbed a shot for the only target that offered—the thug's revolver—and found it, along with the fist that gripped it.

There was a shriek as the crook came floundering forward, knocking the stack of tires ahead of him, sending them rolling on the floor. His companions, turning to wage combat with The Shadow gave up the idea and thought in terms of a getaway, instead.

One was beside Matt's car; the fellow jumped to the wheel and started the coupé ahead. The others, including the wounded man, were diving beyond the car, and they sprang on board it as it went by.

One fired wildly back. Wheeling to another angle, The Shadow clipped him in the shoulder, sagging him half into the car. Hearing the shot and seeing the result, the driver did not wait for anyone to open the front door, toward which the coupé was headed. He smashed right through the flimsy barrier and kept on going, carrying his three companions with him.

The Shadow turned to meet Matt, expecting to settle him easily. Matt had looked very groggy after The Shadow sideswiped him, but the sudden departure of his yellow companions had come like a douse of cold water. Matt was fully on his feet, driving in so viciously that The Shadow had barely time to wheel aside.

Matt's gun blazed shots at the spot where The Shadow had been; then, sighting his foe in black, the desperate thug changed direction and flung himself squarely on his cloaked foe.

The Shadow met the onslaught with a grapple that should have curbed an opponent of Matt's caliber. Trapping Matt's gun hand, The Shadow sledged a hard blow with his automatic, but Matt not only warded it, he hooked The Shadow's arm in a hard grip of his own. The earlier stroke that Matt received had evidently knocked all caution from his brain.

DESERTED by the recruits that he had sought to enlist for future service, Matt knew that his own career depended upon escape from The Shadow.

To Matt, his taste of The Shadow's slugging skill was indication that he would be completely through if he lost this struggle. Moreover, The Shadow's efforts to take Matt alive, that he might talk, were misinterpreted by the thug. He thought that he had found The Shadow's weakness.

Grimly, the pair reeled across the garage floor, The Shadow as determined to take Matt alive as Matt was to see The Shadow dead.

To an ordinary observer, the grapple would have appeared a toss-up; if anything, Matt seemed to have the edge. As they tightened, Matt was actually forcing The Shadow backward, straining to get in a slug at the cloaked fighter's head, and at moments, almost succeeding.

Moe Shrevnitz, however, was no ordinary observer.

Popping suddenly into sight from the rear of the garage, the cabby viewed the clutching fray. Generally, Moe stayed in the offing, at The Shadow's order, but the time lapse since the gunfire and the flight of the thug-manned car had brought Moe to the scene.

Moe was carrying a monkey wrench, and could have hurried across the floor to land it on Matt's head; but he didn't. Moe recognized The Shadow's game.

There was a shriek as the crook came floundering forward, knocking the stack of tires ahead of him, sending them rolling on the floor.

The cloaked grappler was letting Matt carry the fight, and Matt was doing it, to such a strenuous extent that shortly he would be exhausted. Every twist, every lurch, was tiring him. Soon, he would wilt suddenly, as Moe had seen others do. The cabby relaxed, watching with quick, understanding eyes, until he spotted something else.

Matt's efforts were not all sheer folly. In pressing back The Shadow, Matt could see beyond his adversary. Over The Shadow's shoulder, the gunman had spied a perfect pitfall for The Shadow. It was the grease pit over which Matt had driven his car. Matt's car was gone, taken by the men who had deserted him, and the pit yawned wide!

Yielding purposely, The Shadow was only a few yards from the menacing hole when Moe saw the danger. About to spring forward and steer the pair away, Moe halted, hearing another clatter. A door in a corner of the garage had opened; through it was coming a rangy man who flourished a .38 revolver.

Moe guessed instantly that this was the driver of the other car that had trailed The Shadow to the Cobalt Club, and later continued along the path that Matt had furnished. Moe was right; the man was Blandle.

Determinedly, Blandle pointed his revolver at the pair of strugglers. At that moment, it was difficult for him to pick his target, for The Shadow and Matt were twisting, swaying, as they neared the grease pit.

It wouldn't make sense to allow Blandle to insert a shot, so Moe, monkey wrench in hand, went after the rangy man. But as he went, Moe remembered the gaping grease pit and shouted the words: "Look out!" to The Shadow.

It wasn't a well-timed yell. The Shadow, with a sideward glance, saw Blandle and naturally supposed him to be the menace that Moe indicated; hence, all reference to the grease pit went unheeded. But Moe, in calling to The Shadow, had also warned Blandle of coming interference, and the rangy man, instead of lingering with his aim, began to speed it.

If ever things looked black for The Shadow, it was then.

Still, The Shadow was master of blackness.

He did what in Moe's opinion was the worst thing possible. He took quick back steps, hauling Matt with him. In his turn, Matt lunged all the harder, and so swift did it happen that the pair were actually at the pit before Blandle could fire. But where Moe's warning of the pit had failed, The Shadow found one of his own, which Matt—like Moe—had overlooked.

The grease pit had a raised metal rim, a guide to keep car wheels from sliding into the hole when people drove across it. The Shadow's heel encountered that flange. It told him exactly what was to be expected.

The Shadow twisted. His strength was suddenly at the full. Matt came flying about like a straw figure, as The Shadow, his heel actually hooked to the pit's rim, made an incredibly swift pivot.

Moe was hurling the monkey wrench, but the flying missile didn't stop Blandle. He tugged his gun trigger more than once, in quick succession. But his bullets did not reach The Shadow. Instead, they found the body of Matt Mardan, for The Shadow had wisely whirled his human burden in Blandle's direction.

The shots almost ripped Matt from The Shadow's grasp, but their jolts only increased Matt's hold. Instead of shying on the pit brink, Matt took the plunge, and The Shadow had no choice except to go with him, which wasn't a bad one, considering that Blandle was still at large with a very active gun.

MATT landed first in the bottom of the pit. His own fall buffered, The Shadow sprang upward and around, coming over the top of the pit, automatic first. He wanted to aim for Blandle, in case the rangy man started shooting at Moe; but all The Shadow saw of Blandle was a slamming door.

Chance of pursuit was gone. Before The Shadow could climb from the pit, the roar of a motor outside told that Blandle was leaving in his car. The Shadow called to Moe, telling him not to attempt a useless chase. Stooping, The Shadow then bent above Matt Mardan.

The crook's eyes opened. Words croaked from his lips.

"Hello, Shadow!" Matt's clucking tone was ugly. "I know what you want ... the name of the guy you heard me call. I'll give it ... to you. His name is Thor—"

With the broken croak, Matt's eyes went shut. Climbing from the pit, The Shadow studied the crook's prone form. Matt looked dead, but he might be faking. With a gesture, The Shadow ordered Moe down into the pit, to make sure.

With rapid strides, The Shadow crossed to the office and picked up the newspaper that Matt had dropped there. Moe was climbing from the pit, shaking his head, when The Shadow returned.

Matt was dead; Blandle was gone. Sounds of approaching sirens meant that police had been attracted by the gunfire and that rapid departure would be the only way to avoid much trouble and delay.

Beckoning to Moe, The Shadow hurried the cabby out to the rear street. They made a swift start in Moe's cab, while the police were coming through the front of the garage.

Crossed battle had produced regrettable results. The fact that Blandle had revealed himself meant little, because the rangy man had staged a getaway. Offsetting it was the death of Matt Mardan, which might prove very serious. Matt had deserved what he received, but he was no longer an informant. The words that Blandle's shots had stifled on Matt's lips were but a part of what The Shadow needed to know.

Turning on the reading lamp in the cab, The Shadow studied Matt's newspaper as he rode along. It was a small-town newspaper from a place called Kronskill, not far from New York. The Shadow recognized the name, for the town was where the Asbestile Co. was located.

Thumbing through the thin newspaper, The Shadow found what he expected—a story that concerned the Asbestile plant.

It stated that Asbestile had increased the daily shifts; that the factory would be working until nine o'clock every night, including Sundays.

That item had significance for The Shadow. The Asbestile plant, though owned by Jarvis Fralingham, was a key company in the setup of Universal Industries, a weak link in the chain that Oswald Kelber controlled. Certainly a suitable target for Jerome Thorden, should he seek to ruin Universal Industries.

Nine o'clock.

It wasn't far to Kronskill. The Shadow could be there before nine. Nothing could happen within the Asbestile plant before the closing hour. It was well guarded, and it would be difficult for anyone to start destruction among fireproof materials. The danger, as The Shadow saw it, would be after nine o'clock. The clue in Matt's newspaper, therefore, could be a valuable one.

It happened that The Shadow had let one clue distract him from another. He was to learn that fact later.

CHAPTER VIII
DEATH FROM THE HILL

IN his race to Kronskill, The Shadow made much better time than he had anticipated. Before reaching the limits of Manhattan, he stopped to put in a call to Burbank. It was an order for Harry Vincent to follow Moe's cab in The Shadow's roadster, on the chance of overtaking the cab.

The roadster was a road-burner. Given any breaks in traffic, it would show its superspeed. Harry found the breaks, and he overtook the cab halfway to Kronskill. Transferring to the roadster, The Shadow took the wheel. He kept Harry with him, but ordered Moe back to Manhattan.

Shortly after eight o'clock, The Shadow swung in sight of Kronskill. Beyond the glimmering lights that strewed a sizable valley, he saw the glow from the Asbestile factory, off to the left at a slightly higher level.

It wasn't necessary to go through the town to reach the factory, and the shortcut would further reduce The Shadow's running time. By the dash light, Harry picked out the route, and the distance indicated that they could get to the plant by quarter-past eight.

Curving along a paved road, The Shadow asked Harry about other routes, close by. Harry found that a connecting highway passed just beyond the Asbestile factory.

Considering that The Shadow had plenty of time, it would be easy to swing to the connecting road and pull up on the other side of the plant. However, since terrain was rough, it seemed better not to approach the factory on foot, since delay would be inevitable. The Shadow decided to drive directly to his destination.

He revoked the decision as soon as he had made it.

The Shadow's change of mind came when a great sweep of light illuminated the sky, revealing the entire landscape. It was sheet lightning, followed by a rolling peal of thunder.

Lightning!

Most potent of all the angles that concerned current crime was Margo's report of a mysterious lightning stroke the night before. The Shadow had not seen the shaft that destroyed the car that carried Wilbert and Quade, but he credited Margo's story.

The lightning that The Shadow saw tonight was real, and seemingly distant, at least to Harry, who regarded sheet lightning as indication of a faraway storm. But the glare that brightened the sky told another story to The Shadow, as did the prompt response of the thunder.

The storm was quite close. The reason why the lightning showed in a sheet, instead of streaks, was because of a high, intervening hill. The view that the lightning gave disclosed the entire slope, and The Shadow saw that the Asbestile plant was located on the near side of the hill, while the blackish clouds were approaching over the brow!

There was menace in that lightning.

The Shadow knew.

Quick in his conclusions, The Shadow recognized a menace coming from the hill, and he saw but one way to offset it. That was to reach the hill, instead of the Asbestile plant, before the storm really arrived.

From Harry's report of a road beyond the factory, The Shadow knew that the highway in question must skirt the brow of the hill. He promptly changed his course and increased the roadster's speed.

AS they swung into the cross highway, the lightning ripped anew. This time, it was closer, and directly visible. It was forked lightning, and the storm was coming with real fury, much closer to the hill.

Why The Shadow had suddenly decided to run a race with a thunderstorm, especially to a spot beyond his intended goal, was quite a mystery to Harry.

In fact, Harry was thinking of the factory, not the storm. The lightning flash gave him a sideward view along the slope. He saw the factory at closer range, and recognized what it must be.

The Asbestile plant was an old and rather decrepit mass of buildings that had been taken over for new industry. It looked like the sort of plant that might experience trouble from a thunderstorm.

Still, Harry couldn't quite size the menace.

Lightning could knock shingles from a farmhouse roof, but it could hardly damage an industrial plant, even an old one. As for starting fires, lightning was noted for that sort of business, but a plant that made fireproof materials would certainly prove immune.

The trouble was that The Shadow did not seem to agree with those opinions. Harry stared questioningly at his chief. As if reading his agent's thoughts, The Shadow spoke.

"Somewhere along this road," he told Harry, "we are going to encounter enemies. Men who are working with a strange design. Last night, they struck from a clear sky. Tonight, they hope that the storm will cover up their work."

There was another flash of lightning, much closer. The storm was almost at the hill, yet The Shadow was outracing it. In a very few minutes, he would be at his new goal: the center of the hill on the slope above the Asbestile factory. Harry heard The Shadow's whispered laugh, strangely sinister. He knew that his chief foresaw success.

"We shall meet a man named Oliver Bayruth," declared The Shadow. "An almost forgotten man, once famed as an electrical wizard—"

Another flash of lightning interrupted. Vivid, it outlined the entrance to an old dirt road less than a hundred yards ahead. The road was steep, for it came down from the hill. It also revealed the paved highway, with The Shadow's car hurtling along it at a speed which seemed amazing, considering that the motor's tone was a smooth purr, not a roar.

In fact, any noise of the engine was completely drowned by the roll of thunder that followed close after the lightning. But no one had to hear The Shadow's car. Sight of it was enough.

Like a thing produced from nowhere, an old sedan shot down from the dirt road. Hurling itself into the glare of The Shadow's headlights, the ramshackle heap of junk blocked off the speedy roadster from the highway ahead!

The Shadow performed double miracles with brakes and steering wheel. He couldn't possibly get past the blocking car, for it went clear across the road; but what he did do left Harry awed and breathless.

A jab of the brake pedal lifted the roadster over a slight hump, on what seemed a take-off. A twist of the steering wheel pointed the car toward rocks and trees, but this time there was no jagged obstruction to receive the bounding front tires.

Another application of brakes, with a deft swing of the wheel, and the car was pivoted the other way. Again, The Shadow diverted it in bouncing fashion.

The roadster was doing ninety when The Shadow went into those gyrations. How he ever managed to cut down that breakneck pace was something that Harry never did understand. But the final result was a shriek of tires, a heave that almost toppled the stout car over.

Then, with a jolt, The Shadow and Harry were right beside the sedan, so close that they could almost touch it.

THE junk pile was disgorging men from the far side. Men with guns, who thought that The Shadow would wreck his own car against their sedan and make himself a helpless target for their weapons.

Instead, The Shadow completely reversed the situation. Not only did he avoid the fatal crash; he came to his stop before the thuggish clan had time to turn around and aim.

The Shadow had a gun talking before others could begin. The menace was the other way about, and had happened so quickly, that foemen had no time to scatter. Harry saw figures plunge, as another glare of lightning lit the scene. The Shadow plunged, too, but not to the ground. He sprang from his own car to the hood of the sedan, to shoot across it. The stabs of his gun sent more men sprawling

Out from his own side of the roadster, Harry rushed around the front, to find The Shadow on the far side of the sedan. Oddly, The Shadow seemed to be overrunning his mark. He was beyond his opponents, giving those that could a chance to get back into their car.

But it proved to be part of The Shadow's strategy. He *wanted* thugs to get back into their car, and flee in it, so that the road would be clear for him.

Men did reach the car. They started it, but not along the road. A wounded man was at the wheel; his sagging hand couldn't turn it, though his foot

The Shadow sprang from his own car to the hood of the sedan.... The stabs of his gun sent more men sprawling.

was strong enough to push against the accelerator. The sedan shot forward with its load of desperate thugs, whose ardor was only on escape.

It made a slight swerve, then crashed a flimsy fence on the far side of the road and went plunging through, to roll down a jagged slope, sending back a chorus of shrieks.

Lightning showed the sedan's plunge. Thunder, hard upon the flash, drowned the cries of crooks who had made their own rocky bed of death. The Shadow leaped back to the roadster, and Harry followed him, but they reached the car too late.

By then, the storm was full upon the hill. New shafts of lightning were rending the sky, and thunder was blasting with them. Through a clearing in the trees, The Shadow and his agent saw the devastation that occurred.

Those shafts of lightning were not coming from the sky. They were being hurled from the brow of the hill itself, at some point farther along the road, as if some thunder god were throwing them!

Down came a lurid flash, a man-made arrow of ten million volts. Like The Shadow, Harry was a witness to its effect. The lightning struck one corner of the Asbestile plant, just down the slope, and ripped away a chunk of wall. Another of those shafts broke loose and cracked the very center of the brick-walled building!

Like a giant among pygmies came another flash of genuine lightning, with a mighty smash of thunder, directly overhead. But it was nothing but a cover-up for the man-made efforts that immediately followed it. The real lightning did not strike the red-brick plant; the human product did.

Crash—crash—crash!

Bolts smashed from the brow of the hill with the power of great volleys loosed from howitzers. Each stroke ripped walls to chunks, showed staggering human figures coming from the Asbestile plant. That horror was followed by other roars, not crackly like the thunder that accompanied the man-made volts, but hollow, sullen, the smothery tumble of collapsing walls.

Those sounds kept echoing; they had almost ended when a glare spread across the sky.

The flash told that the storm had passed. All that it did was give a view of the location where the Asbestile plant had stood. Instead of closely cluttered brick-walled buildings, the illumination from the sky showed a pile of sagging ruins. The first of Kelber's key industries had found its finish.

Quiet came again, broken only by the occasional rumbles of the departing storm. Drenched by a torrent of terrific rain, Harry Vincent stood stunned amid the blackness.

From beside him came a strange, solemn tone, chilling and mirthless, carrying one theme only: vengeance.

It was the laugh of The Shadow!

CHAPTER IX
THE SHADOW WAITS

HARRY wondered what The Shadow intended to do next. The answer came, quite promptly. Reaching from the roadster, The Shadow drew his agent into the car; then backed into the dirt road from which the sedan had come, only a few minutes before.

Only a few minutes.

In that short space of time, Harry had witnessed events which passed belief. He had seen destruction wrought so rapidly that he felt he needed another look to make sure that the Asbestile plant was really gone. Harry couldn't take that look, for it was his task to remain with The Shadow. So he used his imagination, instead.

He tried to imagine what the Asbestile plant would look like if lightning had struck it repeatedly, and with directed force. From that picture, Harry recaptured the scene that had actually been on display before his eyes. He knew the truth of crime, tremendous though it was.

Another recollection came to mind.

Harry thought of Oliver Bayruth, the famous electrical wizard. Bayruth was the man responsible, yet the wizardry could not be called his own. He had simply applied a known device, that of man-made lightning, a thing which science had often demonstrated for public display.

True, Bayruth's bolts had been formidable; greater and more numerous than any used in exhibitions. But, to date, artificial lightning had never been employed as a destroyer. No, Harry was wrong. It had been used for such last night. Lightning from the bridge of the superhighway had doomed two men who knew too much: Wilbert and Quade.

Recalling how he had driven Margo from the scene of that disaster, Harry recalled some words that she had spoken. Talk that had seemed incoherent at the time about lightning striking from the sky. He hadn't credited it at the time, for last night the sky had been clear.

It didn't matter, starlight or clouds, when Bayruth's mechanism was in action, except for one point. A real thunderstorm could cover up the deadly work of the artificial lightning. Bayruth had risked that point last night. Tonight, he had not.

Harry's mind came from its whirl. He began to wonder why The Shadow was waiting on a dirt road, in a torrential rain, after having witnessed such crime as the total destruction of the Asbestile plant. It might be that The Shadow, himself, had been dazed by the procession of horrendous events.

Usually, The Shadow went after perpetrators of crime without delay. Harry turned to his chief, a question on his lips. An afterthought made him restrain his query.

The Shadow didn't have to go after Bayruth and the other hands of crime.

They were coming to The Shadow!

It was logical that they would come in this direction. They had planted the sedan to cover up their work. The men in the sedan were stationed for two purposes: one, to block off troublemakers; the other, to pass the word along, in case such persons came.

But The Shadow had banished the sedan and its crew. The car was over the cliff, and no one had given Bayruth the news.

Soon, the wizard of destruction would be coming in this direction, to find The Shadow waiting for him!

AS Harry formed that conclusion, a rumble sounded from somewhere along the road. It increased, and with it, headlights sliced through the rain. The glare became more brilliant, and finally materialized itself in the shape of a huge, double-sectioned truck that rolled by at considerable speed.

As soon as the ponderous vehicle had passed, The Shadow slid the roadster into gear and took up the trail.

Harry expected The Shadow to drive without headlights, a system which The Shadow often used to keep close behind an unsuspecting car.

It would have been easy in this instance, for the truck's lamps were huge and powerful, cutting a strong swath along the highway ahead. In addition, the trailer portion of the lumbering vehicle was well sprinkled with taillights, glimmering blobs of red that made guideposts in themselves.

Nevertheless, The Shadow turned on the roadster's headlights, and after a mile or two it dawned on Harry why he had done so.

Bayruth and his crew of evil-working technicians would naturally expect the cover-up crew to follow along in the sedan. If they didn't see headlights behind them, they would suspect something. So The Shadow had supplied the lights, as a necessary item in this case.

The great truck was heading west. Off to the south, the last flashes of lightning from the parting storm disclosed stretches of rugged landscape, and at one spot, Harry observed great metal towers approaching the highway at an angle, and carrying wires across it. Towers and wires represented a high-tension power line, that continued back past the demolished Asbestile plant.

Harry remembered a similar line in New Jersey, not far from Highway 95. He could understand how the makers of man-made lightning obtained the power for their terrific volts. They simply tapped the high-tension systems and accumulated the electricity that they needed. This necessarily limited the scope of their activities; but, so far, it had not hampered them.

Last night, they had picked a suitable spot: somewhere along the route to Bayruth's headquarters, which must be in New Jersey. Tonight, they had experienced no difficulty, because they had probably scouted the Asbestile plant in advance. If the high-tension line had not been close enough, they could have planted longer extensions beforehand.

From Harry's glance toward the high-tension poles, and the silence which followed that observation, The Shadow divined that his agent had fathomed one part of the game. In a steady tone, The Shadow supplied further details regarding the production of artificial lightning, first mentioning facts with which Harry was familiar.

"Margo spoke of towers above the superhighway bridge," stated The Shadow. "What she saw were metal columns extending up from the truck. Those columns were used again tonight. They are made in sections, so they can be telescoped. They are called 'capacitors,' and they store up electrons through transformers.

"When fully charged, the capacitors spill lightning, which can be directed to its mark. In laboratory demonstrations, ten million volts have been employed, with an energy equal to the muzzle of a sixteen-inch gun. Such voltage is about one tenth of a natural lightning bolt."

There was a pause, while The Shadow followed the truck across another high road, carefully slowing pace to keep an even distance behind it.

"Original tests with artificial lightning," continued The Shadow, "produced only a few hundred thousand volts. Its power was increased to two million volts, covering a distance of about five feet. Voltages of ten million represent a greatly increased range; still, they could hardly account for the destruction that we witnessed tonight.

"Therefore, we may assume that Bayruth has devoted his scientific abilities to the further development of artificial lightning. Statistics, themselves, prove that its limit has not been reached. Those bolts of his were higher-powered than any ever displayed to the public."

THE final statement was emphatic. It made

Harry wish that he could see the inside of the huge mystery truck. In fact, he might within the course of the next few hours, considering how capably The Shadow was keeping to the trail.

Rather than start battle on the road, The Shadow was endeavoring to reach the base where Bayruth housed the big truck, and thus clean up the entire case.

Evidence was needed that would go beyond Bayruth, the misguided scientist, and reach the real brain of destruction. For Bayruth, despite the power that he exerted, was a mere tool in the game. His experiments in doom would be impossible without the necessary capital to build bigger and more formidable lightning machines.

Harry recalled facts that The Shadow had mentioned: how Jerome Thorden denied all knowledge of Bayruth's whereabouts, and belittled the scientist's efforts. Disclaiming all connection with Bayruth would be good policy on Thorden's part while Bayruth was knocking down plants that were important to Universal Industries, the chain controlled by Thorden's financial rival, Oswald Kelber.

As for Thorden's claim—to Cranston—that Bayruth specialized in impractical ideas, it was completely belied by this evening's demonstration.

Harry couldn't doubt that Thorden was behind Bayruth's work, but he knew that tangible evidence would be needed to clinch the fact. Evidence such as the letters that Wilbert and Quade had gone after when they started their ill-fated journey, only to find doom awaiting them from Bayruth's well-timed shafts.

Red lights, blinking ahead, brought Harry from his reverie. The truck was signaling to the car that followed it, and The Shadow was trying to interpret the blinks. He moved up closer, but the flashes continued, so he dropped to the rear. The red lights steadied, then blinked again, calling for even more distance.

It was about time for the truck to head for New Jersey. Perhaps it didn't want the cover-up crew to be too close; indeed; Bayruth might be signaling for thugs to drop off altogether. Getting a good look at the road, The Shadow decided to drive blind and come up behind the truck.

There was a bend just ahead, and the truck was beyond it. Lights off, The Shadow picked his way uncannily through the darkness. He spotted red lights at a crossing ahead; they veered to the right, and The Shadow neatly trailed them. He was right under the rear of the truck for the next few miles, until it crossed a narrow bridge.

By the truck's lights, Harry saw a bridge sign that stated: "Limit, Six Tons," but didn't appreciate its full significance until The Shadow spurted forward. As the road widened, the roadster's lights came on, and The Shadow whipped past the truck, cutting in front of it to halt the big vehicle, or drive it off the road.

The truck jerked to a stop. Men sprang from it, with revolvers, and began a wild fire in the roadster's direction. They would probably have employed accuracy instead of haste, had they known who was in the roadster. The Shadow's laugh challenged their fire, and the staccato barks of his automatic backed up his mirth.

His shots were to the mark. Three men had leaped from the truck; all fled as they heard the Shadow's taunt. His bullets sprawled two, the third man escaped only because he managed to dive from the road, into bushes that hid him, while The Shadow was clipping the other two.

Harry was shooting with The Shadow's third shot, but by then, further fire was useless. Together, The Shadow and his agent reached the wounded men, who were lying in the glow of their own headlights. The Shadow sprang into the truck, while Harry was stopping by the two thugs who had sagged in the road. Promptly, The Shadow returned.

"A substitute truck," he told Harry. "Waiting at the crossroad until Bayruth's truck passed. Bayruth must have suspected us, so he gave those signals to urge us farther back. It's too late, now, to regain his trail."

The bridge sign had been The Shadow's clue. Bayruth's truck, with its tons of lightning machinery, could not have crossed a bridge that would take only a six-ton load. Questioning the wounded thugs, The Shadow found that they knew nothing of value.

They were small fry, who had been told to bring this truck, a big but very light vehicle, to the crossroad and wait there until its twin went past; then lead followers on a false trail. The thugs weren't badly wounded, for The Shadow's shots had neatly skimmed them.

After giving them first aid, The Shadow packed them into the dummy truck and told Harry to take it back to town. Harry would have no trouble with the prisoners. The Shadow had bound them.

THE truck pulled away. The Shadow gave a low, grim laugh. It didn't concern the losing of Bayruth's trail; he was thinking of an earlier clue that had slipped.

Stepping into the glow of the roadster's headlights, The Shadow consulted the newspaper that had belonged to Matt Mardan. This time, he ignored the item concerning activities at the Asbestile plant. It was the thing that had misled him.

The Shadow found another item, so obvious,

that he had previously overlooked it. It was the weather report for Kronskill and vicinity. It predicted heavy thunder showers early in the evening. That was why Matt had been so anxious to sign up new recruits. He had known that Bayruth would strike, and therefore it would be his opportunity to bring the new men and join up with the regular crew.

Though The Shadow had practically wiped out all mobsmen who covered Bayruth, he wasn't satisfied. Disaster had struck despite The Shadow. One course alone remained: to wait. Only by such policy could The Shadow trap Bayruth in new crime.

The Shadow hoped to accomplish more. Next time, if possible, he would avert disaster and carry the trail through Bayruth, to the real head of the game!

CHAPTER X
CRIME'S RESULTS

NEW YORK newspapers were filled with graphic accounts of havoc wrought by lightning at the Asbestile factory. The descriptions were wrong in certain essential details. The heavens hadn't hurled down horror, as one journal put it. Destruction had come from the hill, not from the sky.

Nor had the wrecked car, toppled from the road, its occupants dead, been demolished by another lightning shaft. That car happened to be the crook-manned sedan which had crossed The Shadow's path and kept on to its own destruction.

In his sanctum—a hidden, black-walled room somewhere in the heart of New York City, wherein he planned moves against men of crime—The Shadow studied newspaper clippings and referred to reports from agents. Harry and others were over in New Jersey trying to trace Bayruth's headquarters; so far, without result.

Unfortunately, The Shadow could only direct that quest by blocking off sections of a large-scale map, and phoning new instructions to Burbank.

The Shadow had appointments in Manhattan which he had to keep as Cranston. Leaving the sanctum, he stepped into the daylight of afternoon and started on his rounds.

His first stop was at Kelber's. Things looked very gloomy in the fortieth-floor offices of Universal Industries. A secretary even hesitated at calling Kelber to tell him that Mr. Cranston had arrived, but finally did so.

Entering Kelber's private office, The Shadow could hear the magnate's booming tones. He found the bulky man loosing a tirade upon another visitor, a wizened man who was gasping as Kelber stormed.

Pausing, Kelber changed his scowl to a very poor smile, meant as a welcome to Cranston. He gestured toward the wizened man, who was taking time out to get a pair of glasses back on his nose, from the ribbon on which they dangled. Bluntly, Kelber introduced the earlier visitor:

"This is Jarvis Fralingham."

The Shadow shook hands with the owner of the Asbestile Co. By then, Kelber had broken loose again.

"I warned you, Fralingham!" he argued. "I showed you Wilbert's report. It said that your factory was an old one, that needed further reconstruction. You should have had such work done immediately."

"But ... but"—Fralingham was stuttering—"I couldn't believe that lightning—"

"Your plant was insured, wasn't it?" demanded Kelber. "That proves the danger existed."

"Danger *always* exists," returned Fralingham. "You see, it was imperative to turn out Asbestile in a hurry. We were just on the point of proper production. Other matters had to wait."

Kelber paced the floor in his caged-lion manner.

"Other things could wait," he growled. "Now, we'll get no Asbestile. I can't do without it!"

Fralingham spread his hands, pathetically.

"I've offered you my formulas," he insisted. "The contracts that I had are now yours, Kelber. The insurance has covered my losses. You can turn out Asbestile."

"How?" queried Kelber. "It requires a plant equipped to apply your chemical process and render building materials, from wallpaper to partitions, entirely fireproof. We've salvaged enough of your

BURBANK

materials, Fralingham, to last a week. After then, where do I stand? I'll tell you!" He gestured from the window to the street, far below. "Down there—in a breadline!"

FRALINGHAM went to a chair picked up a briefcase and opened it on Kelber's desk.

"Here are the formulas," he said, "and the contracts. You're a man of genius, Kelber. Surely, you can do something with them, now that they are yours. I equipped the old factory in a month."

"In a month! I have only a week!"

"But we had nothing to start with," Fralingham insisted. "I had to buy rollers and compressors. I had to install vats. If only—"

Kelber interrupted with a snap of his fingers.

"Rollers!" he exclaimed. "Compressors! I have them! Ones that I don't need, at my Pennsylvania wallboard factory. Vats! Let's see the specifications, Fralingham. Hurry!"

Digging through the briefcase, Fralingham found the specifications. Kelber gave a triumphant whoop

"The dye works down in Delaware!" he shouted. "Working on part-time, with only half its vats in use. I can move the machines from the wallboard plant and install them in the dye works! Give me those formulas, quick!"

Kelber pounced for the telephone and began bombarding it with long-distance calls. He talked with chemists, superintendents, shippers, and finally lawyers. When he finished, he sank behind his desk, so heavily that the chair creaked.

"My attorneys are coming over," he told Fralingham. "You can sign a release on the Asbestile process to cover my contracts. I'll be able to deliver, Fralingham!"

Fralingham was hugely relieved. He knew that the fortunes of others hinged upon the situation. Fralingham's interests were but a portion of the Universal Industries chain, and he was glad that he was no longer the weak link.

Kelber turned to The Shadow.

"This will stop Thorden from taking over my contracts," asserted Kelber, triumphantly. "Do you know, Cranston"—Kelber was pursing his bushy brows in reflective style—"if anything but lightning had struck the Asbestile plant, I'd have believed that Thorden was in back of it! By the way, how did you fare when you called on Thorden?"

"Quite well, while I was there," replied The Shadow, calmly. "But I was followed after I left his house."

"Because Thorden suspected that you came from me!" exclaimed Kelber. "Tell me, Cranston, what did you do?"

"I went hack to the club," said The Shadow, idly. "It is always a good place to spend a quiet evening."

Kelber nodded, then stroked his heavy chin. He studied Cranston from under his large brows.

"You wouldn't care to call on Thorden again?" queried Kelber. "To find out his present reactions? I would deem it a favor, Cranston."

An interested spectator, Jarvis Fralingham was pleased when he saw Lamont Cranston nod his willingness. But it was after The Shadow had gone that Fralingham, about to make his own departure, remembered a point that Oswald Kelber had failed to mention.

"Cranston said that he was followed from Thorden's," reminded Fralingham. "Shouldn't you have advised him to note if the same thing happens again?"

"I should have," agreed Kelber. Glum for a moment, he brightened. "I think we can depend upon Cranston to observe that for himself, since he did before. Somehow, Fralingham"—Kelber smacked a fist into the palm of his other hand—"Thorden seems to be conniving something. Yet it can't be. No man on earth could have arranged the destruction of your plant at Kronskill, in the manner that it happened."

UNNATURAL dusk was again clouding Thorden's mansion when The Shadow arrived there, as Cranston, an hour later. The dusk, of course, was due to higher buildings west of the house, so it was therefore man-made. The Shadow noticed the analogy. Last night's lightning had been man-made, too.

Perhaps Jerome Thorden had often observed the early gloom that came to the windows of his residence. But it was scarcely likely that such had given him the idea that nature could be improved upon by other man-made devices: specifically, artificial lightning, capable of terrific destruction.

The power of artificial thunderbolts had probably impressed many persons who viewed public demonstrations in which they were used. Almost any person, bent upon creating disaster, could picture himself a human Jupiter, hurling lightning shafts at will, provided he could find a Vulcan to forge such bolts.

Oliver Bayruth, the electrical wizard, was just such a Vulcan, but he was being allowed to play at Jupiter, as well, to satisfy his crazed vanity.

It would take more than haphazard investigation to link Bayruth with the brain that controlled him. The Shadow had that thought quite in mind when he entered Thorden's house, on this second occasion, and was conducted to the financier's upstairs office.

From the rather cryptic smile on Thorden's

face, The Shadow recognized that certain news had reached him—which was proof, in itself, that Thorden had ways of getting information. Though only an hour had passed since Kelber found out how to offset the loss of the Asbestile plant, Thorden knew all about it.

"I thought that Universal Industries would be through," said Thorden, smoothly. "But I was wrong. It may interest you, Cranston, to know that Kelber pulled a rabbit out of his hat. He is going to manufacture Asbestile himself."

The Shadow showed traces of surprise. Thorden let out a slight chuckle.

"It should please you, Cranston," Thorden added. "Since Kelber is still in business, and even stronger than before, he should be in a position to buy some of your imports. I would advise you to call on him."

"But how—"

"How did Kelber counteract misfortune?" queried Thorden. "Very simply. He is combining a pressed-wood factory with a dye works, to produce an Asbestile plant. Something he could have done originally, if he had controlled Fralingham's fireproofing formulas.

"Frankly, I am sorry that Kelber saw such opportunity. I still feel that Thorden Enterprises should have the contracts which went to Universal Industries. Kelber's total bid was too low for proper profit.

"Ah, well"—Thorden gave a shrug—"he may still realize that he has undertaken too great a problem. When he does, he will be glad to turn his white elephant over to me."

Since Thorden wasn't interested in the purchase of imported goods, there was no occasion for The Shadow to prolong his visit. He chatted casually, in Cranston's style, for a short while; then took his leave.

As soon as the visitor was gone, Blandle came from behind the paneled wall, to join Thorden by the window. Through the webby curtains, the two watched Cranston stroll down the front walk to his limousine.

"No need for you to follow him, Blandle," said Thorden. "I can keep check on Cranston, through others. You might get into further difficulties, considering that the curious masquerader who calls himself The Shadow is interested in Cranston's affairs, and those of people who trail him.

"You are too valuable to take the risks, Blandle. I want you to contact Bayruth, instead. Not from here, of course, because the telephone wires may be tapped. Make all your calls from outside.

"When you talk to Bayruth, assure him that I am giving new consideration to his plans for perpetual motion. I am quite sure that such a message will have a marked bearing on the future."

By then, The Shadow had reached his car. Seeing Cranston's tall form enter the big limousine, Thorden turned from the window. Even the deepening dusk could not hide his satisfied smile.

Something else would have.

Thorden's plans for the future might have undergone a rapid change, had he and Blandle kept closer watch on Lamont Cranston, otherwise, The Shadow!

CHAPTER XI
MARGO TAKES A TRIP

WHEN Lamont Cranston entered his limousine, he underwent a rapid change. The drawer beneath the sliding seat was already slightly open, and the tall passenger, snapping from his leisurely manner, flipped a cloak from it in a swoop that carried the garment over his shoulders.

The twist took him toward the speaking tube, where, in Cranston's tone, he ordered Stanley to start for the Cobalt Club. While giving that order, The Shadow was clamping his slouch hat on his head and kneeing the drawer shut. Still on the spin, he went out through the far door, slapping it shut as he struck the street.

The Shadow was beyond the mansion gate, where Thorden could hardly have seen him, even if still on watch. But that drop to the street, the fading glide that followed it, were meant to deceive observers closer by—and did. The Shadow had timed his drop to the moment when the limousine veered out from the curb; hence, men in another car did not notice the flips of the far door. That action, alone, could have told them that the passenger was gone. For The Shadow, thanks to the gloom that came so early to the street, was no more than a flitting creature that vanished into the hovering bulk of an old building across the way.

The limousine rounded the corner, with another car trailing it. The Shadow glimpsed faces that looked thuggish, though he couldn't view them closely. Two men were taking up the duty that had previously been Matt Mardan's—that of following Cranston's big car to the Cobalt Club

From another car, a watcher saw the double departure. The watcher was Margo Lane, and she was quite perturbed. Not long ago, Cranston had phoned her, asking her to wait for him outside of Thorden's in her coupé.

Hence, Margo, seeing Cranston come from Thorden's gate, had expected him to join her. She would have been irked at his neglect, had not the sight of the trailing car worried her.

Margo didn't know whether to follow, or wait.

She took the latter choice, purely because she couldn't make up her mind. By the time she changed it and decided to get started, she found a new reason to wait. The door opened on the curb side of her car and Lamont Cranston entered and calmly sat down beside her!

"Sorry, Margo," he said, affably. "I forgot our appointment until I was around the corner. I had Stanley drop me, so that I could come back."

Margo did not doubt the statement. She had been debating with herself long enough for Cranston to return in the style that he claimed. Nor did she see the cloak and hat that he carried on his arm. The Shadow was keeping those garments to the door side.

In addition, Margo was inspired by something more important. She gripped Cranston's arm, the one that wasn't draped with cloak and hat.

"You were followed, Lamont!" she exclaimed. "Didn't you see the other car? It went right after the limousine!"

The Shadow gave a casual laugh.

"Funny, now that you mention it," he remarked. "I must have dropped off without those fellows noticing it. I did see a car, with two men in it. It came around the corner just after Stanley had dropped me."

"But what are you going to do about it?"

"Do about it?" The question seemed to puzzle Cranston. "Well, I suppose I shall have to go to the club, since those chaps will probably report that I checked in there. Too bad, Margo. It will spoil our evening."

For the moment, Margo was angrily inclined; but she cooled quickly. This was the way Lamont often acted when something more important was involved. It made her think that The Shadow would soon appear upon the scene, and she wanted to see Cranston vanish first.

BUT Cranston didn't vanish.

He offered Margo a cigarette, and took one for himself. Snapping his cigarette case shut, he proffered a flame from the lighter that topped the case. Margo noted Cranston's face as he obtained his own light. His impassive features revealed nothing, yet Margo was convinced that he had more in mind than a mere trip to the Cobalt Club.

Suddenly, Cranston extinguished the lighter. His eyes gazed sharply through the windshield. For a passing moment, Margo thought that she could see those eyes glint, as though retaining the reflection of the dead flame.

"That chap who just came from Thorden's gate," remarked Cranston. "Does he remind you of Wilbert?"

The question made Margo shudder. The man *was* reminiscent of Wilbert. He happened to be Blandle, but Margo could not see his face. His build was rangy, and his shoulders had a stoop as he sidled to a car across the way. Those characteristics were too similar to Wilbert's to suit Margo. Then, tensely, Margo said:

"He *couldn't* be Wilbert, Lamont. Wilbert is dead—"

"Of course," interposed Cranston. "You misunderstood me, Margo. I meant: would you class him as a man of Wilbert's type?"

"Why, yes—"

"Wilbert was working for Kelber, as a private investigator. Perhaps this fellow, whoever he is, may be serving Thorden in the same capacity."

Blandle's car was starting. Instinctively, Margo put her coupé in motion. She heard Cranston's mild, but approving laugh.

"Adventurous as ever, Margo," he chuckled. "I suppose you will insist upon following the chap and finding out who he really is. Drop me off somewhere, so that I can get to the club. If you learn anything interesting, call me there. But stay away from places like Highway 95."

"Don't worry," returned Margo. "Maybe you've forgotten that I'm leaving at midnight on my vacation. I have the Pullman ticket right here in my purse, and tomorrow, I'll be with a hiking party somewhere in the White Mountains."

"Still a girl scout at heart," approved Cranston, in a bantering tone. "Ah, here's a red light, and I see a taxicab around the corner. So I'll drop off. Send me some picture postcards of rugged mountain scenery, so I can appreciate how nice it is to stay in New York."

MARGO did not notice the cloak and hat that Cranston carried, bundled, as he stepped from the coupé. She was too interested in following Blandle's car.

As the trail continued, Margo did look into the mirror, on the chance that Cranston might have decided to follow her in the cab that he had taken. But the cab had gone in another direction. Cranston was actually going to the Cobalt Club, as he had stated.

Keeping well behind Blandle's car, Margo managed to hold sight of it. When it parked near a side-street restaurant called the Platinum Grill, Margo was lucky enough to find another space for her coupé. She also caught a glimpse of Blandle's face as he entered the lighted restaurant. He didn't even glance back in Margo's direction.

Entering the restaurant herself, Margo felt quite free of any danger, provided that she used good sense. She was quite sure that Cranston's departure to the Cobalt Club was tacit agreement on that point.

Tonight's events could not, in Margo's opinion, lead to any scene of disaster as had her trip to Highway 95, a few nights ago. She'd simply find out what she could about the rangy man who had come from Thorden's, call it an evening, and take the midnight train.

Margo only hoped that she would learn something important enough to telephone Lamont and stir him out of his indifference.

Inside the Platinum Grill, Margo saw Blandle at a table, talking to a waiter who was shaking his head. Taking a nearby table, she overheard their undertoned conversation.

"I haven't seen him, Mr. Blandle," the waiter was saying. "If he's back in town, he hasn't stopped in here. He was always irregular, anyway. Maybe he's using one of the other eating places, like down in Greenwich Village. He went there a lot."

Blandle nodded, with no change of his poker-faced expression. Margo, meanwhile, was congratulating herself. She had learned Blandle's name. The next point was to learn the name of the person who was the subject of Blandle's conversation with the waiter.

When the waiter turned to Margo's table, she ordered a sandwich and some coffee. Meanwhile, Blandle went to the cigar counter, changed a quarter into nickels, and entered a telephone booth. He evidently intended to put in calls to several places.

Margo waited until her order arrived, then called after the waiter, asking him to get her some cigarettes. But she didn't call loud enough for him to hear, and since his back was turned, he couldn't see Margo beckon.

All that was for Blandle's benefit, if he happened to be glancing from the phone booth. Deserting her table, Margo went to the cigar counter and bought the cigarettes. She asked for an obscure brand, and while the clerk was hunting for it, Margo inclined toward the phone booth.

Blandle was making his fourth call, and, having a poor connection, he raised his voice.

"You say Bayruth will be back?" Margo heard him query. "Maybe in an hour? Good! Have him call the Platinum Grill... Yes. He is to ask for Blandle—"

Margo was back at her table, when Blandle arrived at his. Instead of giving an order, Blandle confided in the waiter.

"I've found out where his nibs was," said Blandle. "They say he's due back in an hour. But you know how the old guy changes his mind. I'm going to make the rounds and see if I can find him. I'll be back in an hour, but if he calls up in the meantime, find out where he is and tell him to wait there."

The waiter nodded. Rising from his table, Blandle took a long look at Margo. There wasn't a touch of suspicion in his gaze; instead, his eye showed a glimmer of approval. He gave a glance at the waiter, who shrugged.

Quite obviously, Blandle was questioning if Margo was a regular customer at the Platinum Grill, in hope of a future introduction. The waiter's shrug meant that he had never seen the girl before.

MARGO fumed inwardly as Blandle left. Not because Blandle had deliberately eyed her, for she had already typed him as a man who would seek that mode of acquaintance. The trouble was that Blandle would remember her, which made it impossible to follow him when he "made the rounds" in search of Bayruth.

Even worse, Margo couldn't stall around the restaurant until Blandle returned, because he would recognize her.

Finishing sandwich and coffee, Margo paid her check and stopped at the telephone booth, to call the Cobalt Club. She learned, worse luck, that Cranston had been there, but had left a few minutes before.

He had left word that Margo could reach him at the office of the Orvis Engineering Corp., in the Mohawk Building. In her turn, Margo left a message for Cranston.

"If he calls back," she said, "tell him that Mr. Blandle expects to meet Mr. Bayruth this evening."

Hanging up, Margo wondered if she should call the Orvis Corp. She was looking up the number in the phone book, when the bell in the booth began to ring. Margo took a quick look, saw that Blandle's waiter friend had gone to the kitchen. The man at the cigar counter glanced at Margo as though he thought the return call was for her. So she took the receiver off the hook and gave a cool: "Hello!"

"Hello." The voice was sharp and crackly. "I want to talk to Mr. Blandle."

"He just left," returned Margo. "He told me to take any message that came."

There was a pause; then the voice quizzed:

"Who are you? Blandle's secretary?"

On the point of saying "yes," Margo paused. It might be a catch question. Very probably Blandle didn't have a secretary. Margo was sure that Bayruth was the speaker at the other end, and he probably knew a great deal about Blandle. That probability, in itself, gave Margo an excellent inspiration.

"No," returned Margo. "I work for Mr. Thorden. He told Mr. Blandle that I had better come along"—Margo's tone was becoming strictly confidential—"just in case we had difficulty in finding you."

She was practically telling Bayruth that she

recognized his voice, and she heard a pleased chuckle in return. Margo had scored another point. Anyone in Thorden's employ might logically recognize Bayruth's voice, since the electrical wizard, himself, had previously worked openly for Thorden.

"Very well," crackled Bayruth. "Tell Mr. Blandle to meet me at the side entrance of the Cartwyn Building. I shall be there within twenty minutes. I shall wait until he arrives."

As she hung up, Margo shuddered. Bayruth's verbal crackles had reminded her of something; she now remembered what it was. His voice was like the sharpness of the lightning that had ripped down from a starry sky to overwhelm Wilbert and Quade in their doomed car. Even as an echo, it wasn't a pleasant recollection.

Leaving the grill, Margo stepped into her car and decided to drive to the vicinity of the Cartwyn Building. She could look the place over before Bayruth arrived, and give Cranston a call at the Orvis office. It would only be a short trip and a safe one; a good way of killing time until Lamont reached his own destination.

Margo was doubly wrong. She wasn't beginning a short trip; she was starting on a long one. A trip that would be fraught with menace, even after she completed it. As for killing time, something far more important was at stake, to which the term "kill" aptly applied.

The lives of men were on the verge of sacrifice, and among those slated for sudden doom was Lamont Cranston, otherwise The Shadow!

CHAPTER XII
THUNDER OVER MANHATTAN

THE Mohawk Building was an old one, a five-story relic, in one of those halfway areas where old Manhattan blended with the new. The boom days of the '20s had raised much taller structures in the neighborhood; then the building wave had stopped, leaving an unsightly architectural medley that people had begun to regard as permanent.

Rent was cheap in the Mohawk Building, and the top floor had skylights, as well as windows, which was why Martin Orvis had located his offices there. The Orvis Engineering Corp. employed a corps of draftsmen, and they found the skylights helpful to their work.

The drafting rooms were located on the side away from higher buildings. Orvis' own private office was in another corner, and from its window he could look across the street to the blank wall of a thirty-story building, which made the Mohawk Building look like a pygmy beside a giant.

An elderly man, with a tired expression, Orvis often commented on the blank view from his window.

At present, Orvis had a visitor named Cranston, who had never been in the Mohawk Building before. Quite naturally, Orvis was pointing out the view across the way.

"I like it," said Orvis, "because it cuts off my view of everything else. If it didn't, I would have to look at the architectural monstrosities in this neighborhood. How I hate them!" He shuddered, as if the mere thought grated his nerves. "I have to walk with my eyes set straight ahead, every time I enter this building or leave it."

Cranston gave a sympathetic nod. He glanced at two other men in the office. One was Orvis' nephew, Claude Orvis, a junior partner in the business; the other, the head draftsman, Tilton. In Cranston's tone, The Shadow inquired:

"How soon do you expect Mr. Kelber?"

"Almost any time," returned Martin Orvis. "He is stopping off to get Fralingham and Darrison. Do you know"—Orvis wagged his head seriously—"I think that Kelber is bringing Fralingham here to impress both myself and Darrison."

Cranston's eyes went quizzical. Orvis explained.

"Kelber warned Fralingham to protect the Asbestile plant," stated Orvis. "Nevertheless, disaster struck it. Universal Industries lost a most important adjunct as a result, but Kelber managed to find a way out. He has taken over the Asbestile formula, and will be able to manufacture the product himself.

"But he is worried about these plans." Orvis spread large sheets of drawings that were on his desk. "They cover the cantilever construction for the bombproof manufacturing units that Kelber has to build. They are practically complete, and though Kelber does not need them until the end of the month, he is afraid that something may happen to them.

"How could anything happen? I know every detail of these plans. So do Claude and Tilton. I told Kelber that there is no need for worry. He has approved the rough plans in duplicate, and knows that we can deliver everything they call for. It is the most profitable job that we have undertaken; so naturally, we are anxious to complete it."

The Shadow's thoughts retained one phrase: "until the end of the month." He agreed with Kelber's opinion that something might happen. One link in the Universal Industries chain was gone: the Asbestile Co. Kelber had managed to replace it; could he do the same again, if anything ruined the Orvis Engineering Corp.?

While waiting for Kelber to arrive with Fralingham and Darrison, The Shadow decided to call the Cobalt Club. He used Orvis' telephone, and received the brief message that Margo had left for Cranston.

The simple statement that Blandle intended to meet Bayruth, could only mean that Blandle was the name of the rangy man whose trail Margo had taken. It seemed a conclusive link between Thorden and Bayruth.

Unfortunately, Margo hadn't added that she had completed that link, and was taking on a self-appointed assignment. The Shadow was confident that Margo, having been told where Cranston could be reached, would send word of any new developments.

Not only did Margo intend to do so; she was much closer at hand than either she or The Shadow supposed.

IN fact, Margo was right outside the Mohawk Building, within hail of the office windows of the Orvis Engineering Corp., but she didn't know it.

Margo was more interested in the thirty-story building across the street. It happened to be the Cartwyn Building, where Bayruth was to wait for Blandle. Margo had parked her coupé at a rear corner, from which she could watch the side entrance of the Cartwyn Building, as well as the street in back.

From the backstreet, Margo heard a rumble which gave her a chilling reminder, because it was vaguely like thunder. She stared, saw a truck roll away, a great truck built in two sections, with a blaze of red taillights. The truck looked empty, from the way the trailer section swayed. It had evidently been unloading in back of the Cartwyn Building

Again, the rumble, very faint and from another direction. This time, it was thunder, and immediately afterward, through a space between two buildings, Margo caught a blink of lightning. It was one of those sudden storms that often arrive unnoticed, over Manhattan.

It was approaching, for Margo heard the thunder again, low and sullen, soon after the lightning flash. She would neither have seen the lightning nor heard the thunder had she been indoors, for the storm was low over the river, off beyond massed buildings. But Margo, since her New Jersey adventure, had become quite allergic to thunderstorms.

She decided not to wait and watch for Bayruth. She started the motor hastily, intending to drive from this neighborhood and reach a telephone, from which she could call Lamont. At that moment her eyes, roving the street, saw a startling surprise.

Across the street was an old five-story building which had lights on the top floor. Its front door was also lighted, and it bore the name:

MOHAWK BUILDING

This was luck, indeed! To find the building where Cranston had gone almost directly opposite the side entrance of the Cartwyn Building, where Oliver Bayruth was to appear.

Thinking that she could get quicker results without telephoning, Margo sprang from her coupé and hurried toward the entrance of the Mohawk Building. Dribbles of rain flicked her face as she dashed. The sudden storm had arrived from the river.

Margo was halfway across the street when a closer flash of lightning rendered the scene brilliant. Margo thought she heard two hoarse voices; they were drowned out by a roll of thunder that seemed to follow in along the street. But the voices were real, as Margo promptly learned.

Amid the return of darkness, two men sprang out from the shelter of the Cartwyn Building and cut across Margo's path.

They nabbed the brunette without a struggle. Wrenching from one pair of hands, Margo was tripped by the other. She threw her arm forward to shield herself from the curb, and only partly succeeded. Her head took a thump that half wilted her. As captors lifted her limp figure, she was vaguely conscious of their voices:

"Maybe this is the dame that talked to Bayruth —"

"Even if she ain't, we'd better grab her!"

"Yeah! She was headed for the wrong place!"

"Maybe she's wise that something is due to hit —"

All during that talk, Margo was being carried to the back of the huge Cartwyn Building, to the very loading entrance that the truck had used. Her head was swimming; she seemed to be sinking, until something jarred her upward.

Then, from a gradual floating impression, Margo realized that she was in a darkened elevator, being carried to the top floor of the tall Cartwyn Building!

THE same lightning flash that betrayed Margo, was observed by The Shadow up in the Orvis office. To his view, it was a glare that filled the street, whitening the blank wall of the building across the way. The earlier flashes had not been visible to The Shadow. That this one was quite close was evident from the immediate arrival of the thunder, which was the first rumble that he had heard.

Immediately, The Shadow galvanized to action. No longer the lackadaisical Mr. Cranston, he showed a speed that startled Martin Orvis right out of his chair; which helped. For The Shadow was grabbing at Orvis' shoulder, to yank him toward the door.

"Out of here! Quickly!" ordered The Shadow. His tone, still Cranston's, had a commanding snap. "Don't stop to ask questions. Get clear of this building, if you want to live!"

Propelling Orvis to the door, The Shadow was beckoning for Claude Orvis and Tilton to come along, confident that they would follow when they saw Orvis go. Claude was present, but Tilton was gone. He had left the office during The Shadow's call to the Cobalt Club.

The Shadow's words were grim, in Cranston's tone.

"Where is Tilton?"

"In the drafting room!" exclaimed Claude. "I'll get him in a hurry!"

There was a vivid flash of lightning, followed by heavy thunder, as The Shadow reached the head of the stairway and pointed the elder Orvis down. In another minute, the storm would be directly overhead.

The Shadow heard Claude's shouts to Tilton; then came thumps against a door near the stairs, a short route out of the drafting room. They couldn't get it open.

Springing for the door, The Shadow grabbed the knob and gave a titanic wrench that ripped the door wide. Both men were gone, the pound of their footsteps telling that they were taking the longer way, around through the private office. Hoping that they wouldn't be too long delayed, The Shadow turned to the stairs to follow Martin Orvis.

But Orvis wasn't going down.

He was on his way back to his office, shouting that he had forgotten the precious plans. On the stairs, The Shadow called for Claude and Tilton not to worry about the plans. They were coming out of the office, and, by all rights, they should have swept Orvis right along with them in response to Cranston's ardent beckon.

In fact, Claude did try. It was Tilton who wavered, as he heard Orvis screech frantically that he must save the plans. Tilton's hesitation produced a clutter in the doorway, and before The Shadow could spring to untangle them, it was too late.

The great clap came.

A smash from the sky above. Vivid lightning, and an instantaneous crash of thunder. But that stroke of nature was only the harbinger of destruction. It announced the real devastation, which was produced by man.

Except for The Shadow, those in the building thought that the sky lightning did the work. So did witnesses along the street, persons who had taken shelter in doorways to avoid the storm.

Only Bayruth and his fellow tools of disaster were in a place where they could really see their deadly work. They were atop the Cartwyn Building, among a cluster of squat skeleton towers that they had set up.

Those towers were flanked with rows of great metal spheres, the capacitors that were loaded with electricity. Timed to the great flash from the sky, Bayruth, a sharp-featured man with apish crouch, released the load.

Arrows of lightning streaked downward with an accuracy unmatched by nature. The crackles those bolts produced drowned Bayruth's laugh, for they were a thousand-fold greater, though in the same key.

Shafts ripped the skylights from the top floor of the puny Mohawk Building, tearing segments of the roof. The offices of the Orvis Corp. were bared to a bird's-eye view, showing tiny human figures fleeing for the stairs.

Another bolt cleaved the walls; the roof broke apart, and the great rift revealed the stairway. The top offices were withered under the electrical barrage; the furniture vanished into splinters, and with it, the precious plans were consumed upon the desk where Orvis had left them.

Another streak of devastating voltage knifed down into the split building, chopping through wooden floors as though they were cardboard. That crash sprawled human figures, as it took the stairs from under them.

Dollish forms, representing Orvis, his nephew, and Tilton, went tumbling headlong into the debris below. One tiny fugitive, alone, had outraced that electrical volley. He was Lamont Cranston, The Shadow.

Still on his feet, The Shadow was near the ground floor, ahead of the crashing wreckage that carried human shrieks, when the last jab of lightning came. It found a weak spot in the building wall, and the whole front of the structure gave. A great curtain of masonry shivered, then toppled inward, engulfing helpless victims beneath its collapsing tonnage.

A great sheet of lightning flickered from the heavens, as though some thunder god had winked an eye. That flash, and the roaring peals that followed, marked the passing of the storm. They were the final cover-up that nature supplied upon this scene where man's evil had triumphed.

A cackle from a thirtieth-floor roof, lost in the wail of wind and splash of rain—such was Bayruth's gloat over the destruction that he had wrought in the service of a hidden, ruthless master, who had ordered this disastzer.

Well might men of evil gloat. This deed had succeeded to the fullest measure. Orvis, his associates, and their plans were gone forever, and within the ruin that human thunderbolts had caused, crime's archfoe, The Shadow lay entombed!

CHAPTER XIII
MARGO'S MESSAGE

SEVERAL blocks from the ruined Mohawk Building, a limousine had paused beside the curb to await the passing of the torrential rain. One of its three passengers was Oswald Kelber. He addressed his companions impatiently.

"First you delayed us, Darrison," he told a heavy-set man at his right. "We should have left your apartment earlier."

"But you were in no hurry, then, Kelber—"

"Perhaps not," interposed Kelber. "We still had time to keep our appointment. I suppose we can blame Fralingham"—he glanced to his left—"for becoming skittish in this storm."

"I merely asked that we drive cautiously," put in Fralingham, adjusting his ribboned glasses on his wizened nose. "I thought it would be better to arrive late, than not at all."

"Very well," grumbled Kelber. "The rain is letting up. We can proceed."

They proceeded, but not to the Mohawk Building. Police cars blocked them off before they reached it. The *clang* of fire trucks came from another street, heading in the direction that Kelber had expected to go.

Showing alarm, Kelber inquired where the fire was, and was told of the destruction that lightning had produced. Immediately, Kelber furnished facts to the law.

"The Mohawk Building!" he exclaimed. "Why, there must be three men trapped there! Orvis, his nephew, and their head draftsman, Tilton. No, four—if Cranston happened to arrive ahead of us!"

Out of their limousine, Kelber and his companions were allowed through the fire lines. They found firemen digging into the massed debris that had been the Mohawk Building. One look convinced the arrivals that no one could have survived the crash, but the firemen speeded their efforts, upon learning that there were victims in the building.

"They'll never even find the bodies!" wheezed Fralingham. "This is worse than the tragedy at my plant. There, at least, most of the workers had a chance to escape."

Kelber was watching the proceedings, his bushy eyebrows furrowed in gloom. He turned to Darrison, beside him.

"First Fralingham's plant," said Kelber. "Now, this! Orvis and his plans—obliterated! I wonder, Darrison—"

"If I'm next?" broke in Darrison. "Impossible, Kelber! These things were accidents."

"But two of them—"

"Mean a most unfortunate coincidence. You've a problem ahead, Kelber, now that you have lost Orvis. But if you can solve it, there's no need to worry about me. I'll turn out all the air-conditioning equipment that the contracts demand."

Doubtfully, Kelber shook his head.

"We're safeguarded at our plant," insisted Darrison. "Vortex Circulators are manufactured in modern surroundings. We have taken every precaution against all dangers. Lightning might knock some shingles off our roof; nothing more."

Fralingham excitedly announced that the firemen had found a body and were bringing it out. Approaching, Kelber and Darrison saw the smoke-eaters lever up a battered door frame, while others reached for the figure beneath it.

"It's Cranston!" exclaimed Kelber. "My friend Cranston, dead!"

A TAXI driver was shouldering his way among the firemen. How he had managed to pass the lines, no one seemed to know. He was the first, however, to argue that the victim was still alive, a point which the firemen doubted.

It happened that the cabby was Moe Shrevnitz, and he couldn't believe that anything could permanently halt The Shadow's career.

"Get him into my cab," insisted Moe. "I'll have him to a hospital before you can get a call through for an ambulance."

The cab drove off carrying Cranston, with a fireman in the rear seat. They had just reached the hospital, when the fireman suddenly agreed with Moe's hunch.

"Say, this guy *is* alive!" exclaimed the fireman. "I don't think he's even hurt bad. You know why? He must've grabbed that door when it was coming in at him along with the wall. He could've hung right in the middle of it and let it take the bricks. Luck, that's what!"

Not luck, in Moe's opinion. He'd seen his chief make drowning grabs at cables and come up with a rope in his fist It was just one more instance of The Shadow's ability to offset any disaster that overwhelmed him.

Others, however, had not fared so well. Back at the ruined building, Kelber turned away when he saw firemen reclaim the mangled remains of three other humans. Both members of the Orvis partnership, and their chief assistant, Tilton, were in an unrecognizable shape.

Observing that both Fralingham and Darrison looked very sick, Kelber suggested that they go back to the car.

They rode in silence to Kelber's offices, which were open evenings, and working overtime. From the fortieth-story window, Kelber studied the sparkling carpet of Manhattan as if searching for a black gap in its midst, the spot where a building had been chopped to chunks. He swung suddenly and faced Darrison.

"Fralingham will bear witness to what I say," declared Kelber. "Cranston was here this afternoon. He testified that on a visit to Thorden's, in my behalf, he was followed when he left the house. Am I correct, Fralingham?"

Fralingham nodded.

"Cranston went to see Thorden again today," continued Kelber. "When I called him at the Cobalt Club, he stated that his car had been followed again. That is why I wanted Cranston at our conference with Orvis. I wanted him to drive home the danger that I believe exists.

"If Cranston is still alive, you will hear his testimony later. But how can we doubt the menace, after seeing what happened to the others? A coincidence: the destruction of Fralingham's plant and Orvis' building? Bah! Lightning doesn't strike twice!"

Kelber repeated the phrase, as though it impressed him. Picking up the telephone emphatically, he told his companions, "I'm going to call Thorden. I'll tell him that lightning doesn't strike twice. We'll see what he says."

The phone call wasn't much of a success. Kelber reached Thorden, but the latter professed ignorance of the Orvis tragedy. Kelber had to tell him all about it, before breaking loose in wrath. Finally, however, he inserted his choice remark.

"I'll tell you just this, Thorden!" he boomed. "Lightning doesn't strike twice!"

Kelber listened to something from the other end. Thorden's statement finished with a harsh *clack* of his receiver. Kelber's face looked somewhat blank when he turned to Fralingham and Darrison. They both wanted to know what Thorden's comment was.

"He told me I was wrong," said Kelber, slowly. "The old saying is that lightning doesn't strike twice in the same place. Thorden insists it didn't, in this instance. He said that Orvis' building wasn't your factory, Fralingham. He laughed when he hung up.

"But he won't split hairs with me!" Kelber pounded his desk so hard that he had to clutch his fist with his other hand. "Before I'm through, I'll *prove* that Thorden had a hand in these disasters!"

HOW Kelber intended to prove it remained a puzzle. Only one person was in a position to reveal the inside of the lightning-making game, and she was, at present, quite helpless.

MOE SHREVNITZ

Bound and gagged in a darkened office on the thirtieth door of the Cartwyn Building, Margo was watching men who worked in the gloom, dismantling the telescopic columns they had brought down from the roof.

Bulky electrical contrivances were also being removed, and being crated in sections, with Oliver Bayruth cackling orders to his crew.

Hours had gone by, when word came up that the firemen were gone from the ruins of the Mohawk Building. Bayruth promptly used a telephone to summon the truck.

Margo was taken down on the last load that descended in the freight elevator, along with a cargo of cable that had been used in supplying power to the capacitors. She understood why Harry Vincent and the others had failed to locate Bayruth during their New Jersey search. The canny electrical wizard had doubled into New York, there to make ready for tonight's job.

That done, he was going back to New Jersey. Riding in the truck, Margo could tell when they were going through the Holland Tunnel. After that, she was unable to calculate their direction, or even guess the running time.

Finally unloaded, she was carried from what seemed an underground garage into a cell-like room, where Bayruth arrived and ordered that her bonds and gag be removed. Margo saw that he was carrying her purse.

"We picked this up, Miss Lane," spoke Bayruth,

eyeing Margo with a cunning gaze. "Your car has been taken to its proper garage, and your bag reclaimed from the Grand Central checkroom. The bag is over there in the corner."

Margo looked, saw the suitcase.

"You were going on a trip," continued Bayruth. "We found your railroad ticket. It is possible that you might want to write to certain friends—Mr. Cranston, for example?"

Margo started to say something, then stopped.

"Picture postcards would be appropriate," chuckled Bayruth, as though reading Margo's mind. "So I shall supply some, later, and have them posted from the proper towns.

"In advance, I might mention that we have samples of your handwriting, taken from your driver's license and other papers in the purse. When the time comes, you will write the postcard exactly as you normally would."

Dully, Margo sank back in the chair where she had been placed. She tried to gather her wits, to think of some way in which she might trick old Bayruth, whose sharp eyes and apish grin took away all the dignity that his snow-white hair gave him. Watching Margo craftily, Bayruth queried suddenly:

"There was something else, Miss Lane?"

"Why... no—"

"Perhaps there *is* something else!" Bayruth's tone became a snarl, accentuated by fangish teeth, as his lips opened in a leer. "If there is"—he was approaching viciously—"it would be wise for you to tell me!"

"Only one thing!" blurted Margo. "The telegram ... it's Lamont's birthday tomorrow. He'd expect a telegram. I ought to send him one—"

"That will be done," interposed Bayruth, easing his forward creep. "Quite easily, Miss Lane. We shall have the telegraph company send one of its form telegrams to your dear friend, Mr. Cranston."

With that, Bayruth turned on his heel and left the cell. He slammed the door, and Margo heard a bolt grate on the other side. How long she would remain a prisoner, Margo could not guess, but she hoped it would not be many days.

Margo was depending on The Shadow.

CHAPTER XIV
THE SHORTEST WAY

FROM his hospital cot, The Shadow took a new look at the world. It wasn't very bright outside the windows, and his first thought was that it was early morning, only to decide that it was late afternoon. Piecing his recollections, he kept his final verdict.

The Shadow could remember a long, drowsy spell, broken at intervals. He recalled that he had seen drawn window shades whenever he opened his eyes.

He recalled the crash of the night before, and knew that he must have received a brain concussion when the top of the door frame hit his head. But in return for that slap, the door frame had certainly stopped a lot of harder blows from falling masonry.

At any rate, the hospital had supplied its new patient, Lamont Cranston, with the usual treatment—that of keeping him quiet in a darkened room. They'd probably want him to stay a few days more, but that was something The Shadow couldn't tolerate. He'd have to get in touch with Dr. Sayre.

Seeing a bell beside the bed, The Shadow thumped it. He expected a nurse to arrive; instead, Sayre appeared.

Dr. Rupert Sayre was Cranston's physician, which meant, in a sense, that he was in The Shadow's service. In fact, if it hadn't been for The Shadow, Dr. Sayre would never have had Cranston as a patient. Nor would Sayre have had the very fine practice that came from Cranston's friends.

In fact, Sayre wouldn't even be alive. He owed his life to The Shadow, who had pulled him out of a very bad jam several years before.

As a result, Sayre was always ready to do favors for The Shadow, or for Lamont Cranston, for he knew that they were either one and the same man, or very closely associated.

Hearing that Cranston was in the hospital, Sayre had dropped everything else, to come there and wait until his star patient improved.

"You've got to get me out of this, Sayre," said The Shadow in Cranston's calm tone. "So go to it."

"I think that you have sufficiently improved," decided Sayre. "At least, enough for me to convince the chief resident physician. But you still need rest. Knowing how deeply you get into certain matters, I'm afraid you'll overdo this one if I get you away from here."

"Just a few loose threads to gather," returned The Shadow, wearily. "I'm too weak to do anything more, Sayre."

Sayre wasn't entirely bluffed; nevertheless, he compromised with himself, by deciding that he would accompany Cranston and watch him gather up the few loose threads. Soon, Sayre and Cranston were in the latter's limousine, riding downtown to visit a man named Oswald Kelber.

In Kelber's office, they met Fralingham and Darrison. Both were impressed by Cranston's description of disaster at the Orvis office. But they were even more interested in his emphatic statement that his car had been followed by two thuggish-looking gentry, after leaving Thorden's the day before.

"You see?" said Kelber to the others. Then, turning to Cranston: "Thorden thinks he has me licked. But be hasn't! Look at these, Cranston!" He spread sheets of rough plans on the desk. "Orvis sent these to me yesterday, which is something that Thorden didn't guess.

"These plans are good enough to work from. I own a bridge-building works, the Criterion Constructors. They're building approaches to the new industrial units that I have to complete. This cantilever stuff was not in their line, but it is now. My engineers say that they can take over from where Orvis left off. It means that I can fulfill the contracts after all, and beat Thorden at his game!"

Triumphantly, Kelber paced his office; then, stopping short, he said:

"But how can I prove the incredible? How can I make anyone believe that Thorden was behind those disasters? I'll admit it sounds impossible. I may be a fool to even think it. But you can help me, Cranston—"

"In what way?"

"By calling Thorden. Make another appointment with him. If men follow you again, find out what you can about them. Thorden can't possibly suspect that you know about the men who were on your trail."

The Shadow didn't entirely agree; nevertheless, the suggestion intrigued him. He reached for the telephone, despite Sayre's warning hand, and called Thorden. After a short, friendly chat, he hung up the telephone.

"It's all right, Doctor," he said to Sayre. "I arranged it for the day after tomorrow. Suppose we go to the Cobalt Club for dinner, and then you can see me off for home—early."

Sayre nodded, and stepped to the door. The Shadow found time to turn to Kelber and undertone:

"Not the day after tomorrow. Tonight, at ten o'clock."

THEY dined at the Cobalt Club, The Shadow and Dr. Sayre. From the way his patient seemed to tire, Sayre was quite convinced that Cranston would be glad to leave for home at an early hour.

They were finishing their dessert, and yawning, when a trio of telegraph messengers clattered into the grillroom, much to the annoyance of the fussy club members.

Lining up in front of Cranston's table, they began to sing a "happy birthday" song. They were badly off key and rather ragged when they sang "dear Lamont," but they rallied toward the end. Then, in chorus, they chimed the signature:

"Margo!"

The Shadow was still smiling when the messengers had gone. He turned to Sayre.

"That's enough for one night," he decided. "Give me a help upstairs, Sayre. I'm a bit shaky. I'd better start home."

"I didn't know it was your birthday," said Sayre, as they reached the foyer. "Rather a good joke on Margo's part, having a lot of messengers blossom into the sedate Cobalt Club and disturb its serenity with a birthday song."

"A *very* good joke" was Cranston's chuckled reply. "A much better joke than you think, Sayre."

They were going through the door, when Sayre inquired why.

"Because"—The Shadow paused, about to step into his limousine—"it doesn't happen to be my birthday!"

Leaving Sayre standing quite nonplussed, The Shadow wearily ordered Stanley to drive home. Around the corner, he countermanded the order and told the chauffeur to go to the Hotel Metrolite.

There, The Shadow picked up Harry Vincent, who was back from the hunt for Bayruth's headquarters.

"We've narrowed down the range," said Harry, glumly, "but we still have a lot of territory to cover."

"Central Park, Stanley," said The Shadow, in Cranston's tone, through the speaking tube. Then, in a whisper more his own, he stated cryptically to Harry: "Find Margo and you'll find Bayruth."

"What? You mean—"

"They trapped Margo, last night. I'm sure of it. She had to find a way to reach me and let me know something had happened. She managed to send through a phony birthday telegram."

"We'll have to move fast, chief." Harry's tone was worried. "Margo must be in a bad spot."

"I don't think so," returned The Shadow. "She was tagging Blandle, Thorden's prize snooper. He was trying to get in touch with Bayruth. I don't think they'll harm Margo, until they know just how much she knows about Blandle and Thorden."

"But if they make her talk—"

"Trust Margo to handle that," interrupted The Shadow. "She has a perfect out, and sense enough to use it. She can tell them that her friend Cranston is the one who really knows. I am quite sure they will believe her."

The limousine had reached Central Park and was following the drives. Having a few hours until ten o'clock, The Shadow leaned back, closed his eyes, and began to analyze the case, for Harry's benefit.

FROM the start, Harry was intrigued by the fine points; the way The Shadow simplified and interpreted them.

It began with the first time that The Shadow, as Cranston, had visited Thorden. Two persons had picked up the trail. Matt Mardan and Thorden's snooper, Blandle. Matt, in particular, had been too obvious. On Cranston's next visit, only yesterday, another thug, evidently Matt's successor, had promptly followed the limousine from Thorden's. Blandle, however, had gone on another mission.

It seemed that Matt had purposely let it be known that he was on Cranston's trail. Certainly, the car that followed yesterday had made no effort to hide the fact that it was tagging the limousine. On the first occasion, Matt's trailing of Cranston had brought The Shadow to the old garage, where he had ruined Matt's rather makeshift effort to trap him.

"Because of what happened to Matt," concluded The Shadow, "those men who followed this limousine last night could well have known that by trailing Cranston, they might end by having The Shadow trailing them. If so, there is but one answer.

"Last night, a trap was set. A real one, much better than Matt's makeshift. But the men who were to bring me to it found themselves ignored. Nevertheless, they are likely to try again. Tonight, if they follow Cranston from Thorden's, they will expect—"

The Shadow's words ended in a low, sinister laugh—his own, though it came from Cranston's lips. Harry knew that thugs would again expect The Shadow, and that this time, they would not be disappointed. The Shadow would arrive.

Harry linked other points. No one—Kelber, his rival Thorden, nor the latter's snooper, Blandle—had proof that Cranston was The Shadow. Even Bayruth, the human tool of murder, could not be positive of that fact. But they did regard The Shadow as Cranston's protector. Blandle, most certainly, could testify to that effect.

Men of crime were seeking a showdown with The Shadow. Their idea of a showdown meant death. The Shadow was willing to accept the challenge.

Why?

Harry received his answer from the solemn, subdued laugh which he heard The Shadow utter. That mirthless tone provided the complete solution.

No longer could The Shadow waste time in a search for Bayruth's headquarters. He was seeking actual contact with men of crime as the shortest way to reach his goal, the hidden place where Margo Lane was a prisoner!

CHAPTER XV
THE MURDER MACHINE

THE big clock in Bayruth's laboratory pointed to the hour of nine, but Margo Lane wasn't looking at the clock. She was too busy staring at the contrivances which Bayruth had on display. Never had Margo seen such an odd exhibition.

The place frightened her, even though Bayruth had been polite enough in inviting her to see the lab. All around were electrical devices, with huge switches, large coils and multitudes of wires.

One, which had a pair of squat posts a few feet high, topped by large metal spheres, was certainly a portable lightning maker, though it couldn't compare with the mighty contrivance which Margo knew was packed in Bayruth's big double-sectioned truck.

Bayruth could be pleasant when he so chose. But in the sharp-faced wizard's smile, the crackly laugh that accompanied it, Margo sensed menace, accompanied with insanity. At present, Bayruth was trending toward the latter. He had forgotten his electrical contrivances, to enthuse over his perpetual-motion machine.

It was a great wheel, and had cups at the end of each spoke. Smiling at Margo, Bayruth placed a rubber ball in the topmost cup, but held the wheel steady.

"When I release the wheel," he declaimed, "the weight of the ball will carry it around. Then, after the ball has passed the bottom, the wheel will bring it up again. Ah, you think I am crazy, as they all do. Watch! Learn why I am right."

He released the wheel and the ball carried it downward, but when it neared the bottom, the cup flipped and the ball scaled out at an angle. It struck the table on which the machine stood, and being of rubber, the ball bounced upward at an angle. By then, the wheel had passed it; the next cup in line scooped the ball and carried it up to the top.

Around and around went the wheel. Each time, near the bottom, the ball left it and made the same bounce. The timing was perfect: the scooping cup next on the wheel took the ball deftly and carried it along.

Margo was so fascinated that she began to forget her present predicament.

"They argue soundly," declared Bayruth, "when they say that friction will prevent the wheel from bringing up the same weight that carries it down. My answer is to remove the weight during a portion of the revolution, thereby lessening the burden of the wheel."

The wheel was slowing slightly, and Bayruth gave it an annoyed stare. He was muttering something about "poor balance," and "too much friction," when a rap came at the door. Bayruth answered it, to admit a flat-faced man, one of his technicians. The fellow saw the revolving wheel and didn't like it. In guttural tone, he said:

"We are waiting for you, Mr. Bayruth. Remember you have orders from Thor—"

He chopped off suddenly as Bayruth gave a gesture in Margo's direction. Seeing the girl for the first time, the technician was quick to smother any mention of names.

"You have work," he corrected. "Important work. When it is done, you can again test your wheel."

Bayruth nodded his shaggy head.

"Very good, Klegg," he said. "The truck is ready?"

Klegg nodded.

"I have come for the portable machine," he said, indicating the small-sized lightning maker. "You are taking it to New York, you know. You are to meet me, afterward."

"I remember," Bayruth acknowledged. "Put the portable machine in my car. Then start out with the truck."

Klegg brought in another man to help carry the portable device. Studying them both, Margo could understand their association with Bayruth. These men had the Fifth Column brand; they were the sort who would try to cripple American industries if they could. They were finding such opportunity, through Bayruth.

Though Bayruth happened to be the user of the secret weapon in the duel between two industrialists, Oswald Kelber and Jerome Thorden, he was also accomplishing work that foreign agents sought to do.

Margo promptly credited Thorden with having hired such apprentices to serve Bayruth. Ordinary thugs would do for outside work, but these were more efficient in schemes of huge destruction.

HAVING heard that Klegg was taking out the truck, Margo became apprehensive. Knowing that Bayruth had already eliminated two key members of Kelber's Universal Industries chain—the Asbestile Co., and the Orvis Engineering Corp.— she was certain that a stroke was due against the third weak link. That would necessarily mean trouble for Roy Darrison, owner of Vortex Circulators.

But how to get such word to The Shadow?

Margo was puzzling over that problem, when Oliver Bayruth supplied the answer in his sharp, crackling tone.

"If you have any message for The Shadow," he gibed, "I shall be pleased to carry it. I expect to meet him within the nest few hours. You saw the portable machine that Klegg took to my car. I intend to test it against The Shadow and his guns!"

The words stunned Margo. She could only stare.

"With The Shadow eliminated," added Bayruth, "we shall have little worry regarding your other friend, Lamont Cranston, who luckily escaped death last night. In fact"—Bayruth tilted his head to study Margo—"you will be our only problem. We shall keep you here, to produce you if needed. But after that necessity is ended—"

Bayruth finished with a gloating cluck that promised Margo a one-way ticket in the wrong direction. By then, the girl's nerve returned. Margo sprang for the door, intending to block off Bayruth.

She was going to fight it out with the crazed inventor, who considered murder a pleasant pastime. Not just for her own life, but for the lives of others. Most specifically, for one life, that Bayruth seemed to think was two: that of The Shadow and Lamont Cranston.

Margo needed a weapon, and found one in the shape of a thing that looked like a table lamp; it had a red bulb, but no shade. She grabbed it, bringing its wire along, and swung it at Bayruth's head.

He made a dive for the wall, and pressed a switch which Margo thought would extinguish the laboratory lights; something that wouldn't matter, because she was sure she could reach Bayruth in the dark.

But the lab lights didn't go out. Instead, the red bulb in Margo's light came on. With its glow, the girl received a sudden shock from the metal standard that she gripped. Tumbling to the floor, Margo was shaken and jounced by the current that came through the wire to the lamp.

The red bulb didn't break when it battered the floor. It was of unbreakable glass, and Margo couldn't let go of the lamp because of the current.

Bayruth kept cackling in great glee at Margo's contortions. Finally, he turned off the current and watched the girl settle in limp relief.

"Fortunately for you, Miss Lane," he said, "I am careful never to use a high current on my laboratory devices. That lamp is one that I was testing as a method of disposing of troublesome persons. You can imagine how effective a full charge would prove."

Margo could do more than imagine it. She hadn't any fight left in her. Bayruth opened the door and summoned two of his men. Margo was so weak that they had to carry her back to her cell. There, they dropped her in a chair and departed without ceremony, bolting the door behind them.

Quite wilted, Margo heard the rumble of the

big truck when it left, and also the lesser roar of Bayruth's car. She could only revert to her original hope that The Shadow, in some way, would prove himself a match for the best of Bayruth's efforts. But she knew the truth, and did not like it.

Unquestionably, tonight, The Shadow would walk into a trap, there to meet with Bayruth's portable lightning maker, which was designed to kill within a required range. In picturing such a trap, Margo could think of no place more ominous, and therefore suitable for murder, than the gloomy Manhattan mansion where Jerome Thorden lived.

SO far as Thorden's house was concerned, Margo should have set her mind at ease. When Lamont Cranston entered that residence at ten o'clock, he wasn't even carrying a gun.

It was the last place where The Shadow would look for trouble. Thorden might be twice the monster that Kelber made him out to be, and still have judgment when dealing with visitors to his own preserves.

Tonight, however, Thorden could not quite veil his actual sentiments. He received Cranston with a show of mock politeness, which was practically an open statement that he knew his visitor came from Kelber. In fact, The Shadow for once seemed to lack the full poise of Cranston. He didn't know quite how to explain his visit.

Smoothly, Thorden waived that point.

"You had a lucky escape last night," he said. "I was very glad to learn that you were still alive. Too bad about Orvis. I suppose that his death was a very great shock to Kelber."

Before The Shadow could offer a reply, Thorden modified the statement.

"I don't mean in a business way," he added. "I wouldn't do Kelber an injustice, even by supposing such a case. Besides"—Thorden's tone had an oily irony—"I understand that Kelber has quite recovered from his loss. Clever, the way in which he managed to salvage the Orvis situation.

"Perhaps Kelber is more lucky than clever. It was luck that he happened to have those rough plans that his own constructors could decipher. I'm beginning to believe that Kelber is a hard man to beat. I really think that if Vortex Circulators went out of business tomorrow, Kelber would find some substitute method of filling those key contracts."

Cranston's expression was becoming weary. He asked Thorden to excuse him. He was trying to remember why he had made this appointment, at all, and his recollections were very hazy.

In a tired tone, The Shadow remarked that he should have followed his doctor's advice and postponed all business appointments for a few days.

"I had something to discuss," he said, "but it's gone from my mind, Thorden. I think I'd better be getting along."

Ringing for a servant, Thorden insisted that Cranston accept help in going downstairs. On the way, The Shadow stumbled twice, while Thorden watched.

While the servant was piloting Cranston out through the front door, Thorden returned to the office. Blandle was standing near the window. Both watched from deep behind a curtain. From the light above the front door, they could see Cranston walking unsteadily toward the gate.

"Cranston was badly off form," observed Thorden, dryly. "I didn't believe that he could bluff so poorly. Unless—"

Thorden paused; his eyes took on a shrewd look. He heard Blandle query:

"Shall I follow him, like I did the first time?"

"No," decided Thorden. "Sometimes, Blandle, an act can be so bad that it is good. I think it applies in Cranston's case. He was giving us the come-on."

"Then why not take it up?"

"It might not prove healthy, Blandle." Thorden clapped his hand on the rangy man's shoulder. "That is, not for you. I wouldn't care to have you in another mix-up with The Shadow. I am quite sure that he will appear upon the scene after Cranston leaves it."

THORDEN'S prediction was correct. Riding to the Cobalt Club, The Shadow saw a rakish car take up the limousine's trail just around the corner from Thorden's. The other car made no effort to conceal its presence.

Arriving at the club, The Shadow alighted as Cranston and sent the limousine away. He saw the rakish car roll slowly past; it actually lingered at the next corner.

There was a side exit from the club. Coming from it, still in the guise of Cranston, The Shadow stepped directly into a coupé, where Harry Vincent was at the wheel. He was using Harry in preference to Moe Shrevnitz because the latter's cab might prove too conspicuous along the coming trail.

The Shadow had a package with him. He told Harry to cruise along and find the rakish car; meanwhile, The Shadow was unwrapping the package. In a side glance, Harry saw black garments within—the cloak and hat with which The Shadow intended to obliterate the guise of Cranston.

Then they were past the corner and Harry's eyes were straight ahead, seeking the trail of the car that had been sent to decoy The Shadow to his doom!

CHAPTER XVI
JOLTS OF DEATH

THE trail was easy, so easy that it worried Harry. The thugs in the car ahead did everything except reach out and wave. From the moment that Harry's car eased up in back of theirs, they were sure that The Shadow had found them, and they made the most of it.

However, Harry noted that the decoy crew was skittish. They preferred streets that offered a clear path ahead, in case The Shadow should begin to open fire, or try to overtake them. Every now and then, the driver showed tendencies to spurt, until his companions evidently restrained him. Probably they pictured The Shadow half leaning from a window, a ready gun in his hand.

The Shadow wasn't leaning from the window. He didn't even have a gun in his hand. He was putting on his black garments—rather painfully, Harry thought, which made him wonder if his chief had sufficiently recovered from last night's ordeal to take on the present quest.

Usually, The Shadow slid into hat and cloak so rapidly, that they swished. Such wasn't the case tonight. He was wrapping the cloak in flabby fashion, and he couldn't seem to get the hat properly settled on his head. He kept tugging it down and tightening it.

When cloaked, The. Shadow generally became so silent, that Harry almost forgot his presence. On this occasion he seemed fidgety, and Harry was conscious of it.

The car ahead began new tactics. It had reached a dismal section of the city and was increasing speed, while it made devious turns into side streets. It wasn't trying to shake the trail; rather, it was seeking to increase the distance, and keep farther ahead of Harry's car. The reason was explained when the decoy car suddenly swerved into an alley.

As Harry came to the opening, he and The Shadow saw taillights ahead. The red gleams were suddenly extinguished.

The Shadow whispered for Harry to ease past the mouth of the alley and wait on the street, itself.

It was plain that the alley was a blind one; therefore, the decoy crew must have deserted their car. But they wouldn't be waiting for The Shadow in a blind alley. Obviously, they must have some outlet which they could go through, although their car could not.

Harry watched The Shadow step from the coupé, saw him trip over the dangling folds of his cloak. Stooping, The Shadow spent some time in adjusting the garment's hem, which worried Harry badly. Harry was just about to protest against his chief undertaking a fool's venture, considering his condition, when The Shadow moved off into the darkness. From then on, Harry could only wait.

Entering the blind alley, The Shadow plodded slowly, instead of moving with his typical swift glide. Nevertheless, he was up to par when it came to concealment. He had merged completely with the blackness; he made no sound whatever, as he neared the deserted car at the inner limit of the cul-de-sac.

Past the car, The Shadow found the route that thugs had taken. It was a door in the corner of the wall, leading down into a basement. A tiny flashlight pressed between gloved palms, The Shadow directed dots of light along the floor, which was of cement. The passage ended in a flight of wooden stairs that led upward.

Squarely at the top was another door. The Shadow tried it; the door yielded, opening inward. Stopping short on the top step, he viewed a feebly lighted room, where a shaggy-haired man sat in a chair beside a table. The Shadow saw a sharp-featured face, with bright, but watery eyes, above a pair of huddly shoulders. Lips, with a crazed smile, uttered a crackly greeting.

There wasn't a doubt as to the man's identity. He was Oliver Bayruth.

"WELCOME, Shadow!" voiced Bayruth. "Won't you walk into my parlor? I am only the fly, you know. You are The Shadow. To be frank"—Bayruth's tone went suddenly solemn—"I have very much to tell you. Facts I have been afraid to reveal, about crimes for which I was not responsible."

The Shadow's figure was but dimly outlined. He took one step forward, so that Bayruth could see him better. As proof of his real regard for Bayruth, The Shadow extended two automatics, one in each hand.

The right gun covered Bayruth; the left was aimed toward a door in the far corner of the room. It was the only place that the vanished thugs could have gone.

Though he preferred to take Bayruth alive, The Shadow was willing to show short shrift to lurking thugs. One tremble of that door, and it would be blasted with bullets from the gun that pointed toward it.

Just within the door, where The Shadow could reach it with a few paces, was a table that bore the portable death machine that Margo had seen in Bayruth's lab. Noting the squatty columns, with the metal spheres that topped them, The Shadow recognized the device as a lightning maker, capable, perhaps, of hurling a half a million volts—enough to demolish an elephant, with a direct hit.

"It is yours, Shadow," declared Bayruth, earnestly. "I am giving it to you as evidence against the evil master who has done great crime through my inventions, and who hopes to place the blame upon my shoulders."

Bayruth's tone was piteous. His shoulders looked too scrawny to support any burden. He was so far removed from the portable lightning maker that he couldn't reach the switch which projected from the front of the machine. Bayruth extended a scrawny hand to the cord of a lamp beside his chair.

"I'll give you more light, Shadow," he insisted, "so you can see everything quite plainly."

The Shadow took one step toward the lightning machine. As he did, Bayruth pulled the lamp cord. The two happened to be connected by a wire beneath the carpet.

Terrific was the flash that came, its horrendous crackle drowning Bayruth's gleeful laugh. The two capacitors, loosing their killing load, hurled zigzag shafts straight at The Shadow. The natural targets for those streaks of man-made lightning were The Shadow's steel guns.

Striking them with a tremendous jolt, the charge hurled The Shadow's arm upward, flaying his body with it. Amid a peal of instantaneous thunder, that actually rocked the room, The Shadow went backward in a flying somersault that carried him through the door and down the steps.

Out of the thunderous echoes came Bayruth's high-pitched laugh. He could still hear the downward tumble of the falling form in black, but The Shadow's plunge, even though it might be of the breakneck variety, was quite inconsequential to Bayruth. He knew the power of his lightning bolts.

Bayruth had placed the machine at just the proper distance from the stairway door. No living human could have received the charge within that range and survived the stroke. Some persons, perhaps, credited The Shadow with being more than human. Not Bayruth. He had seen the results.

So had the crooks who stepped from the other door. Nevertheless, they gave anxious glances toward the stairway. Bayruth laughed as he studied their three faces.

"Fools!" he exclaimed. "The Shadow is dead. He was killed the moment that those lightning bolts hit him. Come! I am going out through the front, to my own car. Jerry will accompany me. You two, Spike and Ringo, will bring the machine."

BAYRUTH went through the far door with Jerry. Sniffing the ozone that filled the room as a result of the electrical charge, Spike approached the lightning machine a bit gingerly, and began to unclamp it from the table. He heard Ringo gloat from the stairway door:

"Take a look, Spike."

Approaching, Spike took the flashlight from Ringo's hands and gazed along the path of light that it projected downward. At the bottom of the stairs, they saw what was left of The Shadow, a huddled blotch of black against the stone floor.

"Croaked!" rasped Spike. "Just like Bayruth said. Only, there's one thing his nibs forgot."

"Yeah?" queried Ringo. "What?"

"When the cops find the body," returned Spike, "they'll know what hit it."

"But Bayruth followed orders. He got them from Thor—"

"Never mind that," interrupted Spike, his voice raspy. "We're supposed to use good sense, ain't we? I'm going to load The Shadow with a gatful of slugs so the bulls will think that gunzels snuffed him. What's more, if The Shadow still has life in him, he won't have after I finish blasting!"

Deliberately, Spike aimed his gleaming revolver downward. Ringo was watching his companion's trigger finger when the first shot roared. But Spike's finger hadn't moved, nor did his gun spurt. In fact, the gun burst didn't come from the top of the stairs; it was delivered from the bottom!

Nor did Spike shoot at all; instead, he staggered backward, his gun slipping from his hand. Spike had taken a bullet right in the wrist.

The flashlight, sliding from Spike's other hand, gave a last flickering view down the stairs. In that gleam, Ringo saw the incredible. It wasn't some newcomer who had beaten Spike to the shot. It was The Shadow! The black-cloaked fighter was rising from the stony floor, a smoking automatic in his gloved fist!

Before Ringo could believe his eyes, the view was gone. But from the lower blackness came new proof that The Shadow still lived. It was a laugh that came upward with an increasing taunt, a challenge of vengeance from The Shadow to the men who thought they had slain him!

Ringo was sure that The Shadow was coming up the stairs, for the mocking mirth was rising in volume. But The Shadow had darkness at his service, and Ringo couldn't risk staying in the light, to become a target like Spike.

Dashing across the room, Ringo ducked for the far door, turning as he went through, to take quick shot at The Shadow if the revived fighter appeared.

The Shadow did appear, too soon for Ringo. At the head of the stairs, The Shadow dropped below the level of the top step. Ringo's frantic shots whizzed high above his cloaked adversary's head. The single shot that The Shadow fired clipped Ringo's shoulder, caught the crook off balance and snaked him right out of the doorway, sprawling him on the floor of the room.

Footsteps were pounding up the stairs. Harry Vincent had arrived, having heard the gunfire. Crossing the room, The Shadow sped through the far door, leaving Harry the task of gathering up the revolvers dropped by Spike and Ringo before the wounded thugs could crawl and get them.

Reaching the front street, The Shadow was just too late to open fire at a car that whizzed the corner. His parting laugh, however, was a memory that Bayruth could cherish. It was no farewell, that mirth. It was a token that The Shadow still lived; that he expected to meet Bayruth soon again.

RETURNING to the lightning room, The Shadow found Harry quizzing the sullen prisoners. They wouldn't talk to Harry, but sight of The Shadow, the tone of his sinister laugh, unloosed their tongues. He reminded them that he could send them where they thought that he had gone: into the realm of death.

"Bayruth deceived you," added The Shadow, sardonically. "After that, he deserted you. I shall find him"—his tone was positive—"and when I do, I shall remember whether or not you supplied me with information. Suit yourselves."

The Shadow was turning away. Outvying each other, Spike and Ringo spilled all they knew. They couldn't give The Shadow the location of Bayruth's New Jersey hideaway, because they hadn't been there. But they did know where Bayruth happened to be going first.

"He's going to knock off another plant," blabbed Spike. "The Vortex Circulators—"

"And the truck is waiting for him," broke in Ringo. "With a guy named Klegg in charge of it!"

The Shadow drew Harry to a corner, gave him instructions regarding the prisoners, the removal of the portable lightning machine, and other matters to follow.

They were in better light, and Harry could see The Shadow's face beneath the brim of the slouch hat. The face was odd, expressionless, which puzzled Harry, until he saw that it wasn't a face at all.

It was a rubber mask!

Harry eyed the cloak and hat. They were of rubber, too, which explained why they hadn't swished! Hat, mask and cloak were all one piece, as were the rubber gloves, which Harry at last observed. The Shadow was wearing rubber shoes with spreading tops, like boots, that became a part of the cloak. He had been fixing them when Harry thought that he had stumbled, just outside the car!

Expecting a meeting with Bayruth, The Shadow had come equipped to meet any bolts that the lightning maker might hurl. Fully insulated, he had taken the jolts of death, unscathed. The Shadow had overlooked one trifling detail: his guns.

Because of his grip upon them, The Shadow had been hurled backward when the guns received the lightning thrusts, which accounted for his unexpected tumble down the stairs. He'd needed a breather after that plunge, so had taken one. Ready for new action, The Shadow had supplied it when the time came.

Thus had The Shadow nullified the schemes of a superfoe who had sent Bayruth to murder him. As Harry pieced those facts, he heard The Shadow's whispered laugh, a token of departure. Then, with a half-plodding glide, the rubber-cloaked fighter was gone, down into the darkness of the stairway.

The Shadow was bound for new combat with Oliver Bayruth, the human tool responsible for mighty crimes!

CHAPTER XVII
TRAILS TO DISASTER

IN the massive mausoleum that he called a mansion, Jerome Thorden was seated at his desk, drumming it with his fingers.

Blandle, watching him, could see shrewd changes in Thorden's Napoleonic expression, but they did not reveal the deep thoughts that they indicated. Blandle, with his poker-faced manner, could not equal Thorden when it came to hiding unexpressed opinions.

At last, Thorden spoke, his tone smooth.

"Kelber is indeed a problem," he said. "Ever since he underbid me on those contracts, I've expected him to cry for help; but he hasn't. The man is tenacious to the last degree. The loss of the Asbestile plant should have sunk Universal Industries, but it didn't. Nor did the loss of Orvis and his construction plans.

"There is one weak link remaining: Vortex Circulators. If it snaps, Kelber is through. Frankly, Blandle"—Thorden gave a shrewd smile—"I want to see it break. I've made my plans that way. And yet"—his lips stiffened—"if Kelber finds a substitute, my efforts will prove useless."

Blandle had an idea.

"It might be," he said, "that the best way would be to handle Kelber direct."

Slowly, Thorden nodded.

"You are right, Blandle," he decided. "I used the wrong tack. I worked on the assumption that Kelber would begin to lose money through Universal Industries, and would call on Thorden Enterprises as a last resort. But I've just begun to realize that Kelber is in a position to *make* money.

"Sometimes"—Thorden eyed Blandle cannily—"it is easier to force a deal when a man's business is on a rise, instead of a decline. I have an idea that it will prove that way with Kelber. But I shall wait, until I learn what happens with Vortex Circulators. It won't be long, Blandle."

The ensuing pause was broken by the ringing of a telephone bell. Thorden made a quick reach for the telephone, then shook his head.

"It might be Kelber," he remarked. "I don't want to talk with him yet. You answer it, Blandle."

Blandle answered the call. With his first words, the snooper lost his poker-faced manner. Clapping his hand over the mouthpiece, he turned to Thorden and exclaimed:

"Bayruth!"

Thorden took the telephone. His voice was oily, but pleasant. At moments, he seemed to be talking to a child, in humoring fashion.

"So you are making further progress?" Thorden inquired. "Good! ... What? Not going quite so well as you expected? Don't be discouraged, Bayruth ... Yes, I am sure that you will have no further difficulty...

"Yes, I have the utmost confidence in you, Bayruth. Of course, I sometimes ask too much, but I am a businessman. You are the true genius... Tonight? Why, certainly! Since you are sure the work will be completed, it is just the time for us to get together—"

Thorden was making notations on the memo pad beside his telephone. He tore off the sheet and pocketed it.

"We are going to Bayruth's place in New Jersey," Thorden told Blandle. "He will have much to tell us."

Blandle's face steadied. "About the perpetual-motion machine?" he asked.

"That's right," returned Thorden, with a smile. "Didn't you hear how I was humoring him? You may wonder at my interest, Blandle, but there are many things that you do not know, even though your business is to find out facts. However, I know that I can trust you. Tonight may explain a few riddles that you haven't yet solved."

QUITE in contrast to the discussion at Thorden's was the conference going on in the offices of Universal Industries, where Oswald Kelber held sway. Kelber was with his earlier companions, Fralingham and Darrison. They were talking, but the big man looked uneasy.

"I wonder why we haven't heard from Cranston?" boomed Kelber, suddenly. "I'm not surprised that he didn't come back, but he certainly should have called us after he saw Thorden."

"Maybe he hasn't found out what we wanted," put in Fralingham. "You wanted him to check on any persons who followed him."

"Of course," agreed Kelber. "A simple matter."

"Perhaps not," ventured Darrison, uneasily. "It may be that Cranston put himself into trouble."

The lift of Kelber's bushy brows indicated alarm. He reached for the telephone and called the Cobalt Club, only to learn that Cranston had left an hour before. A call to Cranston's home produced no results.

Kelber was wondering if he should call police headquarters, when a secretary entered to announce a visitor who claimed to be one of Cranston's friends.

The friend was Harry Vincent. He introduced himself, and his frank manner impressed Kelber and the others. But Harry didn't do much to clear the Cranston situation. He simply said that Cranston had left the Cobalt Club on what seemed a very important mission, and had asked him to stop in at Kelber's, to assure the latter that everything was working out well.

However, Harry was glancing about in apprehensive fashion, as though he expected to see his friend Cranston, which rather offset his favorable report.

"Tell me, Mr. Vincent," queried Kelber. "Had Cranston been to see Jerome Thorden?"

"I believe so," replied Harry. "I was outside the club when Cranston arrived. What puzzled me was the fact that a car was following him."

"From Thorden's!" exclaimed Kelber to the others. "As we thought it would! Did you see the men in it, Mr. Vincent?"

"Yes. I didn't like their looks."

That statement did not relieve the tension.

Glancing at his watch, Kelber observed that it was after eleven o'clock. He began to chide himself on letting Cranston pursue such a dangerous errand. When his impatience reached the breaking point, Kelber decided to call up Thorden and have a showdown.

"If he knows what happened to Cranston," declared Kelber, grimly, "I'll make him tell me. When I mention that Cranston, himself, testified that people trailed him from the house, it will put the shoe on Thorden's other foot. He won't dare to harm Cranston when he hears such facts."

There was no answer to Kelber's call. He tried the number again, without result, and finally shoved the telephone aside. His bushy brows thickened.

"Thorden must have gone out," Kelber decided. "I wonder why. Could it be that some new catastrophe is due? Tell me, Darrison"—he swung to the thickset man—"has there been any trouble whatever at your plant?"

"None at all," assured Darrison. Then, with a slight laugh. "Thorden tried to annoy us, but failed."

"Tried to? How?"

"You remember, Kelber. He insisted that Vortex Circulators be put to the test that the contracts specified. We have to demonstrate that they can clear out inflammable gas from underground rooms."

"Oh, that!" exclaimed Kelber. "You certainly had no trouble with such simple tests."

"We won't have," corrected Darrison. "So far, we haven't made the test. The materials weren't delivered until today, and the government inspectors won't come until next week. It is a trifling matter, Kelber."

Darrison had strolled to the window. He was looking westward, across the Hudson, to the Jersey shore. The hill on the other side blocked off his view.

"If we were about twenty stories higher," Darrison estimated, "we could see my plant over on the Jersey meadows. But I don't have to see it. The plant is safe. It is surrounded by a high-wire fence, and I have special guards on duty. Not a single source of danger in the place."

Kelber was on his feet.

"Those materials for the test," he queried. "Just what were they, Darrison?

"Gas bombs, I suppose," returned Darrison. "Of the incendiary type. There was a truckload of them; we put them in the storeroom—"

DARRISON ended his statement with a gulp. Kelber's eyes, as much as his own words, made him stop. Darrison realized that he had belied his former statement that everything was safe in the Vortex Circulator plant.

"Get them on the phone at once!" roared Kelber. "Tell them to clear those bombs out of the storeroom and chuck them in the meadows! My word, Darrison! If they ever went off, they'd melt your plant and all its equipment! Incendiary bombs could turn a cold-storage plant into an incinerator!"

Seizing the telephone, Darrison called the plant, and finally received an answer from the night superintendent. Stammering the news of danger, he ordered immediate removal of the bombs. As soon as Darrison had given that word, Kelber told the others:

"We know where Thorden has gone—out to see havoc ride over Darrison's factory! Come! We're going out there, too. We'll prove that Thorden's hand is behind these recent disasters. This time, he'll be caught on the scene!"

As Cranston's friend, Harry joined the others as they rushed from the office. They had cars downstairs, and the trip to the plant on the Jersey meadows could be made in less than half an hour. Kelber didn't have to convince Harry that a stroke was due against the Vortex Circulators factory.

The prisoners that Harry had stowed away had already told The Shadow. Somehow, Harry felt that Darrison's call to the factory would be too late to save the situation. His only hope was that The Shadow had already reached the place where doom was due.

Though the case was more desperate than even The Shadow knew, Harry still believed that his chief could find some way to halt disaster from the sky!

CHAPTER XVIII
THE SHADOW'S EXIT

HAVING left Harry the car belonging to the wounded thugs, The Shadow was using his agent's coupé for a swift trip to the Jersey meadows.

Cutting away from a superhighway, The Shadow saw two roads across the flats. One was a level route, to the left, straight to the Vortex Circulators factory, which was located against a hill that stood like an island in the meadows.

The other skirted the hill itself, and evidently connected with a roadway to the top. The hill was something like a knoll, and it was plainly visible, for it had great advertising signs on the brow, illuminated for the benefit of railroad passengers who might chance to read them while passing across the meadows.

The Shadow could see other lights moving up the slope—the lights of a car, unquestionably Bayruth's. The Shadow had gained on the crazed inventor, but to follow him would be folly. Bayruth would have men posted to block the road, and it would take too long to shoot a pathway through them.

Something better might be done at the Vortex plant, itself. At least, it would offer access to the front of the hill, the one direction from which Bayruth's tribe would not expect attack.

Sullen clouds hung over the meadows. They didn't have the look of thunderheads, but that wouldn't worry Bayruth. This was the last job that his master had ordered, and he would certainly go through with it. Later, people could try to explain the phenomenon of a lightning flash descending from clouds that hadn't shown previous symptoms.

Bayruth wouldn't care. The duel between Thorden and Kelber would be at an end, so far as destruction was concerned.

But destruction was the very thing that The Shadow wanted to prevent. He had to defeat killers tonight, and throw them into confusion. It was the only way to make sure of following their trail.

That trail would lead to Margo. The Shadow was still thinking in terms of the shortest way to his most important task—the rescue of the girl who had so faithfully tried to aid him, only to become a helpless prisoner.

It wasn't dark across the meadows, despite the sullen sky. Railroads crisscrossed the flats, and the great headlights of heavy freight locomotives cut moving lines through the darkness. Many factories were at work, some gushing flames from their chimneys, to cast lurid reflections against the sky.

Besides, there was plenty of glow at the Vortex plant, enough for The Shadow to see the gate and the buildings beyond it without relying only on the headlights of Harry's coupé.

The Vortex factory was modern, compact. Its buildings made a stout mass against the knoll. There were open spaces in among the buildings, but the whole plant was surrounded by a high meshwork fence. The gate was metal, and closed, with men on guard there. They sprang out with rifles, warningly, to challenge The Shadow's car.

He didn't wait to argue. Gates often had a weak spot: their center. Those at the Vortex factory were no exception. The Shadow took them right in the middle, split them apart, ripping them from the hinges.

Thinking he would stop before he crashed, the guards had sprung out to stop The Shadow. They had to dive away as he roared through, with the wreckage of the front bumper jammed across the coupé's radiator. In diving, the guards didn't have a chance to use their rifles.

WHEELING in among loading platforms, The Shadow came upon a beefy man in shirtsleeves, who was unlocking the door of a storeroom, while others stood about. He was the night superintendent, and he couldn't see what had happened to the front of The Shadow's car, because the gleam of the twisted headlamps blinded him.

Taking it that the car had been sent by Darrison, the beefy man hurried over as soon as he had unlocked the storeroom door.

"We're getting the inflammable stuff out," he reported. "But it's stored under a lot of new materials that came in this afternoon. It will take us half an hour—"

He stopped, quite amazed. He saw The Shadow. Having discarded his rubber outfit, The Shadow was normally cloaked as he stepped from the car. Whether he was man or ghost, the superintendent could not tell, but his reaction was the sort that The Shadow wanted. This man would listen.

"I'm here to help you," The Shadow told him. "Send away the guards from the gate. I hadn't time to stop and chat with them. You say the storeroom contains inflammables—"

The superintendent nodded. He was explaining the matter of the test bombs, while he waved back the arriving guards. The facts learned, The Shadow cut the speaker short.

"All will be over in half an hour," informed The Shadow, grimly. "We must do something sooner. Do you have a good supply of insulated cable?"

"Plenty of it!"

"Take men with you. Attach the cables to your plant dynamos. Run them to the fence and make connections. You can do it in ten minutes?"

"In less!" exclaimed the superintendent. "Do you know why we have so much cable? Mr. Darrison wanted to electrify the fence to protect the plant. He thought better of it, later, because of the danger to employees. We'd already run the cables, but we never connected them."

"Connect them at once. Send the juice through, and keep it running."

The beefy man sent others to the fence, while he hurried to the dynamo room to await the word for the current. Meanwhile, The Shadow was beckoning to the guards, who came on the run, having accepted this cloaked stranger as a leader somehow appointed to handle the coming emergency.

In five minutes, the juice was on. Meanwhile, men were getting to the inflammables, to bring them out to the loading platform. It was Darrison's order, so The Shadow let them proceed. Besides, the incendiary bombs might prove useful later.

Five minutes more. All the while, The Shadow kept under the projecting roof of the storeroom, to avoid notice from the hill above. The first of the incendiary bombs was coming out of the storeroom.

Nobody was near the great wire fence that surrounded the yard, for the current was constantly going through it, rendering it quite dangerous.

That thought brought a whispered laugh from The Shadow. Darrison's idea had helped, though The Shadow's ten-minute estimate still held. But Darrison had intended the electric fence to ward off prowlers. The Shadow was putting it to a much greater use. The test would soon come.

NONE of the workers at the storeroom realized what terrific things were due to happen. They learned, a few minutes later, when they saw the first flash from the hillock and heard the mighty crackle it produced.

Down spurted a wave of man-made lightning that ripped the big advertising signs to shreds, for the great truck was located just behind them. There was plenty of smash to that stroke, for the capacitors had been feeding from one of the many high-tension lines that crossed the meadows.

Millions of volts were directed toward the weak spot of the Vortex factory—the storeroom, with its inflammable materials.

But for The Shadow, those bolts would have found their mark, and more. Men would have been stunned by the stroke. The fact that they were removing incendiary bombs would have meant their positive doom. The emergency measure ordered by Darrison was a misguided idea. At present, it did not matter. The lightning missed its target.

Instead of striking the heart of the plant, the forked terror found the electrified fence. The surrounding meshwork blazed, while balls of lightning danced merrily along from post to post. More lightning thundered from the sky, to increase the vivid spectacle, as weird as a pyrotechnic display. But the fence was absorbing every volt that Bayruth's great machine could throw!

Amid the thunderous crashes, The Shadow laughed.

He had introduced a system used in the protection of oil fields—a method of diverting lightning from a vulnerable spot. Electrified fences were lightning attractors, and this one was serving its duty perfectly. But it wasn't staving off chance strokes from the sky. This fence was offsetting the deadly work of scheming men.

Snatching a rifle from a stupefied guard, The Shadow wheeled out to the very center of the loading court. He could see the spurts of lightning as they darted downward, and he took their source as a target.

With his long-range weapon, The Shadow opened fire on Bayruth's truck. Others saw what he was doing, and came dashing out to join in the fire.

Immediately, the lightning hurling stopped. Bayruth knew its uselessness. Guns began to answer from the brow of the hill, but they were puny revolvers. The guards, with their rifles, held the full advantage. But The Shadow couldn't count upon them to prevent the flight of Bayruth and his crew.

Hurrying to the storeroom, The Shadow scooped up a pair of incendiary bombs. Coming out, he met the superintendent.

"I'm going through the back," The Shadow told him. "Signal when you cut off the juice; then start it again in fifteen seconds."

From a small gate in the rear fence, The Shadow saw the beefy man lean from the dynamo room and wave. Whipping through, The Shadow clamped the gate behind him. Clambering up the slope, he could hear the whine of rifle bullets above his head. Revolvers still were answering; their punches were louder as The Shadow neared the brow of the hill.

OVER the top, The Shadow flung the first bomb at the hazy outline of the truck. It struck the side of the vehicle and went off with a great gush of flame, lighting the whole scene. The Shadow saw the open back of the truck, with Bayruth in it, huddled beside the transformers of his great lightning maker. The Shadow chucked the second bomb for the interior.

Bayruth must have guessed that it was coming. He yanked one half of the double door, and was lucky enough to pull the right section. The bomb struck the closing barrier and glanced aside with another burst of flame.

In that lurid light, Bayruth saw The Shadow swooping forward. Quickly, the apish man grabbed for a switch and tugged it.

Puny revolver shots, aimed for the spot where The Shadow had last been seen, were useless and as nothing, compared to the last bolt that Bayruth delivered. A shaft of lightning skimmed the hill brow, blasting away chunks of rock and stumps of trees. In that blaze, Bayruth saw the flying pieces of debris, any one of which might have been a figure cloaked in black.

If caught by that charge, The Shadow could have survived only if clad in rubber, as before. But it was doubtful, even so, that he could live after a plunge down the craggy knoll.

Quite confident that he had finished The Shadow, one way or the other, Bayruth called for his men to board the truck.

They groped to it and climbed inside. Wires were hauled in, and the truck made for the slope. Rifle shots faded in the distance.

Peering out, Bayruth was troubled only when he saw the gleam of car lights from below and knew that they were trying to take up the trail. But that seemed trivial to Bayruth and his companions, who were grouped in the darkness of the truck.

What they were listening for was the laugh of The Shadow. The weird mockery did not come. Bayruth delivered a crackle of mirth instead.

It was his token of victory over The Shadow, telling his companions that they need have no worry for the future.

CHAPTER XIX
RIVALS MEET

SILLY though it seemed, Margo was pounding anew at the door of her cell. She had been hammering, at intervals, for hours, and no one had answered. But she wouldn't give up. Margo remembered stories of prisoners who had dug underground for years, to quit when they had but a few feet to go. She wasn't going to make the same mistake.

Apparently, Bayruth had taken all of his technicians with him, but there was a chance that someone might return. Perhaps such a person might heed Margo's knocks, and be just the one who would listen for her plea to be released. So Margo rapped, and then went back to her chair.

As she sat down, she was sure that she heard echoes beyond the door. At first, they were vague, as though her strained imagination fancied that her own knocks were returning. Then she recognized that the sounds were footsteps. They approached the door; she heard the bolt grind back. Springing to her feet, Margo was at the door when it opened.

She recognized the man who confronted her. Blandle!

The poker-faced man had a companion, almost out of sight beyond Blandle's rangy form. Margo saw a darkish face, with keen eyes, and knew that the man must be Jerome Thorden.

She gave him a polite smile over Blandle's shoulder. It might have been of some avail with Thorden, if Blandle hadn't recognized her as the girl from the Platinum Grill.

"So it's you," said Blandle, coolly. He turned to Thorden: "This is the girl I mentioned. No wonder I didn't hear from Bayruth, after I came back to the Platinum Grill."

"Ah, yes," observed Thorden, stepping forward. "Quite charming, isn't she? I don't blame Bayruth for keeping her locked up while he is away."

Indignation flashed from Margo's eyes, but it impressed neither Thorden nor Blandle. Their politeness seemed a form of mockery, and when Thorden began smoothly to question her, Margo decided not to reply at all.

He was asking her what she knew about Bayruth, and why the inventor had imprisoned her. To Margo, those oily questions were simply the first steps to more important ones.

From queries regarding Bayruth, Thorden could lead to others that concerned Cranston, and before she knew it, Margo would be telling him too much. After a certain point, even her silence would become a giveaway.

The Shadow was quite right in telling Harry Vincent that they could rely on Margo's judgment. Margo had one very excellent system, which was to say nothing until the pressure became too strong. Since neither Thorden nor Bayruth were inclined to use pressure, her silence served quite well.

Both men had guns. They suggested that Margo accompany them around Bayruth's preserves, so she complied. The guns were a good argument, and Margo was quite glad to get out of her cell.

Thorden suggested that she walk ahead of them; Margo did so. She was quite sure that the guns were close in back of her, so she made no false moves.

They arrived in Bayruth's laboratory. Thorden saw the perpetual motion machine and stepped past Margo to examine it. He gave one of his crisp laughs.

"So *this* is the great invention!" he remarked. "Do you know how it operates, Miss—"

He paused, as though expecting Margo to supply her name—as if he did not know it. Just another wedge to get her talking, so Margo met Thorden's gaze with frozen silence. She stepped to the big wheel and started it revolving. Thorden and Blandle watched the bouncing ball, and soon recognized its purpose. Blandle, particularly, was impressed.

"It works," he declared, reluctantly. "Maybe there is something in this perpetual-motion stuff."

"Something, indeed," agreed Thorden. "My money, Blandle! I paid Thorden to produce other things, and he kept reverting to this. He is welcome to keep this brainchild."

Thorden threw a sidelong glance to Margo, to see if his statement impressed her. She was still doing an imitation of a wooden Indian.

"Suppose you chat with the talkative lady, Blandle," suggested Thorden. "I want to look around."

Margo ignored Blandle, to watch Thorden while he looked around. He came to a metal cabinet in the corner, tried to open the drawers, but found them locked. He was still rattling them, when a rumbling sound interrupted.

It was Bayruth's truck, returning. It rolled into the cavernous garage outside the laboratory, and Margo gave a weary sigh. She had just been on the point of suggesting that Thorden and Blandle examine a couple of odd-looking lamps.

Both were connected with the wall switch, and Margo had hoped to set the two men hopping under an electric current. Bayruth's return put the end to that little scheme.

BAYRUTH was the first man to drop from the truck. The white-haired inventor looked anxiously about, saw the lights in the lab and hurried there, closing the door behind him. He thrust out a scrawny hand to Thorden.

"I knew you'd be here!" wheezed Bayruth. "How do you like the place? Very nice, isn't it, out in the New Jersey hills? Ah! You have met Miss Lane. I'm so glad you released her. I had to lock her up because she didn't want to stay."

Mention of a lock reminded Bayruth of something else. He brought a key from his pocket and unlocked the filing cabinet. Out of one drawer, he brought an envelope and flourished it toward Thorden.

"The plans for my great invention," began Bayruth. "But wait!" He thrust the envelope into his pocket. "I can show you the apparatus, itself."

Bayruth was stepping toward the revolving wheel, when Thorden halted him.

"Miss Lane has already shown us the perpetual-motion machine," said Thorden, using his crisp tone. "There are other matters that I would prefer to discuss, Bayruth."

"Of course," acknowledged Bayruth. "But first, I must take Miss Lane back to her cell—"

"Not necessary, Bayruth," Thorden interrupted, as the inventor grasped Margo's arm and drew her toward the door. "I would like Miss Lane to hear what I have to say. I have an idea"—his tone was thoughtful—"that she is well acquainted with a certain Mr. Cranston."

All through that discourse, Margo was becoming rather bewildered. This byplay between Thorden and Bayruth couldn't all be for her benefit. Somehow, it must be leading to a climax; though what it might be, Margo could not imagine. She did not have to imagine, for the climax came quite suddenly.

Bayruth, with one hand upon the door, the other gripping Margo's arm, saw Thorden moving toward him, followed by Blandle. Perhaps Bayruth was a creature who formed sudden mistrusts, even toward those with whom he was closely associated. It might have been that he didn't like to be outnumbered, two to one.

At any rate, he corrected the latter situation by taking Margo on his side, though she was an unwilling ally.

Bayruth did two things at once. He yanked the door open as he pulled Margo toward him. With a quick shove, he sent the girl stumbling toward Thorden and Blandle as they sprang forward.

Throwing out her arms to prevent a sprawl, Margo involuntarily blocked the two men. They spun her aside, and she landed in a corner, knocking over a table and bringing a lamp down upon her shoulders. Fortunately, the lamp wasn't electrified.

Out through the door, Bayruth was actually darting away from Thorden and Blandle, the men who had come here specially to see him. But they weren't following Bayruth. Instead, they were dropping back.

Bayruth's men—Klegg and several others, among them Jerry—were out of the truck, brandishing revolvers. One word from Bayruth was the only signal they needed to cut loose.

Bayruth *was* crazy. That was the way it struck Margo. Sprawled in the corner, her head against the wall, one foot on top of the overturned table and the other tangled in the lamp cord, she was in a most ludicrous position, one that had suddenly become a vantage point, for she could see all that was happening and still be out of harm's way. To her, it looked like mutiny.

If Bayruth had simply forged the lightning bolts, while Thorden had reserved the privilege of hurling them, this might not have happened then. But Bayruth, so far, had been the whole show. Apparently, he wasn't going to play second fiddle in any more of Thorden's machinations.

CACKLING gleefully, Bayruth was retiring to a waiting car, and his men were backing with him, still keeping their guns toward the lab door where Thorden and Blandle were rooted.

Yes, Bayruth was going his way, leaving Thorden in possession of all the equipment, which only Bayruth himself could handle and which no longer was needed. Maybe he *wasn't* crazy. He was abandoning his perpetual-motion machine, which, to date, he had valued more highly than anything else.

All that Bayruth was taking was time. Too much time. Before he and his men could get to their car, Margo heard shouts from the entrance to the cavern that served as the garage. While Bayruth's men were turning, others lunged into sight.

They were uniformed guards from the Vortex plant, and county deputies, who had joined in pursuit of Bayruth. Behind them, Margo saw a smaller cluster that included Oswald Kelber.

Bayruth crackled out a wild order, calling upon his men to open fire. Margo started to close her eyes, so she would not see the horrible results.

As she did, she heard a laugh, far louder than Bayruth's cry. Grim mirth that froze the men who heard it, for it rose, like a voice from the dead, in a crescendo challenge that stirred the cavern with its weird reverberations.

Margo's eyes came open very wide. Only one being could deliver mockery like that. The Shadow. Staring, Margo hoped to see the fighter in black. She did; he was coming from the last place that she expected.

Out of the great truck which Bayruth had used as a lightning-bearing juggernaut sprang The Shadow, a pair of automatics in his fists!

CHAPTER XX
MASTER OF THUNDER

GUNS were blazing from every direction, their stabs so sharp and frequent that Margo wondered how anyone could survive the outburst. Most of all, she was concerned about The Shadow, for he was the logical target for every man who represented crime.

Disentangling herself from the corner, Margo landed on her hands and knees and decided to go no farther.

She saw The Shadow.

He was in the truck no longer. He had gone from it, in a long leap, amid the first volley of wild shots that missed him. He was weaving across the cavern, jabbing straight shots at Bayruth and the band that served the white-haired inventor.

They were maddened at the way The Shadow had tricked them back on the hill. Too well, they realized how he had survived.

Diving toward the truck when Bayruth had released the last batch of lightning, The Shadow had reached it safely, and had been the first to board the vehicle. He had ridden along with crooks to crime's headquarters. He had tricked them then, and he was tricking them now, by drawing their shots in his direction.

For Bayruth's men of murder were spilling faster than The Shadow could drop them with his guns alone. In going after The Shadow, thugs had exposed themselves to the fire of pursuers who had come from the Vortex plant. Of that evil tribe, only one man was still on his feet: Oliver Bayruth.

Having left battle to his henchmen, Bayruth, surprisingly agile, was trying to leap into a car, even though it would be impossible to make a getaway. Wheeling suddenly, The Shadow sprang across the rolling forms of men like Klegg and Jerry, to overtake the frantic inventor. Just then, a revolver spoke.

It was Kelber's gun. He had thrust through the ranks, to put in a timely shot that wasn't really needed. Close behind him, Harry Vincent tried to jog his arm, for Harry saw that The Shadow was already after Bayruth.

But Harry wasn't there in time. Kelber scored a hit. His shot dropped Bayruth from the car step and sprawled him on the stony floor.

The Shadow was stooping over Bayruth, when Kelber and others arrived. Dying, his eyes glassy, Bayruth glared upward. He tried to speak a name as he wagged one hand, and slid the other weakly toward his coat pocket. Each time Bayruth crackled a syllable, his voice broke.

"Thor—" he gulped. "Thor ... Thor—"

The third croak was his last. Bayruth's glassy eyes still stared up toward the faces that peered at him. His smile was venomous—an accusation—but it had become a dead man's leer.

"He means Thorden!" boomed Kelber suddenly, swinging from the group. "I'll settle scores with that man!"

Kelber pivoted toward the laboratory, where Thorden was struggling against heavy odds. Blandle was already overwhelmed, with four men taking credit for his capture; but in going after the rangy man, the attackers had neglected Thorden.

He was still clutching his gun and trying to twist free, when Kelber picked him as a target. Finger on trigger, Kelber was ready to drop the man who had been marked as the master of murder.

A gloved fist tightened on Kelber's wrist, so powerful that it stayed the big man's trigger finger. From crouched position, The Shadow was halting Kelber's shot. With his other hand, The Shadow plucked up an envelope that had dropped from Bayruth's pocket.

Releasing Kelber's wrist, The Shadow rose to full height, dipped his free hand to his cloak, and with the other extended the envelope.

Staring at the envelope, Kelber saw the batch of letters that poked from its unsealed flap. He heard The Shadow's strangely whispered query:

"Have you forgotten these, Thor?"

The name "Thor" jolted Kelber, as though he had stepped in the way of a few hundred volts. Uttered by The Shadow, it had a new significance. It didn't come in hurried fashion, as though it were a single syllable, the first part of a name. It was a name in itself, one that The Shadow repeated:

"Thor!"

The name of the great lightning god, master of destruction from the heavens. No title could be more apt for the man higher up, the real head of crime, whose purposes Bayruth had served.

Thor, the thunder king!

Not Jerome Thorden, whose name had been neatly paraphrased, in part; but Oswald Kelber!

KELBER was the man who had been known to his followers as Thor. Only Bayruth could denounce him, and he had tried, when he found himself double-crossed.

Bayruth's dying stare had been fixed straight upon Kelber, and The Shadow had observed it. He had seen something else. Bayruth's plucking at the envelope. Its evidence would do, even though Bayruth now lay dead.

Kelber's booming defiance suited the title of Thor. With his sudden bellow, the thunder king took a new hold on his gun and aimed for The Shadow.

It was what The Shadow wanted—a move whereby Kelber would openly betray his guilt. As for damaging The Shadow, Kelber did not have a chance. His hand was more numbed than he supposed, and before he could pull his trigger, The Shadow was away.

As he twisted from Kelber's path of aim, The Shadow whipped a gun into sight, bringing it in the hand that was dipped against his cloak. So swift was the gesture, that he had Kelber covered and helpless before the master of thunder knew it. Others failed to observe it, too. The Shadow was too swift for them; they saw only Kelber and his attempt to aim his gun.

Thorden, wrenching from hands that had suddenly loosed him, jabbed the first shot at Kelber. It clipped the big man and jolted him, serving as an example for a dozen other marksmen. Shots rang out from every direction, and all were aimed at Kelber. They stretched him lifeless on the floor, across the body of Bayruth, whose death had represented Kelber's final murder.

The Shadow was gone, into the black edge of the cavern, when others began to look for him. It was Harry Vincent who met Margo, when she came from the laboratory, and suggested that she ride back with him to New York. On the way out, Thorden detached himself from a group, to insist that they stop at his mansion, later.

This they did, after Harry had taken Margo to dinner, to make up for the stingy meals that she had received while Bayruth's prisoner.

When they were ushered up to Thorden's office, they found Lamont Cranston seated there, resting wearily in a chair. Thorden explained that he had called Cranston's home and asked him to come into town.

"Do you know, Cranston," expressed Thorden, "I really believe that you saw through this business more clearly than I did. I should have taken you into my confidence. The trouble was, I mistrusted you."

The Shadow nodded.

"I mistrusted you, too," he said, in Cranston's style. "But not for very long. I was soon convinced that Kelber was the brain in back of Bayruth."

"Just how?"

"Kelber had as much to gain as you—and more," returned The Shadow, calmly. "The real profit for Universal Industries lay in those key contracts held by Fralingham, Orvis and Darrison. Kelber took over Asbestile, and the Orvis proposition. He was after Vortex Circulators tonight. We can be quite sure that he had a substitute for Vortex Circulators."

It was Margo who showed sudden surprise.

"But, Lamont!" she exclaimed. "What about Wilbert? He was working for Kelber—"

"Until he met up with Quade," interposed The Shadow. "Do you remember the correspondence they discussed? Thorden has it. Here, you can see it."

THORDEN passed Cranston the envelope that had come from Bayruth's pocket. He opened it to show the letters. They were addressed to Bayruth, and they concerned the lightning machine, but they bore Kelber's signature, not Thorden's.

"Wilbert was with Kelber," analyzed The Shadow, "and Quade was with Bayruth. They got together and arranged a little plan. Bayruth was keeping Kelber's letters, just in case of a double cross. Quade wanted him to sell them back to Kelber. If he wouldn't pay enough, Thorden naturally would have."

Margo nodded understanding.

"Kelber must have suspected that Wilbert and Quade were framing something," The Shadow added. "Maybe Bayruth told him, without furnishing full details. However, Kelber needed Wilbert no longer, and Bayruth had no use for Quade. So Kelber had Bayruth wait for them along Highway 95."

Easing back in his chair, The Shadow gazed at Thorden and smiled.

"Call in Blandle," he suggested. "He deserves congratulations."

Thorden winced; then he laughed in friendly tone. It was sufficient for Blandle. He stepped from his listening post behind the wall.

"Just force of habit, I assure you," said Thorden, in a tone of apology. "This Kelber business had us worried. We hadn't an idea of how it really operated. We were trying to get hold of Bayruth and make him explain. When he called me tonight, I thought he was coming back to my side, so I humored him."

"Without suspecting," inquired The Shadow, "that it was Kelber's way of framing you?"

"Stupid of me, but I didn't," admitted Thorden. "Nor did I realize that my insistence on a test of Vortex Circulators was a play into Kelber's hands. If it hadn't been for The Shadow, Kelber would have pinned the entire game on me. I had a close call, Cranston."

The Shadow supplied a Cranston smile, and said: "I fancy that The Shadow had several close calls."

"He must have," agreed Thorden. "Blandle helped him out of one. Blandle was following you, Cranston, and saw another car upon the trail. He stayed with the other car and wound up at an old garage, where a thug was trying to fling The Shadow into a grease pit. Blandle put a few bullets into the thug to turn the fight The Shadow's way."

It happened that Thorden was telling something that The Shadow already knew. The Shadow had recognized Blandle's real intent, after the struggle with Matt. It had been an important point in swinging The Shadow's suspicion from Thorden to Kelber.

The visitors were about to leave, when Cranston remembered something else. He mentioned it to Thorden when they were standing by the door.

"The night I called on Orvis," he said, "when Margo was so near, and yet so far. The thunderstorm that came up must have worried Kelber badly. He knew that Bayruth was all set to deliver, and Kelber hadn't expected a storm so soon.

"He had to do some clever stalling with Fralingham and Darrison, to keep from getting there before the lightning struck. He was in a bad spot, because he wanted my testimony to help frame you later; but he couldn't warn me, or I would have known that he was Thor."

THAT paradox intrigued Thorden. He was still thinking of it when he stood, with Blandle, at the upstairs window watching Cranston help Margo into the limousine, while Harry was walking away to get his own car.

The webby curtains were drawn aside, for Thorden wanted his friends to see him, if they looked back, and know that his spying ways were ended.

They didn't look back, yet when the limousine had started, Thorden still stared, feeling that eyes must be watching him from somewhere in the darkness. For Thorden was sure that he heard a strange sound from the night, like an echo from the past.

He looked at Blandle, but his companion's face was unchanged. Thorden decided that his imagination must have tricked him. Yet he was not sure.

For the sound that Jerome Thorden fancied that he heard was a fleeting laugh; solemn, like a knell. It could have been The Shadow's final tone of triumph over Oswald Kelber, the master of crime who had styled himself Thor, the thunder king!

THE END

INTERLUDE by Will Murray

This long-overdue volume of The Shadow is dedicated to Margo Lane, who debuted on *The Shadow* radio program 75 years ago in 1937.

Not for four years did Margo surface in the pulp magazine where the Dark Avenger had been forged from a laughing narrator without substance into an iconic force for vigilante justice.

Early in 1941, Street & Smith began celebrating the tenth anniversary of *The Shadow Magazine*. It was a stellar year for the character. His radio show was the top-rated daytime series, a Shadow serial starring Victor Jory had been a hit, and the Avenger of Crime was appearing in newspaper strips and a best-selling Street & Smith comic book of his own.

Central to all of these incarnations was the woman who debuted when The Shadow's long-running dramatic radio series began in the Fall of 1937. This was socialite Margo Lane, who functioned as Lamont Cranston's presumably platonic girlfriend. Her primary role was to give Cranston someone to talk with while formulating his criminological theories, and to occasionally fall prey to various evildoers, allowing for a climactic rescue. As a female, Margo also provided necessary voice contrast to the actors playing Cranston. She was never mentioned, even in passing, in *The Shadow Magazine,* in any of the 200-odd novels printed during the 1930s.

Over time, with the radio program increasing in popularity, S&S began receiving letters from new readers wondering: Where was Margo? It's doubtful that long-time readers cared. But in that tenth anniversary year of 1941, a wave of publicity began drawing new readers to the magazine. They noticed a complete absence of the famous Margo Lane in its pulpy pages.

Introducing Margo into the pulp magazine was not Walter Gibson's idea.

It's not clear that editor John L. Nanovic wanted it, either. No doubt someone higher up at S&S decided this was the optimum time to bring Maxwell Grant's stories in line with the radio program. This had already been imposed upon Gibson in the scripts he was turning out for the newspaper strip and comic book incarnations of the Dark Avenger A year before her pulp debut in *The Thunder King*, Walter had begun using Margo regularly in Street & Smith's *Shadow Comic*s, as well as in the newspaper strip, both of which he scripted as "Maxwell Grant," though he never considered either to be canonical.

No doubt this official was S&S president Allen L. Grammer, who soon after taking over the company in the Fall of 1938, began pushing to showcase Street & Smith properties in other media, principally radio.

Certainly there was no great clamoring for Margo among faithful longtime readers, although newer ones may have been taken aback by her notable absence.

In one 1941 issue, a reader wrote, "The radio program is coming along nicely, except that Margo Lane should be removed and The Shadow's agents should be inducted for service on the radio."

That was probably the prevailing feeling among the Shadow faithful.

At the end of 1940, the decision was made and Gibson dutifully started work on *The Thunder King*. It was a big shift. Walter was on the cusp of celebrating ten years of writing The Shadow. Up until this point, virtually all the creative invention surrounding the character emerged from his novels. Now, the radio program would drive his depiction of the character he brought to life.

"Margo Lane was introduced to meet the exigencies of the radio program," Gibson later explained. "They liked a 'running' heroine in both senses of the term. So we tied her in with the pulp stories."

*The Thunder King** marked the first time Street & Smith and Walter Gibson lost control over the famous series. One would think that editor Nanovic would have played up Margo Lane's pulp debut in his next-issue teaser. Here is what he wrote:

> Before we close up this column, we must remind you of the honey of a yarn that's coming through in our next issue. It's "The Thunder King," and it's a smashing, roaring novel of a murderous villain who gets control over a terrific force that he seeks to use for evil purposes. Only The Shadow knows what is really behind the campaign of terror that the Thunder King wages, and only The Shadow can fight through to the solution. But before he reaches the end, he knows he's been in a terrific battle.

But no, Nanovic did not mention Margo. When the issue in question rolled around, Nanovic gave this pivotal story an even greater buildup. But it's more significant for what is not in it than what is:

> "The Thunder King" is the complete novel in this issue. It packs as big a kick as the biggest thunderbolt you've ever heard, we'll wager! We've been trying hard to get the very best stories possible for these months which mark our tenth

---

*The Thunder King and his super-weapons were well suited for the comic strip format, and the master villain returned as Althor in the newspaper strip and comic book storylines that introduced reformed moll Valda Rune as another distaff agent (and a rival for Margo Lane).

The Thunder King returned as Althor in *The Shadow* newspaper strip in

> anniversary, and all of you readers have certainly shown your enthusiasm for them thus far. "The Thunder King" will not let you down, and there are even better ones coming along.

Puzzling, but it may be a reflection of Nanovic's editorial concerns that readers might not fully embrace Margo.

He was right. They did not. One reader wrote:

> Maxwell Grant is certainly an excellent author, however, I wish that he would chuck Margo Lane out and make The Shadow mysterious again as he once was and should be. I think that the character of Margo Lane detracts a great deal from an atmosphere of mystery.

Another reader concurred:

> Why do you not leave Margo Lane out of your magazine altogether? I agree with reader Marx of New York in hoping that hereafter you do not print any more stories with her in them.

Yet another wrote:

> I seem to disagree with some of the readers who object to Margo. I believe that she should be a part of The Shadow magazine and she should be described more vividly. I mean her beauty and intelligence. Keep Margo, by all means.

Over the succeeding months, opinion began to diversify. The first significant pro-Margo communication came from Robert Sherwood of New Jersey, who wrote:

> And now—I don't mind Miss Lane in the stories (though I was startled when I read "The Thunder King"), so long as Maxwell Grant doesn't drag in any of that invisibility nonsense heard in the inaccurate radio versions. Miss Lane adds to the human interest, although she may cause complications. The Shadow is really Kent Allard, after all, and the original Lamont Cranston—well! Maxwell Grant could evolve some pretty clever mix-ups in personalities (and I hope he does!)... Margo Lane would add some pulchritude if she were given an individual cover sometime, also.

Sherwood went in to suggest that Margo be properly introduced, a suggestion Nanovic showed to Gibson. The result was *The Hydra*, which sealed Margo as a permanent member of the cast.

Gibson recalled that story this way: "Of course, when I put Margo Lane into the stories, a lot of readers began to scream. In fact, a lot of them said she was a troublemaker. That's true. That was the comic relief. That thing that really satisfied them was the way The Shadow happened to get her, which was she met Lamont Cranston on a cruise, and she looked him up when she got back to New

the storyline that introduced Shadow aide (and Margo's rival) Valda Rune.

York and she found The Shadow instead! She never knew the difference. So, that satisfied the old readers."

In the year or two that followed, the letter columns were filled with pro and con letters, many from female readers:

> I have just read "The Thunder King." It was a good story except for the presence of Margo Lane. I do not think it right to have a woman mixed up with The Shadow. It's bad enough to have her on the radio instead of one of his regular aides.

> I am now reading "Gems of Jeopardy," which is quite good except for Margo Lane, who ever since her introduction in the magazine harmed it, as far as I am concerned. I have stood her in the radio, funny books and the shows, and now I have to stand her on The Shadow magazine.

> I've read The Shadow for quite a long time, and I like it very much. Most of your male readers complain of Margo. But I think she helps the magazine because she always bungles a job The Shadow gives her, and he always takes time off to save her, which makes the story last longer.

> There seems to be some question about having Margo Lane in The Shadow stories. Well, I think she keeps the story going along. I also like her, for she seems like a real American woman. I would like to read more about her. You have her as Cranston's girlfriend in the movies and radio, but you didn't even mention her in the books for quite a while.

> Margo Lane is all right provided you emphasize she's just an agent, nothing more. If you're going to have woman agents, though, I personally would prefer Myra Reldon.

Over time, the pros won. Or maybe it was that once having introduced Margo, there was no turning back. And since that was the case, Gibson took her more and more seriously as time went on. She stayed with the series clear up to 1949, when it ended.

Margo aside, *The Thunder King* is a shattering story of a gigantic threat to New York. Written in December 1940 as "Master of Thunder," it appeared six months later in the June 15, 1941 issue. It also marked the first time that Maxwell Grant hinted that the Master of Darkness possessed mind-clouding powers similar to those displayed by the radio Shadow. He was careful to draw a parallel, not state this outright. S&S's Shadow was still the pulp version—even if loyal cab driver Moe Shrevnitz more and more came to be called "Shrevvy" after his radio counterpart.

Immediately thereafter, Gibson turned in *The Star of Delhi*. Also written that December, it saw print in the issue dated July 1, 1941. Here again, Margo was central to the story. There was no interval allowed to await reader reaction. S&S had committed to Margo Lane, apparently as part of their tenth anniversary publicity push.

Yet, once again, the teaser for *Star of Delhi* fails to mention Margo:

> In the next issue, we have "The Star of Delhi," a novel that has mystery, excitement, and action packed into it from start to finish. There is always something about big, important jewels that appeals to the public. Generally, there is a history connected with such gems—a history of blood and death, most likely. Why is this? Is there something in these gems that influences conditions for the people who wear then or own them? Or is it just common, ordinary greed, resulting in attempts at the destruction of the owner of the gem; destruction either physically by murder, or destruction in spirit by ruining the wealth, social

position, or mental condition of the person? The Star of Delhi is a gem that is one of the outstanding treasures of the world, and therefore a great deal will be done to grasp the fortune which it gives to anyone who owns it, and there are other things which make the story even more interesting—purpose and cross-purpose which make you wonder just where it will all end. It all ends with the criminal—and you'll be surprised at who the criminal really is!—brought to justice by The Shadow, and the reader taking his first long breath of relief when it is settled.

Nor did Nanovic deign to acknowledge her in the introduction to the story:

> There's always something exciting, something pulse-stirring, about precious stones, especially if they are large and famous precious stones. You've probably had that feeling even when looking at a particularly large diamond on some fair lady's finger (or maybe the fair lady influenced your heartbeat, too!) or seeing a collection of jewels on display. We know we had that feeling, along with tens of thousands of others, when looking at the jewel exhibit at the World's Fair a year ago; or any time we go down to the diamond center to check on some material for stories. We got it especially strong at an exhibition at Cartier's, New York's glamorous jewel house, just yesterday, in which many of the world's great gems, including the Hope diamond, were on display.

The Shadow arrives to rescue Margo Lane (Marjorie Anderson) in a 1940s MBS publicity photo.

> So, with that tingling sensation as a head start, you'll know why "The Star of Delhi," the complete novel ... of this issue, will give you all that you are looking for in the way of excitement and interest. Maxwell Grant knows jewels well; he knows the history of all famous gems, much of it never published but gathered from personal contact with people who have such gems. He's put all that feeling into this yarn, and you can bet it's a honey!

Nanovic didn't begin acknowledging Margo's presence until his editorial for *The Devil Master*, in which Margo first met Myra Reldon, a previously established agent of the Dark Avenger. Here he gave readers his take on the new wrinkle in The Shadow's cloak:

> Here a story in which Margo plays an important part. Some of you readers have expressed various opinions as to The Shadow's female helper. She's familiar to everyone through the radio programs of The Shadow, and the general opinion is that she is an improvement in the stories. Some don't quite agree because this is the first time The Shadow has taken a girl as an agent; however, many of those who didn't like the idea at first find her more enjoyable and are really her boosters!

After a period of uncertainty, Margo graduates from being a version of the radio Margo Lane, mixed with a dash of Superman's Lois Lane, finally maturing into a capable agent of The Shadow who knows—or thinks she knows—that The Shadow is really Lamont Cranston. Gibson went back and forth on that point for quite a while.

"I put Margo into the stories judiciously," Gibson claimed. "She would figure in certain ones if they were that type of whodunit stories."

The Star of Delhi has another distinction: It was a story often referred to by Walter Gibson in later years as one that was prophetic. The theft of the fabulous gem described in this mystery seemed to come true in real life.

"*The Black Hush* foreshadowed New York City's 'blackout' by thirty years," Gibson once related, "while another novel, *The Star of Delhi*, called the tune on a jewel robbery that occurred two decades later."

Walter was referring to the infamous theft of the gem on which his mythical star sapphire was based. On October 29, 1964, the Star of India was lifted, along with several other famous gems, from the American Museum of Natural History in New York. The chief perpetrator was Jack "Murph the Surf" Murphy. He was captured within days of the heist, and the Star of India was subsequently recovered.

Read *The Star of Delhi* and see how close Maxwell Grant came to foreseeing the future of this fabulous gem. •

CHAPTER I
THE SECRET SIX

"THE Star of Delhi!"

The man who spoke the words pronounced them with a tone of awe, as well he might. Resting in the white plush of the opened jewel casket was a magnificent sapphire, the largest that he had ever seen.

It wasn't surprising that he recognized the gem, for it was Raymond Walder's business, as head of Walder & Co., noted New York jewelers, to identify precious stones.

But he hadn't expected to find the Star of Delhi in the possession of Armand Lenfell. Though a financier, wealthy enough to buy the Star of Delhi many times over, Lenfell had never rated as a jewel fancier in Walder's opinion.

Hence, Walder's thin features, usually drab and expressionless, were registering amazement. He looked toward Lenfell, saw a smile on the financier's broad, heavy-jowled face. Then Walder's eyes returned to the Star of Delhi, as though drawn by a magnet.

It was certainly a remarkable gem. Dome-shaped, its curved surface smooth, the Star of Delhi was large enough to fill the space between Walder's thumb and forefinger, had he placed them tip to tip. But color and size were not the features that gave the sapphire its fame.

Deep within the gem, Walder saw straight lines, streaks of light that radiated like the spokes of a wheel. Those scintillating shafts were the marks of the true star sapphire, a much-prized type of gem.

His breath returning, Walder began to express congratulations. Lenfell cut him short with booming tone.

"Convince yourself, Walder!" he said. "Make sure that this is actually the Star of Delhi."

Walder lifted the sapphire from its plush nest and calculated its weight. He produced a jeweler's glass and studied the gem through the magnifying lens. He held the Star to the light for a time, and finally returned it to the jewel case with a satisfied nod.

Then, quite suddenly, Walder became nervous. He glanced at the windows of Lenfell's study as though wondering if the shades were fully drawn. He stared over his shoulder toward the door, which was closed. He even gave a doubtful glance at Lenfell's modern safe, which stood behind the desk.

Lenfell inserted an indulgent laugh.

"I know what worries you, Walder," he said. "There have been many jewel robberies lately. But that is no cause for alarm. No criminals know that I have the Star of Delhi; hence they will not come here to find it."

Walder's eyes were still on the door. His face looked strained, for he was sure that he heard creeping footsteps in the hallway outside. He remembered his surprise when he arrived at the house a short while before, to find only one servant on the premises where usually there were many. Moreover, Walder recalled that Lenfell had promptly told the lone servant to take the evening off.

Yet the creeps from the hall were real! They had increased too noticeably, to be the product of Walder's imagination. Hoarsely, the jeweler began:

"Someone has entered the house, Lenfell—"

"I know it," interrupted Lenfell. "They are friends of mine. I want you to meet them, Walder. But first, you must prepare yourself for another surprise."

Lenfell stepped to a corner of the room. From a closet, he brought out a long dark coat, which he put on. Then, from a shelf, he produced a black hood that had two eye slits cut in it. Lenfell slid the hood over his head and peered through the slits.

Instead of the broad-faced financier, he had become an ominous figure from which Walder instinctively shrank. Then, feeling Lenfell's friendly clutch upon his arm, hearing the familiar voice from within the hood, Walder regained some of his composure.

"Come, Walder," said Lenfell, his tone reduced to mildness. "There is nothing to fear, I assure you."

The jeweler gave a pinch-faced smile. He wasn't going to be frightened by a mere masquerade. Lenfell was his friend, and was merely taking Walder to meet others who wanted to see the Star of Delhi, for Lenfell had closed the jewel casket and was bringing it along. The friends were obviously in Lenfell's library, for the hooded financier was taking Walder in that direction.

Then, on the very threshold of the library, Walder gasped with horror and would have sagged to the floor if Lenfell's strong hand had not stayed him. Within the dimly lighted book-lined room, Walter saw Lenfell's friends. To a man, they were hooded like their host, and there were five of them!

With Lenfell, the group formed a secret six, as forbidding as a semicircle of inquisitors. Eyes glistening from hood slits were fastened upon the slumping jeweler, as though accusing him, judging him, and condemning him, all on sight!

AIDING Walder to a chair, Lenfell placed the jewel casket on a table and opened it. Walder saw the gleam of the Star of Delhi, like a great blue eye, shining up to greet the strange band of hooded men.

Lenfell's voice, modulated to a kindly tone, gave Walder a vestige of relief, enough for him to glance upward. Then his courage returned. One man of the throng had unmasked: Lenfell. Sight of the financier's smiling face steeled Walder against the terror that his view of the rest produced.

"Be tranquil, Walder," said Lenfell. "I tried to ease the shock, by letting you see me in full regalia before meeting the rest. These men are friends, but of the group, I am the only who can unmask. I shall explain why."

Walder listened. He was getting used to the eyes about him. No longer did he imagine that they glared. They were becoming milder each time he studied them. All the while Lenfell's voice, easy but emphatic, was disclosing facts that Walder could comprehend.

"We are a syndicate of six," Lenfell explained, "who have contributed our wealth to buy gems from foreign refugees. Our purpose is to convert those jewels into cash, through private sales, giving unfortunate persons a fair return on the possessions that they are forced to sell.

"Of the six, I alone am known to the other five. Since they meet here in my house, I can unmask when occasion demands."

Walder was nodding, actually smiling at the members of Lenfell's secret six.

"We have met with an obstacle," proceeded Lenfell. "There have been so many jewel robberies of late, that wealthy customers are doubtful of our bona fide gems when approached, confidentially, by my associates. Buyers fear that the refugee story is false; that we are trying to unload stolen gems.

"Since we must do something to prove our status, we have decided to cut the Star of Delhi, one of our most important purchases, into six parts. Each of us will wear a ring containing a star sapphire from the famous Star of Delhi. That fact, alone, will mark us men of integrity. However, we do not care to take such a step without proper advice. We are asking yours, Walder."

Drawing himself together, Walder looked about the group; then stared at the Star of Delhi. He shuddered, not through a return of terror, but at the thought of cutting such a rare gem into smaller ones. Then, slowly, a canny look spread over Walder's features. His business sense outmatched his love of gems.

"The Star of Delhi is unique," conceded Walder. "It might be worth half a million dollars, to the proper buyer. But I doubt that you could find anyone nowadays who would pay more than a mere fraction of that sum.

"Cut into smaller stones"—he eyed the great gem appraisingly—"each a perfect star sapphire in its own right, the Star of Delhi would be more salable. Each of the six rings would be worth at least fifty thousand dollars to its owner. There is merit in your plan, Lenfell."

Buzzes came from five hooded men; all those buzzes were approving. Lenfell heard them and took the murmurs as a vote in the affirmative. He simply said:

"We shall have the stone cut."

Still staring at the great Star, Walder was thinking of another factor. Quite accustomed to the hooded men by this time, he expressed his theme.

"You must find some way," he said, "to let people know that the Star of Delhi is in America, and that it has actually been cut into smaller gems—"

Lenfell was interrupting with a smile that Walder noted.

"We are counting upon you to help us," said Lenfell. "You have seen the Star of Delhi, Walder. Your word is beyond reproach. We have hoped that you would see fit to exhibit the six rings, stating their origin, without naming the man who placed them in your custody: that is, myself."

THE idea startled Walder for the moment. As he looked about, he fancied again that eyes were glaring at him from the hoods. But Walder's business acumen came to the fore. He visualized the publicity that such an exhibit would bring to Walder & Co. Gradually, he nodded his willingness.

There was a wave of Lenfell's hand. One by one, the members of the hooded group departed, until all were gone save Lenfell. Walder could hear their creeping progress down the stairs—some by the front, others by the back, one by a side stairway that was little used. Then, back in Lenfell's study, Walder gave a smile of real relief to find himself alone again with Lenfell, the Star of Delhi lying on the desk between them.

While Lenfell was putting away his coat and hood, Walder made a suggestion.

"You may entrust the cutting of the stone to the proper man," he said. "I would say that there is only one such man in New York."

Lenfell paused while opening the safe, where he intended to replace the Star of Delhi.

"You mean Roger Sherbrock?"

"I mean Sherbrock," replied Walder. "Of course, there are foreign experts here—better men, perhaps, than Sherbrock. But they are men who have lost fortunes and might prove bitter. They would be dangerous. You can rely on Sherbrock. I repeat, he is the only man."

"I shall see Sherbrock," decided Lenfell. The safe was open; he put the jewel casket in it. "You will hear from me later, Walder. Meanwhile, accept my thanks for your kind co-operation. It is hardly necessary"—he was extending his hand—"for me to add that I sent the servants out tonight so they would not happen to see any of my hooded visitors."

Lenfell personally conducted Walder to the front door. Outside, the jeweler looked back at the large old-fashioned mansion and gave another shudder at sight of its gloom and bulk. Into that shiver, Walder put memories of the creeping sounds that he had heard, those weird indications of the advent of Lenfell's hooded friends.

Then, briskly, Walder walked to the next corner to find a cab.

There were creeping sounds again in the old mansion. Armand Lenfell was making them himself as he returned to his study. He didn't mind them; indeed, he rather enjoyed the weird sound, for Lenfell was smiling, more noticeably than before. His smile had become a leer of an insidious sort, as he stooped at the safe to reopen it.

Then, with the Star of Delhi again on his desk, Armand Lenfell sat back and waited, his leer taking on a satanic touch as he gazed at the blue gleam from the great Star of Delhi. His head was tilted, for Armand Lenfell was listening for new creeps in the hallway.

Creeps that would announce another visitor, less fearsome in appearance than the members of the secret six, but one who would understand Lenfell better. Lenfell had spoken truly, in stating that his hooded associates were banded together in a cause of good. His one lie had been his inclusion of himself in such a worthy purpose.

Alone, unobserved by either Walder or the secret throng, Armand Lenfell could relax and reveal himself for what he really was—a man with crime at heart. He was waiting for another of that same ilk, that together they might plot an underhanded scheme involving the much-valued Star of Delhi!

CHAPTER II
BAIT FOR CRIME

THE exhibit of the six star sapphires, when announced a week later, was promptly heralded as the event of the New York jewelry season. Raymond Walder, true to his word, surrounded it with integrity and mystery.

Walder's statement that he had seen the Star of Delhi, was something unimpeachable. His declaration that he could not name its owner provided the mystery. He added, of course, the news that the Star of Delhi had been cut into six parts, and other jewelers agreed that the process would render the gem, or segments of it, more salable.

But Walder did not state who had cut the sapphire. He simply invited the public to view the sextuple result.

Few persons in New York were more interested in Walder's coming display than was Lamont Cranston. A millionaire collector of rarities, including jewels, Cranston seemed disappointed only because the Star of Delhi had been reduced to a sectional form. He tried to treat the matter lightly, but he did not deceive Margo Lane.

She could tell Lamont's mood, when they lunched together on the day of Walder's exhibit, and from remarks he dropped, she was quite sure that he would have prized the Star of Delhi for his own collection. It was too bad, Margo thought, that Cranston had not learned that the great Star was for sale before it was hacked to chunks.

Calm-mannered, his hawkish face often masklike, Lamont Cranston seldom revealed his inner thoughts, even to an attractive and sympathetic brunette like Margo Lane. But it was plain, on this occasion, that Cranston should normally have stayed away from the exhibit at Walder's.

Mere sight of six lovely star sapphires, in place of one unblemished marvel, would certainly pain him. Margo knew that Cranston was going to the exhibit purely from sense of duty.

That was because Margo also knew that this man who posed as Lamont Cranston was actually The Shadow, master fighter who battled crime. As The Shadow, he couldn't afford to miss the Walder exhibit, because it was the greatest bait for men of crime that had been offered in months.

The newspapers were full of jewel robberies. A few had occurred in New York, despite the vigilance of The Shadow, but the rest had happened in other cities. Though the mob, like the mastermind who handled the game, was probably in New York, no leads were yet available. Stolen stuff, if peddled, had been artfully fenced without being traced; all the more reason why The Shadow should be on the job.

Therefore, Margo was quite sure that Cranston wanted to visit Walder's to look over the customers as much as the sapphires. He knew that crooks couldn't resist the lure that the exhibit offered.

It was fairly late in the afternoon when Cranston and Margo finally arrived at Walder's. The exclusive jewelry store was under heavy guard. Armed guards stood outside, and others were posted at strategic spots inside the store itself.

All other jewelry, the usual Walder stock, had been put away for safekeeping, except for cheaper items that would interest the general public. Emphasis was upon the six sapphires.

The stones that represented the famous Star of Delhi were in a special burglarproof case in the exact center of the store. The box, bolted into a stone pedestal, had a top surface of bulletproof glass, protected by photoelectric devices connected with burglar alarms.

Sometimes, such cases had lights inside them. This one did not. The sapphires scintillated under the beam of a spotlight focused from a ceiling dome.

Even in sixes, the sapphires were marvelous to view. They were the size of large peas, and quite as much alike. Each had its identifying touch—the star formation—and all were set in rings of the same type: heavy, plain gold.

People passed along the rail that fronted the display and gave gasps of appreciation, so that the vaulted space of Walder's jewelry store echoed constantly with one repeated simper.

MARGO was pleased to observe a flicker of passing interest on Cranston's immobile features. The perfect match of the six sapphires intrigued him, as did the provisions taken for their custody.

But when he had finished looking at the gems and drawn away to the outskirts of the throng, his mind went back to the persons present. Close beside him, Margo caught Cranston's undertone.

"Look for others who are staying around. People who seem too sure of themselves."

Margo looked. If her opinion had counted, The Shadow would have had about fifty suspects. Knowing there couldn't be that many, Margo gave it up.

"I'm no good, Lamont," she confessed. "If you can pick any goats from these sheep—"

"I see one goat," interposed Cranston. "Look over by that notion counter, Margo. You'll recognize him."

Margo's eyes almost popped as she studied a young man whose face, though somewhat hardened, looked to be the result of dissipation, rather than crime. She caught herself just in time to keep from exclaiming his name too loud:

"Dwig Brencott!"

Handsome in his way, black-haired, with a complexion that would be defined as dark, rather than sallow, Dwig was the pride of the nightclubs. A member of café society, he never appeared in public until afternoon and, from then on, could be seen in what some columnists considered the "best places" in town.

Dwig was in and out, from one spot to another, until the closing hour, which was usually five in the morning. It hadn't occurred to Margo, until Cranston mentioned it, that such a practice might be Dwig's alibi. Dwig had a way of being somewhere else, very often. There were many times when he might even have been out of town.

It could be that Dwig was the mainspring of the jewel mob, so far as actual robberies were concerned. If so, he was falling for the blue bait. Whether or not he intended to go after the six sapphires, Dwig hadn't been able to resist the temptation of looking over the situation. The Shadow's theory was right; not only that, it was proven.

Of all people, Dwig Brencott wouldn't be hanging around the cheap jewelry counter, striking up an acquaintance with a melancholy-looking clerk, unless he had some purpose in mind. He would be more likely to chat with Raymond Walder, who was standing behind the sapphire exhibit, except that Walder was getting attention from socially prominent visitors, who might remember Dwig if he made himself too noticeable.

"At seven o'clock," Margo heard Cranston say, in an even undertone, "the sapphires will be removed in an armored truck. It will be dark at seven, and the truck will be the natural target for an attack. It might be well for someone to follow the truck."

Margo nodded. She could think of someone perfectly qualified: namely, The Shadow. Hence, Cranston's next words rather surprised her.

"Tackling an armored truck would be too difficult," he said indifferently. "There will be no trouble outside. It would be interesting, though, to know where the sapphires go. Suppose you stay around, Margo. Then you can follow the truck, and find out."

STILL wondering if her ears were hearing right, Margo forgot to use her eyes. She was looking at Cranston, not at Dwig. But, in his turn, The Shadow was watching Dwig Brencott. He saw the sleek man turning away from the counter, about to leave Walder's store.

Outside, accumulating dusk promised Dwig an easy departure. It also offered The Shadow an excellent chance to follow him; hence The Shadow's casual instructions to Margo.

Before Margo could argue that trailing trucks was not her idea of a pleasant evening, Cranston strolled away as if the whole matter had been settled. It was then that Margo discovered the coincidental departure of Dwig Brencott, and understood.

In giving her one trail, Lamont was taking up an earlier, and more difficult one. He was following Dwig Brencott, on the chance that he might learn enough to stifle coming crime before it even began.

In either event, whether crooks planned to move tonight or not, Margo's task of trailing the truck would be reduced to a matter of routine. Should any threat of actual danger arrive, The Shadow would be the one to accept it.

Of course, Cranston had neither stated nor implied that fact. He had a way of treating The Shadow as a different personality than himself, even though Margo had long identified them as the same. It was just another proof of The Shadow's perfect tact.

Considering how crooks were always gunning for the black-clad avenger who so often crossed their paths, it was wise policy for The Shadow to deny the Cranston link, even among friends.

Proof of his sagacity was being evidenced outside of Walder's store, where Dwig Brencott, turning to walk along the avenue, was taking a shrewd backward glance into the jewelry house. Had Dwig even suspected that Cranston could be The Shadow, he might have noticed Margo's hawk-faced friend strolling out with others who were leaving the exhibit.

As it was, Dwig simply classed them all as curiosity seekers who had seen enough of the sapphire display. The sleek man was on lookout for persons who might be detectives, and he was quite sure that none such had followed him from the store.

In the back of his mind, perhaps, Dwig might have been looking for a stealthy figure clad in black, but the lighted doorway of the jewelry store could have offered no concealment, even for The Shadow.

When such a figure did appear, he came from across the avenue, where Cranston had gone, unnoticed. Stepping into one door of a taxicab, Cranston had entered as himself, and come out the other side as The Shadow, all in a matter of mere seconds.

He was on the west side of the avenue, where the buildings cut off the last rays of sunset. Under the shroud of dusk, The Shadow was gliding, unseen, from doorway to doorway, keeping pace with his quarry, Dwig Brencott.

Cloaked in black, a slouch hat drawn down across his eyes, The Shadow wore the famous garb that enabled him to stalk an unsuspecting prey. With darkness on the increase, every minute was improving the conditions that the cloaked investigator needed in his present expedition.

With nearly an hour until seven o'clock, The Shadow was confident that he could learn the essential details of any crime with which Dwig Brencott, might be concerned.

That was why a whispered laugh came from The Shadow's hidden lips. It was a tone that presaged trouble for men of evil, the sort of trouble that The Shadow could provide. As bait for thieves, the six sapphires had come up to The Shadow's expectations. The rest would lie in his hands.

Perhaps The Shadow's tone would have lacked the prophetic touch had he known the full story of the Star of Delhi and the six blue gems that Raymond Walder was exhibiting as the carved components of the famous sapphire.

That story could have given The Shadow an index to the startling and unexpected turn that crime was to produce at seven o'clock; events that even The Shadow would not quite fathom when they came!

* *

As a mongoose whips a cobra—as a cowboy throws a wild steer—as a lion springs on its unwary prey—so, too, does The Shadow attack the hordes of crime and thwart their evil ends! Master of Darkness—Crime-fighter Extraordinary—The Shadow, by wits and thundering automatics, overawes those who seek to break the law and those already beyond its pale!

In his never-ceasing campaign to deal justice to crooks and honest citizens alike, The Shadow at times assumes the role of Lamont Cranston, globe-trotting millionaire. With this disguise, The Shadow makes his ends to meet unbeknownst to denizens of the underworld. There is a real Lamont Cranston; but he is a man of deep understanding, and it is with his tacit permission that The Shadow adopts his identity.

CHAPTER III
CRIME IN REVERSE

"AT seven o'clock, in front of Walder's."

It was the fourth time that Dwig Brencott had given those simple instructions from the telephone booth near the cloakroom in the Club Cadiz, which was one of the nightspots that Dwig frequented.

Just past the cloakroom was a stairway, and under its shelter The Shadow was listening to Dwig's smooth-purred tone, hoping that he would specify further details; but Dwig didn't. Furthermore, The Shadow had encountered another handicap.

From his listening post, he could hear Dwig's voice, but the *clicks* of the phone dial were not audible enough to be translated into numbers, a favorite trick of The Shadow's. Hence, when Dwig left the phone booth and went to the bar to get a drink, The Shadow had gained a rather frugal net result.

He knew only that Dwig had called four men, all obviously tools of crime, instructing them to be outside Walder's at the time when the six sapphires were to be taken away. Perhaps those four would bring others; in any event, the thing fitted with The Shadow's previous calculation that Dwig intended to trail the truck that came for the sapphires, either to take a crack at its contents, or to learn the truck's destination.

At the bar, Dwig was chatting with cronies and building up something of an alibi. He was telling them other places where he intended to go, even suggesting that some come along with him and make the round of the hotspots. They were all promising to meet Dwig later, the very point for which he had been playing.

Seven o'clock was drawing close. By then, Dwig would be gone from the Club Cadiz, for the buildup that he was giving indicated, to The Shadow, that the sleek man intended to be at Walder's, too.

But Dwig was making it very easy for himself to drop out of the nightclub picture for the half-hour between seven and seven-thirty, and yet have friends believe that he had been at one place or another all during that period.

Gliding out through a little-used rear exit from the Club Cadiz, The Shadow paused near a darkened corner and blinked a tiny flashlight. Its rays were green, and the flashes caused a parked coupé to come in The Shadow's direction.

The man at the wheel was Harry Vincent, one of The Shadow's capable secret agents. Sliding in beside him, The Shadow instructed Harry to drive over to the avenue and park near the corner beyond Walder's.

The Shadow had a purpose in choosing that

* *

Wherever fliers gather together, whenever the public talks of aviation, the name of Kent Allard is one of the first to be mentioned. World-famous aviator, Allard is a public hero. But what no one knows—save his two Xinca Indian servitors—is that Allard is the real identity of The Shadow!

Assisting The Shadow in his perpetual battle with the underworld is a retinue of aids—men who owe their lives to The Shadow and for whom they gladly do his slightest bidding.

Burbank is the contact man between The Shadow and his aids; through him go all orders and information. Rutledge Mann gives invaluable service to the Master of Darkness through his "front" of investment broker. Harry Vincent is very close to The Shadow, and acts in many cases as his advance man. To Moe Shrevnitz goes the honor of transporting the Crime-fighter to battle—in his taxicab. Clyde Burke, reporter on the Classic, furnishes The Shadow with inside information and advance news.

Cliff Marsland and Hawkeye are purported tough underworld characters; but, in reality, they are aids of The Shadow. When physical strength is needed the Master of Darkness calls on Jericho, giant African, whose muscular power is equaled only by his willingness to fight crime.

These, then, are the aids of The Shadow, characters who are willing to subject themselves to the Master of Darkness because they realize in him a superior force counteractant to crime.

The Shadow knows!

corner. He was certain that the truck would stop at the side door of the jewelry store, on a one-way street, where traffic headed toward thc avenue.

Since Dwig had ordered his men to be in front of Walder's, they wouldn't be in a position to attempt a robbery until after the truck was under way. Then, they would logically come from the avenue and swing in back of the truck, to follow it.

As for making an attack before the jewels left the store, that would be sheer folly. Dwig had looked over the lay; certainly he knew how strongly Walder's was guarded.

Crooks wouldn't get past the front door, if they tried to rush the guards and reach the sapphire display before anyone came for it. Besides, Dwig had specified seven o'clock, which wouldn't give him time to organize such a foolhardy attempt.

SEVEN o'clock.

The hour had arrived. From his vantage point, The Shadow looked back along the avenue and saw a car sliding into a parking space. Evidently, some of Dwig's men had come by car, while others were to join them on foot.

Glancing down the side street, The Shadow saw a small armored truck stopping at the delivery entrance. Men in uniform, coming from the truck, were meeting others from the store.

At the front door of Walder & Co, guards were moving the last patrons out. The last of the lot was Margo Lane, and a taxicab wheeled in to take her as a passenger. The driver of that cab was Moe Shrevnitz, another of The Shadow's secret agents. Margo wasn't surprised to see Moe's cab arrive. It usually showed up whenever Lamont Cranston delegated Margo to special missions.

About to enter the cab, Margo paused, as though she had forgotten something. She had a chance to look back into the jewelry store. The place had cleared, and she saw Raymond Walder superintending the removal of the burglarproof display case that contained the rare star sapphires.

With Walder were a few other jewelers, taking a last look at the much-prized gems. Though those privileged visitors had not handled the sapphires, they were quite convinced that the six stones had been cut from the famous Star of Delhi. To them, the word of Raymond Walder—that he had seen and examined the great sapphire itself—was as good as the gold which formed the rings in which the six gems were mounted.

Margo stalled until she saw the case go out through the side door. From his observation point, The Shadow watched the rapid loading of the truck. Immediately, the armored vehicle moved forward and kept straight across the avenue, along the side street. By then, Moe's cab was under way. It took the corner and followed the truck.

Harry was sliding the coupé into gear. The Shadow's gloved hand restrained the start that the agent was about to make.

Next in order was to be the crook-manned car, and after it passed, The Shadow would follow it. Meanwhile, Moe would be dropping from the

MARGO LANE and MOE SHREVNITZ

trail, for The Shadow had given him a red blink from the little flashlight when the cab swung past the coupé.

With crooks on the truck's trail, as The Shadow expected them to be, Margo wouldn't be needed. That was why The Shadow had ordered Moe to come with the cab. Moe, or Shrevvy, as they often called him, would explain to Margo that The Shadow was taking over.

Like all The Shadow's plans, this one was well laid, but it was destined to go astray. Dwig's car was starting, and the Shadow gave Harry the word to go, but to let the other vehicle swing past him. Then, abruptly, thugs made a stop directly in front of Walder's.

Before The Shadow could do more than reach for the door of the coupé, mobsters were out of their car and across the sidewalk, dashing into the jewelry store. There were six of them, all masked, and their leader was about the build of Dwig Brencott. The Shadow had time only to glimpse the masked crew before they disappeared inside the store.

The whole thing was crazy. Dwig must certainly have seen the armored truck pull away; he surely knew that the sapphires were inside it. This was the unexpected point that The Shadow had in no wise anticipated. Dwig's thrust was an attack upon an empty nest, from which the wanted prizes had been removed!

AT least, Dwig had accomplished one thing. Without knowing that The Shadow was on hand, he had beaten the black-cloaked fighter to his goal—which happened to be Walder's store, not the armored truck.

Dwig had gained a margin of only a few dozen seconds, considering that he and his masked companions were at the store itself, whereas The Shadow was up at the corner ahead. But the time was enough for crooks to get in deadly work.

Guards were gone from the front door, for, with the truck's departure, their duty was ended. Walder held the center of the floor, where he was shaking hands with the visiting jewelers. While there were still some guards in the place, they had gone beyond the counters to change from uniforms to other clothes.

It was Raymond Walder who first saw the invasion and gave a frantic yell to his helpless friends. The other jewelers went ducking for the counters, easy targets for the guns that masked men brandished, had Dwig and his murderous pals wanted to shoot them down.

But they were choosing one victim only, Raymond Walder, and he was even easier than the rest. For Walder, brave when confronted by the grueling test, was holding his ground, shouting for the guards to return and aid him against the attacking tribe.

Six guns spoke almost as one. Walder took the bullets from that firing squad. Riddled by the close-range shots, the drab jeweler was dead before he struck the floor. Inspired by that show of courage, guards were springing across the counters, some still in uniform, others not, but all with guns that they had hurriedly snatched.

Mobsters were ready for them too. The masked leader gave a snarl, that no one could have identified with the smooth, affable tone of Dwig Brencott. Wheeling like a well-trained team, the killers were taking point-blank aim, each at a different human target. They intended to blast the guards as they had finished Walder: to leave no one to hamper their retreat to safety.

It was a moment made for murder, a triumph for these killers who had arrived ahead of The Shadow. But their very surety was to be the factor that would end their delivery of further doom. They had wasted a few vital seconds; those seconds were enough to ruin them.

From the avenue door came a fierce, defiant challenge—the mockery that crimedom feared and hated; the tone that made deep-dyed crooks forget all other purposes and seek only to meet the taunter in a duel of death.

The laugh of The Shadow!

CHAPTER IV
HALF AN ANSWER

DWIG BRENCOTT and his masked companions had staged crime in reverse, by attempting what seemed a robbery in a place where booty could no longer be obtained. To that reverse, The Shadow was adding another twist. Announcing himself with strident, mocking challenge he was inviting enemies to treat him as they had done Raymond Walder.

The trouble was, they couldn't. Though they outnumbered The Shadow six to one, he held advantages which, taken separately, were slim, but added together made a total that Dwig and his pals failed to calculate.

Foremost of those advantages were The Shadow's guns, a brace of automatics, already drawn, that began a pointed tattoo while crooks were on the whirl. Two of the masked men ended their spins in sprawls before they could pull their gun triggers.

Others, too, were at a loss. In Walder, they had found a close-range target who hadn't tried to dive away from their guns. The Shadow was more distant, and crooks expected him to dive. They fired for the doorway, to get him when he tried to fade. But The Shadow's momentary twist was only a feint that came with the recoil of his automatics.

Instead of whipping back through the doorway, he took a long lunge forward, striking almost flat, but catching himself on his elbows as he slid along the tiled floor of the jewelry store. Bullets whizzed above The Shadow's head, high by feet rather than inches, while from the floor level he used each .45 to blaze answers at his adversaries.

The Shadow's shots were quick ones, calculated to make crooks dive, rather than to drop them; but he succeeded both ways. Dwig and two others managed to do a frantic duck, but The Shadow clipped the fourth man. Coming up from elbows to knees, he was ready for more target practice with the remaining three; but, by then, it was unneeded. The final factor had come into the game.

The final factor: namely, the guards who only a few seconds earlier had been facing cold-blooded death. Not only had they rallied, they were right in the paths that Dwig and his two unwounded pals were taking to get away from The Shadow's fire. Two to one, the guards were pouncing on the hapless crooks, intending to suppress them.

Unfortunately, the guards were too ardent, as the crooks had been with The Shadow. While Dwig and the other two were trying to wrest away in among the counters, and losing their guns in the attempt, the guards heard shots.

Wounded men were supplying them from the floor, and the guards didn't wait for The Shadow to suppress those cripples. Instead, they turned to blaze away at the incapable marksmen.

The Shadow cleared a counter in one long leap, his only way to escape the misguided fire that the vengeful guards supplied. Dwig and his two unscathed companions dashed for the front door, hoping only for a getaway, since they were gunless.

Coming up from the counter, The Shadow aimed to stop them, but by then the guards were in the way, closing in upon the wounded men that they had already riddled.

One guard saw the three escaping crooks and yelled. The rest flooded toward the door, firing as they started, thereby ending The Shadow's last chance of inserting timely shots. Once hurried, the guards were even worse marksmen than the crooks.

Two masked men went safely through the door while bullets were cracking show windows on each side. The third of the fleeing tribe—the nervy Dwig—actually made a pause in flight, to pick up a gun that a guard had kicked from the hand of a wounded thug.

Speeding to the side door, The Shadow looked along the street, saw Dwig's car make a two-wheeled turn from the avenue. The guards, by then, were shooting from the front door of Walder's, and a single gun was answering from Dwig's car.

Coolly, The Shadow aimed at the spurting weapon, intending to put Dwig out of action and therewith demoralize the escaping pair who accompanied him. Again, The Shadow was forced to stay a timely shot.

Another car whipped around the corner. It was Harry's coupé, taking up the pursuit, and it cut right into The Shadow's path of aim. The two cars sped along the street, and The Shadow watched them dwindle to a distant corner while the noise of guns trailed back from both.

The chase was far beyond The Shadow's range of fire when he saw Dwig's car swerve around another corner. There were flashes of tiny guns, and Dwig's car was gone, while Harry's coupé kept ahead and climbed a curb. Still watching, The Shadow saw his agent come from the coupé and stoop beside it.

Dwig's shot hadn't clipped Harry; it had taken a front tire instead. But it meant that Dwig was off in the clear, free to make his round of nightclubs, while the two thugs with him could return to hideaways.

Sirens were sounding in front of Walder's, telling that police cars had arrived. With a gloomy departing laugh, The Shadow took his way into paths of darkness.

JUST as Dwig Brencott moved in a fancier sphere than the ratty crooks who had helped him in a scheme of murder guised as robbery, so did The Shadow frequent places much more exclusive than the nightspots that Dwig patronized.

As Lamont Cranston, The Shadow was a member of the Cobalt Club, which numbered many millionaires among its patrons.

It happened that Police Commissioner Ralph Weston belonged to the Cobalt Club, and esteemed Cranston as a bosom friend. Chances were that Cranston would be hearing from the commissioner as he always did when crime reached up from the underworld and bothered high society. So The Shadow went to the Cobalt Club, arriving there as Cranston.

He hadn't long to wait. Notified of a telephone call, the leisurely Mr. Cranston answered it and heard the brusque voice of Commissioner Weston, telling him about the tragedy at Walder's and asking him to come over. Indulgently, The Shadow

The Shadow's guns began a pointed tattoo while crooks were on the whirl.

drawled that he would. A while later, he arrived there in the guise of Cranston.

Instead of six sapphires, there were four bodies on display. One was Walder's; the other three were the crooks that The Shadow had crippled and the guards had slaughtered. All three had been identified as low characters from the badlands, which didn't surprise The Shadow. He was quite sure that Dwig Brencott, crook deluxe, would choose the lowest of companions for criminal forays, just to distract all thoughts from himself.

The man who had identified the three hoodlums was present. He was a swarthy, stocky, police inspector; by name, Joe Cardona. He rated as Weston's ace inspector, despite the fact that Joe and the commissioner were wont to argue.

Usually they had conflicting theories as the cause of their dispute, and they were running true to form now. Both were irked because the three thugs had died too soon to be questioned, but except for that point, the commissioner and the inspector were at loggerheads.

"The case is obvious," growled Weston. "These men belong to the band of jewel thieves who have been operating so extensively. They are of a low type, and their leader was undoubtedly the roughest of the lot. They weren't the sort who could show their faces in a store like this, even before they made their attempt at robbery.

"So they simply waited outside until they saw that the door was clear of guards. Not knowing that the sapphires had been removed, they made the thrust, hoping to grab the gems that they had heard about. Walder tried to block them, so they killed him."

The Shadow knew that Weston's theory was even wider than the shots that the excited guards had fired after Dwig when the crook deluxe departed. Even before they pulled up in front of Walder's, Dwig and his company had been close enough to see the removal of the sapphires by the side door.

They had even waited until the armored truck went across the avenue before making their thrust at the store itself. Therefore, The Shadow was interested to learn if Cardona had a different theory.

Joe did have. It was as far from the mark as Weston's.

"I figure it different, Commissioner," gruffed Cardona. "These gunzels weren't after the sapphires. They'd have been dumb to snatch a load of matched gems like those six blue stars. What they were figuring on was a robbery of Walder's regular stock.

"They doped it that the guards would unlax as soon as the truck pulled away, which is just what did happen. It was a crazy time to stage a robbery, with the big swag gone. Only, like I said, this outfit would have laid off of gems that couldn't be easily fenced. They were pulling a routine job at a time no body figured it would come. That's all."

Recalling Dwig's presence in the jewelry shop earlier, The Shadow could easily have refuted Cardona's theory. Dwig, had seen for himself that Walder, expecting an influx of curiosity seekers, had locked up all of his worthwhile stock and left nothing but showcases of cheap trinkets and notions for visitors to look at, after getting an eyeful of the six star sapphires.

LEAVING Weston and Cardona to argue the merits of their erroneous opinions, The Shadow expressed his regret over Walder's death, and gave a leisurely good night in typical Cranston style. Still retaining his lackadaisical pose, he left the store, entered a waiting limousine outside and rode to his favorite restaurant.

Sight of Moe's cab, parked outside, told The Shadow that he would find Margo inside, which he did.

As they dined, Margo kept watching the immobile face of Cranston, hoping for some expression that would answer the questions that she had in mind. None came, but as they finished dinner, The Shadow spoke in Cranston's steady tone.

"It's too bad, Margo," he said, "that you didn't follow the truck, as I suggested."

"But I did!" began Margo. "Only, I was in Shrevvy's cab, and he dropped the trail. He said that The Shadow—"

She stopped abruptly. There was no use in telling The Shadow something that he already knew. Margo realized that his remark had merely been a statement in keeping with the Cranston pose. It wasn't policy with Cranston to know what The Shadow had planned until someone else told him.

"A peculiar chap, The Shadow," observed Cranston quietly. "He usually succeeds; but tonight he bungled things. He is partly to blame for Walder's death, but I suppose we cannot criticize him. Crime certainly took an unexplainable twist."

Margo arched her eyebrows. So far, she agreed that the attempted robbery at Walder's *was* unexplainable, but she was gaining the impression that Cranston had an answer to the riddle. The way to get an answer was to ask for one.

"Very well, Lamont," said Margo. "Just why did Dwig and his masked crew head the wrong way? We thought that they would go after the truck; instead, they went into the jewelry store. What was their reason?"

Cranston spoke three words:

"To murder Walder!"

The fact was so simple that it took Margo's breath away. She had racked her brain for the answer, and Cranston had provided it in a style that left no room for dispute. The explanation brought a flood of ideas, all in keeping with the theme itself.

Margo realized that the surge of masked men into Walder's couldn't have been a robbery attempt, at all, for she knew the flaws in the theories held by Weston and Cardona.

Not being a robbery, it had been a cover-up for something else. Dwig and his ugly band wouldn't have wasted time at getting to their objective. One use of cover-ups was to make a success look like a failure. Dwig Brencott had accomplished that very purpose.

The one thing that the law did not suspect was the fact that unknown men had sought to slay Raymond Walder, rather than to rob his store or to seize the six sapphires that some wealthy, unnamed patron had asked him to display.

The riddle of seven-o'clock crime was half answered by The Shadow. But in giving half an answer, the investigator who posed as Cranston, was making it plain that the rest had not been learned. The Shadow's regret—that Margo hadn't followed the armored truck—was real, even though he, himself, had taken her off the trail.

Until the owner of the former Star of Delhi was discovered, the reason for Walder's death would remain unanswered. Watching the gaze of Cranston's eyes, Margo could tell that they were visualizing the six sapphires that he had viewed that afternoon.

No longer bait for criminals, those missing gems had become the object of The Shadow's next quest!

CHAPTER V
CREEPS IN THE DARK

SEATED in his study, Armand Lenfell was resting his folded arms upon the desk, listening intently for sounds from outside the room. Beside him lay a stack of newspapers, the accumulation of three days. They showed glaring headlines that concerned the attempted robbery which had resulted in the sudden death of Raymond Walder.

A wince showed on Lenfell's lips, as his eyes drifted to the newspapers. When alone, Lenfell always let his real opinions register themselves upon his face. It was plain that he not only regretted Walder's death, but felt anxious regarding its possible consequences to himself. Lenfell's expression lost none of its troubled air while he was noting the most recent headlines.

A sound brought Lenfell from his reverie. It was the one that he expected, a creeping through the hallway. Not merely a cautious tread like those that had roused Walder's imagination on the night of the jeweler's visit to Lenfell's house, but a creak that was actually ominous. The creeping carried its echoes along the hall, making it impossible for Lenfell to estimate the exact distance of the approaching visitor.

Indeed, Lenfell's eyes were still half closed, his full attention concentrated upon listening to the crawling footsteps, when the door of the room opened as if at its own accord.

Popping upright in his chair, Lenfell stared at the gaping door as though expecting it to devour him. In the dimness of the hall he saw a whitish face that seemed floating there, until Lenfell recognized it. It was his familiarity with the smiling countenance that brought the financier to his senses, making him realize that the face in the doorway had a body attached.

Lenfell sank back in his chair, tugged a handkerchief from his pocket and mopped his forehead.

The man from the hallway entered. He came with a pace that was a cross between a shuffle and tip-toe. His face, as it neared the desk, underwent a variety of changes, due largely to the angles from which the light struck it, for the man, himself, did not outwardly alter his demeanor.

From a white blur, with a slitted smile, the face became a withery, lipless visage spread in a fangish leer. Still nearer the desk, it caught a more flattering light, and lost its venom.

Lenfell's visitor was dryish-faced, rather than withery. He had lips, when one was close enough to observe them. As for teeth, they were prominent, but not ugly when studied in proper proportion to the rest of his face. Indeed, his smile was friendly, though with a cunning touch that Lenfell, no longer perturbed, could appreciate as belonging to a man of his own likes and ambitions.

The visitor's odd gait accounted, of course, for the echoing creeps that had so deceived Lenfell, even in his own preserves. But it only certified the man as one worthy of Lenfell's confidence. Furthermore, the visitor's thin white hair marked him as elderly, and therefore lacking any physical superiority over Lenfell.

Keenly, the white-haired man's shrewd gaze went from Lenfell to the newspapers and back again. The visitor spoke with slight traces of a rattly wheeze; otherwise, his tone was mild and kindly.

"Still brooding over Walder?" he queried. "Come, come, my friend! You can in no wise be held to blame for his death."

"Why not?" returned Lenfell. "I gave him the sapphires—"

The old man interposed a laugh. He tilted his head as he did, and his merriment was genuine, though its rattly wheeze carried too much of the macabre for Lenfell to join in it. Then, lowering his eyes, the old man let them glisten steadily upon Lenfell.

"You gave him what he thought were sapphires," the visitor corrected. "The synthetic gems which I, Jan Garmath, manufactured in my crucible. Not imitations of existing gems"—Garmath smiled proudly—"but conceptions of what the Star of Delhi would look like if divided into sixes."

Lenfell nodded. Then:

"At any rate," he said, "I gave Walder gems that passed as the sapphires and made him the target for crime and death."

"Through no blame of yours," argued Garmath. "According to those newspapers"—he waved a long hand toward the desk—"the murderers were after Walder's own jewels, not your sapphires. The police have not even pushed the case far enough to seek the owner of the former Star of Delhi."

GARMATH'S reassurance restored Lenfell's composure. Catching the contagion of the old man's grin, Lenfell rose from his desk and turned to the safe. It was already unlocked; he opened the door and brought out two jewel cases—a long one, and a square one. He placed them on the desk and opened them.

Set in a row within the long case were the six sapphires that had been exhibited at Walder's. From the square box gleamed the famous Star of Delhi, as large and as radiant as when Walder had first viewed it. So like the great gem were the smaller ones, that the eye could almost identify them as one and the same.

"A marvelous job, Garmath," commended Lenfell. "I doubt that any cutter, even Sherbrock, could have produced as fine a resemblance as you have with these synthetics. They will please my friends when they arrive."

Sounds from somewhere in the hall below caused Lenfell to remember that his friends were almost due. Hurriedly, he closed the case that contained the great Star and replaced it in the safe, spinning the combination dial.

Then, taking the longer case with its six rings, he stepped out into the hallway, closing the door behind him. He was going to the library, to meet the first of his hooded associates.

Immediately, Jan Garmath rose from his chair and approached the door. Opening it a crack, he listened, caught the sound of voices. Then, with his creepy stride, Garmath moved toward the library, but no longer were his footfalls audible. Silent in his creep, Garmath had become a most insidious figure.

Peering between the edge of the library doorway and a curtain, Garmath observed Lenfell and a hooded arrival. Not having considered it necessary to mask on this occasion, Lenfell expected his lone friend to raise his hood, which the other man did.

The two were talking as man to man, Lenfell expressing regrets over Walder's death and bolstering them with the very arguments that Garmath had provided. Garmath saw the unhooded visitor nod his sympathetic understanding; then, when Lenfell opened the jewel case, the man took one of the rings.

That visitor was hooded and on the way out, as other footsteps came up the stairs. Squeezing his frail form deep in the doorway, Garmath waited. He saw another of the hoods enter and unmask to chat with Lenfell. New footsteps were approaching, when the second man took his sapphire ring and departed.

The same process took place with the third; and after a brief wait, Lenfell received a fourth of the hooded group. Having seen all their faces and observed the transfer of the rings, Garmath waited patiently for the fifth man to arrive.

After several minutes, Lenfell became restless. Sensing that the financier might return to the study, Garmath sidled in that direction himself, again making his creak noiseless.

Garmath was seated in his chair, apparently half asleep, when Lenfell arrived bearing the jewel case with two rings left in it. He removed one and slipped it on a finger of his left hand, grinning toward Garmath, who chuckled. Then, surveying the last ring with a frown, Lenfell remarked:

"I wonder why he hasn't come. I know that he was out of town, but he promised to return this evening. I suppose that it can wait—"

Pausing, Lenfell decided otherwise. He took an envelope from his desk, wrote an address on it, and placed the ring inside. Then the thought of sending even a false sapphire by messenger troubled Lenfell. He was shaking his head, when the doorbell rang. Pocketing the envelope, Lenfell gestured for Garmath to remain where he was.

Garmath did. But as soon as Lenfell went downstairs, the white-haired man stretched a long hand to the desk and picked up the blotter that Lenfell had applied to the envelope. The address was plainly legible in reverse, and Garmath read it without the aid of a mirror. The blotter was back on the table when Lenfell returned.

"It was his servant," he said, referring to the last man of the hooded six. "He said his master will not arrive home until midnight, so he called by long distance, telling the servant to come here. I gave the envelope to the servant."

TURNING to the safe, Lenfell unlocked it; from a cashbox, he brought out a sheaf of crisp bills and counted off a stack of large denominations, to the total of six thousand dollars.

"Your fee, Garmath," said Lenfell. "Ten times the value of the rings you made for me, but well worth it. Those imitation sapphires had to stand the test of expert scrutiny, though I saw to it that they could not be handled, thanks to the sealed case in which I delivered them to Walder."

Showing Garmath to the stairs, Lenfell was conscious of the creaky stride that old Jan no longer sought to keep unheard. He was still listening for those creeps as he returned to the study, and Lenfell was at last satisfied that they had dwindled clear to the front door. After a few moments of silence, Lenfell stepped into the study.

He thumbed the remaining bills in the cashbox, counting out a batch which he had promised Garmath as a bonus after a certain transaction was completed. Then, as he replaced the cashbox in the safe, Lenfell stared mistrustfully at the square case which contained the Star of Delhi.

He opened the case hastily, saw that it still held the great sapphire. Closing the safe and locking it, Lenfell picked up the telephone.

Outside Lenfell's door, a man was listening at the crack. The man was Garmath; he had returned, in his silent fashion, by another stairway. Garmath caught Lenfell's tone:

"Yes, yes. I still have the sapphire, the original Star of Delhi ... The exhibit at Walder's? That was merely for our mutual protection ... Yes, poor Walder supplied imitations himself, to help create the impression that the Star of Delhi no longer exists—

"Yes, it was wise, considering those recent robberies... Yes, the fact that crooks sought the smaller gems proves how they would have coveted the Star ... Next Monday? Certainly, I can see you then, Crome—"

As Lenfell's receiver clicked upon the hook, Garmath moved away. By overhearing that telephone call, he had learned what he wanted. Descending the front stairs again, this time in absolute silence, Garmath crept out through the big door and went away from the gloomy mansion.

Quickening his creep into a lengthy stride, Garmath covered a few blocks before stopping in a drugstore to make a telephone call of his own. Even in a phone booth, Garmath was cautious, something that Dwig Brencott hadn't been at the Club Cadiz the night The Shadow overheard him.

Oddly enough, the voice that Garmath heard from the receiver was Dwig's. Placing his thin lips close to the mouthpiece, Garmath spoke in a voice much firmer than the rattly wheeze that he had used before.

Garmath's words were terse. He said:

"Take care of Sherbrock."

CHAPTER VI
THE WRONG FOEMEN

OUT of a rather tiresome evening at the Cobalt Club, Lamont Cranston had at least gleaned one point of information through his friendship with Commissioner Weston. In sifting the Walder murder anew, Weston had called in various jewelers, and the question of the six sapphires had been raised.

None knew who the owner of the gems could be, nor did they consider the matter relative to Walder's death since the exhibited gems were gone when robbery began. They felt that the owner of the sapphires might find himself in a spot like Walder, should his name be learned and made public.

Inasmuch as the police had traced none of the remaining killers, Commissioner Weston was not anxious to add fuel to new crime. He decided to let the subject pass, for the present.

Mention of the six sapphires, however, had turned the conversation to the Star of Delhi. Before they realized it, the jewelers were talking shop. It didn't take them long to agree on the very thing that Walder had said privately to Lenfell—that there was only one expert in New York to whom the cutting of the great stone could be entrusted: Roger Sherbrock.

Whether Sherbrock could have found time for the task was another question. According to the jewelers, the expert cutter was working night and day on orders of long standing.

The technical talk bored Weston, and his friend Cranston walked out in the middle of it. Inasmuch as The Shadow was interested in tracing the past history of the Star of Delhi, a prompt visit to Sherbrock's had become a logical step. Before leaving the club, The Shadow telephoned Margo and asked her to meet him near Sherbrock's place of business.

At present, The Shadow's agents, Moe Shrevnitz included, were busily seeking traces of Dwig Brencott, who had conveniently left town not long after the Walder affair. Upon meeting Margo, who came in her own car, The Shadow explained the new situation in Cranston's style.

He wanted Margo to drive him to Sherbrock's

and wait outside, while he interviewed the gem cutter. Margo observed that Cranston was carrying a briefcase. He opened it, to take out a small bag containing some uncut diamonds which he intended to show Sherbrock.

Margo suspected that the briefcase also contained a slouch hat and a black cloak; but if it did, the garments were packed so deeply that she could not see them.

Sherbrock's place was on the second floor of a rather old and dilapidated building in a fairly disreputable neighborhood. It looked like an ideal place for crime, except that the windows were barred. Lights from the second floor indicated that Sherbrock and other cutters were at work.

Alighting from Margo's car, Cranston strolled into the building, and just as he passed through the doorway the girl noticed that he had taken the briefcase with him.

A blunt-faced husky was in charge of the second-floor portal. He looked like a janitor, but acted as if he were Sherbrock's confidential secretary. Impressed by the visitor in evening clothes, he accepted Cranston's card and took it through an inner door that looked like the entrance to a strongroom.

While waiting, The Shadow observed several other small rooms with heavy doors, evidently the workshops assigned to the gem cutters.

There were large safes around the floor, at least a dozen of them, and when The Shadow was ushered into Sherbrock's own workroom, he saw three more in different corners of the room.

It was an office, also, for Sherbrock was seated behind a desk, going over stacks of correspondence. He looked up, studied Cranston briefly, then dismissed the husky watchman.

ROGER SHERBROCK had a strong, deep-lined face that marked him as a businessman, rather than an artificer; but exacting work had taken its toll of him. Any man who followed the profession of the lapidary invariably acquired a careful eye, and Sherbrock was no exception to the rule of gem cutters.

Nevertheless, he seemed able to take time out from his professional work to talk terms with customers, particularly those who looked as prosperous as Cranston.

Sherbrock was all business when The Shadow mentioned diamonds; but when the gems came from the briefcase, the lapidary promptly reached for a magnifying lens, pressed it to his eye and forgot that he had a customer, in order to examine the uncuts. Meanwhile, The Shadow made a further appraisal of the strongroom.

Behind Sherbrock's desk was a huge door that dwarfed the heavy safes. It was the front of a large vault that measured at least six feet in every direction, something which could readily be estimated, since the door of the vault was partly open.

Since the vault was empty, The Shadow assumed that Sherbrock placed the more valuable gems into some of the smaller safes, and wheeled them into the vault when he closed up shop. A very logical process, since movable safes could be rolled from one workroom to another, whenever required. Such a practice was the perfect way to keep rare jewels under lock, except when Sherbrock's assistants were actually working on them.

The uncut diamonds interested Sherbrock, but he was loath to discuss their merits at so late an hour.

"If you would come back tomorrow, Mr. Cranston," he suggested, in a brisk tone, "I should be glad to examine these diamonds in detail. If you care to leave them, I can give you a receipt for them. You doubtless know that some of the most famous gems in existence have been entrusted to our custody."

There was a keen look in Sherbrock's right eye, the result, perhaps, of its recent association with the magnifying lens. Yet his statement could have been a probing one, an effort to find out if Cranston supposed that Sherbrock had recently handled the cutting of the celebrated Star of Delhi. Certainly, the words offered The Shadow a chance to question Sherbrock on the subject.

But The Shadow ignored the opportunity. He preferred to have a longer chat with Sherbrock before discussing sapphires instead of diamonds. Reaching for the chamois bag that contained the diamonds, he quietly decided to take the uncut gems along with him.

That action, more than a blunt question, produced results with Sherbrock. Following his visitor to the door, the lapidary apologized for having been so abrupt.

"Some gems are coming in shortly," explained Sherbrock, a trifle nervously. "A very special assortment, from Baldwin & Associates, one of the most reliable wholesale houses in the city. They always insist upon a detailed receipt for all the gems they send us.

"Therefore, I shall be very busy for the next hour, at least. Frankly, I do not like to receive shipments so late at night. There have been too many robberies lately, and the Walder affair was so shocking that I have felt uneasy ever since."

Again, Sherbrock was laying a lead that might bring mention of the Star of Delhi. But his tone was such that anyone, even The Shadow, could have accepted it either of two ways.

It might be that Sherbrock knew much about the great sapphire, and was feeling Cranston out; on the contrary, Sherbrock gave something of an impression that he knew nothing of the gem's history and hoped that perhaps his visitor did.

The Shadow's only response was a disinterested nod. He strolled out through the main door, which the blunt-faced watchman held open for him.

As he descended the stairs, The Shadow saw an armored truck pull up in front of the building. It bore the name: "Baldwin & Associates."

It wasn't sight of the truck that interested The Shadow, mostly. The other thing he noticed was a low-built car that cruised past, for no good reason, and swung into an alleyway that led to the rear of Sherbrock's building.

Observing a rear door on the ground-floor passage, The Shadow stepped toward it, only to find it heavily locked. At that moment, two uniformed men came in from the armored truck and started upstairs, carrying a heavy box between them. The Shadow drew back beneath the stairs and heard their footsteps pass overhead.

A third man was overtaking the other two, for The Shadow could hear his quicker, lighter footsteps. Apparently, the burden carriers waited for him, for The Shadow heard voices; then the procession continued.

Meanwhile, The Shadow was sweeping hat and cloak from his briefcase, intending to obliterate the guise of Cranston and make a foray to the rear alley. New footsteps caused him to delay; they were very light and hesitating, as they came in from the front and moved a short way up the steps.

Dropping hat and cloak, The Shadow stepped into sight, as Cranston, just as he heard a girl's low, anxious voice:

"Lamont!"

It was Margo. The Shadow gave a quiet response as he stepped into sight. Margo clutched his arm across the banister. She didn't ask why he had gone from sight when the men from the truck entered. Margo had something more to tell.

"Those men who came in—"

"I saw them, Margo," The Shadow interposed. "The two in uniform."

"But did you see the third?"

The Shadow shook his head.

"I did!" blurted Margo. "He was Dwig Brencott!"

In a style that was rapid for Cranston, The Shadow took a look out to the street. The truck was a short distance ahead, and no one in it appeared to be keeping lookout. Drawing Margo from the doorway, The Shadow pointed her to her car.

"Have the motor running," he said calmly. "Others may be along. If they come too close, get started. Circle the block, and should they follow you, blow the horn. I'll recognize it."

Margo smiled despite her tensity. Her car had a musical chime that played "East Side—West Side," and very probably crooks like Dwig Brencott wouldn't be running around with horns of that type; hence Lamont wouldn't have much trouble identifying the right note.

With Margo gone, The Shadow picked up his cloak and hat in rapid time. He was donning them as he hurried up the stairs. Though speedy, he was quiet, for he wanted to see where the husky guard was. The fellow had gone from the door, leaving the way clear.

Sliding into the large room, The Shadow neared the door of Sherbrock's workshop office and was flat against the wall when the husky guardian came out, leaving the door ajar.

Peering through, The Shadow saw that Margo was right. The third man from the truck *was* Dwig. He was wearing street clothes, and he was leaning over Sherbrock's shoulder while the lapidary sorted a large array of jewelry that strewed the desk. On either side stood the two guards, watching the process.

A gun half drawn, The Shadow was waiting for a timely moment to move in on the conference, when he heard a hoarse shout from the guard at the outer door. As The Shadow turned, a surge of men came straight for Sherbrock's office, hurling the human watchdog ahead of them. So impetuous was their dash, that they flanked in upon The Shadow before he could wheel away.

Twisting back across the doorway, The Shadow tried to trick the sudden attackers by a reverse dive in the opposite direction—a move that would have succeeded, had not one stalwart supplied a lucky flying tackle that carried himself and The Shadow right through the doorway, into the light of Sherbrock's office, where they rolled aside, just clear of the trample from incoming feet.

It was then that The Shadow gave his tackler a further fling and came up, gun in hand, to meet a somewhat dazed opponent who had a revolver, but who was slow in bringing it to aim.

Finger on trigger, The Shadow could have fired, but didn't. He recognized the face of the fellow who had tackled him and come out worse in the sprawl. It was the swarthy countenance that belonged to Inspector Joe Cardona!

These men weren't more of Dwig's mob, coming to aid him in some fell work. The Shadow had encountered the wrong foemen—the police!

CHAPTER VII
PROOF OF CRIME

"LOOK OUT, Sherbrock!"

It was Dwig Brencott who shouted the warning, and his cry took the attention of the invading detectives.

They knew that Cardona had tackled an opponent they had scarcely seen, but supposed that their leader had come out winner. For some reason, Sherbrock was the man they had come after, so they surged straight for him.

But Dwig and his men were quicker. It was Dwig who grabbed Sherbrock and fairly hurled him into the open door, while the two men with him, mobbies in guard uniform, seized the desk and hoisted it at the invading police.

Detectives ducked amid a shower of scattering jewels. They fired as they dived aside, but their shots were wide, for the desk was heavy and they had to avoid it.

By the time Cardona's men had a chance to take real aim, Dwig's uniformed pals were into the vault, too, hauling the big door shut behind them. It had hardly closed, before bullets from police specials began to bash the steel front.

Finding that they couldn't drill the heavy metal, the detectives sprang to the door and tried to get it open. It was locked, automatically, from the inside.

In their futile effort to overtake four fugitives, the detectives left the door of the room quite clear. On his feet, The Shadow whisked out through that convenient exit, seen only by Cardona, who lost

Finger on trigger, The Shadow could have fired, but didn't. He recognized the face of the fellow.

sight of the cloaked fighter between blinks.

Then, seeing what the detectives were about, Cardona found his own feet and started to join them, only to stop short and listen.

Cardona heard a sound which his excited men did not—the rumble of an elevator, coming from the wall that held the vault door. Joe shouted for his men to stop attacking the steel barrier.

"They've taken a way out!" Cardona bawled. "That's no vault. It's an elevator! They're getting to the rear alley. Come on—we're going down to head them off!"

Getting to the alley wasn't so simple as Cardona supposed, considering that all the windows in Sherbrock's place were barred, while the rear passage, downstairs, ended in a heavily locked door.

Bellowing orders as he reached the top of the stairs, Cardona heard responses from officers below: men that he had left down there. They were trying to get through to the alley, and couldn't.

The only thing was to go around by the front, and Cardona beckoned them toward the stairs. Joe was in too great a hurry to think of something that would ordinarily have puzzled him: namely, what had become of The Shadow. Somewhere between Sherbrock's offices and the floor below, the cloaked intruder had mysteriously vanished!

It happened that The Shadow had found what Cardona wanted, a short route to the rear alley.

SHERBROCK'S windows were barred, but others on the second floor were not. Cutting out from Sherbrock's. The Shadow had swung in back

of the stairway leading up to the third floor, on chance of finding a suitable window—which he did.

It was narrow, barely large enough for The Shadow to slide his lithe form through. Once the squeeze was accomplished, he dropped to the ground below, the only token of his arrival being the *swish* of his cloak.

That sound wasn't heard. Others were making a loud clatter in the alley. Out of a rear door that slid suddenly open came Sherbrock, impelled to rapid gait by pressure of Dwig Brencott and the two thugs who wore the uniforms of armored-truck drivers.

There was a car in the alley, the low-built sedan that The Shadow had seen earlier. The fugitives dived into it, scooping up Sherbrock as he stumbled on the step.

The car was in motion when The Shadow turned and aimed low, swift shots at a rear tire. The answer was a *clang*, repeated with each bullet. The Shadow's fire had found an intervening fireplug, invisible against the fenders of the moving car. It was a squat fireplug, wide enough to stop two shots, though The Shadow sliced them at slightly different angles.

Those blasts brought a jolt from the car, as though it had been hit. The driver veered across the street and zigzagged back again, putting all his weight on the accelerator. Off at a wild speed, taking a crazy course, the car was roaring away in a fashion calculated to offset the efforts of any marksman.

The Shadow held his next shots until the car swung the corner. There, the zigzag couldn't help. He ripped a rear tire broadside, and saw the car take a real jounce under the impetus of the bursting rubber. The car disappeared around the corner, but it wasn't going far. The Shadow started on the run to overtake it.

From the sharp crack of the first shots, Cardona recognized that he had heard them through an open window. Still on the second floor, Joe dived beyond the stairs and thrust his head and shoulders out in time to see the effect of The Shadow's second fusillade.

Unable to wedge his stocky form through the narrow opening, Cardona decided to go out by the front way—a wise choice, considering that the fugitive car was no longer in the rear street.

Downstairs, Cardona found police cars and sprang into one, ordering a rapid chase.

Meanwhile, The Shadow had reached the rear corner, where he paused only to pick a darkened course across the side street to the wrecked car, which was tilted high upon the curb. Resuming his dash, he arrived at the sedan and found it empty.

A passageway between two buildings explained where Sherbrock and the crooks had gone. It was very short, and led to a wide street that cut through this neighborhood at an angle. Looking for a car, The Shadow saw one swing hesitatingly toward him. It was Margo's.

With a long leap, The Shadow hooked the door of the coupé, opened it, and dropped in beside the girl, so suddenly that she could only give a breathless gasp. Margo had been looking for Cranston, but by the time the door had slammed, she wasn't surprised to see The Shadow, instead.

In sharp, whispered tone, he was questioning if she had seen the fugitives. She hadn't, but she had spotted something else.

"The armored truck!" Margo exclaimed. "It started away before I did. It was gone when the police arrived. But I saw it again, just now, going around the next corner!"

THE SHADOW ordered a chase. As Margo put speed into the coupé, she realized that the armored truck must have picked up the fugitives that The Shadow was after. A few turns and she saw the truck once more, as did The Shadow. It was taking a corner and guns spouted from its loopholes. Wide shots, that didn't damage Margo's coupé.

Leaning from his window, The Shadow responded, aiming for the tires. His aim was accurate, but the truck's tires were bulletproof, as The Shadow expected, though he considered it worthwhile to test them. Then The Shadow's free hand, lunging to the left, shoved the wheel from Margo's control and sent the coupé skewing around a nearer corner.

Margo caught the idea as The Shadow let her resume control. He wanted to pursue the truck along a parallel street.

Across their path flashed a police car. Rapidly, The Shadow yanked the wheel again, thus informing Margo to follow the prowl car.

The police car was speeding for a corner where the armored truck was due, but The Shadow didn't wait for the fugitive vehicle to arrive. He blasted shots at the rear tires of the police car, and, fortunately, they didn't stand the gaff. The police car hit the curb at the corner just as the armored truck zoomed across.

If The Shadow hadn't halted them, Cardona and his companions would have been juggernauted by the heavier, more powerful vehicle.

It was The Shadow who resumed the chase alone, telling Margo to keep a respectful distance behind the armored truck, since it was impregnable, whereas her coupé was not. Gaining a big lead, the truck went through a swirl of traffic on an avenue.

Had Moe been at the wheel, and this car his specially geared cab, he might have followed through; but Margo and her coupé were not equal to the job. Halted by the traffic, Margo turned to The Shadow and began words of apology, that she did not complete.

The Shadow was gone.

At Sherbrock's, half an hour later, The Shadow arrived as Cranston, to find Weston in charge. He had called the Cobalt Club and learned that his friend, the commissioner, had left a message for him.

Order was restored in Sherbrock's office, and Cranston showed some surprise to find Weston sorting batches of jewels which lay on Sherbrock's desk. They happened to be the same lot that Sherbrock had been pawing over with Dwig.

"It was a tip-off, Cranston," informed the commissioner. "Someone called the club and told me that Sherbrock was fencing stolen gems. I have an idea that the person who called me might have been one of the jewelers who were at the club earlier. They left soon after you did!"

The Shadow didn't comment on that point; in fact, he rather doubted it. But the gems couldn't be overlooked. Weston had already checked them as loot that unknown crooks had acquired in the recent robbery of a Midwestern jewelry store.

"Very clever, Sherbrock was," continued Weston. "He had deliveries made in regular jeweler's trucks. The one that came tonight, bringing mobsters as its crew, bore the name of Baldwin & Associates. We've called them, and learned that both of their trucks are stored for the night. The one that came here was a fake."

"A fake, all right," put in Cardona, who was standing by. "It ducked away before we got here. We ran into it later, after it picked up Sherbrock and the other crooks."

Weston eyed Cardona, somewhat sharply.

"What about The Shadow, Inspector?"

"He was here," replied Cardona, laconically. "We ran into him at the office door. He slid out, and later he popped the tires on our car, just when he saw the truck."

"Rather odd," observed Weston, "for The Shadow to act in such fashion."

"Not at all," returned Cardona. "He was probably after Sherbrock, too. We met up with him by mistake. I figure he shot our tires so we wouldn't get into trouble with the truck."

THE explanation suited the commissioner. He reverted to the subject of Sherbrock.

"Here is full proof of crime," asserted Weston. "Stolen jewels in Sherbrock's possession; his flight through a secret rear exit; use of a fake truck that offered battle when it fled. Roger Sherbrock is unquestionably the head man behind the mob of jewel robbers. As an expert gem cutter, he was equipped to unload stolen goods by changing the appearance of the gems."

It was a strong indictment, one that The Shadow considered in detail when he was riding back to the Cobalt Club with Weston. But through that chain ran one important thread: every whit of evidence against Sherbrock was purely circumstantial.

Dwig Brencott could have brought the truck on his own. On such short inspection, Sherbrock couldn't have known that the jewels were stolen ones. The elevator in the big vault might well be a device that Sherbrock had installed as a way out if crooks invaded his premises, more logically than something that he had planned as an aid to crime.

As for his flight, Sherbrock hadn't any choice. He'd been rushed by Dwig and the uniformed mobbies, men that he might have supposed were actually from Baldwin & Associates. They hadn't given Sherbrock time to identify Cardona and his squad of detectives as men from police headquarters.

The Shadow could readily take that view, inasmuch as he had built up a circumstantial case against himself by first blocking Cardona's squad, and later wrecking a police car. Weston had dismissed those facts, because he regarded The Shadow as a foe to crime. Had it been anyone else, the commissioner would not have been so lenient.

Maybe Sherbrock's case deserved the same consideration that The Shadow's had received. The Shadow, deeply involved in the matter and a witness to occurrences at Sherbrock's, was definitely of that opinion. He wasn't willing to concede that Roger Sherbrock was the real head of the jewel-robbing outfit.

The Shadow's trail remained the same as before: to find Dwig Brencott and seek facts concerning six matched sapphires that had formerly been one great gem, the Star of Delhi!

CHAPTER VIII
REIGN OF MURDER

ALL during the next day, The Shadow kept in touch with Commissioner Weston. It didn't surprise the commissioner that his friend, Lamont Cranston, should drop into the office in the morning, suggest that they lunch together and, later, ride back to the office again in Weston's car. Contrarily, it rather pleased the commissioner.

Weston was a social climber and regarded Cranston as a good friend to have. Since Cranston was indifferent toward furthering acquaintances, it was usually Weston who insisted that the two go places together. Thus, on those rare occasions when Cranston cultivated Weston's company, the commissioner took it that his much-prized friend was coming around to Weston's own views.

Never did Weston guess that these periods really indicated Cranston's deep interest in some criminal investigation that the police were conducting; yet such was invariably the case. As Cranston, The Shadow had the habit of appearing quite bored at too much mention of current crime.

It was to Margo Lane that the quiet Mr. Cranston expressed the purpose of his frequent meetings with Weston during this important day. Cranston met Margo in a café lounge during the cocktail hour, and smiled approvingly when she ordered a Mirage, a pinkish drink that looked quite powerful, but did not have a drop of liquor in it.

"Good judgment, Margo," said Cranston, quietly. "I may be needing you later."

"After you've seen the commissioner again?" bantered Margo.

"Exactly!" Cranston glanced at his watch. "He will be at the Cobalt Club at half-past five. I want to be there when he arrives."

Margo took a sip of the Mirage, then queried:

"Why all this sudden interest?"

"Because of Sherbrock," replied Cranston. "I think that he may be innocent. If such is the case, crooks are holding him. Therefore it is important to check anything that the police learn about Sherbrock."

"So that you may get a trail to the guilty men—for instance, Dwig Brencott? Is that it, Lamont?"

For reply, Margo received a headshake.

"I can leave the guilty to The Shadow" was Cranston's laconic reply. "I merely felt that I, in my feeble way, might aid an innocent man."

Margo was still thinking that one over, when she saw Cranston stroll out to keep his appointment with the police commissioner. She approved Lamont's policy of discussing The Shadow as a distinct personality, but it did not deceive her. Margo had learned enough to understand the full extent of the present case.

With agents still on the hunt for Dwig Brencott, who had ducked away again without being recognized by Cardona and the detectives, The Shadow was personally keeping tabs with developments from the Sherbrock angle.

It was true that Cranston wanted to aid Sherbrock; equally certain that The Shadow could uncover mobsters if Sherbrock happened to be found. Hence, Margo could find no flaw in Lamont's statement.

Cranston would search for the innocent, and The Shadow would find the guilty. One and one made two—which happened to be one and the same.

Another point occurred to Margo. If Sherbrock happened to be the real head of the jewel mob, as the police believed, The Shadow—through his Cranston guise—would get to the guilty, anyway. But Margo accepted Lamont's opinion of Sherbrock at its face value. She only wished that she had asked him something else: his present views regarding the six sapphires, formerly the Star of Delhi.

Margo had come to the adamant conclusion that those gems, when located, would provide the complete answer to crime's riddle.

MATTERS promised well, as soon as The Shadow reached the Cobalt Club. He found Joe Cardona there, and the inspector was glad to see Weston's affable friend, Cranston, who was one man who often sided with Joe's opinions when they conflicted with the commissioner's.

Soon after, Weston arrived in a hurry, steered both men to a corner and spoke brusquely to Cardona:

"Well, Inspector, let me see the message!"

Inferring that Weston wasn't keeping secrets from Cranston, Cardona produced the message, explaining it as he did.

"It's a letter," said the inspector. "It came into Sherbrock's office today, in the last mail. Sent last night, according to the postmark, before Sherbrock's mob knew we got a tip-off."

"A letter?" demanded Weston bluntly. "Then why did you call it a message?"

"Because it looks like one, Commissioner."

It did look like a message. It was a half sheet of paper, folded twice, and its brief statement was typed in capitals that bore no signature. Weston read it, then showed it to Cranston. The message stated:

> H. J. COMING INTO NEW YORK TOMORROW. DON'T WORRY. EVERYTHING IS FIXED. JAKE WILL TAKE CARE OF HIM AT FIFTY-FIVE.

The commissioner grunted, then queried:

"What do you make of it?"

He put the question to Cranston, but it was Cardona who answered. Joe already had a theory.

"I'd say it meant five minutes to the hour," declared the inspector. "But which hour—that's the question. Unless the guy that wrote it was smart and tried some double talk. He might mean five-fifty. That would be ten minutes of six."

"Ridiculous!" snapped Weston. "Fifty-five is an address. Probably a number on some street right here in New York."

"There's more streets than there are hours, reminded Cardona. "With only twelve hours to pick from—"

"Twenty-four," corrected Weston. "Two sets of twelve."

"That's right," agreed Cardona. Then: "But there's two sets of streets, too—east and west. It doubles up on you, too, Commissioner."

The Shadow smiled at the final quip, but his face was turned away. He was going to a phone booth; he called Margo and suggested that she meet him promptly, outside the Cobalt Club in her coupé. Of course, his tone was Cranston's.

He was still Cranston as he stepped from the booth to find Weston and Cardona beckoning to him. From Weston's manner, The Shadow guessed that the commissioner had won out despite Cardona's neat dig.

"We're going on a tour," declared Weston. "We're going to zigzag across Fifth Avenue looking at all places that have the address of No. 55. Would you like to come along, Cranston?"

After brief consideration, The Shadow shook his head.

"It would take too long a time," he said, as he strolled with the others toward the door. "Besides, I'm expecting Miss Lane. We're going to have dinner at a nightclub. I don't know just which one—"

They had reached the street when Cranston's tone took its pause. His companions stared, wondering what had struck him. Slowly, he said:

"I wonder—"

Another pause, during which Margo's car swept into sight around the corner. Then Cranston added:

"I wonder if fifty-five could mean a street, rather than a building number?"

Weston shook his head; then, observing Cranston's fixed expression, the commissioner demanded why his friend had put the query.

"Because fifty-five would then mean Fifty-fifth Street" was The Shadow's reply. "As I recall it, there is a nightclub up there that took its name from the number of the street. It is called Club Fifty-five."

That was enough for Weston. He exclaimed the name, "Fifty-five!" and Cardona echoed it. Both were anxious to get started, but since Margo had by then arrived, Cranston decided to go in her car, saying that Club Fifty-five would be a good place to dine in case the lead proved worthless.

BOTH cars reached Club Fifty-five at the same time. By then, Cranston had explained matters to Margo; while Cardona, in his turn, had been expressing ideas to Weston.

Joe was so enthused that he started into the nightclub ahead of the others, flashed a badge at a startled head waiter and demanded:

"Who's Jake?"

"Why ... why everything's jake!" the head waiter began. Then, properly comprehending the query, he added: "I guess you mean Jake, the barkeeper—over there."

There was just one barkeep on duty, a beefy man who was serving a drink to a rather drowsy customer perched on a stool, with head tilted against his arm. Cardona was about to start toward the bar, when Cranston's hand restrained him.

"Perhaps it would be better," suggested The Shadow quietly, "if one of us stopped there first. Myself, for example—or Miss Lane."

With Weston nodding, Cardona agreed, realizing that it would give him a chance to cover Jake without the barkeeper knowing it. The Shadow turned toward Margo in Cranston's polite manner. With a smile, the girl said:

"Very well, Lamont."

Reaching the bar while the others watched, Margo took a stool and ordered a drink. She was trying not to stare at Jake; hence her eyes went to the tipsy-looking customer who was slouched upon the bar.

She saw the drink that Jake had served the fellow, just beyond the reach of the man's outstretched hand. Before making Margo's drink, Jake tapped the lounging customer on the shoulder.

Rather fascinated, Margo watched the man's hand move automatically toward the waiting glass, as though he saw it without lifting his eyes. The horror of the thing didn't grip her, until that moving hand had slid past the drink without touching it. By then, his shoulders were on the move, slumping downward. His head turned as he started a contorted sprawl from the bar stool.

Margo shrieked even before the toppling body hit the floor, for on the way, she saw the tumbling man's face as it tilted away from his arm.

The face was bloated, its lips spread in a frozen grin. Eyes were glazed and glaring, like objects of stone. Mere sight of them gave Margo the terrifying truth.

The man was dead!

Cranston, Weston and Cardona were springing toward the bar, when Margo loosed the scream. But they were arriving on the scene too late. A reign of murder had begun!

CHAPTER IX
DEATH FINDS DEATH

"YOU'LL talk, Jake!"

Cardona had been repeating the same words for nearly half an hour, but without result. Jake, the barkeeper, had done all the talking that he could. Jake had tried to bolt when the dead man hit the floor, but he claimed he didn't know that the customer had died.

It was the sight of others coming to grab him that worried Jake. He had something of a criminal past—he admitted it—but he had been going straight for the past few years.

Cardona wasn't convinced, which was why he kept on quizzing Jake; but The Shadow, silent as he posed as Cranston, was quite sure that the barkeeper told the truth.

The dead man had been poisoned, which made it look bad for Jake, though the beefy bartender swore that he hadn't slipped anything lethal into any of the three drinks that the man had taken.

"This is a reliable place," Jake insisted. "We wouldn't even hand a tough guy a Mickey Finn. What would I gain sticking around, if I'd croaked the guy?"

That was just it. What would Jake have gained? Nothing, in The Shadow's silent opinion. He saw what lay behind the message that had come to Sherbrock's.

It was a fake tip-off, like the one that the police received the night before. Real murderers had known that a victim would die at Club Fifty-five, and were trying to plant the job on Jake because of the bartender's questionable past.

The dead man's name was Howard Jorton, which fitted the initials "H. J." mentioned in the note. He was well-dressed, had plenty of money in his pocket, and was fairly well-known at Club Fifty-five, where he often came to spend the late afternoon.

Jorton was in the rug business, as evidenced by cards found on his person, but his office was closed when Weston tried to reach it by telephone. Apparently, Jorton had lived at some hotel, because there was a big key in his pocket with the number 331 on it; but it didn't bear the name of the hotel.

Having called headquarters to make a general checkup on hotels, Weston began an examination of Jorton's effects. Money, cards, and other items were spread along the bar, when Cranston called attention to a ring that Jorton wore on a finger of his left hand.

It was a gold ring, with a fair-sized stone that had no color. Weston drew it from the man's finger, which was rather difficult, since Jorton's hands were swollen. The police surgeon, recently arrived, attributed the swelling to the effect of the poison, which had not yet been identified.

"A cheap stone," declared Weston, as he held the ring to the light. "Too sparkling to be glass, but not good enough for a genuine diamond."

"A variety of quartz," identified The Shadow. "Such stones are often sold under the name of Brazilian diamonds. You are right, Commissioner—they are very cheap, though persons are sometimes deceived by them."

A telephone bell was ringing. Taking it to be a call from headquarters, Weston answered. His voice immediately became both brisk and eager.

"Yes, yes!" he exclaimed. "Mr. Jorton is here ... He's to call Mr. Bayle? Which Mr. Bayle? ... I see, Moreland Bayle. May I ask who you are? ... You're Bayle's butler—"

A second later, Weston was hammering at the receiver hook. The speaker at the other end had hung up very suddenly. Pouncing for the phone book, Weston was trying to find the name of Bayle, when Cranston reached across his shoulder and pointed it out for him.

"Moreland Bayle—"

After the name, Weston repeated the number from the directory. But when he called Bayle's number, he received no reply, not even from the mysterious butler, a point which troubled The Shadow. The call had all the earmarks of another so-called tip-off, designed by crooks. It produced the sinister picture of further crime to come.

THERE was nothing to do but go to Bayle's, so Weston started, taking Cranston and Margo along in his official car, while Cardona remained at Club Fifty-five to clear up what little he could in the Jorton case.

Bayle's address turned out to be a small apartment house, a converted dwelling, and Weston was pressing at the button which bore Bayle's name, when a taxicab pulled up in front.

It was The Shadow who stepped out to meet it, when he saw the driver give a puzzled stare into the rear seat. Before the driver could object, Cranston was opening the rear door of the cab.

The act brought another shriek from Margo, who was standing by, though she managed to stifle the cry somewhat. However, it was enough to bring Weston full about in time to see the reason.

A body was rolling from the cab, to hit the curb and stretch flat before The Shadow could stop the force of its dead weight. Arriving at Cranston's side, the police commissioner stared down at a horrible, grinning face, quite as bloated as Jorton's.

Then came Cranston's calm-toned statement of identity:

"Moreland Bayle."

The Shadow was correct. Examination of the victim's pockets proved him to be Moreland Bayle, traveling representative of a large paper company. The gulping cab driver declared that he had picked up his fare at the Pennsylvania Station, from an incoming train.

It was plain to The Shadow that murderers had not cared just where Bayle died, though they would probably have preferred him to fall from a cab, the way he had. The pressing question was whether or not Bayle's death would produce another planted lead, as Jorton's had.

No other name was indicated among Bayle's effects, but the man was wearing something which, to The Shadow, was a menacing token.

The object was a cheap ring, but its stone was Spanish quartz, rather than Brazilian. Almost colorless, the so-called gem had a faint tint of amber, which might have led a person of credulity and imagination to accept it as a topaz. It wasn't in keeping for Bayle to be wearing such a ring, any more than Jorton.

Accepting Cranston's suggestion that they go up to Bayle's apartment, Weston was going through the door of the house, when his friend stopped him. In the slit of Bayle's mailbox The Shadow observed the mere corner of a sheet of paper, and drew it out.

The paper had a calling card attached to it by a paper clip. It bore the printed name: "Arthur Halden." Down in a lower corner was the name of a hotel, the Marwood.

It wasn't far to Halden's hotel. Having hailed a patrol car and putting the officers in charge of Bayle's body, Weston suggested a quick trip to the Marwood. The place turned out to be a small one, and an affable clerk nodded as soon as Halden's name was mentioned.

"Mr. Halden is in," the clerk said. "He called me a while ago. At least, he started to, and then hung up. I'll ring him."

"We'd better go up," decided Weston. "Give me a passkey."

THEY reached Halden's room. While Weston was unlocking the door, Margo stepped forward, only to be pressed back by Cranston's arm. That left it to Weston to utter the gasp of horror, when he pressed the door wide.

The commissioner voiced Cranston's name, and his friend stepped calmly past him, to view a sight which he fully expected.

Flat on the floor lay a tall man, his face turned toward the doorway, his features skewed in a one-sided smile that was very far from pleasant. But it wasn't the glimmer of bulging eyes that attracted The Shadow's chief attention.

He had expected to find Arthur Halden dead. More important was the gleam that came from the finger of the man's stiffened hand, the one that clamped the telephone, which Halden hadn't quite been able to put in use for a frantic call.

The gleam was of a slightly pinkish hue, produced by a stone which The Shadow classed as rose quartz, quite as cheap as the settings in the finger rings worn by the two previous victims, Jorton and Bayle.

Again, death had arrived ahead of both The Shadow and the law. Murder still reigned; how many more victims it would take was a matter for conjecture, even by The Shadow.

He, the investigator who had so often run down crime, could only hope that the toll of dead men would stop before it reached the total of six!

CHAPTER X
THE STOLEN LINK

THE clerk at the Hotel Marwood was a better informant than either the bartender who had seen Jorton die, or the cab driver who had brought Bayle's body home. The clerk knew quite a lot about Arthur Halden. The dead man, he said, was a former stock broker who had retired during a flush period of more than ten years before.

Halden was quite wealthy and still had dabbled in the market, advising friends, as well. However, he was living on his investments, which weren't paying the old-time dividends; hence he preferred a reasonably priced hotel like the Marwood.

In trying to recall the names of Halden's friends, the clerk promptly remembered one. The man in question was Kirk Raft, who had a real-estate office on upper Broadway, not far from the Marwood. The clerk remembered Raft, especially, because there had been a phone call from the realtor's office while Weston and his friend, Cranston, were coming down from Halden's apartment.

Since Raft's office was near, Weston suggested an immediate trip there. On the way, he confided:

"This is horrible business, Cranston, but we're getting to the heart of it. I wouldn't be surprised if this man Raft is the murderer!"

The Shadow deemed quite otherwise, but did not express his real opinion. As they were alighting from the commissioner's car, he helped Margo out and remarked that she was looking pale.

"You'd better stay outside," said The Shadow, "and get some fresh air."

"A good idea," returned Margo. "I'll walk to the corner, Lamont, and get some cigarettes."

A gesture of The Shadow's hand had given her the cue. As Margo stepped away, she heard Cranston's undertone:

"Try to get Shrevvy here."

Margo knew how that could be accomplished. It meant a call to a man named Burbank, who always seemed to be on duty. He was a contact with Harry Vincent, Moe Shrevnitz, and other agents. If they were available, Burbank would summon them. But Margo really felt sick as she walked toward the store.

She'd received her first indication that Cranston did not consider the chain of death ended. She realized that he was hoping for another link from Raft's, further on, and that this time he would seek some pretext to get away from Weston and speed ahead of the commissioner, in an effort to forestall some other tragedy. That was why Shrevvy would be required. His cab would help.

Meanwhile, Commissioner Weston was striding into Raft's real-estate office with an air of self-satisfied importance. He saw a girl seated at a desk and introduced himself, along with Cranston.

The girl said that Mr. Raft was working late and didn't like to be disturbed, but that she would ring his private office. Stopping her, Weston said that he would go into the other office without such unnecessary formality.

The commissioner drew a gun as he opened the door. Just why he pictured Kirk Raft as a hand in crime was something that Weston couldn't explain afterward. His mistaken confidence, however, reversed itself in a fashion that jarred him worse than at Halden's. Half into the lighted office, Weston actually dropped his gun and clamped a hand to his dampening forehead.

KIRK RAFT was a worse sight than any of the former victims. He was a scrawny man, with tight-skinned face, and the effects of the poison had changed his dead face into a human skull.

Lips were scarcely visible above and below his grinning teeth. His eyes seemed sunken in their sockets, but small though they were, they carried the ugly death glisten that Weston had viewed before.

One of Raft's hands, his right, was stretched so far across the desk that it dangled from the edge. Its fingers were spread like a starfish, but none of them wore a ring. However, the left hand was still to be considered. It was doubled beneath Raft's slanted body, quite out of sight.

Helping Weston to a chair, The Shadow rounded the desk and started to draw the doubled left hand into sight. It was then that Weston's wits returned.

"No, no, Cranston!" he exclaimed, rising. "Touch nothing for the present! I must call Inspector Cardona and have him catch up with us, bringing the police surgeon. Four deaths within a half hour! They are more than I can stomach!"

The Shadow could have suggested that Weston get over his weakness and prepare for further shocks, but he was more interested in the ring, that now showed on Raft's partly raised left hand.

It was another specimen of cheap jewelry, a smooth, roundish stone like those that had adorned the other victims, but this one had a trifling lavender tinge. It was a poor variety of domestic amethyst, nothing more, and as The Shadow tilted a light toward it, what little color the stone had faded very promptly.

The girl was coming from the front office. The Shadow stopped her on the threshold. He used Cranston's way of breaking the news calmly, but he was glad when Margo appeared, for Raft's helper had gone white and limp, even without seeing her employer's body.

Margo produced some smelling salts, but before bringing the stenographer from her fainting spell, she thought it wise to mention something that Cranston wanted to know about.

"You can expect Shrevvy," she whispered, "in about ten minutes."

Back in Raft's office, The Shadow found Weston rummaging through the realtor's desk. He'd reached Cardona by telephone, and the ace inspector was on his way. When things became desperate. Weston sometimes relied on Cardona's hunches—for which Joe was famous; though, ordinarily, the police commissioner scoffed at guesswork.

Being in one of his hunch-accepting moods, Weston still insisted that Raft's body be left untouched, on the chance that Cardona might learn something when he viewed it as it was.

The wait actually worried The Shadow. He was looking at Raft's right arm; beneath its elbow, he saw something that appeared to be a memo pad. It was very possible that such a pad would show a notation leading to someone else. However, since The Shadow was depending upon Moe's cab, it was as well to wait.

Had Moe arrived first, The Shadow might have done some deft work, sneaking the telltale pad from under the dead arm. But it happened that Cardona was the first man to appear. He entered the office and stared glumly at Raft's body. The Shadow was about to point out the memo pad, when an interruption came.

A telegraph boy had entered the real-estate office and was arguing with officers outside. They sent him in to the commissioner, and the messenger stared blankly at Raft's body.

He was an oldish chap, the messenger, well over twenty-one, of the jockey type that never seemed to outgrow the job of delivering telegrams. He handed the telegram envelope to Weston, mentioning that it was for Mr. Raft.

The telegram wasn't very important. It was from an upstate real-estate concern, quoting prices on some lots. Cardona crowded in to have a look at it, while the commissioner was showing it to Cranston.

The messenger inquired drearily if there was a reply. When Weston told him no, the fellow shambled from the office, clamping his hat upon his head.

Looking outward, The Shadow saw Moe's cab pulling up in front. Officers were going out to order it away, and it was Cranston's part to explain the cab's arrival.

He motioned Margo toward the outer door as the messenger passed through; then, following, The Shadow quietly told the officers that the cab had come for Miss Lane.

HELPING Margo into the cab, The Shadow was about to tell her to have Moe cruise around the block, when a better idea occurred to him. In this weird trail of death, the merest trifles might prove important. Certainly, anything that the police ignored was worthy of observation.

At the corner ahead, The Shadow saw the telegraph messenger turning from sight, whistling as he went. On a hunch less justifiable than most of Cardona's, The Shadow said to Margo:

"Have Shrevvy follow him."

Returning through the outer office, The Shadow indulged in one of the slight smiles that sometimes showed themselves on the usually immobile lips of Cranston. He'd supplied another little touch, to dispel Margo's long-held belief that Cranston was The Shadow.

Sending her with Moe along the route of a sauntering messenger boy wouldn't strike Margo as worthy of The Shadow. She would regard it as real stupidity on Cranston's part, when the trail wound up at a telegraph office.

Of course, the cab would then return, and The Shadow would have it later; at least, so he thought, until he reached Raft's private office again. He came just in time to see Cardona reach for the dead man's right arm, raise it and look beneath.

The memo pad was gone!

Only one person could have taken it: the telegraph messenger! Small wonder that he had looked so old; the fellow was a fake, a crook disguised in uniform, like the men in the truck at Sherbrock's!

The Shadow recalled instantly how Cardona had blocked his view of the messenger while the fellow was in Raft's office. That was when the pretended messenger had snagged the memo pad and slipped it into his cap!

Like other planted clues, the memo pad had been a link arranged by murderers to carry the death trail farther. For some reason, men of crime had found it necessary to eliminate that lead. But the stolen link still existed, and The Shadow had sent Margo along the trail!

It was fortunate that she was in Moe's cab, for Shrevvy was a very clever hackie, a good man at dodging trouble. Nevertheless, The Shadow promptly told Weston, in Cranston's calmest manner, that four deaths were enough for anyone.

Weston agreed. He couldn't blame Cranston for deciding to go back to the club.

Thus did The Shadow manage to be on his way, to again become a figure clad in black, a hidden crime hunter who would be in readiness for whatever word might reach him, regarding the trail of the stolen link to death!

CHAPTER XI
THE BATTLER IN BLACK

MARGO LANE was more than ever convinced that Lamont Cranston was The Shadow. Only The Shadow could have snapped up so innocent a trail as that of a loitering telegraph messenger and picked it as a prize.

For two blocks, Margo had felt herself upon a stupid quest, wondering why Moe, the patient hackie, was falling for the joke and sneaking the cab at a snail's pace along the curb.

Then, when the messenger looked back from another corner, Margo's opinion reversed itself. He didn't spot the cab, for Moe had it out of sight between two other cars that were parked on the street. But Margo saw the messenger's face, with its ugly, triumphant leer. She also spied him start into a run as he took the corner.

Moe followed after him. Around the corner, the fake messenger was peeling off his uniform jacket as he sprang into a waiting car manned by other thugs. From then on, Margo was glad that she wasn't at the wheel of her own coupé, trying to trail the group ahead. Shrevvy was much better qualified for that very ticklish job.

He let the other car get out of sight before its passengers could notice the cab behind. Then, taking cross streets, mingling with traffic, Moe picked the right car from a dozen others and was back on the trail again.

Not only on the trail, but free to follow closer, because the men ahead did not suspect his cab. Of all vehicles, taxicabs, the commonest type in Manhattan, were the best to use in work like this.

Margo was gradually piecing facts together. She knew that each murder had been the lead to the next, and reasoned that, in this case, something different had occurred. It could only be that the fugitive messenger had taken the clue that linked Raft's death to one to follow.

But Margo couldn't quite figure why crooks had planted something and then removed it. She felt sure, however, that The Shadow could answer that question, and probably would—through Lamont Cranston—when she met him later.

Events caused Margo to drop that problem. The trail was leading into a rather sinister portion of the East Side, where shabby old buildings ranged on each side of an elevated line. Such neighborhoods were all right normally, but when mobsters dived into them, every house became menacing.

When the car ahead rolled into a side street that stretched, dark and gloomy, toward the river, Margo felt that they were near the end of the ride.

She was right. Crooks halted their car and disembarked, while Moe deftly extinguished the cab lights and slid into a parking space some distance behind. Margo watched slinky figures cross the sidewalk and sneak into a basement. She couldn't even tell which one had been the messenger boy.

The fact pleased her. It meant that the sidewalk was dark enough for her to do some stealthy work on her own. She opened the rear door of the cab, caught a warning gesture from Moe. Coolly, Margo said:

"It's all right, Shrevvy. I'll be careful."

"They may have a lookout," voiced Moe, shrewdly. "Those guys can konk you quick. I ought to know."

He rubbed his head, as though recalling a few such experiences. Margo laughed lightly, though she was taking the words to heart.

"I'll be very careful, Shrevvy."

MARGO was true to her word. She was wearing a dark dress, which enabled her to keep nicely unobserved as she moved along the line of basement fronts. But, as she neared the one where the crooks had entered, she remembered her promise to Moe.

It was well that she did. As Margo waited, one doorway short, she saw a huddling man shift from the adjoining doorstep.

Drawing back, Margo felt quite secure, though annoyed because she couldn't get closer. This was really a job for The Shadow, and Margo realized it. There was just a chance that luck might come her way—and it did.

The reason that the lookout had shifted was because a door was opening. Men emerged in a shaft of dim light, and Margo was able to overhear their voices. Not only that, she saw a face exceedingly like the sleek but sallow countenance of Dwig Brencott.

The sleek man spoke.

"A couple of you lugs cruise around," he said. "The Shadow has got wise to too much, and even when The Shadow learns too little, he knows too much. So keep cruising for a half hour; then duck out. I'll call you later."

As the door closed, Margo walked away. She was trembling during the return trip to the cab, fearing every moment that hands might fling from a doorway and grip her. Straight opposite the cab, she was afraid that some clatter from her high heels might betray her, so she took off her shoes and carried them as she stole across the sidewalk.

In the cab, her nerve returned. She was putting on her shoes again, as she leaned to the front seat and said:

"We'd better start, Shrevvy—"

It was then that a real horror overwhelmed Margo. The cab no longer had a driver!

Sinking back, the girl opened her purse and tried to draw out a small automatic that she had there; but her fingers were gone numb.

Not that Margo was short on nerve; she could take care of herself in a pinch; otherwise, she wouldn't be working for The Shadow. But the belief that she might first have to rescue Shrevvy from the clinches of a mob was enough to mentally stun her.

Someone bounded into the cab from the street side and took the wheel. Margo caught a grip on the gun and shoved it forward, saying boldly:

"Don't move!"

A voice answered. It was Moe's. He thought that Margo meant the cab, not himself.

"O.K.," he said. "What are they doing? Prowling around?"

"They may be." Margo slid the gun back into the bag. She was glad Moe hadn't spied the weapon. "Only they're in a car—the ones we've got to avoid."

Moe gave a grunt, as though he expected what Margo told him. Then:

"Find out anything?" he asked.

"Dwig is in the hideaway," replied Margo. "He'll be there for the next half hour."

"Good enough!"

With that, Moe started the cab. It dawned on Margo that he must have called Burbank, saying that he thought they had located Dwig and that the wanted crook would be around awhile.

Guesswork on Moe's part, but the sort The Shadow liked, because it could be promptly countermanded if it turned out wrong. Otherwise, it would stand, and was a great timesaver, for, if right, such guesses would enable The Shadow to make prompt plans.

There was one point, however, that Margo couldn't fathom. As they turned into an avenue, she questioned:

"Where are you taking me, Shrevvy?"

"To keep your date" was the reply. "The one you made with Mr. Cranston. He said to meet him at the Hotel Metrolite, didn't he?"

Lamont hadn't said anything of the sort, but Margo did not dispute the matter. She was sure that Moe had been told to remind her of the imaginary date. Since it was certainly time for dinner, Margo relaxed, while the cab zigzagged from street to avenue.

As they swung a corner sharply, she landed half around in the rear seat and had a look through the back window.

WHAT she saw, worried Margo. A coupé was jabbing past the same corner, acting very much as if on the cab's trail. Thoughts of the cruising car rang home to Margo. She exclaimed to Moe:

"They're following us! Like we followed them!"

Taking a look in the mirror, Moe certified Margo's statement and sped the cab ahead. He was neatly in advance when he reached the side door of the Metrolite, but he didn't stop.

Instead, Moe whizzed past, went along the darkened street and swung around the block. He went by so fast, that Margo did not get a look at the hotel's side door.

A man was lounging there: Lamont Cranston. He not only saw the cab, he observed that a suspicious car was trailing it.

Things happened while those cars were rounding the block. Cranston became a figure in black: The Shadow. He signaled some blinks with a tiny flashlight; they were seen across the street. The Shadow had merged with darkness, away from the hotel door, when Moe's cab came past again.

This time, Moe slackened, and Margo thought that he intended to stop; but, instead, he kept on. Of course, the trailing coupé slowed when the cab did, but it didn't resume its speed.

A door yanked open on the driver's side of the coupé. Something hit the thug and sent him clear across the car into his companion's lap. Before the other hoodlum could get rid of the burdening driver, his head took a hard jolt, too.

By then, there were three in the car, and the driver was The Shadow. He pulled to the far curb and stepped out. Harry Vincent promptly joined him; The Shadow blinked the flashlight on the faces of the stunned men. Seeing that they would stay put awhile, he turned the car over to Harry, who drove away.

Finishing another tour around the block, Moe stopped at the Metrolite and let Margo out. Very anxiously, she looked back toward the corner, then decided that Moe must have managed to slip the trailing car. Margo went into the hotel, while Moe was looking at a green blink from a flashlight, farther down the street.

Wheeling over, Moe picked up The Shadow and made a brief report. The Shadow ordered a prompt return to Dwig's hideout.

"Sorry about Miss Lane," informed Moe. "She's expecting to meet Mr. Cranston at the Metrolite."

"Rather odd," returned The Shadow. "He didn't tell her that he would be there."

"No," Moe admitted. "But I did."

"Then Cranston can blame it on you?"

The Shadow's tone ended with a whispered laugh that carried nothing more significant than the fact that Margo Lane might have a very long wait before she dined with her friend Lamont Cranston.

CHAPTER XII
THE FIFTH VICTIM

IN his squalid basement hideaway, Dwig Brencott was talking on the telephone, while other men stood by.

Sleek, suave of tone, Dwig was a contrast to his companions. They were husky, but dumb-faced, recruits that Dwig had signed to take the place of the lamented gunzels who had suffered, permanently, from meeting with The Shadow and the police.

Except for the telephone, the hideaway had no furnishings other than a table and some broken-down chairs. It was quite apparent that Dwig, when he gestured for his tribe to follow him, intended to abandon the place. The Shadow could tell that from the looks of the place.

For The Shadow was present, though unseen.

The cloaked investigator had entered the hideaway from the back.

Peering through a partly opened door, he heard Dwig say: "Let's go!" Then, followed by his small but tough crew, Dwig went out through the front.

Even though he glanced back, Dwig did not see The Shadow. Motionless in the other doorway, the cloaked observer had benefit of darkness; but that was not all. It was unlikely that Dwig *could* have seen The Shadow.

Using the system of remaining absolutely immobile, with even his thoughts fixed, The Shadow was practicing the ways of the Tibetan mystics.

It was their belief that such concentration could produce the equivalent of invisibility. Through experience, The Shadow had demonstrated that complete immobility did reduce an observer's chances to almost nil.

It produced the semblance of a power through which he could cloud men's minds; and many of The Shadow's enemies had sworn that he had suddenly appeared in the midst of a lighted room before their startled eyes.

Only a few could claim that they had seen The Shadow vanish, for the simple reason that it was much more difficult the other way about. Though The Shadow could fade rapidly into darkness, he required ideal conditions if he sought to remain on the very ground, unnoticed. Once crooks saw The Shadow, their minds became too excited to be readily quieted.

If Dwig had any suspicions that The Shadow might be about, they were so vague that they did not bother him. His mind was at ease and tending toward other matters.

Had The Shadow spoken at that moment, in ventriloquial style, he could have startled Dwig into absolute bewilderment. In fact, Dwig would have imagined The Shadow almost anywhere except at the spot where he actually was.

But The Shadow did not speak; nor did he choose to reveal himself. He simply waited, motionless, until Dwig had followed the others outside. Then came the slightest stir amid the darkness, the merest *swish* of a black cloak, as The Shadow made his own departure from the rear of the hideout.

Moe's cab was waiting in the next street; from then on, it became the medium whereby The Shadow kept close to Dwig and his crew without being discovered.

The fact that his cruising bruisers had not returned was proof sufficient to Dwig that the way was clear. He'd told them to go their way, and it didn't occur to him that The Shadow might have put them out of the picture by virtue of a surprise attack. Hence, Dwig was going his own way also and providing The Shadow with a very easy trail.

Where that trail would lead was no mystery to The Shadow.

Analyzing the matter of the stolen message more deeply than Margo had, The Shadow reduced it to but one solution. Mobsters had been forced to remove the link to a fifth murder because, somehow, that particular crime had fallen through. If the police had found the name on the memo pad beneath Raft's elbow, they might have been able to forestall a coming crime.

That, in itself, was an important point.

The very oddity of the four deaths—all by poison, and striking almost at an appointed hour—indicated definitely that they were prearranged. Therefore, Dwig had probably supposed that the fifth man was dead, too, until some last-minute information had indicated otherwise. Naturally, since a murder scheme had slipped, Dwig, at present, was out to amend it.

Dwig and his mob were actually leading The Shadow to the fifth victim *before* death was delivered. Somewhere along this trail, The Shadow would have to pass the killers and be the first to reach the helpless man they sought!

THE trail narrowed suddenly, as the car ahead stopped near an elevated railway station. Moe parked on the other side of the avenue, and The Shadow glided from the cab, prepared to follow an elusive course beneath the el pillars, in case Dwig tried a sudden move.

Crooks were watching the steps that came down from the elevated station; it might be that they intended to waylay their quarry when he descended from the platform.

A man appeared from that direction. He was well-dressed, fairly tall, and with an intelligent square-jawed face. His lined features marked him past middle age, but his gait was agile. His expression was a troubled one—that of a man who was bound upon an unpleasant duty; but The Shadow noticed no trace of fear.

Reaching shelter beside the el steps, The Shadow pointed an automatic for the window of the sedan in which Dwig and the other thugs were seated.

The mere glint of a revolver barrel would have meant a bullet for the man who showed the gun; but no one in the car tempted The Shadow's aim. Dwig and his watchers let the square-jawed man go past them, but when he had walked a half block, their car moved slowly in the same direction.

It appeared that they preferred to trail their prospective victim to some place where they could kill him with less notice.

Back in Moe's cab, The Shadow had his driver proceed along the same trail. Lights extinguished, the cab sneaked neatly up behind the sedan. The other car stopped; Moe did the same.

The walking man had stopped at a dingy brick house. Abruptly, he went up the steps and into the place. Dwig's car started away, but The Shadow told Moe to wait. He foresaw what the crooks intended. They were going around to the back, to find another way into the house.

Inadvertently, they were giving The Shadow the very chance he wanted. By using the front door, The Shadow could overtake the victim first.

Swiftly, The Shadow left the cab; fleetingly, Moe saw him on the house steps. Then, entering a gloomy hall, The Shadow heard creaks from the floor above and went directly for a flight of stairs.

By the time he had reached the second floor, the man ahead was on the third. As The Shadow neared the top of the next flight, he saw his man stop at a door.

After a few sharp knocks, the man spoke a name:

"Glevin!"

There was no answer. The man rapped again, spoke louder. His tone had an accusing note.

"Glevin!" he repeated. "This is Mr. Talney. Louis Talney. I want to speak to you!"

There was no response. For the first time, Talney exhibited actual hostility. Clamping his left hand firmly on the doorknob, he prepared to drive his shoulder forward, while his right hand drew a small, stubby revolver.

"I'm coming in, Glevin!"

Turning the knob, Talney jabbed his shoulder hard. Whether he expected to crack the rather flimsy door, or merely alarm Glevin, was difficult to tell. In fact, The Shadow did not have time—or need—to decide the question. The door was unlocked, something that Talney had not suspected. Swinging inward, the door carried the tall man on a long lunge.

Talney must have caught himself as he gasped. But it wasn't his near sprawl that brought the odd sound from his lips. The word that Talney gasped was proof of some different sort of shock. The word was a name:

"Glevin!"

FROM the doorway, The Shadow viewed the sight that had so horrified Talney. Small wonder that the tall man was aghast, for it was his first view of the sort of death that The Shadow, as Cranston, had seen on display four times upon this very evening.

Upon a cot that stood beyond a strip of frayed green carpet lay a dead man who stared straight toward the ceiling—a corpse with staring, glassy eyes and bloated features that bore only a grotesque resemblance to anything human. Yet Talney had managed to recognize the face as Glevin's, which proved he must have known the man well.

Standing beside the cot, Talney reached gingerly and lifted Glevin's left hand. From it, he removed a finger ring, which he held toward the gaslight. The ring had a roundish stone, as colorless as a chunk of glass. Stunned by the tragedy of Glevin's death, Talney spoke half aloud:

"I trusted you, Glevin, as a faithful servant. Yet you stole ... a worthless ring."

Had The Shadow been acquainted with plans of Armand Lenfell, he would have known that Louis Talney was the fifth member of the secret six; also, that Glevin was the servant who had come in Talney's stead to receive a sapphire ring from Lenfell.

Jorton, Bayle, Halden, Raft—they were the four hooded men who had received rings. Talney was the fifth. Yet *none* of those rings bore the blue hue of a sapphire, whether real or imitation; nor did *any* show the peculiar star formation that should have been their characteristic!

Talney's bewilderment proved The Shadow's present theory: that all five of the worthless rings had once been valued as precious. So stupefied was Talney that The Shadow ended his immobile vigil and moved into the room, approaching the dumfounded man beside the cot.

Once in motion, The Shadow ran the risk of detection; but it seemed slight, considering that Talney was still staring at the ring.

It was the flickering gaslight that betrayed The Shadow. Fanned by a breeze that came through the open window, the flame stretched and wavered, lengthening the streak of approaching blackness that preceded The Shadow.

Staring past the ring, Talney saw the weird, hawkish silhouette that was cast upon the cot where Glevin lay.

Roused from his stupor, Louis Talney uttered a savage cry. Wheeling, he aimed his stubby revolver point-blank for the cloaked figure that was swooping in from the door, and fired!

CHAPTER XIII
DINNER AT NINE

THE Shadow's swoop had become a dive when Talney opened fire. The first shot, therefore, whizzed a full foot above The Shadow's slouch hat; but Talney wasn't deceived.

Knowing that he had missed, he shoved his gun downward, intending to score at least one hit upon the unknown invader, who, in Talney's opinion, must be a foe. Talney's second aim was good, but he didn't pull the gun trigger.

The Shadow's dive was toward the stretch of carpet on which Talney stood. Grabbing the green weave, The Shadow gave a hard yank. Talney somersaulted as the carpet went beneath him, his gun flying to the ceiling. The Shadow was on his feet, picking up the revolver, by the time Talney struck the floor.

It wasn't luck on The Shadow's part. He wouldn't have moved in on Talney if he hadn't seen that the carpet was rightly placed for emergency. In fact, the breaks were all against The Shadow. He had counted upon plucking away the carpet before Talney managed to fire at all. The shot, even though it missed, was disastrous to The Shadow's plans.

Heard below, Talney's gun blast was bringing men up the stairs as fast as they could come. Dwig and his crew, in through the back way, knew that something had happened, and they didn't intend to let Talney, their wanted victim, get clear.

Coming to his feet, Talney launched for the

Roused from his stupor, Talney aimed his stubby revolver point-blank for the cloaked figure that was sweeping in from the door.

door, not knowing that death was hurrying up to meet him. The Shadow reached the door first, slamming it across Talney's path. Twisting about, he blocked off the tall man and whirled him toward the window.

Something thumped the door and exploded with a smash that reduced the barrier to kindling. It was a bomb, chucked by one of Dwig's henchmen. That bunch was out to get rid of Talney without finesse or ceremony.

The door took the shock of the explosion, but before Talney could congratulate himself on escaping one death, he was confronted by another. Headfirst, he was going through the open window, propelled by The Shadow.

Talney thought it would be a thirty-foot plunge to a cement court below. He overestimated by twenty-nine feet, and he was wrong about the cement. Instead of taking off on a long plunge, Talney simply flattened on a fire escape outside Glevin's window.

The Shadow had noticed the ironwork of the fire escape, even though Talney hadn't. Rolling through the window, The Shadow flattened beside the tall man just as another "pineapple" scaled through the shattered door, zimmed across the smoke-filled room and landed beneath the cot that held Glevin's body.

The second bomb took powerful effect. Glevin's cot was hurled to the ceiling; his body, already bloated beyond normal recognition, was mangled by the blast. Walls cracked; great chunks of the ceiling showered down with Glevin's form. The windows ripped outward, showering Talney and The Shadow with a deluge of glass which cascaded from the fire escape, for the iron framework tilted outward at a crazy angle when the bricks that held it weakened.

In time to catch Talney before he rolled from the canted platform, The Shadow, instead of restraining him, steered him to the steps. Badly shaken, Talney no longer offered opposition. He wanted to get away from the exploding room, and was willing to trust anyone who aided him.

Reaching the ground, The Shadow helped the stumbling, horror-maddened man around to Moe's cab. At intervals, Talney faltered as if paralyzed, and during that slow journey The Shadow recognized that there would be no further chance of trailing Dwig and the murder crew.

They had gone down the front stairway, after hurling the bombs. They couldn't have seen who was in the bombed room, for the first of their explosive missiles had struck the closed door; the next had sailed through a clouded atmosphere of smoke.

Having heard the shot, they might suppose that someone was in the room with Talney; but that was immaterial. They would be satisfied that they had delivered death.

THAT fact suited The Shadow.

It meant that Louis Talney was marked off the book. His servant, Glevin, if even considered, was written off, too. But Talney was the one that counted; he was the fifth link in the chain of death. Whether the chain went on from there was the next point to learn. Already sure that it did lead farther, The Shadow now held the proof.

Talney's bewilderment over the cheap ring that Glevin wore fitted with The Shadow's own curiosity concerning the rings on the fingers of previous victims. Those rings should have had sapphires as gems. Furthermore, the fact that they did not contain sapphires pointed to the rings themselves as bearing responsibility for death.

Glevin's case backed that point.

The servant had died instead of his master, Talney, and it was doubtful that human poisoners had made the mistake, since Dwig, very active in the chain of crime, knew what Talney looked like.

However, further speculation was hardly necessary, since The Shadow now held a valuable informant: namely, Talney. Should there be a sixth man listed for death, Talney might be able to name him; but there was no rush, for death, if scheduled, was by this time delivered.

Indeed, rush was impossible with Talney. Getting sense from him was equally difficult, as The Shadow learned while riding in Moe's cab.

Beside him, Talney sat staring, muttering useless words. His mind was still numbed by his recollection of Glevin's body and the startling events that had succeeded it. He didn't even see the black-clad battler who sat beside him. At moments, Talney's eyes lighted, when he opened his hand to stare at an object that he had clutched all through the excitement.

It was the dull, glassy ring that he had taken from Glevin's finger. Momentarily, Talney's eyes would brighten, then fade. This ring was not the one that he expected to see. He couldn't understand it.

The cab pulled up at an address around a corner from Park Avenue. It was the side entrance to the office of Dr. Rupert Sayre, who happened to be Cranston's own physician. Sayre was there, and lost none of his professional calm when he saw the cloaked figure of The Shadow bringing in Talney as a patient.

They helped Talney to a couch and let him lie down; hearing The Shadow's version of the patient's ordeal, Sayre nodded, and made a brief examination.

The Shadow, meanwhile, sat at Sayre's desk in

another corner. Coming over, the physician stated:

"Our patient will need about an hour. Nothing serious; the combination of mental shock and physical exertion was too much—"

Pausing, Sayre stared at the ring that The Shadow held between the fingers of his gloved left hand. It was a very cheap ring, and The Shadow had been examining it with a powerful microscope on Sayre's desk. At present, however, The Shadow was doing something that made Sayre think he might be a better candidate as a patient than Talney.

Having laid aside the microscope, The Shadow had picked up an eye dropper and filled it with ink from Sayre's inkstand. He was carefully inserting the point of the eye dropper beneath the colorless quartz that served as a gem for the cheap finger ring.

The Shadow heard Sayre's voice chop short.

"This stone is hollow," spoke The Shadow, quietly. "It is cut *en cabochon*, as jewelers say, meaning dome-shaped. The microscope shows a special mounting beneath the hollow. Watch this effect, Sayre."

AS The Shadow squeezed the bulb of the eye dropper, the hollow space in the quartz sucked up the blue ink. Only a small quantity, but the effect was splendid. Filled with blue, the worthless gem took on a gorgeous luster. Nor was that all; as The Shadow raised the transformed jewel to the light, Sayre saw scintillating streaks that radiated from the center of the imitation gem.

"A staurolite," informed The Shadow. "The trade name for imitations of star sapphires. Usually a staurolite is easily detected; but this one is different. The liquid deepens the color and magnifies the marked mounting."

It happened that Sayre had stopped in at the exhibit at Walder's. He couldn't fail to recognize the amazing imitation gem that The Shadow held.

"One of the six sapphires!" Sayre exclaimed. "Those that were cut from the Star of Delhi!"

"Supposedly cut from it," corrected The Shadow. "No one examined them. They were in a sealed casket that had no lights beneath its top of unbreakable glass. Let us try another experiment."

He held the ring to Sayre's desk lamp. As the blue stone heated, little dribs of ink began to ooze from it. Sayre watched The Shadow wipe the blue dabs away with his glove, while the slow flow continued. Fading gradually, the stone was a star sapphire no longer, but just poor quartz.

"You can answer the next question," The Shadow told Sayre. "Suppose the ink to be a virulent poison, oozing because of the heat of the finger that wore it, working its way into a man's pores—"

Sayre interrupted. He defined the very poison by its Latin name. The Shadow listened while Sayre gave more facts; how such a poison, slowly administered, would be absorbed through the entire bloodstream, bringing eventual death. In the form of blue crystals, the poison, made into a solution, would have the same hue!

Death's riddle was solved by The Shadow!

Much, however, remained. Foremost was the tracing of the master murderer. The Shadow reached for Sayre's telephone; the physician heard him call the Cobalt Club and ask for Commissioner Weston. For the first time, The Shadow was using Cranston's tone. He seemed startled by what he heard over the phone.

"Another death?" he queried. "A man named Louis Talney killed in an explosion? ... What? Someone called Raft's office ... The last, you think! Well, that is helpful. I see. No other leads beyond Talney ... I'll drop in later, at the club—"

Rising, The Shadow turned toward Sayre, who was seated beside Talney's couch.

"When he comes around," spoke The Shadow, in the whispered tone that suited his cloaked guise, "send him to the Cobalt Club. Tell him not to give his name; he is merely to ask for Cranston."

"But if the commissioner will be there—"

"It will be the last place in the world"—The Shadow's tone was a whispered laugh—"where Commissioner Weston would expect to meet a dead man named Louis Talney!"

The Shadow was gone while Dr. Sayre was considering the unimpeachable merits of that particular plan. With a laugh of his own, Sayre turned again to his patient.

It took ten minutes for Moe's cab to get from Sayre's office to the Metrolite. When The Shadow alighted at the hotel, he was Cranston again. Inside the Metrolite, he found Margo waiting, and quietly apologized, as any gentleman would have, for coming to dinner at nine when he should have arrived at eight. Margo accepted the apology and asked no explanation. But while they dined, she gained the definite impression that Lamont Cranston, though as leisurely as ever, expected to keep further appointments before this night was ended.

CHAPTER XIV
MASTER OF CRIME

COMMISSIONER WESTON was very disappointed by the sudden way in which his friend, Lamont Cranston, lost all interest in the strange chain of quintuple death. Dropping into the club at about ten o'clock, Cranston listened to all that Weston had to say; then he yawned and decided to go home.

"But these are unexplainable riddles!" Weston exclaimed. "Men slain by a subtle poison administered in an unknown manner. We must solve these deaths! Think of the menace of a type of murder that never fails!"

"It failed the last time," reminded Cranston, "in Talney's case."

The statement carried far more truth than Weston suspected. The commissioner did not catch the point behind it.

"Talney died!" he insisted. "He was blasted out of existence. Don't you realize it, Cranston?"

"Of course I realize it. Again, I say the perfect murder failed. They had to bomb Talney, instead of poisoning him, and that, I hope, will be the end of it."

Accompanying Cranston out through the foyer, Weston stopped impatiently while his friend paused to shake hands with a man who was waiting for him. Cranston didn't bother to introduce his acquaintance. He just waved to Weston and went out with the arrival.

The commissioner noted that the man had a solemn, squarish face, but soon forgot it. As yet, Weston had seen no photographs of Talney, a matter on which The Shadow had checked while chatting with the commissioner.

In Cranston's limousine, Talney showed quite plainly that Sayre had brought him fully around. He was very voluble in describing all that had happened, including his recollections of The Shadow.

"Dr. Sayre said that you might help me," concluded Talney. "He spoke of previous deaths and told me that you knew something about them, since you were a friend of the police commissioner."

"I do," returned The Shadow in Cranston's tone. "Five men died, all wearing rings with colorless gems.

"Not rings with star sapphires?"

"No. Rings like the one you said your servant wore. Wait—I think I can recall their names—"

He spoke off the list, keenly watching Talney. Though the man recognized none of them, he was definitely ill at ease. Suddenly, Talney blurted:

"Sayre said the rings could have been poisoned!"

"Poisoned?"

"Yes!" Talney was trembling. "He said it might account for them changing from blue to some other color."

Cranston's face registered amazement. Talney gripped his new friend's arm.

"There is much I have to tell you!" he confided. "Dr. Sayre preferred that I should talk to you, as he is very busy. You must hear it all!"

With that, Talney unfolded the history of the secret six, the group that Armand Lenfell had sponsored for the worthy purpose of selling refugee gems, at proper prices, throughout the country. Talney, of course, was a member of the group, but he had known only Lenfell.

"Only Lenfell." Talney's tone was hollow. "The same was true of the others. Until tonight, I had no idea who the rest might be. But from what you tell me, I am sure that they were four of the men who died so mysteriously."

LINKED deaths!

Those had been a problem, even to The Shadow, but now he understood. It showed the craft of a mighty mind behind the reign of murder. Except as members of the secret six, Talney and the four victims had been definitely disassociated. That was why steps had been taken to link them!

It was a move that led the law in the wrong direction, not the right. It made it seem that they had known one another, instead of being men who met only incognito. In Cranston's deliberate style, The Shadow suggested it to Talney, and the living dead man responded by ejaculating the very name that The Shadow expected:

"Armand Lenfell!"

Coolly, The Shadow inquired:

"You think that Lenfell is the murderer?"

"Who else could be?" demanded Talney. "He knew us all, he alone. It was his idea to cut the Star of Delhi into six portions and have Walder exhibit it. But he kept the real Star for himself, and had five poisoned rings made instead!"

"There were six rings—"

"Yes," interposed Talney. "Lenfell kept one, but obviously, he would not have filled it with the same deadly liquid. That ring, however, will prove Lenfell to be a murderer! We must stop and call the police at once!"

Talney saw Cranston stare idly from the window of the slowly rolling limousine, which was piloted by a very patient chauffeur.

"We are in Central Park," came Cranston's tone, "with no phone booths near. But it would be unwise to call the police. They believe you dead, Talney."

"I shall come to life—"

"And make yourself a target again?" Cranston's head shook slowly. "Quite unwise, Talney. The Shadow might not arrive, the next time, to save you!"

Talney slumped back into the cushions. He rallied, suddenly, to announce:

"I shall go direct to Armand Lenfell!"

"To accuse him?" interposed Cranston. "That would be dangerous. You would be giving away the fact that you live, straight to the man that plotted murder. He wouldn't have to wait for the police to proclaim the fact."

"But someone must go to Lenfell!"

The Shadow nodded, as he pretended to give the statement deep consideration. Then, in Cranston's slowest tone:

"I shall go," he said. "Lenfell will not suspect me. Stanley, my chauffeur, will take you to my home in New Jersey, and you can remain there, Talney, as long as it is necessary to play dead. I shall tell you later how I make out with Lenfell."

SOON after sending Stanley home, with Talney as a passenger, The Shadow approached Lenfell's gloomy house, but not as Lamont Cranston. The Shadow was cloaked, the proper guise for this occasion. In a way, he had borrowed an idea from Talney, based on the latter's tale of the secret six.

Since hooded men had moved in and out of Lenfell's practically at will, a cloaked visitor should find the same process satisfactory. But The Shadow was not taking this expedition as a sinecure.

From Talney's account, he inferred that Lenfell had given the servants evenings off whenever he expected his hooded friends—or dupes—to visit him.

Lenfell's house was an index to that fact. It was not as gloomy or formidable as Talney had described it. The Shadow saw lights that appeared to be in the kitchen; others, on the third floor. Unquestionably, there were servants about. But when The Shadow glided to the side door and tried it, he found it unlocked.

The Shadow paused just inside. If Lenfell expected no more visits from his five companions in the secret six, why was the door unlocked? There was a plausible answer: the servants.

Probably Lenfell locked the doors himself; otherwise the servants, in the past, might have unwittingly blocked out the hooded visitors. It wouldn't be wise for Lenfell suddenly to change that policy overnight, particularly on a night when murder was rampant.

Finding Lenfell's study was doubly easy. Talney had mentioned its location; from outside, The Shadow had seen a light in the room. Of all mysterious visitors who had entered Lenfell's house, none moved with more stealth than did The Shadow as he took the side stairway to the second floor. None, that was, except Jan Garmath, on the occasion when the elderly gem maker had returned to eavesdrop at Lenfell's study.

So far as the servants were concerned, The Shadow's stealth was superfluous. None was close enough to overhear his approach to the study. The Shadow was thinking purely in terms of Lenfell, and when he reached the study, his gliding arrival gave proof of dividends. Through the door, which was ajar, The Shadow saw Lenfell seated at the desk.

Only a lamp gave light. It was on the desk, and its rays were directed toward a sheaf of letters. Lenfell was leaning forward in his chair, one elbow on the desk; his face, though away from the light's glare, was plainly directed toward the stack of letters. His other hand gripped a fountain pen, ready to affix a signature.

Easing the door open, The Shadow performed a quick, roundabout glide, skirting the desk in darkness. An automatic drawn, he approached Lenfell and stopped short of the seated man's shoulder. One nudge of the gun muzzle, Lenfell would be helpless.

But The Shadow did not touch Lenfell with the muzzle. He did not even brush the back of the chair. He did feel a floorboard give loosely beneath his foot, but he suppressed its creak by adding pressure.

That same board ran beneath a leg of Lenfell's chair. It might have jarred the chair a fraction of an inch, but not enough for Lenfell to have noticed it, because a slight shift of his own body would have produced the same motion. In fact, Lenfell did not notice the effect at all; nevertheless, the result was large.

Lenfell's pen hand slid across the desk. It flopped past the edge, and its weight carried him with it. Rolling from the chair, the financier struck the floor and stretched there. His broad face, though turned upward, was not in the light, but his left hand was. It lay across his chest, and upon the third finger The Shadow saw a ring.

Not a ring with a sapphire, real or synthetic. The ring contained a specimen of very pure glass, as colorless as other worthless pieces of junk jewelry that The Shadow had viewed earlier.

Normally broad, Lenfell's face did not look bloated away from the light, but when The Shadow tilted the lamp toward it, the condition was plainly discernible.

The Shadow had come to meet the master of crime. He had found Armand Lenfell. The two were not the same, however deep Lenfell's schemes, no matter what part he had played in the strange plot of murder. For no man of hideous crime would have numbered himself among the victims.

Armand Lenfell was stone dead, struck down by the same virulent poison that had taken the lives of others whose fingers bore rings of doom!

A low, grim laugh whispered in the darkness above the dead figure on the floor. It was still The Shadow's task to find a mastermind of murder!

CHAPTER XV
CREEP OF DOOM

UNDER the lamplight, Lenfell's face seemed

to grimace upward at the eyes above it, as though the man enjoyed the death that had come his way. Certainly, Lenfell had more cause to grin in death than in life. Had he been living at this moment, he would not have grinned at all.

There wasn't a doubt that Lenfell had betrayed the trust that others had placed in him. But his crimes did not include murder. Lenfell, alone, could point the finger upon the master plotter who had gone still further, to trick him along with his dupes.

Lenfell's knowledge, however, was locked as tightly as the teeth that gritted from the midst of his wide death grin.

The trouble was that Lenfell had known too little. Had he known enough, he would not have been lying dead.

Thinking in terms of the unlocked door below, The Shadow came to a new conclusion. There was another reason why that door was open, and a good one. It could mean that Lenfell still expected visits from members of the secret six, not knowing that death was to befall them. A good explanation, since it gave a plausible reason for Lenfell's own death.

Considering the complexities that Lenfell's death produced, The Shadow turned toward the large safe that stood at the rear of the financier's study. Catching the glow of the lamplight, the glistening bulk added challenge of its own.

Like its owner, Lenfell, the safe refused to talk. But it might be possible to pry facts from the safe, instead of Lenfell's grinning jaws. Stepping to the safe, The Shadow crouched, pressed his gloved fingers against the dial.

Before he could test the intricate combination, The Shadow was attracted by a sound outside the study. It came as a slow creeping, and it was close, yet elusive, as it traveled along the hall.

Having heard no creaks from the stairs, The Shadow was sure that the creeping arrival must have been cautious while coming up from the ground floor, only to drop the guarded manner as he neared Lenfell's study.

Adding that to previous facts, The Shadow found the answer.

The man whose creeps were coming closer was the murderer of Armand Lenfell!

Such logic was perfect. In his own approach, The Shadow had moved silently all the way. The newcomer had done the same only as far as the second floor. He was taking pains to avoid being heard by servants in the kitchen, but once near Lenfell's study, he did not care what sounds he made. It meant that the approacher *knew* that he would find Lenfell dead.

Properly translated, the facts proved that this was Lenfell's murderer. If not, the creeper would still be using caution.

Turning from the safe, The Shadow sidled into darkness, drawing an automatic, to await the appearance of the creeping criminal who was in the hall. Yet, even to The Shadow's skilled ears, the approaching sound was elusive. At moments, it seemed close, then far away until, when The Shadow did not actually expect it, a huddling figure showed itself within the doorway.

Even when close, the creeping man's face could not be distinguished. The Shadow, himself, was partially to blame. He had turned the lamp so it no longer shone toward the door. Creeping footsteps entered, their maker with them, and the huddling man kept looking toward the desk for a sight of Lenfell. The action turned his face away from The Shadow.

Of one thing only was The Shadow certain: that this was not Dwig Brencott, nor any of the slick crook's crew. This was the master criminal, in person, the conniver who had somehow managed to pass death along with the faulty sapphires that Lenfell had given out.

So far, the chief criminal had not shown his hand on other scenes of death, but he obviously had business here in Lenfell's study.

Drawing still farther into darkness, The Shadow watched. He saw the crouched man reach the safe and begin to thumb the dial without the need of extra light. Evidently, the interloper knew the combination, which indicated that he had visited these premises while Lenfell was alive.

What the murderer was about, The Shadow did not fully know, though he could guess. To substantiate his opinion, he glided forward, moving close behind the man at the safe.

Never before had The Shadow sought to trap an intruder who possessed such sharpened senses. Only the most suspicious of eyes could have spied the glide of darkness across the already dimmed floor. Few ears could have caught the slight *swish* of The Shadow's cloak.

Perhaps the crouching safe-tapper possessed some uncanny ability to recognize the approach of a challenger. Whatever the case, he sensed The Shadow's presence.

LIKE an uncoiling snake, the crouched man unlimbered. Spinning around, he flung himself straight for The Shadow, whipping out a revolver as he came. There wasn't time to sight the man's face, for the light was behind him. All that The Shadow could do was meet the lightning attack by as quick a counterthrust.

Swinging his gun hand in a wide arc, The Shadow outdid his foe in point of speed. Guns clashed, automatic against revolver, before the unknown man could give a trigger tug. The force of The Shadow's stroke slashed the weapon from his adversary's hand.

With the blow, The Shadow delivered a low but recognizable laugh—a taunt that would have fazed an ordinary criminal. The mirth did not work with this man.

His gun lost, the creeper simply took advantage of his weaponless condition. In bashing the revolver, The Shadow had swung himself off balance, and quick eyes noted the fact. Long arms shot forward; one hand caught The Shadow's wrist, while the other sped to his throat. His own gun forced upward, The Shadow hadn't time to fire.

He did the next best thing. A quick twist, a backward fling, and The Shadow was starting his opponent on a jiu jitsu flip that should have carried him to the wall. But the master criminal performed an amazing gyration in midair and did a side twist of his own. Though he struck the floor, the twist that he gave The Shadow's wrist was sufficient to yank away the cloaked fighter's automatic.

Undaunted, The Shadow drove anew for his foe. By then, they were halfway to the door, well distant from the desk lamp.

In this first battle with Jan Garmath, the creeper who had come to Lenfell's study, The Shadow was meeting with surprising opposition. But it wasn't the sort that could continue. Clutching his snakish adversary, The Shadow managed to get his gloved hands on the man's neck.

A quick choke and Garmath would be helpless, his identity revealed as soon as The Shadow could drag him to the light. But Garmath, tugging at the gloved hands that throttled him managed to raise an outcry. He shouted, not in his own voice but in excellent imitation of Lenfell's tone:

"Help! Andrew—George—help! They are murdering me!"

In the midst of his cries, Garmath managed a side twist toward the desk. He was still wrestling hard against The Shadow when Lenfell's servants arrived. They came with a promptitude that The Shadow had not expected.

Piling through the door, they saw a writhe of blackness blocking off the light from the desk lamp. Hurling themselves upon The Shadow, they tried to haul him from a victim that they thought must be their master, Lenfell.

The servants were only half successful, but Garmath supplied the rest. Out of The Shadow's clutch, he ducked around the desk leaving the cloaked fighter in the hands of Andrew and George. They were too ardent in their attack to observe Garmath's quick flight.

Only The Shadow saw the running man who scooped up the revolver from the floor and kept on his way. But The Shadow had no chance to spy Garmath's face. The smart crook did not show it.

Flinging Andrew in one direction, George in the other, The Shadow recovered his automatic and went after Garmath, with George and Andrew following. Garmath was at the bottom of the front stairs when The Shadow reached the top; he was slamming the front door when his cloaked pursuer arrived at the bottom of the stairway.

Having a similar lead on Lenfell's servants, The Shadow seemed free for uninterrupted pursuit; but he was due for unexpected opposition. Garmath was across the street by the time The Shadow sprang from the front door, and from an arriving car blockers sprang up to cut off The Shadow's course.

Had they been mobsters, like Dwig and his outfit, The Shadow would have dealt them a proper dose of bullets. But these weren't crooks; they were detectives, backed by none other than Inspector Joe Cardona!

GUNS talked, as The Shadow jogged the hands that held them. Recognizing The Shadow, Cardona was shouting orders that the barking revolvers drowned. From the doorway of the house, Lenfell's servants were shouting: "Get the man in black!" Their cries were louder than Cardona's, after the roar of the guns ended.

Tripping one detective and tumbling him across the other, The Shadow made a dive for darkness, hoping that Cardona wouldn't suddenly change his opinion and decide that, for once, The Shadow might be in the wrong.

Joe didn't decide so, but he wavered, and that was why The Shadow took to the darkness of the side passage leading past Lenfell's, instead of going across the street in chase of Garmath.

Out back, The Shadow found Moe's cab and sprang into it, ordering the speedy hackie to round the block and try to pick up the trail of another car. But the lost time proved costly.

Garmath was gone when Moe made the circuit. The only car that hove into sight was the official one belonging to Commissioner Weston. Sight of that bulky vehicle was cause enough for Moe to veer off in another direction, without awaiting The Shadow's bidding.

The scene that Weston viewed in Lenfell's study was not a great surprise. The commissioner had come to Lenfell's in response to another tip-off. Weston was puzzled merely by the statements of the servants and the detectives. They all insisted that a black-cloaked fighter had fled the house, one who answered far too closely to the known description of The Shadow.

When Cardona listened to those statements, he caught a glare from Weston. Remembering the alibi that he had given The Shadow at Sherbrock's, Cardona was definitely perturbed. With Lenfell's body in plain view, and The Shadow the only intruder on the premises, the cloaked investigator's reputation was encountering a severe strain.

Joe only hoped that Weston would not think back to the Sherbrock case. To forestall such a prospect, Cardona gestured at Lenfell's safe.

"Maybe we'll find the answer there," he said to Weston. "Whoever came here might have been after something important. Suppose we see what's inside."

The idea appealed to Weston and took his full attention, for it wasn't easily accomplished. None of the servants knew the combination, and Weston's guesswork at the dial proved quite unavailing.

Cardona, meanwhile, was consulting a little book that contained the phone number of a specialist in safes. The man proved to be at home, and he agreed to come right over.

It took the legitimate cracksman fifteen minutes to arrive; another quarter-hour to solve the combination of Lenfell's safe. When the big door came open, Weston poked head and shoulders through and pounced upon the first object that he saw, which happened to be a squarish jewel case.

Opening the box, Weston was too surprised to speak. Cardona had to look over his shoulder to observe what the commissioner had found.

Gleaming from within the box, catching the focused lamplight with radiating streaks, was a giant star sapphire that answered the description of the famous Star of Delhi.

It was little wonder that Weston was surprised. Had Lenfell's body come suddenly to life, it couldn't have amazed the commissioner more. For the Star of Delhi, according to the unimpeachable word of Raymond Walder, the now-dead jeweler, had been divided into the six gems that Walder himself had exhibited in his store!

SUCH astonishment was something that Weston had to share. When he arrived back at the Cobalt Club, he made a call to New Jersey and spoke to his friend Cranston, who answered in a very sleepy tone.

"Another murder, Cranston!" exclaimed Weston. "With it we have found the Star of Delhi!"

"Good!" was Cranston's reply. "So you've solved everything. Good work, Commissioner."

"But that only increases the mystery," Weston insisted. "The Star of Delhi was supposed to be cut up. But we've found out that it wasn't."

"Too bad," responded Cranston. "I thought it was cut up. Saw it myself, all in pieces. How are you going to find the Star of Delhi when there isn't any Star of Delhi?"

"But we *have* found it—"

A *click* interrupted from the other end. Evidently, Cranston was too opinionated to give any credence to Weston's statement. At his end of the phone, the commissioner fumed and muttered a few comments regarding Cranston's obstinacy. He was sorry that he had bothered to call his friend at all.

The Shadow wasn't sorry.

At his end of the line, The Shadow stood with half-closed eyes, picturing the possible results to which the finding of the great sapphire might lead. Then, from the fixed lips of Cranston, came a grim but softly whispered laugh.

It was the laugh of The Shadow, presaging new and curious quests along the trail to strangely hidden crime.

CHAPTER XVI
TRAILS DIVERGE

IRKED by Cranston's indifference to the finding of the great sapphire, and desirous of showing some success on an evening when murder had reigned, Commissioner Weston lost no time in informing the press that the Star of Delhi had been recovered in its original shape.

The news created a vast sensation, and somewhat counteracted public criticism over the matter of six mysterious deaths.

It was the sort of story that the newspapers liked. Every great gem had some curious past history, and the Star of Delhi was no exception. Journalists dug for facts, and produced them.

Once famous as the principal gem in a Hindu rajah's crown, the Star of Delhi had undergone a century of travel and transfer, leaving slaughter and rebellion in its wake. Reaching the possession of a European collector, it had brought him ill luck, including the forced sale of the prized blue jewel.

The jinx was still at work, and the fact that it had cost the lives of six men could be attributed to the greed of all. Each man, it so seemed, had shared a sinister secret—that of six false sapphires which had passed as portions of the Star of Delhi.

How much Walder, the dead jeweler, had known; how deeply Sherbrock, the missing lapidary, was involved were perplexing questions that bothered the press quite as much as the law.

Certain it was that six smaller gems had been exhibited as parts of the great sapphire, stones so well matched that they must have been of the same origin. The question of the false gems led to a discussion of synthetic sapphires, which offered the only solution to the fraud.

At late breakfast in the quiet of his New Jersey home, Lamont Cranston read the newspaper reports and made comment to Louis Talney, who was seated across the table.

"They seem more stirred by the finding of the Star of Delhi," said Cranston, "than by your death, Talney, and those of six others."

"Five others," reminded Talney. "I wasn't killed."

"Six others," Cranston corrected. "You are forgetting your own servant: Glevin. It seems that his body was found, but was mistaken for yours."

Talney's face showed an expression of relief. As circumstances stood, he preferred to be counted as dead.

"Any other news?" he queried. "Anything about the man who fled from Lenfell's?"

"You mean The Shadow?" queried Cranston, glancing at the newspaper. "No. They aren't sure that he's to blame. His case doesn't puzzle me so much, Talney."

"Why not?"

"He may have gone there investigating the chain of crime. What does surprise me is the matter of the poisoned rings."

"You're surprised because the police have not suspected them?"

"No." The Shadow shook his head in a leisurely fashion. His steady tone was Cranston's. "I can't quite understand why murder was so necessary."

The remark was meant to draw an opinion from Talney. It succeeded.

"I understand," expressed Talney. "There wasn't any need for Lenfell to murder us. We trusted him too much. But whoever else wanted to steal the Star of Delhi had to kill Lenfell in order to get the gem. That meant murdering the rest of us, because we all knew Lenfell."

"Who do you think the murderer is?"

"Probably Roger Sherbrock. Maybe Lenfell made a deal with him, to fake six sapphires instead of cutting the large one. When the police found out that Sherbrock was the brain behind the jewel robberies, it put Sherbrock outside the law. So he decided to go after the Star of Delhi."

The Shadow nodded, even though he knew that Talney's theories were very wide of the mark. In The Shadow's opinion, Sherbrock was quite innocent, though the police, like Talney, thought the opposite. Sherbrock was the scapegoat for the crimes of others, which The Shadow could appreciate, since he was getting into the same class of the falsely accused.

"I'll drop into town," The Shadow decided, "and have a chat with my friend, the commissioner."

"The sooner you come back," returned Talney, "the better I'll like it, Cranston. I'm eager to know what else develops."

DEVELOPMENTS were under way while Cranston's limousine was starting to Manhattan.

In his office, Commissioner Weston was receiving a delegation of prominent jewelers, all eager to see the Star of Delhi. Among them was a dryish-faced man named Jan Garmath, known as an expert on artificial gems. It was Garmath who supplied some facts that Weston wanted.

"Synthetic sapphires are quite common," declared Garmath. "They are produced by fusing aluminum sesquioxide and the necessary chemical coloring. Only under the microscope can they he told from natural gems."

"Ah!" Weston exclaimed. "Then we could detect the six false sapphires, should we regain them!"

"You could," agreed Garmath. "You must look for the structural lines. You will find them curved, instead of straight. Furthermore, synthetic sapphires contain bubbles. Look at the Star of Delhi, Commissioner"—Garmath provided a powerful lens—"and you will see straight lines, but no bubbles."

Weston studied the great gem through the glass.

"You said curved lines," he remarked, "and bubbles. Was I right, Mr. Garmath?"

"Yes, Commissioner. Synthetic sapphires fit that description."

The commissioner was idly laying down the glass and replacing the Star of Delhi in its plush-lined box. He stopped abruptly, popping up in his chair, looking from one witness to another.

"Synthetic!" he exclaimed. "Did you say synthetic?"

"I said—"

Garmath couldn't complete it. Others were pouncing for the Star of Delhi, all bringing out their magnifiers. In half a minute, Weston's office was teeming with confusion. The great sapphire, seen under the glass, had curved structural lines and bubbles.

The Star of Delhi was a fake!

Never before had these jewelers seen such a large imitation gem. Theories were popping thick and fast, all to one conclusion. Facts had been reversed, with but one possible explanation, according to the experts.

Roger Sherbrock must have cut the real Star of Delhi into six matched gems. That was the really clever part of it. Small sapphires were more apt to be suspected than one so well described as the Star of Delhi.

Probably Sherbrock had sold the imitation Star, a wonderful replica of the original, to Lenfell. He had then disposed of the six matched gems to Walder, who had probably learned that they were the portions of the real Star and had advertised the fact.

Threatened with exposure by Lenfell, the man he had swindled, Sherbrock had been forced to murder his dupe and other men who knew about the crooked sale. It was a sound theory, and one that pleased Weston as well as Cardona who was present, for it cleared The Shadow.

Undoubtedly, Sherbrock had come to Lenfell's last night to steal back the fake Star of Delhi, thereby disposing of evidence against himself. The Shadow had been on hand, crossing Sherbrock's trail again, as on a preceding night. Weston was mentioning this in an aside to Cardona, when The Shadow himself appeared in the office.

Of course, he came as Cranston. Out of the hubbub, he learned of the recent discovery, and looked at the Star of Delhi for himself. Turning to Weston, The Shadow inquired quietly:

"Who detected the fraud?"

"I did!" bragged Weston. Then, noting glances from some jewelers: "Thanks to Jan Garmath."

"Which man is he?"

Looking about, Weston couldn't find Garmath. It turned out that Garmath, like some of the other jewelers, had supposed that the conference was ended, and was therefore gone. When Weston asked where Garmath could be reached, no one knew. Garmath, it appeared, had a large fortune which he had brought from Europe, and was retired, rather than active, as a jeweler.

"It sums up to this, Cranston," declared the commissioner, no longer interested in Garmath. "Six real sapphires have gone back to their original owner, whoever he may be. We believe that those stones were cut by Sherbrock from the actual Star of Delhi. We shall try to find the owner and question him—confidentially, of course—in hopes of evidence against Sherbrock."

"Naturally, the owner of the six sapphires may be loath to declare himself, for fear of death. Nevertheless, we know what we are after—and that it is the first important step."

LATER that afternoon, Lamont Cranston met Margo Lane and calmly told her how Louis Talney was a guest at his residence, sent there by The Shadow. After piecing Talney into the picture, Cranston remarked:

"I shall have to call him later. He will be interested to hear about the Star of Delhi."

"How it was really cut into six smaller gems," nodded Margo. "I read all about it in the early afternoon editions. Clever of your friend, the commissioner, to find out that the large sapphire was an imitation. Well, it's up to the police to look for the six small stones."

"Which they can never find."

"Can never find?" Margo echoed. "Why not?"

Seldom did The Shadow put so much emphasis into the tone of Cranston as he did on this occasion, in response to Margo's query.

"It was Garmath, not Weston," he said, "who exposed the great sapphire as a synthetic stone. After that, Garmath conveniently disappeared. It is Garmath who must be found. I believe that he manufactured the synthetic gem."

"And sold it to Lenfell?"

"No. Lenfell already had it. He wanted to keep it and dupe Talney and the rest into thinking that it had been cut. So he needed six small, synthetic stones, and asked Garmath to make them."

"Which Garmath did—"

"Which Garmath did not!" Cranston interposed. "He made six poisoned rings, instead. Knowing that Lenfell had a sale for the real Star of Delhi, Garmath naturally kept it. He made the large synthetic sapphire to dupe Lenfell. The poison worked too soon for Lenfell to ever take it to his customer."

It all struck home to Margo. Trails had diverged; the one that the police sought was quite different from The Shadow's quest. The law was after six real sapphires, whereas The Shadow wanted to uncover a single stone, the great Star of Delhi itself. The law's trail did not exist, but The Shadow's did!

Arriving late at the commissioner's conference, The Shadow had lost his opportunity to trail immediately the daring supercrook, Jan Garmath, who had personally given Weston the wrong start. But The Shadow would soon find a way to pick up Garmath's trail.

It wouldn't be through the two thugs captured the night before. At dusk, when The Shadow, fully cloaked, appeared within his sanctum, the hidden room where he formulated campaigns against crime, he found blank reports awaiting him. Harry Vincent and other agents had been unable to locate Dwig Brencott through the prisoners.

But there were other sheets of consequence, supplied by Rutledge Mann, an investment broker in The Shadow's service. Those sheets listed the names of wealthy men who were investors in gems, as well as stocks and bonds.

Less than an hour after he had left Margo Lane, The Shadow completed a checkup of the lists.

The Shadow had rated them in order of importance, intending to investigate them, each in turn. He felt sure that one of the first four would prove to be the man who could supply much-needed information.

In that surmise, The Shadow was correct: Second on the list was the name of Uriah Crome.

It should have topped the list, as The Shadow was soon to learn!

CHAPTER XVII
A MATTER OF PRICE

WHILE The Shadow was still busy in his sanctum, Uriah Crome was receiving a visitor, which was something very unusual. Though he lived near the center of Manhattan, Crome was twin brother to a hermit. His penthouse, located on the flat roof of an antiquated eight-story office building, might well have been a cave in the middle of a wilderness.

Old, dyspeptic, as bald as an eagle and beak-nosed as a vulture, Crome had only two delights in life: jewels and milk toast. He liked gems because they glittered, and appealed to his miser's sense of ownership. He preferred milk toast because it was the only fare that did not cause him indigestion.

Crome's penthouse could only be reached by an elevator that had a night operator especially for service to the top floor. Since Crome owned the office building, it was impossible for anyone to come upstairs without his permission. The night man always telephoned up first, to make sure that Crome would receive any candidate for admission who happened to be downstairs.

On this evening, Crome was seated in an oak-paneled room which he termed his den, when one of his several servants entered with a note. After reading it, Crome placed bony fingers to his thin chin, pondered for a few moments, then ordered:

"Show the visitor up."

The visitor was Jan Garmath, and Crome received him alone. While he finished his milk toast, the vulturous man kept surveying his dry-featured visitor with a look that would have suited a bird of prey.

Crome's gaze, however, was actually defensive. He regarded Garmath as the vulture; himself as anything from a worm to a fat-sized guinea hen, or whatever sort of tidbit a vulture might choose.

Crome opened negotiations with a sharpish query:

"You have come regarding the Star of Delhi?"

"I have brought the Star of Delhi," returned Garmath in the mild tone he so often used. "I thought that you would be pleased to view a price-less gem that happens to have a price."

Producing a small jewel case, Garmath exhibited a great blue gem, which, to all appearances, was the synthetic replica that Commissioner Weston had taken credit for detecting that afternoon. Crome had evidently read the newspapers, for he shook his head as he held the jewel to the light.

"Bah!" he snorted. "This sapphire is false!"

"It happens to be real," returned Garmath. "The synthetic stone is now in the possession of the police."

"But this could be an imitation, too."

"There could be another imitation," agreed Garmath, "had I chosen to manufacture two, instead of only one. But one"—he gave a dry cluck—"was all I needed. This is the genuine Star of Delhi!"

BUSY with a microscope, Crome was learning for himself that Garmath spoke the truth. He pressed a button on his desk. One of the wall panels swung about, becoming a jewel case with shelves of resplendent gems that gave a great glitter to that side of the room.

"Bah!" Crome pressed the button again, to turn the shelves away from sight. "I must have these buttons marked. I pressed the one that controls the emerald showcase, by mistake. Here is the sapphire button."

He pushed it. A block of shelves swung from another panel, creating a bluish shimmer as they came. Hobbling over to the display, Crome compared the Star of Delhi with other large sapphires. The comparison was in favor of the great gem that Garmath had brought. Coming back to the desk, Crome planked the Star in front of him and said to Garmath:

"I want it!"

"Of course you want it," chuckled Garmath. "Otherwise, you wouldn't have made a deal with Lenfell. Let me see"—Garmath faked a tone of recollection—"what was the price he wanted? Three hundred thousand dollars?"

Garmath was simply making an estimate, for he had not heard Lenfell mention price to Crome during their phone conversation. Garmath calculated that if six smaller sapphires would have rated fifty thousand each, Lenfell certainly would not have set the price for the Star of Delhi as less than the sum of the smaller stones, had they been cut from the great gem.

Garmath's own deals with Lenfell had been strictly limited to the providing of six small synthetic sapphires; nothing more. But he wanted Crome to think that there had been a closer association.

The estimate was near enough. Early in negotiations with Crome, Lenfell had mentioned three hundred thousand dollars as a suitable price. Hence, though Crome shook his head, he did it slowly.

"Two hundred and fifty thousand dollars," Crome told Garmath. "That was the most that I would have paid Lenfell. But my present offer"—he dug clawish fingers into the desk and leaned across with a triumphant grin—"is only two hundred thousand!"

Garmath's eyes showed surprise, so well feigned that Crome was deceived. His beakish face agleam, Crome gloatingly detailed why he expected the Star of Delhi at a bargain price.

"I knew Lenfell's ways," asserted Crome, "the measures that he was taking to acquire the Star of Delhi as his own. He was betraying his associates; more than that, he was actually swindling them! That, of course"—Crome shrugged—"was not my affair. It was Lenfell, not I, who had to cover up what he had done.

"Nevertheless, his failure to do so could have caused me certain difficulties, should it become known that I owned the real Star of Delhi. I insisted that Lenfell take that into consideration, and he did.

"Now, in your case, Garmath, men have not merely been swindled; they have died! Too bad"—Crome was clucking as though really sorry—"but it means that you will have to give some *extra* consideration to the matter of price, in selling the Star of Delhi."

Crome meant "extra" to the tune of fifty thousand dollars, which he expected to retain, at Garmath's expense, in return for silence regarding Crome's own suspicion of the murders that Garmath had maneuvered. He was reaching to a desk drawer, bringing out crisp currency in bills of a thousand-dollar denomination and higher.

"Ten, twenty, thirty—" Crome had come down to the mere thousand-dollar bills, when he finally said: "Two hundred." He extended that sheaf to Garmath, while he put other bills away. Garmath merely folded his arms.

"My price," he said, "is half a million."

"What!" exclaimed Crome. "Preposterous!"

"Not at all," remarked Garmath mildly. "I reason rationally, not the other way about, as Lenfell did. The greater the crime, the greater the risk, and therefore—the greater the price!"

Crome swept back the money and dumped it in the desk drawer. Garmath was not at all annoyed. He simply leaned forward and added, pointedly:

"And the more certain the sale!"

THE words crept home to Crome as insidiously as the creep of Garmath's footfalls had once impressed Lenfell. Crome's hand had made an involuntary gesture toward the telephone. Garmath waved for him to complete it.

"Call the police," suggested Garmath. "Tell them that you intended to buy the Star of Delhi. When you do so, you will implicate yourself, not in five swindles, but in six murders! The police will find you, Crome, but they will not find me!"

Crome sagged back into his chair.

"No police?" queried Garmath. "Then call your loyal servants and, have them eject me, while you keep the Star of Delhi for yourself. That is as far as you would dare go, Crome, for neither you nor your servants are of sufficient grit and caliber to go through with murdering me.

"But *I* specialize in murder, Crome!" Garmath's tone had a snap as pronounced as the glint from his eyes. "I, and the men in my employ. Remember that, Crome, if you do not buy the Star of Delhi. Should you buy it"—his tone was easing—"you can remember that I also give protection to those that I think deserve it."

Crome's breath came back with a great gasp.

"You mean that if I buy the Star of Delhi at your price, no one will ever know of the transaction?"

"Not through me," returned Garmath. "Moreover, should anyone learn the fact"—his chuckle became raspy—"I can guarantee that they will never tell. Whatever service you may need from me goes with the sale, as a matter of good will."

Good will from a master of evil!

The paradox struck Crome hard; nevertheless, he felt forced to take Garmath's word. His numbed expression showed that Crome was reasoning matters slowly, but he was coming to a sound conclusion.

Good will or evil, Garmath's word could be relied upon. It would have to be so; otherwise, he couldn't have kept the confidence of murderous accomplices to the extent that he undoubtedly had.

With trembling hands, Crome reached for the money drawer, brought out the cash and began to count it. He made up a total of some three hundred and sixty thousand dollars, and looked worried about the remainder, when Garmath suggested:

"Your check will do, or—better—*checks* for some odd amounts, made out to cash. I understand that you often purchase jewels in amounts up to fifty thousand dollars. So keep the various checks below that sum."

Crome wrote out the checks and handed them along with the cash. After counting up to the total and finding that it made exactly half a million, Garmath arose with a gratified smile. He pointed to the Star of Delhi, then gestured to Crome's showcase.

"Put it with your other sapphires," Garmath said. "You can feast your own eyes upon the prize as often as you wish. But do not let others see the Star of Delhi. I spoke of protection. I have already given it. The police do not know that the Star of Delhi still exists.

"Hence, you are quite safe—while they are looking for six sapphires, matched ones that can never be found. However, as part of our bargain, I shall call you occasionally, beginning with tomorrow night. Good evening, Crome."

Rising, Garmath went to the door and Crome

noticed the creeping sound of the murderer's departure, recalling, numbly, that his visitor had entered in the same style, though Crome hadn't regarded it as insidious, then.

A servant was outside the door; hastily covering the Star of Delhi with one hand, Crome gestured with the other, signifying for t xhe man to show Garmath out.

When Garmath reached the ground floor, he went out by the back way, as there were two exits from the office building. His creeping walk, which he did not try to hide, echoed uncannily back through the passage, bringing shivers to the elevator man who was seated in the car with the door open.

The elevator operator wasn't the only one who heard those sounds.

FROM a limousine that had just stopped out front, a tall man in evening clothes was entering the building. He was Lamont Cranston, coming from a chat with one millionaire jewel collector, to call upon another. With the head man off The Shadow's list, Uriah Crome was next in line.

The Shadow heard Garmath's last evasive creeps just as they faded, with a quickened touch, from beyond the closing rear door. Before he could snap from Cranston's leisurely pose and move in the rapid style of The Shadow, he was confronted by the elevator man, who, hearing new footsteps from the front, was peering out to see what they meant.

Easing into Cranston's manner, The Shadow nodded to the elevator man and announced himself, saying that he had come to see Mr. Crome. He knew that the name of Cranston would carry weight with the old collector, for, though they had never met, Cranston had sometimes outbid Crome's representatives when they appeared at jewel auctions.

As one collector to another, Crome couldn't afford to entirely ignore Cranston. Within a few minutes, they were chatting with each other over the telephone, and though The Shadow detected a tremolo in Crome's tone, it was one that could have been attributed to his advanced age—as the old man, himself, was smart enough to recognize.

But The Shadow, having heard the creeping below, had quite another explanation for the wavering tone that he heard across the wire. In his turn, he did not drop one whit from Cranston's quiet form of speech; nevertheless, his words made a hard dent on Crome.

The old collector was saying that it was too late for him to receive a visitor; that he would be glad to have Cranston call some other time. Pressing the point, The Shadow set the meeting definitely for the morrow; then he sprang a neat surprise.

"I am calling on behalf of a friend," he stated. "One who is very anxious to meet you, Mr. Crome. I may not be able to come tomorrow, but I would appreciate it if you would receive my friend."

"Of course, of course," interposed Crome, hastily, his voice betraying only a slight touch of its quiver. "Any friend of yours will be welcome here, Mr. Cranston. But about this friend—"

"He is deeply interested in gems," came Cranston's interruption, "particularly in rare sapphires. He hopes that some well-informed person, like yourself, can give him the advice he needs. Good night, Mr. Crome."

Upstairs, Uriah Crome was half slumped at his desk, his shaky hand barely able to replace the telephone on its stand. He had an idea who Cranston's friend might be: Police Commissioner Ralph Weston. The very thought horrified Crome; he wished with all his might that Jan Garmath had still been around when Cranston's call came through.

Then, gradually, Crome's nerve returned; he managed to force a laugh between his trembling lips. Let Weston come! As Garmath had said, the police were thinking in terms of six small sapphires, not one large gem. He'd talk in terms of small sapphires, too, Crome would, and thus veer the trail still further from himself.

Nevertheless, as he stared at the great Star of Delhi, with its rare radiant streaks gleaming up from the jewel case upon the desk, Uriah Crome could find no happiness in possession of the gem that he had so long coveted.

CHAPTER XVIII
CROME'S WAY OUT

IT was singular, to Margo Lane, the way that Lamont Cranston suddenly lost interest in the Star of Delhi and the chain of murder which the famous gem had caused. For all of Cranston, the police could keep on hunting for six lesser stones that didn't exist, while he kept his own opinions to himself.

That, at least, was Margo's conclusion while she lunched with Lamont. He was so totally indifferent to the case, that when he did glance at the newspaper, he turned to the sporting pages. There he found something that intrigued him. Margo guessed that it had to do with polo.

"Well, well!" exclaimed Cranston. "Another old friend has arrived for the matches. I'll have to drop around and chat with him. Here is his picture."

He passed the newspaper to Margo, who expected to see a photograph of some wealthy polo player from the Argentine, since Cranston was well acquainted with many members of

South American teams. The picture that Margo did see rather amazed her.

She saw a handsome, darkish man who wore a turban; the rest of his attire was a military uniform, well sprinkled with medals. Beneath the picture, she read the name: "Rajah of Lengore."

"Fancy the rajah being in New York," chuckled Cranston. "With all his palaces and possessions, you'd suppose he would never leave India. I remember his great jungle estate, so large that we were lost for three days while on a tiger hunt."

With sharp gaze, Margo tried to pierce Cranston's impassive front. When looks failed, she tried words.

"The rajah has many jewels, I suppose?"

"What rajah hasn't?" queried Cranston calmly. "I saw his rubies, the real Oriental kind, as large as marbles. Emeralds, too, and diamonds—"

"What about sapphires, Lamont?"

"Sapphires?" Cranston gave an indulgent head-shake. "Too common. Only the rajah's servants would wear them. He might use them for coat buttons."

Cranston was reaching for the newspaper again. Margo couldn't curb her patience any longer.

"What about sapphires like the Star of Delhi?" she demanded. "Wouldn't such stones interest this all important rajah?"

The question actually took away some of Cranston's calm, but Margo recognized that his sudden interest must also be a pose. He'd just been waiting for her to bring up the question that was already in his mind, and he was letting her take the credit for it.

"A real thought, Margo!" Cranston exclaimed. "I'll speak to the rajah about the Star of Delhi, and tell him that it was your idea. He'll be so pleased that he'll want to meet you. So there's your reward, Margo—a meeting with a real rajah."

During the afternoon, while still waiting to hear further from Cranston, Margo tried to convince herself that rajahs meant nothing in her life; but despite such efforts, she had to concede that a meeting with the handsome Rajah of Lengore would be an interesting experience.

When Cranston called up, later, and said he'd arranged it for early in the evening, Margo couldn't control the enthusiasm that she felt.

"The rajah will call for you," Cranston told her. "By the way, I sent a package over to your apartment, along with a note. Sorry I can't see you, or go along, this evening. The commissioner insists upon my meeting him at the club."

AT her apartment, Margo found the note and the package, and didn't know whether to be irked or intrigued.

It seemed that Cranston had arranged some scheme with the rajah that probably involved the Star of Delhi, though the note did not specify it. At any rate, the rajah was going somewhere with his niece, a Hindu princess.

Not having a niece who was a Hindu princess, the rajah had been stumped, until Cranston elected Margo for the part. So the package contained the costume that the girl was to wear, and with it, Cranston had sent along a bottle of makeup dye which he guaranteed would furnish Margo with a delicately dusky complexion.

At first Margo rebelled; then, having intended to get dressed for the evening anyway, she decided to try the Hindu costume. Having put on what there was of it, she took a look at the effect in a full-length mirror. Except that it made her feel like a prospective guest at an artists' ball, Margo rather liked it.

The costume had very ornate slippers, a pert jacket studded with real jewels, and a split skirt that gave the effect of bloomers. The skirt was filmy, even away from the light, and though not exactly daring, wouldn't do for street wear in New York.

However, Margo decided that a Hindu princess would probably be privileged to wear a fur coat in a cool clime like America, so she proceeded to dye her face and neck.

The effect was good, and she added the brownish hue to her arms and hands.

She was just finished, when the apartment bell announced the Rajah of Lengore.

Margo met her escort in the apartment lobby. He was as handsome as his photograph, and quite tall. His smile of greeting was a bit troubled by sight of Margo's fur coat, but when she explained that she was wearing the Hindu costume, too, he gave a pleased nod. The rajah, himself, was wearing his uniform and a compact turban.

They stepped into a waiting limousine, and as they rode away together, the rajah produced an array of rings and bracelets for his niece to wear.

There was an anklet, too, the most expensive item among all the jewelry. Of gold, studded with diamonds and rubies, it was so heavy that when Margo crossed her knees, she found it more comfortable to keep her left foot on the floor, since the band of gold was on her left ankle.

When they reached their destination, Margo was rather surprised to find it an old-fashioned office building. A man stepped from an elevator to give the Oriental visitors a curious look, but when the rajah announced in slow but perfect English that he was Cranston's friend, the elevator man took them up.

At the top, Margo saw an elevator door which had a pane of thick bulletproof glass. Peering through, a servant studied the visitors, then opened the door.

They were ushered into a room of paneled oak, where a crabby old man sat behind a desk on which rested a tray with a half-finished bowl of milk toast. The servant was already helping Margo remove her fur coat, when the old man looked up. The expression of annoyance that Uriah Crome was showing to impress Commissioner Weston, took a very sudden change.

Open-mouthed, Crome scanned the uniformed Rajah of Lengore, then, let his widening eyes take in Margo from head to foot. The rajah was introducing himself, and announcing that the lady was his niece, which Crome could readily believe.

Margo's complexion looked about the same hue as the rajah's, and her bizarre Oriental costume revealed a shapeliness that suited the specifications of a Hindu princess. But the feature that overwhelmed Crome, and won him to immediate belief, was the display of jewelry that Margo flashed for his especial benefit.

The rajah had placed a necklace of emeralds and diamonds around his niece's neck, and those gems made a wonderful splash. Bracelets and rings attracted Crome's down-sweeping eye, and when he saw the anklet, with its sparkle of diamonds and fire of rubies, he drew a long, amazed gasp.

The bitter flicker to his lips was just a recollection of the half million dollars that he had spent, under forced pressure, for the Star of Delhi.

IF the Rajah of Lengore intended to pawn his niece's gems, and had asked her to wear them here for the effect on Uriah Crome, it was certainly a case of super-salesmanship. Already, Crome was wishing that he could afford to purchase those adornments wholesale.

Catching the covetous glint in the old man's eye, Margo began to picture herself peeling off layers of jewels and dropping them on Crome's desk, while the rajah would be counting money in return.

It made her angry at Lamont, and at the rajah, too. Cranston's helping the rajah to sell jewels to Crome was fair enough, but Margo didn't like the idea of being used as an attraction to raise the price. She could imagine how a real Hindu princess would feel if called upon by an avaricious uncle to make a public sacrifice of her personal jewels, to impress an old miser like Crome.

She intended to tell Lamont what she thought of him, when she met him. Meanwhile, she'd act the part that she was playing, even though it was helping the very cause that she considered detestable.

Then, as the Rajah of Lengore spoke in a slow, musical tone, Margo was overwhelmed with remorse for having formed so wrong an opinion of Cranston and his Hindu friend.

The rajah, too, had observed Crome's gaze and was politely telling the old collector that none of his niece's jewels were for sale. Instead, the Rajah of Lengore had come to buy gems from Uriah Crome, and had requested his niece to accompany him, that she might compare with her present adornments whatever items Crome offered.

Indeed, the rajah's tone implied a doubt that Crome had many jewels that the princess would care to own.

It was the right way to deal with Crome. Testily, the old collector pressed buttons on his desk and started panels spinning all about the room. Bobbing about like a jack-in-the-box, he pointed his visitors to one display case after another, trying to impress them with his marvelous collection.

They went from topazes to opals, past shelves that teemed with specimens of turquoise and amethyst. On beyond an array of diamonds, to emeralds and rubies, finally stopping at a case of sapphires. It was there that the rajah made his closest study; he shook his head in disappointment.

"I had hoped to find the one gem that I wanted," he announced. "The great Star of Delhi."

Never had any man been taken more off guard than Uriah Crome. Margo looked quickly at the old collector, saw his face go as purple as the shelves of sapphires. Crome's lips were wagging, but no words came from them. It was the Rajah of Lengore who spoke.

"In my land," said the rajah sagely, "we regard no gem as worthy of importance unless men have died in quest of it. Every great ruby can be said to own its color from the blood of those who have warred for its possession. The green of emeralds comes from the grass that grows above the graves of those whose lives were lost in seeking to gain, or keep, the stone they so prized.

"Seldom has any sapphire brought murder to its owner. But the stars of the sky have now looked down upon six scenes of death. I would like the Star of Delhi, itself, to speak its story, like the stars of the firmament. In my land, we believe in the stars. They have told me that the Star of Delhi was not destroyed—"

"No, no!" interrupted Crome. "It was cut, I tell you, into six smaller sapphires!"

"Such could not be," inserted the rajah, while Margo stared, enraptured by his manner. "No man like yourself, Mr. Crome, would have allowed such a crime to happen. Such a crime, I mean, as the ruin of the priceless Star of Delhi. I would only like to see the gem, to know if it could have a price."

THE rajah's definition of crime was the point that made Crome capitulate. He felt, at last, that he had found a friend in whom he could confide. Weighed down by the secret of the Star's true story, craving to be rid of the purchase that Garmath had forced upon him, Crome staggered to a safe and opened it.

Not only did he show the rajah the Star of Delhi, he poured out the whole history of Lenfell's swindle and Garmath's double-cross. With it, Crome swore that he had known nothing of impending murder until after the deaths had been delivered. Garmath's visit had been his first meeting with the master killer.

Margo believed him, as did the rajah. Finding them sympathetic, Crome added to his tale of woe.

"If I sell the Star of Delhi," he said hoarsely, "Garmath may kill me! He knows that I am worried—"

The telephone bell began to ring. The start that Crome gave convinced Margo that the old man expected a call from Garmath. The Rajah of Lengore was of the same opinion. He stepped close to Crome.

"Tell Garmath that you are glad you bought the Star," advised the rajah. "Say that all you want is a way out, in case anyone accuses you of owning it."

"But—how?"

"Garmath made one replica of the Star of Delhi," returned the rajah. "Ask him to manufacture another. It will be your alibi. You can produce it, upon demand; when it is examined and found to be synthetic, you will be regarded as another dupe, like Lenfell; nothing more."

His lips tightening in a wise smile, Crome picked up the telephone. His voice firmed as he chatted with Garmath. In the course of conversation, Crome put the request that the rajah had suggested. His call finished, he hung up, still retaining his smile.

"It will take forty-eight hours," he declared. "Then, Garmath will deliver the replica. After that, I can sell you the Star of Delhi. I shall put the false stone with my other sapphires, where anyone can view it, while I smile. Anyone, including Jan Garmath, should he visit me!"

Margo thought that the visit was completed, but she was wrong. For the next fifteen minutes, the Rajah of Lengore continued to talk terms with Uriah Crome regarding the future sale of the real Star of Delhi.

When she left with the rajah, Margo felt nervous. As they rode in their limousine, she was sure that another car was following them.

A word from the rajah to the chauffeur, and the big car pulled suddenly into an obscure parking place. Looking back, Margo saw a car round the corner and roll past. After it came a taxicab that looked very much like Moe Shrevnitz's. Margo turned to speak to the man beside her. Her new friend, the rajah, was gone!

The cab was slowing, but only for a moment. As it picked up speed, Margo saw blackness within its door, which had opened, and now was closing as if of its own accord. It was Moe's cab, and it had picked up a cloaked passenger, to take him along a new trail.

Alone in the limousine, Margo Lane, the erstwhile Hindu princess, realized very suddenly that Lamont Cranston couldn't have gone to the Cobalt Club this evening. Instead, he had come to take her to Crome's.

For Lamont Cranston had played the part of the imaginary Rajah of Lengore; now both—Cranston and the rajah—had merged into the cloaked personality of The Shadow!

CHAPTER XIX
CRIME'S FORCED THRUST

IN a little boxlike room, Jan Garmath sat at a desk studying an array of gems. He recognized the knock at the door and spoke for his visitor to enter. Dwig Brencott stepped into sight. Without looking up, Garmath used a pair of tweezers to lift a fair-sized ruby and hold it into the light.

"How do you like it?" queried Garmath. "I fused it from three smaller stones. One good way to dispose of stolen goods at high prices. This work intrigues me, Dwig—"

"Trouble, chief," Dwig interposed. "Thought I'd better tell you."

"Is it Sherbrock again?" snarled Garmath. "We've been too lenient with the fellow. Maybe he realizes that we are feeding him well, and keeping him in good health, so they will not believe him should he claim that he was kidnapped."

"We can put Sherbrock back in circulation soon enough," affirmed Dwig. "He's the fellow to take the rap for all the job's we've pulled. But Sherbrock isn't the trouble. It's Crome."

Garmath perched his thin chin in his hand and gave Dwig a very dubious stare.

"Listen, chief," Dwig insisted earnestly. "You've got to take this seriously. Only two nights ago, I tried to trail the Hindu who stopped in at Crome's—"

"And failed—"

"Yes," Dwig conceded, "I failed. But suppose The Shadow was around. What if *he* trailed *me* back here?"

Garmath shook his head, as though the argument wearied him.

"If The Shadow had located us," declared Garmath, "he would have attacked at once. Calm yourself on that point, Dwig. Now—what about Crome?"

"I called our lookout over there," replied Dwig. "He says that Commissioner Weston just dropped in for a chat with our dear friend, Uriah Crome!"

There wasn't a flicker of alarm on Garmath's dryish features. Rather, the situation intrigued the master murderer. He drew a watch from his pocket and noted the time; then remarked:

"Only an hour more—"

He shrugged, as though a trifle disappointed. Then, gathering his fused gems into a box, Garmath considered the changed situation. He finally explained it, for Dwig's benefit.

"I had intended to let you deliver the synthetic sapphire that Crome wanted," Garmath said. "Partly as a test; also, so that you could get a good look at his premises. Had he decided to sell the Star of Delhi to the Rajah of Lengore, it would have meant the end of my promise to protect him. I planned to wait and see."

"And send me to Crome," reminded Dwig, "if you found out he'd double-crossed you."

"Precisely! His receiving the police commissioner is the equivalent of a double-cross. It gives us the privilege of reprisal. Go there at once, Dwig, with your crew, and settle scores with Crome."

"We're to handle the commissioner, too?"

"Of course! By this time, Crome is probably telling him the whole story. Bring back all of Crome's jewels, including the Star of Delhi."

With Dwig, Garmath walked from the tiny room into a larger one. Lights showed a stone-walled passage just ahead. This hideaway was underground. Dwig started out through the passage, then paused.

"If I pull away the whole crew," he reminded, "the place won't be safe—"

"Anything unknown is safe," interrupted Garmath testily. "Try to forget The Shadow, Dwig. However, you may leave one man, to answer the signal when you return. Of course"—he nudged toward a narrow stairway that led upward—"I still have Krem. He is worth half a dozen of your men."

Dwig didn't dispute the question. He went out by his own route, taking along five men who were waiting in another room. Cautiously, they left by a steel door and came up to the level of the sidewalk. Sending four men across to a darkened alley, Dwig told one to wait.

"We're going on a job," Dwig informed the guard. "Three raps—two quick, then a slow one"—Dwig illustrated, by clanking a revolver butt against the door—"means we're back. Don't waste time letting us in. We may be in a rush."

Dwig waited until the guard had gone back into the hideaway and bolted the door, then he joined his companions, glancing along the street as he crossed to the alley. He didn't observe the long, black form that detached itself from the wall beside the door to the hideaway.

The Shadow was here!

QUITE in variance to Garmath's theory, the cloaked investigator had attempted no invasion, even though he had discovered the hideaway two nights before. Garmath had disregarded one very vital point: the fact that Sherbrock was a prisoner.

Perhaps Garmath thought that The Shadow didn't know it. Possibly, Garmath's own disregard for human life was so inbred that he couldn't credit The Shadow with changing vital plans on the slight chance that a man like Sherbrock might be still alive.

But The Shadow was gambling much on that possibility. He was making himself a double task, just on Sherbrock's account.

Having reasoned that Garmath would treat Sherbrock well if he kept the prisoner alive at all, The Shadow had seen no need to hurry a rescue. He wanted to make the rescue sure, and the departure of Dwig's crew increased that prospect.

Yet there was something else to do before attempting to aid Sherbrock. Gliding in the other direction, The Shadow passed beneath the abutment of a great East River bridge. He reached a car of his own and started a quick trip around by streets that led up to the bridge itself.

The hideaway was on the Long Island side of the river. As The Shadow sped up the approach, he saw Dwig's car ahead, but paid it small attention. He was more interested in taking another look at the top of Garmath's hideaway, which squatted just below the bridge, visible in the glow of lights that lined the approach.

It was a squatty, concrete structure, simply the windowless foundation of a building that had gone no further in construction. In the top was a black square that represented a trapdoor, but from one angle the bridge lights gave that patch a silvery glisten. The trapdoor was covered with steel, making it too stout a barrier for ordinary attack.

Certainly, Jan Garmath had chosen himself an unusual hideaway; a veritable stronghold. Whether or not it would come up to the conniver's expectations was something that The Shadow hoped to settle later. For the present, his thoughts reverted to Crome.

Giving his car speed, The Shadow whizzed past Dwig & Co, who were in another traffic lane. Men of their ilk never drove too fast across a bridge. Arguments with traffic cops were not to their liking.

The Shadow was the first to reach Crome's. He approached the elevator, gave a low, weird whisper that captured the attention of the seated operator.

Peering out, the fellow met a greeting quite different from the affable one that Cranston had accorded him two nights before. With a sweep, The Shadow gripped the operator, stifled his cries, and hauled him out to the rear street.

Some of The Shadow's agents were waiting there. Turning the elevator man over to them, The Shadow returned into the building accompanied by one agent: Harry Vincent. They went up in the lift. Servants saw its arriving light, peered through the glass-paned door. They were surprised to find the car empty. One puzzled servant opened the door.

For the first time, Garmath's servants learned that there were bind spots at the front corner of the elevator that couldn't be seen through the pane. The Shadow swung from one corner, Harry from the other. Both had guns, and they took the servants flat-footed.

As soon as the three servants had raised their hands, The Shadow marched them to a side room, while Harry took the car down in a hurry. He had left the building when Dwig and the four thugs arrived.

GARMATH had given Dwig diversified instructions about getting up to Crome's—such as phoning the old collector and putting up a bluff, or threatening the elevator man and making him do the rest.

Neither prospect quite suited Dwig, so he was pleased when he found an empty elevator waiting.

Thinking that the operator had stepped out, Dwig hurried his men into the elevator and ran it to the top. When he tried the upper door, it yielded. Dwig didn't guess that its catch had been left loosened. Motioning for his men to follow, he started straight to the room where he knew he would find Crome.

Dwig's spy hadn't mentioned another visitor beside Weston. There was one: Margo Lane. She was listening while Weston questioned Crome about small sapphires, of the sort for which the police were searching.

All the while, Crome was tossing occasional looks toward Margo, as though he vaguely recognized her. So far, however, he hadn't identified her as the Hindu princess who had visited him with the Rajah of Lengore. Margo was beginning to understand the reason for the masquerade of two nights before.

Crome was showing Weston many sapphires, some of the star variety, giving his opinion of how the six portions of the famous Star of Delhi would look. Though Weston didn't detect Crome's worriment, Margo did. Knowing that Cranston was a link between the rajah and the commissioner, Crome had a right to be worried.

Strolling over to a large French window, Margo slid her hand behind her and unloosed the bolt, something that Cranston had told her to do upon this visit. That was just done when Weston turned, to ask suddenly:

"I wonder what's keeping Cranston!"

"I don't know," returned Margo, truthfully. "Lamont simply said that he would meet us here. He insisted that Mr. Crome could help you find the sapphire that you want."

"The *sapphires*," croaked Crome weakly. "There are *six*, Miss Lane. Six star sapphires, each about the size of this one."

He was holding up a small sapphire, to illustrate, when Margo interrupted with a quick cry of alarm and darted for a corner. Weston, wheeling, flung himself the other way, carrying Crome in a sprawl beyond the desk. Five men, all masked, were entering the room with drawn guns.

For the moment, Margo thought that The Shadow's plans had missed, particularly when she saw black emptiness in the doorway behind the invaders. Then, from that very blackness came the challenging tone that made the masked crooks wheel—the laugh of The Shadow!

Five guns blasted as one, all for a target that wasn't there. Those shots were but an added signal to The Shadow's mockery. Amid the gun echoes, the French windows smashed open and in from the penthouse roof piled another squad of men, detectives headed by Inspector Joe Cardona.

Their guns ripped. The leader of the masked tribe wheeled, saw Cardona and tried to fire. Joe beat him to the shot and sprawled him to the floor, where the mask, sliding from above his eyes, revealed the face of Dwig Brencott.

Detectives, meanwhile, were lunging for the other four; whether they'd fare as well as Cardona had was a question.

A question settled by The Shadow.

Swinging in from the side of the door, The Shadow nicked a pair of masked men with two neat shots that, to Margo, seemed simultaneous. They sprawled, those two who might otherwise have done damage. The second pair weren't dangerous. Detectives were quick enough to grab them.

Crome's servants dashed into the room as The Shadow stepped away. He had taken them into his confidence and told them to await his word. They helped the detectives suppress the wounded strugglers. Seeing that victory was won, Cardona turned to the door, as did Margo:

All that either saw or heard of The Shadow was a vanishing trace of black, a strange laugh that trailed back uncannily, to end, suddenly, with the *clang* of the elevator door. That mockery, however, was no tone of final parting.

It told that The Shadow was on his way to some further mission, where he would again summon men of the law!

CHAPTER XX
CRIME'S PROOFS

EVEN more than the timely arrival of The Shadow, the appearance of Inspector Cardona had amazed Commissioner Weston. Commotion ended, Weston demanded to know how and when Cardona had arrived at Crome's. In his turn, Joe was surprised to find his chief on the scene.

Cardona explained that he had received a tip-off from The Shadow, who told him to bring his men to the ninth floor of an adjoining building and stay on watch outside a lighted penthouse. He hadn't known that the place was Crome's, nor that Weston was a visitor.

Those details were scarcely explained before Crome interrupted the discussion. In a high-pitched quaver, the old gem collector was giving his story. Knowing that Dwig and the accompanying thugs must have come from Garmath, Crome felt that his real friend was The Shadow.

Confessing that he owned the Star of Delhi, but swearing that he had played no part in crime, Crome faltered over to his safe and opened it, to fling the half-million-dollar jewel on his desk.

It took some time for Weston to get the coherent details, which included Crome's forced purchase of the gem. Crome was so desirous to establish innocence, Weston so willing to hear such details as Lenfell's proposal of a swindle that had led to Garmath's reign of murder, that neither the commissioner nor the old collector heard the ringing of the phone bell.

Cardona answered, held a brief conversation. He was starting toward the door, when Weston saw him.

"Where are you going, Inspector?" called the commissioner. "This case is only half complete! We've got to find Garmath!"

"That's what I expect to do!" returned Cardona, across his own shoulder. "I've just had another tip-off from The Shadow!"

The elevator was reaching the top floor when Cardona and his squad approached. It was being brought up by a rather dazed operator, who was somewhat surprised to find himself back in the car. Cardona and the detectives entered the car and went down.

OVER at the hideaway beyond the big bridge, the guard posted by Dwig heard the signaling thumps of a gun handle. He peered out cautiously, saw the dim lights of a car parked in the opposite alley.

The lights went out, indicating that Dwig's men were about to follow their leader across the street. But it wasn't Dwig, who had thumped.

Gloved hands hooked the guard's throat and lashed him clear of the partly opened door. A sinister whisper, fraught with mockery, sounded in the thug's ear—The Shadow's whisper—enough to take the fight from any man of crime. Into the arms of arriving agents, The Shadow tossed the limply settling figure of his gasping prisoner.

Then, alone, The Shadow ventured into the hideaway.

It was still no time for a massed onslaught. Alone, Jan Garmath would be a difficult foe. He was the elusive creeper whose footfalls were almost as deceptive as The Shadow's laugh. Once he sensed the approach of enemies, Garmath would employ uncanny cunning. The only policy was for The Shadow to use lone tactics of his own to force a meeting with the supercrook.

Proof came immediately.

Barely started into the passage, The Shadow heard the creep of footsteps and sidled into a darkened corner. His gloved hand motioned a signal back to the door, where Harry Vincent, just inside, pressed the door shut and turned toward it.

From somewhere in the passage, Garmath saw Harry's back and mistook him for the guard.

Footsteps shuffled away. It was impossible to tell their direction, at first; then The Shadow sensed that they were going upward, which meant that Garmath must have come from a lower room and started to a floor above. Silently, The Shadow glided inward, found the stairs and followed.

At the top, he saw a doorless opening into a large room. In one corner was a smaller room, barred like a cell. The Shadow saw Garmath look that way. Through the bars, a white face peered back.

It was the face of Roger Sherbrock, the kidnapped lapidary. The scene was setting itself as The Shadow wanted.

Above, The Shadow saw the glisten of the steel trapdoor, which, as he expected, was double padlocked on the underside. It was in the very center of the large room, about eight feet above the floor.

There was a doorway in another corner, but Garmath did not go that far. Instead, he stopped at a squatty contrivance that looked like an electric furnace. He busied himself there so intently that The Shadow decided to approach.

Exacting in everything he did, Jan Garmath was not the man to let one plan interfere with another. It might be, in his estimate, that Dwig Brencott would return from Crome's with the news that all was well there. Garmath knew how he had personally thrown fear into Crome, and perhaps the old collector would be capable of staging a good bluff.

If so, Crome would deserve the synthetic sapphire that he had requested, as an alibi to cover his possession of the Star of Delhi. That sapphire was ready, in the same mold that Garmath had used to make a similar gem for Lenfell.

HARRY VINCENT

The crucible had cooled; when Garmath opened it, his eyes sparkled as if reflecting the sight he saw.

Shining from its mold was a blue staurolite, as good as the imitation that Lenfell had once mistaken for the original Star of Delhi, and which now belonged to Commissioner Weston. Its color was perfect, a rich deep blue. But as Garmath reached for it, he saw the sapphire darken—something which he couldn't quite understand.

He stepped to one side, to study it from another angle. Garmath's hand brushed the cloth of a cloak sleeve.

Suddenly paralyzed, Garmath felt the cloth slide forward. A gloved hand intervened between his own and the brilliant imitation gem that twinkled from the mold. The hand of The Shadow, whose lips were uttering a taunt in Garmath's very ear. Crime's foe had found crime's maker!

There, in The Shadow's reach, lay crime's final proof. It was evidence that Garmath, free in this hidden laboratory, dealt in the manufacture of great, synthetic gems, while Sherbrock, a prisoner in the same place, was helpless to prevent him!

SO petrified was Garmath that he seemed truly conquered. Then, in an instant, his manner changed. He was whipping away, in snakelike style, uttering a defiant hiss: a new challenge to The Shadow.

Drowning Garmath's tone came a cry from Sherbrock. The prisoner was pointing excitedly to the other corner and its open door.

Through that space lunged a huge figure, Garmath's ace in the hole, the man called Krem. Garmath had credited Krem with being stronger than Dwig's whole crew, and Krem proceeded to back the claim.

Swooping before The Shadow could turn upon him with drawn automatic, Krem clutched the cloaked fighter about both arms. When he found he couldn't keep a grip upon his twisting adversary, the giant flung The Shadow half across the room.

Rolling to his feet, The Shadow looked groggily for Garmath and saw the murderer making for the door that led below. With a spurt of his old speed, The Shadow tried to head off the fugitive; but Garmath stopped short of the door and tugged a switch, set in the wall. A steel curtain slashed downward, blocking the door.

Krem was almost upon The Shadow. Knowing he hadn't time to meet the bone-crushing giant, The Shadow sprang for Garmath, who was drawing a gun. Had The Shadow shot Garmath at that moment, he would never have been able to stop the vengeful Krem.

Instead of shooting, The Shadow spun Garmath about; imitating Krem's tactics, he sent Garmath spinning across the room, which brought Krem to a momentary halt. Making the most of that interval, The Shadow drove straight at Krem, aiming his gun at the huge man, instead of Garmath.

Krem caught The Shadow's arm and shoved it upward. Gleefully, he forced his cloaked adversary back against the wall, expecting Garmath to return and supply the finish with some bullets.

The Shadow was shooting, but his aim was toward the ceiling, and he was foolishly wasting all his shots. So Krem thought, and the giant gave a huge, bellowing laugh.

There were two things that Krem couldn't see. One was where The Shadow's hard fling had sent Garmath—straight to the door of Sherbrock's cell, where the prisoner had clutched his hated captor through the bars and was wrenching his gun away from him, a task made easy, because Garmath had hit the cell door with a force that badly jarred him.

The other thing that Krem missed was the effect of The Shadow's shots. His aim was toward the trapdoor in the ceiling, and his bullets were shattering the padlocks that barred it!

Slumping suddenly, The Shadow went almost to the floor, with Krem pouncing after him. A quick twist, and The Shadow was away. Garmath saw him and wrenched from Sherbrock's grasp, going after the cloaked fighter barehanded, for Sherbrock had obtained the gun.

Not realizing that Garmath was too dazed even to reach The Shadow, Sherbrock fired all the shots he had.

The bullets sprawled Garmath at The Shadow's feet, just as the cloaked fighter, with a sudden twist, was drawing a fresh gun to catch the blundering giant, Krem, from an unexpected angle. The Shadow had finally tricked Krem, though the giant, very shortly before, had seemed too formidable to be allowed his present leeway.

PROOF of The Shadow's foresight came in a barrage from the lifted trapdoor. Cardona and his squad had spotted their goal from the bridge, by following The Shadow's tip-off. With bullets that shattered the padlock, The Shadow had opened the way for the police, since his agents, blocked off by the steel curtain, could not reach the scene from below.

Riddled with bullets that Cardona's squad provided, Krem fell dead before The Shadow could personally settle the giant fighter.

In his fall, Krem sprawled across the body of his dead master, Jan Garmath. Dropped by bullets from his own gun, served by Roger Sherbrock, Garmath had met a proper fate at the hand of the man upon whom he had falsely foisted evidence of guilt.

Down through the trapdoor, Cardona and his detectives were finding crime's real proof. In the open crucible, they saw the false sapphire that only Garmath, free, could have manufactured—a fact which fitted with Crome's recent testimony—while Sherbrock, still a prisoner about to be released, was in a position which fully bespoke his actual innocence.

While the detectives were cracking open Sherbrock's cell, Cardona looked for The Shadow. Joe saw blackness, but it was only the open doorway to the stairway that led below. The Shadow had pulled the switch, raising the steel curtain, and was on his way to rejoin his anxious agents.

Back from the stairway came a sound as strangely untraceable as the creepy footsteps that Jan Garmath would never again provide as symbols of insidious approach. The sound that Cardona heard was not a token of advance. It was a sign of departure.

It was the laugh of The Shadow, fading off into the realm of night, though its echoes seemed to linger, as well they might.

For The Shadow's tone not only signified his triumph over crime. It was a reminder that with such conquest, he had solved the last riddle connected with the famous sapphire known as the Star of Delhi!

THE END

SHADOWS OVER SALEM

Originally submitted as "The Witch Drums of Salem," the 25th script from the 1938 *Shadow* Goodrich summer season aired in syndication the week of September 11, 1938 under the shortened title, "The Witch Drums," with all mention of Salem removed from the storyline as well, perhaps to avoid offending modern residents. Orson Welles enacted the title role, with Margot Stevenson as Margot Lane (in her penultimate performance as Cranston's "constant friend and aide"), Juano Hernandez as Mowambi and Paul Stewart as multi-generational members of the West family.

Though writer credits don't survive for the 1937-39 *Shadow* broadcasts, "The Witch Drums of Salem" stylistically and structurally appears to be the work of Jerry Devine, who was one of *The Shadow*'s busiest scriptwriters during the 1938 Goodrich season (under the supervision of story editor Edith Meiser). Like several later Devine-scripted *Shadow* episodes, including "The Black Abbot" (October 2, 1938), "Death Rides a Broomstick" (March 2, 1941) and "The Ghost Walks Again" (March 16, 1941), the script opens with a flashback to a Colonial execution and showcases a cross-generational family curse that appears to have dire consequences in The Shadow's time.

"The Witch Drums of Salem" perpetuates a major historical misconception of the infamous Massachusetts witch trials, as Lamont Cranston wrongly maintains that Salem "is the town where they had the quaint custom of burning witches." While accused witches were routinely burned at the stake in Europe, those convicted of the capital felony of witchcraft in Colonial Massachusetts were actually executed by hanging. (However, accused witches' lives were spared if they confessed to the crime, though their property was then forfeit.) Between June and September of 1692, nineteen men and women were carted to Gallows Hill for execution, while another was pressed to death under heavy stones for refusing to submit to a trial. At least five more died while incarcerated. Before the hysteria ended, more than 150 people were arrested and jailed. In 1702, the Massachusett General Court ruled the 1692 trials unlawful. —Anthony Tollin

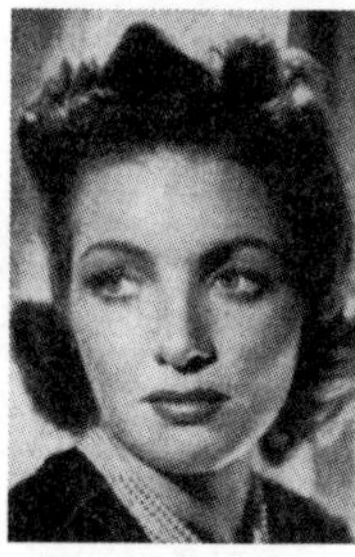

Stevenson

Hernandez

THE SHADOW

"THE WITCH DRUMS OF SALEM"

as broadcast the week of September 11, 1938

(MUSIC UP: "GLOOMS OF FATE" — FADE UNDER)

SHADOW: (FILTER) Who knows what evil lurks in the hearts of men? The SHADOW knows! (LAUGHS)

(MUSIC)

ANNCR: The Shadow, Lamont Cranston, a man of wealth, a student of science and a master of other people's minds, devotes his life to righting wrongs, protecting the innocent and punishing the guilty. Cranston is known to the underworld as The Shadow; never seen, only heard, his true identity is known only to his constant friend and aide, Margot Lane. Today's story—"The Witch Drums of Salem."

(SLOW MOURNFUL TOLLING OF CHURCH BELL—OFF ESTABLISH AND FADE BEHIND FOLLOWING)
(CROWD MURMUR—SULLEN, ANGRY)

MINISTER: (PROCLAIMING) Hear ye ... Hear ye ... (CROWD MURMUR OUT) Hear ye …0 Godly people of Salem Village. Herefore, on this day of June the fifteenth in the year of our Lord, sixteen hundred and ninety two, Dame Anna West, having been tried and found guilty of the practice of witchcraft ... and wherefore, having been sentenced to be hanged and burned ... ye are gathered here on Gallows Hill to witness the triumph of righteousness over the forces of evil!

(CROWD MURMUR)

MINISTER: (SHOUTS) Hear me, Dame Anna West … Recant! Repent! That even in this hour of doom thy soul may yet escape eternal hellfire!

(ANGRY CROWD VOICES)

1ST VOICE: Hang her!

2ND VOICE: Burn the witch!

3RD VOICE: Save our children from her evil kind!

1ST VOICE: Light the fires!

MINISTER: Recant ... Repent ... before it is too late ... Recant ...

ANNA WEST: (BACK—CRIES OUT) I am innocent ... Innocent ... INNOCENT!

2ND VOICE: (SHOUTS) Hang her ... Hang her ...

1ST VOICE: Burn her ... Burn her! Light the fires ...

CAPTAIN WEST: (SHOUTS IN BOOMING VOICE) Stop! Stop! Ye crazed and benighted fools. It is my wife ye would hang and burn!

(CROWD NOISE OUT)

CAPTAIN WEST: What do ye know of witchcraft! By what right do ye condemn the woman of my house .... the wife of my children!

MINISTER: Dame West has had a fair trial before a jury of her peers, Captain West. Ye must abide by their judgment!

CAPTAIN WEST: Aye ... tried by fools such as you, John Cotton! Condemned by the tales of children! Damned by Congo drums which I, Captain Daniel West, brought from Africa with a cargo of slaves.

MINISTER: Be silent, Captain, lest ye share the fate of your spouse!

CAPTAIN WEST: I'll not be silent! Hear me ... Hear me, Minister Cotton … For the deeds of this day let there be a curse on you and your house forever. (SHOUTS WILDLY) Let the spirit of my wife, who is about to die, haunt and torment thy offspring with the madness of the Congo drums, generation upon generation until the last of thy blood kin shall be dead ...

(THROB OF VOODOO DRUMS ....dead … DEAD!

1ST VOICE: (SHOUTS) He has brought the voodoo drums!

2ND VOICE: Stop him! Hang them both ... Kill them!

3RD VOICE: Light the fire! Burn them both ... Burn the cursed drum!

(THROB OF DRUM FASTER AND FASTER BEHIND FOLLOWING)

(CRACKLES OF FLAMES — CROWD NOISE — SCREAMS)

CAPTAIN WEST: (SHOUTS) Aye ... burn us ... burn the Congo drums! It will do ye no good! Not the fires of purgatory nor the march of centuries will wipe out the curse or the sound of the Congo Drums!

(CROWD NOISE—CRACKLES OF FLAMES—DRUMS …)

(MUSIC: TRANSITIONAL BRIDGE)

(SOUND OF MOTOR CAR—ESTABLISH AND FADE DOWN BEHIND FOLLOWING)

VOICE: (NEWS COMMENTATOR OVER FILTER—FADE IN) ... and here's another news bulletin. Flash ... Shanghai, China, With the 1938 Rainy season at its height, the Japanese mechanized armies are bogged down in their efforts to subdue the guerrilla bands of Shansi Province.

MARGOT: Lamont Cranston ... now that we've managed to sneak away for a quiet weekend in Maine ...visiting my Aunt Henrietta ...don't you think you could forget business ... and news …

LAMONT: (CHUCKLES) All right, Margot ... shut off the radio. I just wanted to get the time.

MARGOT: (LAUGHS) Well ... you got it. Didn't you hear that commentator say it was 1938? … Isn't that accurate enough when you're on vacation?

LAMONT: What's the matter, Margot … afraid I'll hear a news report of some crime and go tearing back to the city to try to solve it?

MARGOT: It wouldn't be the first time, Lamont Cranston. Once an amateur criminologist, always an amateur criminologist ... and as for The Shadow ...

LAMONT: (CHUCKLES) I'll try to keep The Shadow in his place ... in the shadows, Margot.

MARGOT: Promise?

LAMONT: I promise ...

MARGOT: Good ... What town is this we're passing through, Lamont?

CRANSTON: Salem ... this is the town where they had the quaint custom of burning witches.

MARGOT: It seems incredible … but then it was a long time ago.

CRANSTON: Less than three hundred years ago ... only a few generations, Margot.

MARGOT: What a stir The Shadow would have caused in this town in those days, Lamont.

CRANSTON: He might have saved quite a few innocent people from being burned at the stake.

MARGOT: Or been caught and burned at the stake himself ... thank heavens this is ... (BREAKS OFF—EXCLAIMS) Lamont … look at that crowd in the yard of that old house just ahead. (CAR MOTOR SLOWS)

CRANSTON: Huh ... looks like trouble of some sort.

MARGOT: Let's stop and see what it is ... What a strange old house.

CRANSTON: All right … but I thought you wanted a quiet weekend ... no excitement.

	(CAR STOPS)
MARGOT:	I know, but just let's see what's going on.
	(CROWD MURMUR—BACK—CAR DOOR—OPENED ON)
LAMONT:	(SHARPLY) Margot ... wait a minute! They're pulling something up out of that old well.
MARGOT:	It's a little boy ... Lamont ... he looks like ...
CRANSTON:	(GRIMLY) Yes ... Dead! Has been for a long time, from the looks of the body. I wouldn't go over there if I were you, Margot.
TOMMY:	(COMES ON SOBBING WILDLY) The witch killed him.... The witch killed him and threw him in the well!
REV COTTON:	(COMES ON) Tommy! Tommy! Wait ... you mustn't say things like that. You mustn't call poor Anna West a witch. You mustn't believe the stories people tell about Martha's great-grandmother ....

Margot Stevenson circa 1940

TOMMY:	(WILD—PANIC) But she is a witch ... she's always scarin' us with those drums she has in the cellar, and now she's killed my brother .... she killed him and threw him in the well!
REV. COTTON:	(PLEADING) Tommy ... don't ... don't make it any harder for me to bear. Don't let mother hear you talk like this.
TOMMY:	But, Dad ....Anna's great granddaddy ... old Capt'n West, put a curse on us. He did! Didn't he? ... Anna's uncle told us about it .. , . ,
REV. COTTON:	Yes, Tommy, but you mustn't believe in things like that ... It was all so long ago.
TOMMY:	Yes ... but ... but Anna's uncle told us to keep away from here ... not to come near when she was down in the cellar beating those awful soundin' old drums ... (WILDLY) And now look at her standing there in the window ... just starin' watchin' them take David out of the well where she threw him ... (WILD SOBBING)
REV. COTTON:	Tommy ... Tommy ... don't ... I know it's hard ... losing your little brother like this ...
MARGOT:	(COMES ON) I'm sorry, Reverend ... We couldn't help overhearing. Is there anything we can do? take him home perhaps?
REV. COTTON:	Thank you, but ...we live just across the street. next to my church. Come, Tommy ... there is nothing more we can do here ....We must go break the news to mother as gently as we can ...
TOMMY:	(SOBS) All right, dad ... but she did it ... I know she did it!
REV. COTTON:	Don't, Tommy ... don't be bitter. Hatred won't bring little David back to us.
TOMMY:	Dad? (QUICK) Let's go home ... Here comes her Uncle. He told us to keep away ... He ...

JONATHAN WEST: (COMES ON) Hold on a minute, Reverend Cotton. I want to talk to you!

REV. COTTON: Not now, Jonathan West, I must go and tell my wife our boy has been ... found ...

WEST: (COLD HARD) What I have to say will only take a minute, and you'll listen ... *now* ... if you know what's good for you *and* your family.

REV. COTTON: Yes, Jonathan?

WEST: Just this — I heard your son accusing my niece and ward of murder ... I heard him calling her a witch!

COTTON: I'm sorry ... he didn't know what he was saying ... try to understand that he's just lost his only brother ...

WEST: (HARSHLY) I know that ... and more. It isn't the first time the children of this neighborhood have stood in this yard screaming "WITCH" ... but it's the last! I'm warning you! There'll be no more of it. My ward, my brother's child, may not be quite normal, but she is not a witch ... even if she is the great-grandchild of one that was condemned and burned at the stake by your illustrious forefather.

COTTON: I'm sorry for what happened so long ago, but you yourself are to blame if that old legend will not die ...

WEST: Legend! Is it a legend that your house and mine has been cursed for centuries by that bloody deed on Gallows Hill?

COTTON: The curse was forgotten until you came back from Africa to rule your brother's home ... send his widow to an early grave and deny his child the right to a normal, happy life ...

WEST: My sister-in-law was mad, and her child is cursed with the same affliction.

COTTON: Then why isn't she being treated? Why do you keep her locked up in that dismal house without companionship, with voodoo drums for playthings ... with her white face and haunted eyes staring from shuttered windows? Is it any wonder that children are afraid ... and call her 'witch'?

WEST: (COLD AND MENACING) Say what you like. Stupid curiosity made one of your sons prowl around the grounds of my property. He fell in that well and was drowned, and now I'm warning you … Keep that boy Tom away from here or … something may happen to him, and the curse of old Captain West will be fulfilled ... (MOCKINGLY) Remember it ... "A curse on your house until the last of your blood kin shall be dead."

COTTON: May the Lord forgive you for your mockery and blasphemy, Jonathan West ... Come, Tommy ... (GOING) We must go to your mother now ...

WEST: (SHOUTS) Remember, Reverend Cotton ... I've warned you! (GOING) ... Keep away from me ... and mine!

MARGOT: (PAUSE—AWED) Lamont … did you see the look in that man's eyes?

CRANSTON: Yes, Margot ... I did. It's been a long time since I've seen such murderous hate in the eyes of any human being.

MARGOT: I wonder if that child's death *was* an accident …

CRANSTON: I wonder ...

MARGOT: Look at that poor girl ... she's still standing by the window ... watching ... Lamont, there's something horrible about all this ... I have a feeling this is the beginning ... not the end of a tragedy ...

CRANSTON:: Margot ... have you forgotten we're on a vacation ... bound for a pleasant weekend in Maine ... You made me promise ...

MARGOT: Do you want to be released from that promise?

CRANSTON: Yes ... I agree with you. There's something going on here ... in that house ... something *horrible.*

MARGOT: Do you think The ... The Shadow could end it?

CRANSTON: Do you want him to try?

MARGOT: Yes ... do what you can, Lamont. Try ... and I'll help you any way I can.

CRANSTON: All right, Margot ... we'll stop here, and perhaps the Shadow can discover what's masquerading in the guise of madness and witchcraft!

(MUSIC)

(DRONE OF MOTOR—ESTABLISH AND FADE BEHIND FOLLOWING …)

MARGOT: What happened at the coroner's inquest, Lamont?

CRANSTON: Nothing ... a routine verdict of accidental death … no wonder there are so many murders in this country.

MARGOT: Why do you say that, Lamont?

CRANSTON: That child was dead before he ever landed in the bottom of that well, and unless I miss my guess he died of strangulation … not drowning. What did you learn about this man, Jonathan West?

MARGOT: Plenty … in my role of inquiring reporter I found a lot of people willing to talk about him. He managed a trading post in Africa in the Congo … came here when his brother died five years ago.

CRANSTON: What about the girl we saw in the window … his ward? And what about her mother?

MARGOT: The mother died a year after her husband … apparently went insane and killed herself.

CRANSTON: And the girl?

MARGOT: Apparently quite normal until two years ago. Then she stopped going out of the house. The neighbors began hearing those voodoo drums … the neighborhood children began to be afraid of that house, and the 'witch tales' started.

CRANSTON: Hmmm … find out anything else?

MARGOT: Yes … one more thing. It seems that Jonathan West brought an old colored woman back with him from the Congo. She's been taking care of the girl … she's always with her.

CRANSTON: Huh … looks like history repeating itself … Old Captain West had a Congo slave woman in that house three hundred years ago … She was the cause of *his* wife's being accused of witchcraft. (CAR SLOWS AND STOPS) Well … here we are.

MARGOT: Be careful of Jonathan West if you go in the house, Lamont. He's dangerous.

CRANSTON: I know, Margot … even a jackal is dangerous if he's cornered.

MARGOT: I'll keep the shortwave tuned in on our regular band … If you run into trouble and need help, let me know right away.

(CAR DOOR OPENED—WIND UP SLIGHTLY)

CRANSTON: All right, Margot … but I think this is one case The Shadow can handle alone.

(THROBBING SOUND OF VOODOO DRUM —OFF)

MARGOT: Lamont … listen … do you hear that?

CRANSTON: Yes … drums, voodoo drums, all right …

MARGOT: Oh … that poor girl … she can't know what she's doing … beating on those drums in that dark house with little David Cotton lying dead in his coffin just across the street.

Paul Stewart doubled as Jonathan West and Captain West.

Orson Welles poses as Lamont Cranston in a 1937 MBS publicity photo.

CRANSTON:	Margot … how old is this girl … this Anna West? I didn't get a good look at her when she was standing in the window this afternoon …
MARGOT:	She's eighteen ... why?
CRANSTON:	It may turn out to be an important factor, Margot. Jonathan West is her guardian and she'll soon be of age.
MARGOT:	Maybe that's it, Lamont … I heard her father left quite a fortune … you wouldn't believe it to look at that house … dismal … dilapidated … Why, they haven't even electricity … just lamps and candles.
	(DRUMS LOUDER AND SLIGHTLY FASTER)
CRANSTON:	So I noticed. (QUICK) But listen, Margot. There's a storm coming up. Don't leave the car … stay here; I'll be back as soon as I find out what's going on in that house.
	(CAR DOOR CLOSED — WIND UP—DISTANT RUMBLE OF THUNDER)
	(MUSIC)
	(THROB OF DRUM DRAWS ON GRADUALLY—WIND UP AND FADE FOR …)
	(BANGING OF LOOSE SHUTTER … WIND AND DRUM SOUND FADE DOWN ....)
WEST:	(COMES ON—CALLING HARSHLY) Mowambi! Mowambi!
	(DOOR OPENED AND CLOSED—BACK)
MOWAMBI:	(COMES ON) (SULLEN—COLORED WOMAN SERVANT) Now, what you want, Meester West!
WEST:	Come here!
	(RATTLE OF LIGHT DOOR OPENED AND CLOSED)
MOWAMBI:	(COMES ON—SULLEN) Mowambi not afraid of big whip, like girl.
WEST:	Hold your tongue! (SHARP CRACK OF BULL WHIP) You'll be afraid of this whip if I give you a good taste of it. (CRACK OF WHIP) After this, you come when I call you, and come quick you, Congo devil!
MOWAMBI:	Mowambi not afraid of you. Mowambi not afraid of any white men … even in her own land … You devil too, Meester West!
WEST:	You hold your tongue and do as you're told, or I'll send you back to Sabu. The authorities would like to get their hands on you for what you did to the commissioner's wife.
MOWAMBI:	I don't kill commissioner's wife … she laugh at Mowambi's magic, and god of Voodoo kill her.
WEST:	Yes … but who's hand held the knife that cut her throat? But never mind that … I thought I told you to keep my niece away from those drums … tonight of all nights.
MOWAMBI:	(SULLEN) I forget.
WEST:	Yes? You're going to forget once too often, Mowambi.
MOWAMBI:	Voodoo drums talk to spirit of dead boy.
WEST:	(SAVAGELY) Listen to me, you dirty heathen … go ahead and talk that rot to Anna … You've got her believing it, but don't try it on me. I know your tricks, you faker.
MOWAMBI:	Voodoo drums say boy *dead* now … but soon *man* die.
WEST:	Huh … All right … if your cursed voodoo drums know so much, what man's going to die?
MOWAMBI:	A man in this house.
WEST:	Why, you treacherous old witch … I'm the only man in this house, and if there's any more killing, it'll be you that'll get it … not me.

MOWAMBI: More than one man in this house … Mowambi know …

WEST: What are you talking about? What's the matter with you? Get down in the cellar and take those drums away from Anna. Take her to her room and keep her there … and another thing … don't give her any more of that stuff you've been feeding her.

MOWAMBI: You say make her life crazy.

WEST: That can wait … There's plenty of time … If only you hadn't let that kid get in the house ...

MOWAMBI: Maybe white police find out how he die …

WEST: They won't. They think it was an accident. They're burying him tomorrow, but we've got to be careful for a while. Now, get down there and stop those infernal drums …

MOWAMBI: Yes ... Mowambi go, but you watch out. Danger close to you ... (GOING) Danger in shadows ... man die tonight …

(DOOR OPENED AND CLOSED ... RUMBLE OF THUNDER)

WEST: Huh ... trying to throw a scare into me ... are you. Well … I'll be finished with you pretty soon … (LAUGHS) You and your voodoo nonsense, Mowambi.

THE SHADOW: (LAUGHS) Voodooism is a dangerous weapon, Jonathan West.

WEST: What? Who said that? Mowambi, you devil .. if this is one of your tricks!

THE SHADOW: Your servant, Mowambi, has nothing to do with my presence in this house, Jonathan West.

MOWAMBI: Then who … She knew ... She warned me.

THE SHADOW: Yes … Mowambi is not a faker. Her powers told her of another presence in this room … she could not see me any more than you can see me now, but she knew I was here ... that's why she left so quickly.

WEST: No... No … this can't be … I'm hearing things … I must be crazy …

THE SHADOW: No … you are sane … quite sane, and I am real ... not the fancy of a mind tormented by remorse ... remorse for the murder of an innocent child.

Mowambi was voiced by Juano Hernandez (far left), performing with Orson Welles as The Shadow (at eight-ball filter mike).

WEST: (PAUSE) Who ... are you?! (DRAWING BACK) How did you get here ... what do you want?!

THE SHADOW: I am The Shadow, Jonathan West … and I have come to take your ward out of this house before she shares the fate of the child you murdered and flung in the well.

WEST: The Shadow …

THE SHADOW: Yes … The Shadow.

WEST: You … you're wrong ... I didn't murder the boy … it was an accident.

THE SHADOW: (MOCKINGLY) Yes … an accident by design, just as all the things that are happening in this house! (LAUGHS) If there is a gun in that desk behind you … don't waste your time … it won t help you …

WEST: If only I could see you …

THE SHADOW: Many a criminal has made that wish.

WEST: You are in this room … not just a voice!

THE SHADOW: The lamplight casts deep shadows …

WEST: (SOUND OF DRAWER JERKED OPEN — RATTLE OF GUN) Now, we'll see if a gun will help me or not!

THE SHADOW: Others have tried … and failed!

WEST: (SAVAGELY) Maybe they have … but I won't fail! Maybe this whip will tell me where you are …

(SUCCESSION OF SHARP CRACKS OF WHIP)

THE SHADOW: You handle a bull whip well ... like a man who has used it often.

WEST: (IN PANIC) You devil … (CRACK) I'll find you … (CRACK) You're here … somewhere … (CRACK)

(CRACK OF WHIP — DULL MUFFLED)

WEST: (EXCLAIMS) So you're there ...

(SHOTS IN QUICK SUCCESSION)

(PAUSE)

(THUD OF BODY FALLING)

WEST: (LAUGHS IN WILD PANIC) Mowambi was right. She was right! She said a man would die in this house tonight! (DRAWS BACK) And that man will be you, Shadow! YOU!

(SINGLE SHOT ... CRASH OF LAMP BREAKING GLASS—QUICK CRACKLE OF FLAMES)

(DOOR OPENED AND SLAMMED)

(MUSIC)

(SLOW THROB OF VOODOO DRUM … DRAWS ON ...)

WEST: (COMES ON) Mowambi! Mowambi! Where's Anna?

MOWAMBI: Be still .. there is death in this house. The gods of voodoo are angry.

WEST: Get away from those drums, you crazy old fool! Where's my ward? The house is on fire! In a few minutes, the whole town will be here!

MOWAMBI: Let them come!

WEST: (SAVAGELY) Listen to me, Mowambi ... If they get in this house and take Anna away … if they get the truth from her you won't have to go back to Sabu to be hung. She saw you strangle the boy ... she'll remember ... Where is she? Quick, tell me! (DRUMS OUT SUDDENLY)

MOWAMBI: If Mowambi die you die too … it is the law of the white man … Mowambi know …

WEST:	Yes … yes … I know! That's why we've got to get rid of her! We've got to do it now! We can't wait any longer ... The house is on fire, I tell you ....Where …
MOWAMBI:	You let her burn in fire like wife of old captain …
WEST:	Yes … no one will know … it's even better than the way I planned. With her out of the way, I'll never have to account for the money her father left her. Hurry up … there's no time to lose … where is she?
MOWAMBI:	Then you give me money to go back to my people …
WEST:	Yes … yes … you'll get what I promised you.
MOWAMBI:	The gods of voodoo say no … say I die soon …
WEST:	(WILD) You and your voodoo gods :.. don't try that stuff on me! You know what I think of voodoo and here's a taste of what you'll get if you don t tell me what you've done with that girl! (CRACK OF WHIP)
MOWAMBI:	(GASPS) No … No … Mowambi tell …
WEST:	Where is she? (CRACK OF WHIP)
MOWAMBI:	(GASPS) In there … In the wine cellar … she can't get out! Door is barred...
WEST:	Good … she can't get out … the whole upstairs is on fire ... Look at the smoke pouring down the stairs. In a few minutes, no one will ever know what happened.
MOWAMBI:	Man who is in house know.
WEST:	(LAUGHS) You were right about that Mowambi, but there's no need to worry about him … He's upstairs … lying on the floor … what's left of him by now!
THE SHADOW:	(LAUGHS) You are wrong, Jonathan West … fooled by the oldest trick in the world. You shot and heard me fall but I was not hit ...
	(ROAR OF FLAMES—OFF—BUILD BEHIND FOLLOWING. SOUND OF POLICE SIRENS AND FIRE ENGINES DRAW ON BEHIND)
MOWAMBI:	(SCREAMS—DRAWS BACK)
WEST:	Oh, no you don't, Mowambi! (CRACK OF WHIP) You're not running out to leave me deal with this Shadow alone … You've been boasting about your voodoo powers … use them now!
MOWAMBI:	No ... No ... it is the spirit of the evil one that speaks ...
	(THROB OF DRUMS..)
MOWAMBI:	Listen … the drums speak but no hands touch them …
THE SHADOW:	Listen, Mowambi ... hear the message of the drums...
	(DRUMS LOUDER AND FASTER)
MOWAMBI:	Death … death for Mowambi...
THE SHADOW:	Listen to me, Mowambi … Listen to me ... you have murdered for Jonathan West … now he means to murder you. You will never get out of this place alive … never ...
WEST:	(IN PANIC) Don't listen to him, Mowambi ... I wouldn't do that. You've served me well ..
THE SHADOW:	But he's through with you. . You've killed for him ... now, he means to kill you. Hear me, Mowambi ... strike first . .. strike first ...
MOWAMBI:	(COMES ON) I hear you ... I hear you, Shadow ... the drums foretold ...
WEST:	(BACKING AWAY) Keep away from me ... drop that knife, you heathen devil ... (SINGLE SHOT)
MOWAMBI:	(GASPS) Strike first ... (WITH EFFORT) strike first ... (THUD OF KNIFE) (CHOKES)
MOWAMBI:	Mowanbi die…but you die too and...and drums speak...(DRUMS BEAT IN QUICK CADENCE THEN SLOWLY FADE OUT BEHIND FOLLOWING...)

(ROAR OF FIRE — OFF — SIRENS AND WHISTLES…OFF MUFFLED POUNDING — DRAWS ON...)

ANNA: (CALLING—MUFFLED) Mowambi … Mowambi ... Let me out ... (CHOKES) Let me out ... I can't breathe …

(DOOR UNBOLTED—OPENED ON RUSTY HINGES)

ANNA: (COMES ON) Mowambi: (GASPS) Mowambi! Uncle Jonathan...

THE SHADOW: They are dead. They meant to kill you ... Quick … get out of this cellar.

(RUMBLE AND OFFSTAGE CRASH OF TIMBERS...)

ANNA: (DAZED AND TERRIFIED) I ... I can't see … (CHOKES) Help me … Help me... I can't …

THE SHADOW: Follow the sound of my voice … Come ... quickly …

ANNA: (GOING) Where are you? Help me!

THE SHADOW: (BACK) This way … follow my voice! Follow my voice and you will be safe!

(ROAR OF FLAMES—UP—SIRENS UP FULL)

(MUSIC)

(DRONE OF MOTOR UP AND FALL BEHIND FOLLOWING)

MARGOT: How did you ever get that poor girl out of that house, Lamont?

CRANSTON: It was easy once I succeeded in turning Mowambi against West. They eliminated each other and saved the state the expense of a trial and execution. How was the girl when you saw her last?

MARGOT: Scared, and she kept talking about a strange voice that led her out of the cellar just before the house caved in … but aside from that she seemed perfectly normal.

CRANSTON: She will be now that … Mowambi is dead. She kept the girl in an hypnotic trance … it would have been only a matter of time before she drove the girl insane with those infernal drums.

MARGOT: Well .. she's in good hands now … Reverend Cotton and his wife have taken her in ... (EXCLAIMS) Look, Lamont … we're passing the city limits...

CRANSTON: Yes, Margot ... the city limits of Salem … where they burned witches three hundred years ago.

MARGOT: Yes, but don't forget, Lamont … Jonathan West and Mowambi died not an hour ago ...

CRANSTON: I know .. but I'd rather think of what's left of our weekend with your aunt Henrietta in Maine ...

(MOTOR UP)

(MUSIC)

ANNCR: The story you have just heard is copyrighted by The Shadow Magazine. The characters in this story are entirely fictitious; any similarity to persons living or dead is purely coincidental.

(MUSIC "GLOOMS OF FATE"—UP AND UNDER)

SHADOW: The weed of crime bears bitter fruit. Crime does *not* pay. The Shadow knows! (LAUGH) •

***Shadow* announcer Ken Roberts**

MARGOT STEVENSON THE *REAL* MARGOT LANE

"The lovely Margot Lane," the only major character in The Shadow mythos that was not introduced and developed by Walter Gibson in his Shadow pulp novels, was inspired by Margot Stevenson, the popular Broadway ingenue who voiced the character during the 1938 *Shadow* summer season sponsored by Goodrich Tires.

Created to provide vocal contrast to Orson Welles' baritone, Lamont Cranston's "constant friend and aide" debuted September 26, 1937 on the premier broadcast of the revamped *Shadow* radio series. The Shadow's "friend and companion" was inserted into later drafts of Edward Hale Bierstadt's radio script by producer Clark Andrews and script editor Edith Meiser (replacing the character of Harry Vincent in the first draft), and named after Andrew's girlfriend, then starring in Kaufman and Hart's Pulitzer-winning Broadway hit, *You Can't Take It with You.*

Margaret Helen "Margot" Stevenson was born on February 8, 1912, the daughter of Charles Alexander Stevenson, an Irish-born actor who had performed alongside the legendary Edwin Booth and cofounded Actors Equity. "He didn't exactly bring me up to be an actress," Margot explained, "but he did believe that the stage was the only place where a woman could carve out a career for herself on even terms with men."

After making her Broadway debut in *Firebird* (1932), Margot Stevenson performed in *Stage Door* before starring as Alice Sycamore in the original Broadway cast of *You Can't Take It with You.* (Margot was cast in the role after Miss Hackett, Kaufman's right-hand woman, observed that the role was "just like you" and very funny.) "Well, the company went to Philadelphia for a two-week tryout," Stevenson remembered. "I was playing a small role and also understudying Margaret Sullavan in *Stage Door* in New York. One week went by. On Monday of the second week I was still in *Stage Door*. On Tuesday I got a hurry call to go to Philly to read for Mr. Kaufman. Luckily I made the grade and stepped into the cast almost then and there."

While appearing onstage in *You Can't Take It with You*, Stevenson did double duty costarring as "the lovely Margot Lane" opposite Orson Welles during the 1938 summer season of *The Shadow*. The character that had been inspired by Margot was first voiced during the initial Blue Coal winter season by Agnes Moorehead, who had patterned her portrayal on the Broadway ingenue who would succeed her. "Agnes Moorehead wanted a vacation, so I took over the role for the summer," Stevenson recalled. "When she had to voice ingenues on the air, I always felt she patterned her performances after me, and especially when she was playing Margot Lane on *The Shadow*. Martin Gabel, who directed the early broadcasts, was my boyfriend's roommate, and I've always suspected that he asked Agnes to imitate me as an inside joke since he knew that Clark had named the character after me.

"*The Shadow* was always great fun to do, because the cast was made up of wonderful, bright and funny guys like Orson Welles and Kenny Delmar, Paul Stewart and Everett Sloane. The series had its pick of the finest actors from Broadway and radio, because it aired late Sunday afternoon when most of the theaters were dark and there were few dramas on the airwaves." Stevenson had previously performed onstage with the young Orson Welles in the 1934-35 Katharine Cornell/Guthrie McClintic productions of *Romeo and Juliet* and *The Barretts of Wimpole Street.*

During the Golden Age of Radio, Stevenson was also heard on many popular network series including *The Silver Theatre* (costarring with Cary Grant in "A Romeo for Juliet"), *Grand Central Station*, *The Molle Mystery Theatre*, *Aunt*

Margot with her parents, Frances and Charles Alexander Stevenson

Columnist Hedda Hopper chats with playwright George S. Kaufman and Margot Stevenson

Margot as Alice Sycamore with Henry Travers as Grandpa in the original Broadway production of *You Can't Take It with You*

Photo by Marcus Blechman

Margot as Scarlett O'Hara in her *Gone With the Wind* screen test

Stevenson was cover featured in 1940 on Street & Smith's *PIC* magazIne.

Jenny's Real Life Stories, The Fat Man, *Life Can Be Beautiful, Stella Dallas* and *Front Page Farrell.*

As one of Broadway's leading ingenues, Stevenson was screen-tested for the role of Scarlett O'Hara in *Gone With the Wind*, and briefly moved to Hollywood where she appeared in a number of classic Warner Bros. films including *Smashing the Money Ring* (costarring with Ronald Reagan), *Castle on the Hudson* (starring John Garfield, Pat O'Brien and Burgess Meredith), *Invisible Stripes* (starring Humphrey Bogart and George Raft), *Flight Angels* (with Jane Wyman) and *Calling Philo Vance.*

During the Golden Age of Television, Margot played Lady Macduff in *The Hallmark Hall of Fame* presentation of *Macbeth* with Maurice Evans, and performed leading roles on *Rheingold Theatre* and *The Philco-Goodyear Television Playhouse.*

Stevenson eventually performed in more than twenty Broadway plays including *Little Women, The Rugged Path* (with Spencer Tracy), Ruth Gordon's *The Leading Lady* (with John Carradine), *Triple Play* (sharing the stage with Hume Cronyn and Jessica Tandy), *Big Fish, Little Fish* (directed by John Gielgud) and *Venus Observed (*directed by Laurence Olivier).

Stevenson was the leading lady for two seasons at Elitch's Garden in Denver, and met her future husband, character actor Val Avery while starring at Pennsylvania's White Barn summer theater.

She later starred in *The Seven Year Itch* and *Sweet Peril* in London's West End.

More than four decades after her Broadway debut in *Firebird*, Margot gave her final Broadway performance in the 1976 production of *The Royal Family*, substituting for Eva LeGalliene opposite longtime friends Rosemary Harris and Ellis Rabb. In later years, Stevenson portrayed Clairee in a tour of *Steel Magnolias*.

Margot also frequently performed at the annual Friends of Old-Time Radio Convention, reprising her famous role as The Shadow's "friend and aide" and voicing the leading role of Mrs. Stevenson in the first stereo production of *Sorry, Wrong Number* (with a supporting cast that included the radioplay's author, Lucille Fletcher). Blinded by macular degeneration, Margot delivered her final stage role as the sightless seer Tiresias in *The Bacchae* in the first FringeNYC Festival in 1997, and performed before an audience for the last time at the 2005 Friends of Old-Time Radio Convention.

The veteran actress was the last surviving star of the *Shadow* radio series and one of the final survivors of the classic Warner Bros. crime films. After a theatrical career that spanned two-thirds of a century, Margot Stevenson passed away January 2, 2011 in her Greenwich Village home, a month before her 99th birthday. —Anthony Tollin

The stars of Warner Bros' *Smashing the Money Ring*: Ronald Reagan, Margot Stevenson and Eddie Foy, Junior.

Virginia Bruce tries to stop a fight between Jane Wyman and Margot Stevenson in *Flight Angels*

James Stephenson with Margot in *Calling Philo Vance*

Photo by Val Avery

Maurice Evans and Margot Stevenson prepare for *The Hallmark Hall of Fame's* 1954 TV presentation of *Macbeth.*

Margot and the London cast of *The Seven Year Itch*

Stevenson and daughter Margot Avery (front row, third from left) with radio-legend Arthur Godfrey and the Bucks County Playhouse cast of *Our Town*

Illustration by Al Hirschfeld

Val Avery and Margot on their wedding day

Margot recreates a radio classic with *Shadow* announcer Ken Roberts